IRWIN SHAW

"A modern-day Maugham ... A master!"

—PLAYBOY

"He has the gift of all great storytellers ... he creates characters as genuine as that odd couple across the street, the curious patrons of the corner bar, the tragic figures from the headlines. They are individuals who walk into the living room of your mind, ensconce themselves, and refuse to be dislodged."

—SATURDAY REVIEW

"Irwin Shaw's short stories are among the best written by anyone anywhere."

—NEWSDAY

"Shaw is the suavest of storytellers, combining romantic themes with an emollient manner, and leaving the reader with a pleasurable feeling of sophisticated satisfaction."

—SAN FRANCISCO CHRONICLE

"Irwin Shaw's latest collection provides ample testimony to his narrative skill ... written with an awareness of the harshness of life today, but also with a bittersweet tenderness."

—BALTIMORE SUN

By the Author

NOVELS

* Voices of a Summer Day
* The Young Lions
  The Troubled Air
* Lucy Crown
* Two Weeks in Another Town
* Rich Man, Poor Man
* Evening in Byzantium
* Nightwork

SHORT STORY COLLECTIONS

Sailor Off the Bremen
Welcome to the City
Act of Faith
Mixed Company
Tip on a Dead Jockey
* Love on a Dark Street
* God Was Here But He Left Early

PLAYS

Bury the Dead
The Gentle People
Sons and Soldiers
The Assassin

NON-FICTION

In the Company of Dolphins

* Available in Dell Editions

IRWIN SHAW

LOVE ON A DARK STREET

A DELL BOOK

ACKNOWLEDGMENTS

"The Man Who Married A French Wife." Copyright © 1962 by The Condé Nast Publications Inc. Reprinted from *Mademoiselle*.

"The Inhabitants of Venus." Copyright © 1963 by The Curtis Publishing Co.

"Noises In The City." Copyright © 1963 by Irwin Shaw. Originally appeared in *Playboy*.

"A Year To Learn The Language." Copyright © 1963 by Irwin Shaw. Originally appeared in *Redbook*.

"Love On A Dark Street." Copyright © 1961 by Irwin Shaw. Originally appeared in *Esquire*.

"Once, In Aleppo." Copyright © 1964 by Irwin Shaw. Originally appeared in *Playboy*.

"Circle Of Light." Copyright © 1958 by Esquire, Inc. Originally appeared in *Esquire*.

"Wistful, Delicately Gay." Copyright © 1954 by The Hearst Corporation.

"Tune Every Heart And Every Voice." Copyright © 1961 by HMH Publishing Co., Inc. Originally appeared in *Playboy*.

"Goldilocks At Graveside." Copyright © 1964 by Esquire, Inc. Originally appeared in *Esquire*.

Published by
DELL PUBLISHING CO., INC.
1 Dag Hammarskjold Plaza
New York, New York 10017
Copyright © 1965 by Irwin Shaw
Dell ® TM 681510, Dell Publishing Co., Inc.
All rights reserved
Reprinted by arrangement with
Delacorte Press
New York, N.Y.
First Dell Printing—September, 1966
Second Dell Printing—July 1976
Third Dell Printing—November 1976
Fourth Dell Printing—July 1978
Printed in U.S.A.

Contents

THE MAN WHO MARRIED A FRENCH WIFE	7
THE INHABITANTS OF VENUS	29
NOISES IN THE CITY	54
A YEAR TO LEARN THE LANGUAGE	66
LOVE ON A DARK STREET	101
ONCE, IN ALEPPO	123
CIRCLE OF LIGHT	164
WISTFUL, DELICATELY GAY	192
TUNE EVERY HEART AND EVERY VOICE	219
GOLDILOCKS AT GRAVESIDE	233

The Man Who Married a French Wife

The habit had grown on him. Now it had assumed the shape of a nightly ritual. When he sat down in the commuters' train at Grand Central, he opened the French newspaper first. He read with difficulty, because he had only begun to teach himself the language after he had come back from Europe, and that was more than a year ago. Finally, he read almost the entire paper, the list of accidents and crimes on the second page, the political section, the theatrical section, even the sports page. But what he turned to first, always, was the account of the attentats, and plastiquages, the assassinations and bombings and massacres that were being perpetrated in Algeria and throughout France by the Secret Army, in rebellion against the government of General De Gaulle.

He was looking for a name. For more than a year he hadn't found it. Then, on a rainy spring evening, as the crowded train, full of suburbia's prisoners, pulled out of the station, he saw it. There had been eleven bombings in Paris the night before, the paper reported. A bookshop had been blown up, a pharmacy, the apartments of two officials, the home of a newspaperman. The newspaperman had been cut around the head, but his days, as the phrase went in French, were not in danger.

Beauchurch put the paper under the seat. This was one newspaper he wasn't going to take home with him.

He sat staring out the window, now sluiced with rain, as the train came up from the tunnel and raced along Park Avenue. Matters hadn't worked out exactly as predicted, but close enough, close enough. He stared out through the window and the year vanished and the tenements and rainy roofs of New York were replaced by the afternoon streets of Paris. . . .

Beauchurch went into a *tabac* and by means of pantomime and pointing got the cigar he wanted. It was the second cigar of the afternoon. At home he never smoked a cigar until after dinner, but he was on holiday, and he had had a fine lunch with two old friends, and Paris was brisk and strange and amusing around him, and the second cigar gave him an added feeling of luxury and well-being. He lit the cigar carefully and strolled along the rich street, admiring the shop windows and the way the women looked and the last light of the autumn sun on Napoleon atop his high green pillar. He looked into a famous jeweler's shop and half-decided to be terribly extravagant and buy a clip for his wife. He went in and priced the clip and came out shaking his head. A little farther on he stopped at a bookshop and bought her a large, beautifully printed volume containing colored prints of the École de Paris. The book was expensive, but it felt like a bargain after the clip.

Ginette wasn't crazy about jewelry, anyway. Luckily. Because until the last year or so, when Beauchurch had been taken in as a partner in the law firm for which he had worked ever since he'd gotten his degree, he and Ginette had had to be very canny about money. What with the children and taxes and building the house near Stamford, there was very little left over for things like diamond clips. Besides, Beauchurch thought, she's so beautiful and smart she doesn't need diamonds. He smiled to himself at this clever and flattering rationalization.

Then, a half-block from the hotel, he saw her. She was about twenty yards ahead of him and there were quite a few people between them, but there was no mistaking that bright, neat head and the straight, disciplined way she held herself as she walked. But she wasn't alone. She was with a man in a raincoat and a soft green Tyrolian kind of hat, and she was holding his arm as they walked slowly toward the hotel on the corner of the Rue de Rivoli. They were talking earnestly, Ginette's face turned to the man, as he guided her among the pedestrians, and from time to time they stopped, as though the gravity of their conversation had halted them.

As he watched them, Beauchurch felt his sense of well-being, of luxury, of pleasure at being in this city for the first time in his life, suddenly sliding away from him. She was so obviously involved with the man in the raincoat, so fixed, concerned, intimate, so patently oblivious of everything else around her, that she gave Beauchurch the feeling that if he went up to her and stood in front of her it would be some time before she would recognize him or acknowledge him as her husband. After nearly thirteen years of marriage, the intensity of his wife's connection with a stranger on a foreign street made Beauchurch feel lost, disavowed, and for one moment he faced the realization that it was possible that one day she would leave him.

He made himself stop and look in a window, to free himself from the coupled image. His reflection in the window was solid, reasonable, reassuring, that of a man in his middle thirties, not bad-looking, in abounding health, with a twist of humor about the mouth. It was the reflection of a man who was plainly not capricious or given to neurotic fantasies, the reflection of a man who could be depended upon in crises to act with intelligence and decision, a man who would not be hurried into hasty judgments or shaken by baseless fears.

Staring into the window, he made himself examine the possible meanings of what he had seen. His wife had said she was having lunch with her mother. Since Beauchurch had already had several dinners with the old lady and since she couldn't speak English and he couldn't speak French, he had felt that his duty as visiting son-in-law had been fairly discharged by now and he had begged off, to lunch with other friends. But it was past four o'clock by now. Lunch was a long time over, even in Paris. Even if she had seen her mother, Ginette would have had plenty of time for other rendezvous between then and now. Ginette had grown up in Paris and had visited France alone twice since their marriage, and the man in the raincoat could have been any one of a hundred old friends or acquaintances met by accident on the street. But the memory of what Ginette and the man in the raincoat had looked like together twenty paces in front of him canceled out the notion of accident and made the words "friend" / or "acquaintance" seem inadequate and false.

On the other hand, in thirteen years of marriage, Ginette had never even for a moment given the slightest indication that she had ever been interested in any other man, and the last time she had been in Paris to see her mother, she had cut her stay short by two weeks because, she said, she hadn't been able to bear to be separated any longer from Beauchurch and the children. And on this visit, which by now had lasted nearly three weeks, they had been together almost every moment of every day, except for those evasive hours when women disappear into hairdressers' salons and the fitting rooms of couturiers.

Another thing to be considered—if she had anything to hide what would she be doing a few doors from the hotel, where she might expect to see her husband at any moment? Unless she didn't want to hide it, whatever it might be, unless she deliberately wanted to provoke . . . Provoke what?

Provoke what?

He made himself remain absolutely still in front of the window, not shifting his weight by so much as an ounce, not moving a finger. He had taught himself this little trick of immobility a long time ago, for the times when he was tempted to lash out, to act rashly, to give way to anger or impatience. As a young man he had been violent and passionate. He had been thrown out of two preparatory schools and one college. He had avoided court-martial in the Army only through the unexpected benevolence of a Major he had grossly insulted. He had been a nervy, blind fighter, a quick maker of enemies, intolerant, sometimes brutal with men and women both. He had made himself over, slowly and with pain, because he had been intelligent enough to realize that he was skirting destruction. Or, rather, he had made over his surface, his behavior. He had known what he wanted to be like, what he had to be like to reach the goals he had set for himself. He was clear, at an early age, what those goals were. They included financial security, a reputation for probity and hard work, a loving, honorable marriage and decent children, and, later on, political power and a high federal judgeship. All these things, he knew, would elude him if he did not keep himself sternly in hand at all times. He had forced himself to act slowly, to swallow fury, to present to the world the image of a calm, balanced, judicious man. Even with Ginette he had managed, almost completely, to preserve that image. The cost was high, but until now it had been worth it. At his core, he still knew himself to be violent, sudden, ready for explosion, fatally ready to destroy himself for the satisfaction of a moment's anger, a moment's desire. The deliberateness of his movements, the softness of his speech, the formal air of privacy with which he surrounded himself were the calculated means by which he preserved himself. Looking like the safest of men, he felt himself continually in danger. Seemingly even-tempered and rational, he fought a daily battle within himself against rage and irrationality, and lived in dread of the day when the useful, admirable, sham character with which he masked his inner turbulence would crack and vanish.

Provoke, provoke . . .

Beauchurch shrugged. He took one last look at the tall, sensible, well-dressed reflection of himself in the window and turned toward the hotel. By now Ginette and the man had disappeared. Beauchurch covered the few yards to the hotel entrance rapidly, threw away his cigar, and went in.

Ginette and the man were standing at the concierge's desk in the lobby. The man had taken his hat off and was turning it slowly in his hands. As Beauchurch came up to them, he heard Ginette saying to the concierge, "Est-ce que Monsieur Beauchurch est rentré?" which was one of the few sentences he could understand in the French language.

"Bonjour, Madame," Beauchurch said, smiling, and carefully keeping his face normal. "Can I help you?"

Ginette turned. "Tom," she said, "I was hoping you were back." She kissed his cheek. To Beauchurch she seemed strained and ill-at-ease. "I want you to meet a friend of mine. Claude Mestre. My husband."

Beauchurch shook the man's hand. The fleeting contact gave him an impression of dryness and nerves. Mestre was tall and thin, with a high, domed brow and smooth chestnut hair. He had deep-set, worried, gray eyes and a long straight nose. He was a good-looking man, but his face was pale and seemed tired, as though he were overworked. He smiled politely as he greeted Beauchurch, but there was an obscure appeal buried in the smile.

"You don't have to go out again, do you, Tom?" Ginette asked. "We can sit down somewhere and have a drink, can't we?"

"Of course," Beauchurch said.

"I do not wish to spoil your afternoon," Mestre said. His accent was strong, but he spoke slowly and clearly, pronouncing every syllable loyally. "You have so little time in Paris."

"We have nothing to do until dinner," Beauchurch said. "I'd love a drink."

They went toward the bar, past a long alley where old ladies were taking tea. The bar was a huge hall, dark, almost deserted, with the tarnished gold-leaf and mahogany elegance of a nineteenth-century palace. Ginette squeezed Beauchurch's arm as they went through the door, which Mestre held open for them. Close to her, Beauchurch was conscious of the strong, pleasing scent of Ginette's perfume.

"How was your mother?" Beauchurch asked, as they traversed the room, toward the high windows which looked out on the Tuileries.

"Fine," Ginette said. "She was disappointed you couldn't come to lunch."

"Tell her, next time," Beauchurch said. They gave their coats to the waiter and sat down. Beauchurch handed the package containing the book of prints to the waiter, too, without telling Ginette what was in it.

"This is rather sinister, this bar, isn't it?" Mestre said, looking around him. "It is rather like a place for ghosts to come and drink."

"I imagine it was pretty gay here," Beauchurch said, "in 1897."

The waiter came and they all ordered whiskey and Beauchurch was conscious again of Ginette's perfume when she leaned toward him slightly to allow him to light a cigarette for her. He saw, or imagined he saw, a cool, speculative expression on Mestre's face, as though the Frenchman was trying to judge the nature of the relations between the husband and wife across the table from him, in the moment in which they briefly approached each other over the flare of the lighter.

There were two large Americans at the bar, their voices making a bass background rumble of sound in the room,

THE MAN WHO MARRIED A FRENCH WIFE

with an occasional phrase here and there suddenly intelligible across the bare tables. ". . . The problem," one of the men was saying, "is with the Belgian delegation. They're sullen and suspicious. I understand perfectly why, but . . ." Then the voice sank back into a rumble again.

"Claude is a journalist," Ginette said, in her hostessy, introducing-the-guests-at-a-party voice. "He's one of the leading journalists in France. That's how I found him. I saw his name in the paper."

"I congratulate you," Beauchurch said. "On being a journalist, I mean. Like everybody else in America, when I was young, I wanted to be a newspaperman. But nobody would give me a job." Saw his name in a newspaper, he thought. I was right. She called him. It wasn't any accidental meeting on the street.

Mestre shrugged. "Perhaps I should be the one to congratulate you," he said. "For not getting the job. There are moments when I consider the man who gave me my first job on a newspaper as a deadly enemy." He sounded weary and disabused. "For example—I could never hope to dress my wife in the charming manner in which Ginette is dressed or afford a six-week tour of Europe in the middle of the Autumn like you."

That's a damned envious, unpleasant thing for a man to say, Beauchurch thought. "Oh," he said. "You're married."

"Forever," Mestre said.

"He has four children," Ginette said. A trifle too quickly, Beauchurch thought.

"I am personally attempting to redress the demographic imbalance that Napoleon left as his heritage to France." Mestre smiled ironically as he said it.

"Have you seen his children?" Beauchurch asked Ginette.

"No," she said. She volunteered no further information.

The waiter came and served their drinks. Mestre lifted his glass. "To a happy stay in this happy country," he said, his voice still carrying the edge of irony. "And a quick return."

They drank. There was an uncomfortable silence.

"What's your specialty?" Beauchurch asked, to bridge the silence. "I mean, is there any particular field that you write about?"

"War and politics," Mestre said. "The prize assignments."

"That's enough to keep you busy, I imagine," Beauchurch said.

"Yes. There are always enough fools and brutes to keep a man busy," Mestre said.

"What do you think is going to happen here, in France?" Beauchurch said, resolved to be polite and keep the conversation going until he could find some inkling of why Ginette had wanted him to meet this man.

"What do you think is going to happen here?" Mestre repeated. "It is becoming the new form of greeting in France. It has practically replaced *Bonjour* and *Comment ça va.*" He shrugged. "We are going to have trouble."

"Everybody is going to have trouble," Beauchurch said. "In America, too."

"Do you think," Mestre fixed him with his cold, ironic glance, "that in America you will have violence and political murder and civil war?"

"No," Beauchurch said. "Is that what you think is going to happen here?"

"To a certain extent," Mestre said, "it has already happened."

"And you think it will happen again?" Beauchurch asked.

"Probably," said Mestre. "But in a more aggravated form."

"Soon?"

"Sooner or later," Mestre said.

"That's very pessimistic," Beauchurch said.

"France is composed exclusively of pessimists," said Mestre. "If you stay here long enough, you will discover that."

"If it does come, who do you think will win?" Beauchurch asked.

"The worst elements," said Mestre. "Not permanently, perhaps. But for a period. Unfortunately, the period will have to be lived through. It will not be pleasant."

"Tom," Ginette said, "I think maybe I'd better explain about Claude." She had been listening intently to Mestre, watching his face anxiously as he spoke. "Claude works for a liberal newspaper here and it's already been confiscated several times by the Government because of articles he wrote about Algeria."

"It is getting so that when an article by me appears and the journal is not confiscated," Mestre said, "that I examine myself for signs of cowardice."

Self-pity, Beauchurch thought, combined with deep self-satisfaction. He liked the man less and less, the more he talked.

"There's something else, Tom," Ginette said. She turned to Mestre. "You don't mind if I tell him, do you, Claude?"

"If you think it will interest him . . ." Claude shrugged. "Americans are not liable to take things like that very seriously."

"I'm a very serious American," Beauchurch said, letting his annoyance show for the first time. "I read *Time* magazine almost every week."

"Now you are making fun of me," Mestre said. "I do not blame you. It is my fault." He looked around him vaguely. "Is it possible to have another drink?"

Beauchurch signaled the waiter and made a circular motion with his hand, indicating another round for everyone. "What's the something else, Ginette?" he asked, trying to keep the irritation from his voice.

"The letters and the telephone calls," Ginette said.

"What letters and telephone calls?"

"Threatening to kill me," Mestre said lightly. "The letters are usually addressed to me. The telephone calls to my wife. Naturally, being a woman, she gets rather upset. Especially since there are periods during which she receives five or six a day."

"Who writes them?" Beauchurch asked. He wished he could disbelieve the man, but there was something about the way he was talking now that put the seal of truth upon what he said. "Who makes the calls?"

Mestre shrugged. "Who knows? Cranks, elderly widows, practical jokers, retired army officers, assassins. . . . They never sign their names, of course. It is not terribly new. The anonymous letter has always played an honorable role in French literature."

"Do you think they mean it?" Beauchurch asked.

"Sometimes." Mestre looked up as the waiter came over with the drinks and didn't speak again until the man had gone off once more. "When I am tired or depressed or it's raining, I think they mean it. At any rate, *some* of them undoubtedly mean it."

"What do you do about it?"

"Nothing," Mestre said, sounding surprised. "What is there to do?"

"You could go to the police, for one thing," Beauchurch said.

"In America one would undoubtedly go to the police," Mestre said. "Here . . ." He made a grimace and took a long sip of his drink. "I am not on particularly good terms with the police at the moment. In fact, I am of the opinion that my mail is often opened and from time to time I am followed and my phone is tapped."

"That's disgraceful," Beauchurch said.

"I like your husband," Mestre said lightly, almost playfully, to Ginette. "He finds things like this disgraceful. It is very American."

"We've had times like that in America, too," Beauchurch said, defending the level of venality of his native land. "And not so long ago, either."

"I know, I know," Mestre said. "I do not mean to imply that I believe that America is a fairyland which is completely untouched by the special diseases of our age. Still, as I say, in America, one would go to the police. . . ."

"Do you *really* think that somebody may try to kill you?" Beauchurch asked. Irrelevantly, he thought, This is a hell of a way to be spending a holiday, talking about things like this.

"Not just now perhaps," Mestre said calmly, as though he were surveying, with judicial impartiality, an abstract problem that had no personal relation to him. "But once the trouble starts, almost certainly."

"Just how do you think the trouble will start?" Somehow, after the weeks of enjoying the peaceful glittering city, with its overflowing shops, its air of bustling activity, its range of pleasures, it was impossible to believe that it would soon be given over to violence and bloodshed.

"How will it start?" Mestre repeated. He squinted thoughtfully over Beauchurch's shoulder into the mahogany depths of the bar, as though trying to formulate there some picture of the future that lay in wait for the city. "I am not in on the councils of the heroes, you understand," he smiled slightly, "so I can only speculate. It depends

THE MAN WHO MARRIED A FRENCH WIFE

upon the General, of course. On the state of his health—physical and political. On his powers of survival. At the moment, we are in a period of *détente*. The plotters are waiting. The murderers remain more or less under cover. But if the General is brought down—by failure, by overconfidence, by old age, by anything—then we can expect certain events to follow."

"What?" Beauchurch asked.

"Perhaps an uprising of the troops in Algiers," Mestre said, "a landing on the aerodromes, a movement among the police, the emergence of secretly armed and trained bodies of commandoes in various parts of the country, to take over the seats of government and the radio and television stations, the capture or assassination of certain leading political figures. The usual. There is no mystery any more about these things. Only the timing is problematical."

Beauchurch turned to his wife. "Do you believe all this?"

"Yes," she said.

"Do any of your other friends talk like this?"

"Almost all of them," she said.

"And you"—Beauchurch turned back, almost accusingly to Mestre—"what do you intend to do if it happens?"

"I shall offer my services to the government," Mestre said. "That is, if I can find the government, and if it has not already locked me up somewhere by then."

"Christ," Beauchurch said, "what a thing it is to be a Frenchman."

"It has its compensations," Mestre said. "Some of the time."

"All right," Beauchurch said to Ginette, "I'm briefed. Only I don't know what for. Why did you want me to hear all this?"

There was an exchange of glances between Mestre and Ginette, and once more Beauchurch had the fleeting sensation of being an outsider, conspired against.

Mestre leaned over and touched Ginette's hand lightly. "Permit me to explain, my dear," he said. He lifted his glass and drank, like an orator playing for time. "Mr. Beauchurch," he began formally, "your wife has been good enough to suggest that perhaps you would be willing to help me. . . ." He waited for Beauchurch to say something, but Beauchurch remained unhelpfully silent.

"It is, unhappily, a question of money," Mestre said.

Good God, Beauchurch thought, all this lead-up to ask for a loan! He was annoyed with Ginette for having gone along with this elaborate manipulation. He could feel his face settling into refusing lines as he waited for Mestre to continue.

"If anything happens," Mestre went on, looking uncomfortable, "as I believe it will, I may have to try to escape from France. Or at least, my wife and my children would be better off out of the country. In any event, I would feel considerably relieved if I had some money safely in another country, to tide me over at least some part of the period of exile that I foresee as a possibility for myself and my family. A numbered account in Switzerland, for example, that either my wife or myself could draw on without formalities. . . ."

"I told Claude we were going to Geneva on Thursday," Ginette said. There was a tone of defiance in her voice, Beauchurch thought, as she said this. "It would be the simplest thing in the world for us to do."

"Now let me get this straight," Beauchurch said to Ginette. "Have you promised your friend that we would lend him a certain amount of money for—" Mestre looked stupefied as he listened, and Beauchurch stopped in midsentence. "Have I misunderstood something?" he asked.

"I'm afraid you have," Mestre said. He seemed embarrassed and angry. "There was never any question of a loan. What right would I have to ask a man I had never seen in my life to lend me even a hundred francs?"

"Ginette," Beauchurch said, "I think you'd better explain."

"A French citizen has no right to take money out of France," Ginette said. "Or, anyway, very little. And since we're going to Switzerland, I thought we could do it for Claude."

"As I understand it," Beauchurch said, "nobody has a right to take much money out of France, not even Americans."

"Two hundred and fifty new francs," Mestre said.

"But the customs people never bother Americans," Ginette said. "They never even open your bags. And if they do happen to ask you how many francs you have on you, you say a hundred or so, and that's the end of it."

THE MAN WHO MARRIED A FRENCH WIFE

"Still," Beauchurch persisted, "technically we'd be breaking the law."

"Technically," Ginette said impatiently. "What difference would it make?"

"My dear friends," Mestre said, "please . . ." He spread his hands above the table pacifically. "I beg you not to argue on my account. If you have the slightest hesitation, I understand perfectly. . . ."

"Let me ask you a question, Mr. Mestre," Beauchurch said. "Supposing we hadn't happened to come to France at this time, Ginette and I, and supposing she hadn't called you up—what would you have done?"

Mestre sucked in his cheeks thoughtfully. When he spoke, he spoke slowly and carefully. "I suppose I would have tried to get someone else to do it for me. But I would be very—very—" He searched for the word. "Very uneasy. As I told you, I am sure that from time to time I am under surveillance. I could only entrust something like this to a very close friend—whose relationship with me would be likely to compromise him. With bad luck, the friend might fall under suspicion, especially if he crossed the frontier to another country. Any Frenchman is likely to be searched upon trying to leave the country. He is likely to be questioned. In the times that I see ahead of us, the questioning that will be taking place here in France is liable to be most strict." He smiled wanly at his understatement. "I would not like to have to depend upon the endurance or the good will or the discretion of any of my friends at that time for my safety. Still, that is no reason for you to concern yourself with me. A man who is in danger and demands help is always such a bore. One has only to remember how annoyed everybody was with the refugees during the war." He looked around for the waiter and signaled him to come over. "I would be most pleased," Mestre said, "if you would permit me to pay for the drinks."

"Wait a minute," Beauchurch said. "How much would you want me to take to Switzerland for you?"

"Four million francs," Mestre said. "Old francs, that is."

"That's only about eight thousand dollars, Tom," Ginette said.

"I know," Beauchurch said. He took the check from the waiter's hand, over Mestre's protest. He paid the waiter and stood up. "Let me think about this and talk it over with Ginette. She has your number. We'll call you tomorrow."

Mestre stood up, too. "If you don't mind," he said, "I would prefer to call you. The fewer calls I get, the better. . . ."

". . . In Africa, for example," one of the Americans at the bar was saying, "the old system of competitive bribery is breaking down. But nobody's found anything better. . . ."

Beauchurch followed Mestre and Ginette out of the room, down the alley of old ladies still taking their tea, solidly anchored among their fur coats, their poodles, their pastries, oblivious to all plots, troop movements, fighting in the streets. A dark phalanx of widows, bedecked with the jeweled trophies of their victories, they remained firm and reassuring against all the assaults of change. In that corridor of elaborately coifed, silvery heads, Mestre's fearful words of prophecy seemed like the insubstantial report of a child's dream.

In the lobby, Mestre kissed Ginette's hand, made a formal little bow to Beauchurch and went off. He was bent over surprisingly, Beauchurch noticed, for a man so young, and his walk was heavy and without resilience. When he put on his soft green hat, he did it carelessly, with no attempt at dash. Whatever he was, Beauchurch decided, he was no professional lady-killer. But when Beauchurch turned toward Ginette, he thought he detected a certain emotion in her eyes, only partially concealed. But whether it was desire or pity, it was impossible to tell.

They went up to their room in silence. The sense of holiday they had shared since their arrival in Paris had entirely gone, and the high-ceilinged old room looked chilly and clumsily furnished in the light of the inadequate lamps. Ginette hung up her coat and pushed listlessly at her hair before the mirror. Beauchurch put the package with the book in it on a table and looked out the window at the gardens of the Tuileries across the traffic-jammed street below him. All the trees were bare and the people hurrying past the newly lit lampposts looked harassed and cold.

Beauchurch heard the bed creak as Ginette sat down on it. "That four million francs," she said. "That's his life savings. That's all he has in the world."

Beauchurch said nothing. He continued to stare out the window at the dark gardens.

"If you won't take it through for him," Ginette said, "I will."

Beauchurch took a deep breath. He turned deliberately away from the windows. "That was a stupid thing to say," he said.

Ginette looked at him coldly, with hostility. "Was it?" she said. "I suppose so." She swung her legs up on the bed and lay back, staring at the ceiling. "Still, I mean it."

"It would make an interesting headline," Beauchurch said. "Wife of New York Lawyer Held in Paris for Smuggling Banknotes. Husband Claims Ignorance of Wife's Activities."

"Does that mean you're not going to help Claude?" Ginette's voice was flat and she kept squinting up at the ceiling.

"It means that in general I am a law-abiding citizen," Beauchurch said. "It means that when I am a guest in a country I prefer not to cheat my hosts."

"Oh," Ginette said. "What a lucky thing it is to be an American. And a Puritan. How convenient it can be."

"It also means that I am balancing the risks against the advantages," said Beauchurch.

"There are no advantages," Ginette said. "There's nothing to balance. A man's in trouble, and we can help him. That's all."

"A lot of men are in trouble," Beauchurch said. "The question is, why do we pick out this particular one to help."

"You didn't like him, did you?"

"Not much," Beauchurch said. "He's self-important and impressed with his own intelligence, and he has a condescending attitude toward Americans."

Unexpectedly, Ginette laughed.

"What are you laughing about?" Beauchurch demanded.

"Because you're so accurate," Ginette said. "That's exactly what he's like. He's the perfect model of the French intellectual." She laughed again. "I must tell him that you ticked him off exactly. He'll be furious."

Beauchurch regarded his wife puzzledly. Her laughter was real, and what she had just said was certainly not the sort of thing a woman would say about a man who attracted her. But against this, there was the enduring vision of the two of them so deeply engrossed in each other on the street in front of the hotel, and Ginette's persistence in pushing Beauchurch to Mestre's rescue.

Beauchurch sat down on the edge of the bed. "The question is," he repeated, "why do we pick out this particular one to help."

Ginette lay quiet for a moment, her arms along her sides, her hands flat on the brocaded bed cover. "Because he's a friend," she said. She waited. Then she said, "That's not quite enough, is it?"

"Not quite," said Beauchurch.

"Because he's French and I was born in Paris," Ginette said. "Because he's talented, because I agree with his politics, because the people who want to kill him are vile. . . ." She stopped and waited again. Beauchurch still said nothing. "That's not quite enough, either, is it?" Ginette said, staring at the ceiling.

"Not quite," said Beauchurch.

"Because he was my lover," Ginette said, without emphasis, looking up at the ceiling. "Did you expect that?"

"I suppose so," Beauchurch said.

"A long time ago," Ginette said. "During the war. He was the first one."

"How many times have you seen him since we've been married?" Beauchurch said. He didn't look at his wife, but he listened intently for a tone of falsehood in her voice. Ginette was not a liar, but a question like this had never come up between them before, and Beauchurch believed that on this subject almost all women, and all men, too, for that matter, lied almost all the time.

"I've seen him twice since 1946," Ginette said. "Yesterday and today."

"Why did you decide, after all these years, to see him yesterday?"

Ginette reached over to the bedtable and took a cigarette out of a pack that was lying there. Automatically, Beauchurch lit it for her. She lay back, her head on the bolster, blowing the smoke straight up. "I don't know why," she said. "Curiosity, nostalgia, guilt—the feeling that middle age was rushing up on me and I wanted to be reminded of a time when I was young—a feeling that maybe I wouldn't see Paris again for a long time and I wanted to straighten out certain memories. . . . I don't know. Don't you ever want to see your first girl again?"

"No," Beauchurch said.

"Well, maybe women're different. Or Frenchwomen. Or me." She squinted at the ceiling through the cigarette smoke. "You're not worried about what went on, are you?"

"No," Beauchurch said. He didn't say anything about the realization he had had on the street that it was possible for her one day to leave him.

"We had two beers at the Dome, because he once took me there on my birthday," Ginette said. "And after the first ten minutes it was all politics and his problem and the thing about Switzerland. Which I brought up, by the way, in case you're thinking of blaming him."

"I'm not blaming him for anything," Beauchurch said. "Still—why didn't you tell me about him yesterday?"

"I was playing with the idea of just taking the money in myself and not worrying you about it at all. Then I decided, today, that that wouldn't be fair to you, and that you had to talk to Claude yourself. I was right about that, wasn't I?" She lifted her head inquisitively.

"Yes," he said.

"I didn't realize that you'd turn so severe," Ginette said. "You didn't behave like your usual self with him at all. You're usually so pleasant with new people. And you were against him from the beginning."

"That's true," Beauchurch said. He offered no explanations. "Look," he said, "you don't have to tell me any of this if you don't want to."

"I do want to," Ginette said. "So you'll understand why I think I have to help him if I can. So you'll understand him better. So you'll understand *me* better."

"Don't you think I understand you?" Beauchurch asked, surprised.

"Not well enough," Ginette said. "We're so reticent with each other, so polite, so careful never to say anything to each other that might disturb or hurt. . . ."

"Is that wrong?" Beauchurch said. "I've always thought that was one of the reasons our marriage has been so solid."

"Solid," Ginette said vaguely. "What marriage is solid?"

"What the hell are you driving at?" Beauchurch asked.

"I don't know," Ginette said listlessly. "Nothing. Maybe I'm homesick, only I'm not sure where my home is. Maybe we shouldn't have come to Paris. Maybe because I was a silly young girl when I was in Paris, I must behave like a silly young girl here, even now when I'm a sober American matron. I *do* look like a sober American matron, don't I, Tom?"

"No," he said.

"I walk along the street and I forget who I am, I forget how old I am, I forget my American passport," she said, speaking softly. "I'm eighteen years old again, there are gray uniforms all over the streets, I'm trying to decide whether I'm in love or not, I change my mind at every corner, I'm wildly happy. Don't be shocked. I wasn't happy because there was a war and the Germans were here, I was happy because I was eighteen years old. A war isn't all one color, even in an occupied country. Hold my hand, please." She put her hand out toward him on the bed cover and he covered it with his, clasping the long, cool fingers, the soft palm, feeling the thin metal of the wedding ring. "We've never confessed enough, you and I," she said. "A marriage needs a certain amount of confession and we've skimped each other." She pressed his fingers. "Don't worry. There won't be any flood. There's no scandalous list. Claude was the only one until I married you. I'm hardly the popular American idea of a Frenchwoman at all. Are you surprised by any of this?"

"No," Beauchurch said. When he had met Ginette, when she had first come over to America on a scholarship, just after the war, she had still been a rather gawky girl, intent on her studies, slender and lovely, but not coquettish or sensual. When they had married she had been unpracticed, reserved, and the sensuality had come later, after months of marriage.

"He wanted to marry me," she went on. "Claude. I was at the Sorbonne. Immersed in Medieval History. It was one of the few safe subjects while the Germans were here. They didn't care much what people said about Charlemagne or St. Louis or the cathedral at Rouen. He was three or four years older than I. Very handsome and fierce-looking. It's not there now, is it?"

"No," Beauchurch said. "Not really."

"How quickly it goes." She shook her head, as though to stop herself from continuing this line of thought. "He wrote plays. He didn't show them to anyone because he didn't want to have any plays put on in Paris while the Germans were still here. Then, after the war, nobody put them on, anyway. I suppose he really wasn't much of a playwright. After the Liberation of Paris, it turned out he hadn't only been writing plays during the Occupation. He'd been in the Resistance and he was put into the Army and that winter he was badly wounded outside Belfort. He was in the hospital nearly two years. They changed him, those years. He became bitter, he hated what was happening to France, to the whole world. He had no hope for anything except . . . well, except for us, him and me. Whatever hope he had in the world he bound up in me. I promised to marry him when he got out, but then the scholarship came along, the chance to go to America. . . . He pleaded with me not to go, or to marry him before I went. He kept saying I'd find someone else in America, that I'd forget him, forget France. He made me swear that no matter what happened I'd come back and see him before I married anyone else. I swore I'd do it. It wasn't hard to do—I loved him—I was sure there'd never be anybody else. Anyway, he was still in the hospital—he had to recover first, establish himself at something, we didn't have a penny between us. Then I met you. I tried. I held back as much as I could. Didn't I?" Her voice was harsh, demanding; before the image of her lover lying broken in his hospital bed so many years ago she was justifying the actions of the girl breaking out of adolescence, newly emerged from the privations and fears of war. "I did everything I could, didn't I?"

"Yes," Beauchurch said, remembering the times he'd been ready to give her up, furious at her hesitations, her incomprehensible fluctuations. Now, after the long marriage, the children, the closely linked lives, they were comprehensible. He wondered if he would have been happier if he'd known, if the marriage would have been better or worse, if he would have behaved differently, loved her more or less. "Why didn't you tell me then?" he asked.

"It was my problem," she said. "It was between him and me. Anyway, I didn't go back. I didn't tell him anything until the day of the wedding. I sent him a cable. I asked him not to write me. I asked him to forgive me."

The days of weddings, Beauchurch thought. The brides at telegraph offices. *Forgive me.* Four thousand miles away. *It is over, it is too late. . . . You were in the hospital too long. Love.* "Well," he said, being cruel to her and to himself, "do you regret it now?" He remembered the phrase Mestre had used. "You could have spent your time redressing the demographic imbalance of France, as the man said."

"It's not too late," she said flatly. "Even now." She was angry and she was reacting to the jibe. "If you must know, he still wants to marry me."

"As of when?"

"As of this afternoon," she said.

"Four children and all?" Beauchurch said. "To say nothing of his wife and your husband and *your* children."

"I told him it was absurd," Ginette said. "We had it all out three years ago."

"Three years ago?" Beauchurch said. "I thought you said you'd only seen him twice since 1946—yesterday and today."

"I was lying," Ginette said, evenly. "Of course I saw him when I was here before. I would have had to be a monster not to see him. I saw him every day."

"I'm not going to ask you what happened," Beauchurch said. He stood up. He felt shaken, confused. The light through the ornate lampshades was dusty and melancholy, and his wife's face, turned away now, was in evening shadow, hidden, unfamiliar. Her voice was cold and distant and devoid of affection. Whatever happened to the holiday? he thought. He went over and poured himself a drink from the bottle on the table near the window. He didn't ask Ginette if she wanted one. The whiskey bit at his throat.

"Nothing happened," Ginette said. "I think I would have had an affair with him, if he had asked me. . . ."

"Why?" Beauchurch asked. "Do you still love him?"

"No," she said. "I don't know why. Atonement, restitution. . . . Anyway, he didn't ask me. It was marriage or nothing, he said. He couldn't bear losing me again, he said."

Beauchurch's hands trembled as he brought the glass to his lips again. A wave of anger toward the man engulfed him, at the arrogance, the egotism, of that permanent, despairing, broken, unwavering love. He put the glass down slowly to keep from throwing it against the wall. He stood immobile, closing his eyes. If he made the slightest movement, he was afraid of what it would lead to. The thought of Mestre and Ginette sitting at café tables during a distant Parisian summer, conferring, cold-bloodedly offering and refusing terms for the looting of his life, was infinitely harder to bear than the thought of their two bodies clasped in bed together. It was less innocent; it lacked the grace and normality of the pardonable weaknesses of the flesh; it ignored, as though they had never existed, the fair claims Beauchurch had established in the years of marriage; it was a conspiracy against him by enemies who were the more hateful because they had never made themselves known to him. If Mestre had been in the room that moment Beauchurch would have gladly killed him. "God damn him," Beauchurch said. He was surprised at how routine, how calm, his voice sounded. He opened his eyes, looked down at Ginette. If she said the wrong thing now, he felt that he would strike her and leave the room, the country, leave everything, once and for all.

"That's why I came home two weeks earlier the last time I was here," Ginette said. "I couldn't stand it any more. I was afraid I'd give in. I ran away."

"I'd prefer it," Beauchurch said, "if you said you ran back."

Ginette turned her head and stared steadily out of the shadows at him. "Yes," she said, "that's better. That's what I mean. I ran back."

She said the right thing, Beauchurch thought. It took a little coaching, but finally it was the right thing. "And in the future," he said, "when you come to France, to Paris, are you going to see him again?"

"Yes," she said. "I suppose so. How can we escape each other?" She lay in silence for a moment. "Well, there it is," she said. "The whole story. I should have told you long ago. Now—are you going to help him?"

Beauchurch looked down at her lying on the bed, the bright hair, the small delightful head, the womanly face with the hesitant touches of girlhood still faintly evident there, the slender, warm, well-known, deeply loved body, the long competent hands lying flat on the bedspread, and he knew there would be no violence, no flight that evening.

He knew, too, that he was more than ever inextricably entwined with her, with her memories, her wounds, betrayals, her other country, with her foreign dangers, her decisions, agonies, responsibilities, her lies, her commitments to renounced loves. He sat down beside her and leaned over and kissed her forehead gently. "Of course," he said. "Of course I'll help the bastard."

She laughed a little, softly, and brought up her hand and touched his cheek. "We won't come to Paris again for a long time," she said.

"I don't want to talk to him, though," Beauchurch said, holding her hand against his cheek. "You make all the arrangements."

"Tomorrow morning," she said. She sat up. "I sincerely hope that package is for me," she said.

"It is," he said. "It is that very thing."

She swung lightly out of bed and crossed the room, her stockinged feet making no noise on the faded old carpet. She unwrapped the package neatly, folding the paper carefully and making a little skein of the string. "It is just what I wanted," she said, as she picked up the book and ran her hand over the cover.

"I was going to buy you a diamond," Beauchurch said. "But I thought it would be crass."

"What a narrow escape," she said. She smiled at him. "Now," she said, "come in and talk to me and give me a drink while I take my bath. Then we'll go out and have a sinful, expensive dinner. Just you and me."

Carrying the book, she went into the bathroom. Beauchurch sat on the bed, squinting at the yellowish patterns of the old paint on the opposite wall, measuring his pain and his happiness. After a while he stood up and poured two good drinks and carried the glasses into the bathroom. Ginette was lying deep in the huge old tub, holding the book out of the water, gravely turning the pages. Beauchurch set her glass down on the rim of the tub and sat down on a chair facing her, next to a large, full-length mirror, whose surface, beaded with steam, mistily reflected the marble, the brass, the shining tiles of the warm, out-sized room, shaped for a more spacious age. He sipped at his drink and looked soberly at his wife, stretched out in the shimmering, fragrant water, and knew that the holiday was repaired. More than the holiday. And more than repaired.

The Inhabitants of Venus

He had been skiing since early morning, and he was ready to stop and have lunch in the village, but Mac said, "Let's do one more before eating," and since it was Mac's last day, Robert agreed to go up again. The weather was spotty, but there were occasional clear patches of sky, and the visibility had been good enough to make for decent skiing for most of the morning. The teleferique was crowded and they had to push their way in among the bright sweaters and anaracs and the bulky packs of the people who were carrying picnic lunches and extra clothing and skins for climbing. The doors were closed and the cabin swung out of the station, over the belt of pine trees at the base of the mountain.

The passengers were packed in so tightly that it was hard to reach for a handkerchief or light a cigarette. Robert was pressed, not unpleasurably, against a handsome young Italian woman with a dissatisfied face, who was explaining to someone over Robert's shoulder why Milan was such a miserable city to live in in the wintertime. "Milano si trova in un bacino deprimente," the woman said, "bagnato dalla pioggia durante tre mesi all'anno. E, nonostante il loro gusto per l'opera, i Milanesi non sono altro volgari materialisti che solo il denaro interessa," and Robert knew enough Italian to understand that the girl was saying that Milan was in a dismal basin which was swamped by rain for three months a year and that the Milanese, despite their taste for opera, were crass and materialistic and interested only in money.

Robert smiled. Although he had not been born in the United States, he had been a citizen since 1944, and it was pleasant to hear, in the heart of Europe, somebody else besides Americans being accused of materialism and a singular interest in money.

"What's the Contessa saying?" Mac whispered, across the curly red hair of a small Swiss woman who was standing between Robert and Mac. Mac was a lieutenant on leave from his outfit in Germany. He had been in Europe nearly three years and to show that he was not just an ordinary tourist, called all pretty Italian girls Contessa. Robert had met him a week before, in the bar of the hotel they were both staying at. They were the same kind of skiers, adventurous and looking for difficulties, and they had skied together every day, and they were already planning to come back at the same time for the next winter's holiday, if Robert could get over again from America.

"The Contessa is saying that in Milan all they're interested in is money," Robert said, keeping his voice low, although in the babble of conversation in the cabin there was little likelihood of being overheard.

"If I was in Milan," Mac said, "and she was in Milan, I'd be interested in something else besides money." He looked with open admiration at the Italian girl. "Can you find out what run she's going to do?"

"What for?" Robert asked.

"Because that's the run I'm going to do," Mac said, grinning. "I plan to follow her like her shadow."

"Mac," Robert said, "don't waste your time. It's your last day."

"That's when the best things always happen," Mac said. "The last day." He beamed, huge, overt, uncomplicated, at the Italian girl. She took no notice of him. She was busy now complaining to her friend about the natives of Sicily.

The sun came out for a few minutes and it grew hot in the cabin, with some forty people jammed, in heavy clothing, in such a small space, and Robert half-dozed, not bothering to listen any more to the voices speaking in French, Italian, English, Schweizerdeutsch, German, on all sides of him. Robert liked being in the middle of this informal congress of tongues. It was one of the reasons that he came to Switzerland to ski, whenever he could take the time off from his job. In the angry days through which the world was passing, there was a ray of hope in this good-natured polyglot chorus of people who were not threatening each other, who smiled at strangers, who had collected in these shining white hills merely to enjoy the innocent pleasures of sun and snow.

The feeling of generalized cordiality that Robert experienced on these trips was intensified by the fact that most of the people on the lifts and on the runs seemed more or less familiar to him. Skiers formed a kind of loose international club and the same faces kept turning up year after year in Mégève, Davos, St. Anton, Val d'Isère, so that after a while you had the impression you knew almost everybody on the mountain. There were four or five Americans whom Robert was sure he had seen at Stowe at Christmas and who had come over in one of the chartered ski-club planes that Swiss Air ran every winter on a cut-rate basis. The Americans were young and enthusiastic and none of them had ever been in Europe before and they were rather noisily appreciative of everything—the Alps, the food, the snow, the weather, the appearance of the peasants in their blue smocks, the chic of some of the lady skiers and the skill and good looks of the instructors. They were popular with the villagers because they were so obviously enjoying themselves. Besides, they tipped generously, in the American style, with what was, to Swiss eyes, an endearing disregard of the fact that a service charge of fifteen percent was added automatically to every bill that was presented to them. Two of the girls were very attractive, in a youthful, prettiest-girl-at-the-prom way, and one of the young men, a lanky boy from Philadelphia, the informal leader of the group, was a beautiful skier, who guided the others down the runs and helped the dubs when they ran into difficulties.

The Philadelphian, who was standing near Robert, spoke to him as the cabin swung high over a steep snowy face of the mountain. "You've skied here before, haven't you?" he said.

"Yes," said Robert, "a few times."

"What's the best run down this time of day?" the Philadelphian asked. He had the drawling, flat tone of the good New England schools that Europeans use in their imitations of upperclass Americans when they wish to make fun of them.

"They're all okay today," Robert said.

"What's this run everybody says is so good?" the boy asked. "The . . . the Kaiser something or other?"

"The Kaisergarten," Robert said. "It's the first gully to the right after you get out of the station on top."

"Is it tough?" the boy asked.

"It's not for beginners," Robert said.

"You've seen this bunch ski, haven't you?" The boy waved vaguely to indicate his friends. "Do you think they can make it?"

"Well," Robert said doubtfully, "there's a narrow steep ravine full of bumps halfway down, and there're one or two places where it's advisable not to fall, because you're liable to keep on sliding all the way, if you do. . . ."

"Aah, we'll take a chance," the Philadelphian said. "It'll be good for their characters. Boys and girls," he said, raising his voice, "the cowards will stay on top and have lunch. The heroes will come with me. We're going to the Kaisergarten. . . ."

"Francis," one of the pretty girls said. "I do believe it is your sworn intention to kill me on this trip."

"It's not as bad as all that," Robert said, smiling at the girl, to reassure her.

"Say," the girl said, looking interestedly at Robert, haven't I seen you someplace before?"

"On this lift, yesterday," Robert said.

"No." The girl shook her head. She had on a black, fuzzy, lamb-skin hat, and she looked like a high-school drum majorette pretending to be Anna Karenina. "Before yesterday. Someplace."

"I saw you at Stowe," Robert confessed. "At Christmas."

"Oh, that's where," she said. "I saw you ski. Oh, my, you're *silky*."

Mac broke into a loud laugh at this description of Robert's skiing style.

"Don't mind my friend," Robert said, enjoying the girl's admiration. "He's a coarse soldier who is trying to beat the mountain to its knees by brute strength."

"Say," the girl said, looking a little puzzled. "You have a funny little way of talking. Are you American?"

"Well, yes," Robert said. "I am now. I was born in France."

THE INHABITANTS OF VENUS

"Oh, that explains it," the girl said. "You were born among the crags."

"I was born in Paris," Robert said.

"Do you live there now?"

"I live in New York," Robert said.

"Are you married?" The girl asked anxiously.

"Barbara," the Philadelphian protested, "behave yourself."

"I just asked the man a simple, friendly question," the girl protested. "Do you mind, monsieur?"

"Not at all."

"*Are* you married?"

"Yes," Robert said.

"He has three children," Mac added helpfully. "The oldest one is going to run for president at the next election."

"Oh, isn't that too bad," the girl said. "I set myself a goal on this trip. I was going to meet one unmarried Frenchman."

"I'm sure you'll manage it," Robert said.

"Where is your wife? Now?" the girl said.

"In New York."

"Pregnant," Mac said, more helpful than ever.

"And she lets you run off and ski all alone like this?" the girl asked incredulously.

"Yes," Robert said. "Actually, I'm in Europe on business, and I sneaked off ten days."

"What business?" the girl asked.

"I'm a diamond merchant," Robert said. "I buy and sell diamonds."

"That's the sort of man I'd like to meet," the girl said. "Somebody awash with diamonds. But unmarried."

"Barbara!" the Philadelphian said.

"I deal mostly in industrial diamonds," Robert said. "It's not exactly the same thing."

"Even so," the girl said.

"Barbara," the Philadelphian said, "pretend you're a lady."

"If you can't speak candidly to a fellow American," the girl said, "who can you speak candidly to?" She looked out the Plexiglas window of the cabin. "Oh, dear," she said, "it's a perfect monster of a mountain, isn't it? I'm in a *fever* of terror." She turned and regarded Robert carefully. "You *do* look like a Frenchman," she said. "Terribly polished. You're definitely *sure* you're married?"

"Barbara," the Philadelphian said forlornly.

Robert laughed and Mac and the other Americans laughed and the girl smiled under her fuzzy hat, amused at her own clowning and pleased at the reaction she was getting. The other people in the car, who could not understand English, smiled good-naturedly at the laughter, happy, even though they were not in on the joke, to be the witnesses of this youthful gaiety.

Then, through the laughter, Robert heard a man's voice nearby, saying, in quiet tones of cold distaste, "Schaut euch diese dummen amerikanischen Gesichter an! Und diese Leute bilden sich ein, sie wären berufen, die Welt zu regieren."

Robert had learned German as a child, from his Alsatian grandparents, and he understood what he had just heard, but he forced himself not to turn around to see who had said it. His years of temper, he liked to believe, were behind him, and if nobody else in the cabin had overheard the voice or understood the words that had been spoken, he was not going to be the one to force the issue. He was here to enjoy himself and he didn't feel like getting into a fight or dragging Mac and the other youngsters into one. Long ago, he had learned the wisdom of playing deaf when he heard things like that, or worse. If some bastard of a German wanted to say, "Look at those stupid American faces. And these are the people who think they have been chosen to rule the world," it made very little real difference to anybody, and a grown-up man ignored it if he could. So he didn't look to see who had said it, because he knew that if he picked out the man, he wouldn't be able to let it go. This way, as an anonymous, though hateful voice, he could let it slide, along with many of the other things that Germans had said during his lifetime.

The effort of not looking was difficult, though, and he closed his eyes, angry with himself for being so disturbed by a scrap of overheard malice like this. It had been a perfect holiday up to now and it would be foolish to let it be shadowed, even briefly, by a random voice in a crowd. If you came to Switzerland to ski, Robert told himself, you had to expect to find some Germans. Though each year now there were more and more of them, massive, prosper-

THE INHABITANTS OF VENUS · 35

ous-looking men and sulky-looking women with the suspicious eyes of people who believe they are in danger of being cheated. Men and women both pushed more than was necessary in the lift lines, with a kind of impersonal egotism, a racial, unquestioning assumption of precedence. When they skied, they did it grimly, in large groups, as if under military orders. At night, when they relaxed in the bars and *stublis,* their merriment was more difficult to tolerate than their dedicated daytime gloom and Junker arrogance. They sat in red-faced platoons, drinking gallons of beer, volleying out great bursts of heavy laughter and roaring glee-club arrangements of students' drinking songs. Robert had not yet heard them sing the Horst Wessel song, but he noticed that they had long ago stopped pretending that they were Swiss or Austrian or that they had been born in the Alsace. Somehow, to the sport of skiing, which is, above all, individual and light and an exercise in grace, the Germans seemed to bring the notion of the herd. Once or twice, when he had been trampled in the teleferique station, he had shown some of his distaste to Mac, but Mac, who was far from being a fool under his puppy-fullback exterior, had said, "The trick is to isolate them, lad. It's only when they're in groups that they get on your nerves. I've been in Germany for three years and I've met a lot of good fellows and some *smashing* girls."

Robert had agreed that Mac was probably right. Deep in his heart, he wanted to believe that Mac was right. Before and during the war the problem of the Germans had occupied so much of his waking life, that V-E Day had seemed to him a personal liberation from them, a kind of graduation ceremony from a school in which he had been forced to spend long years, trying to solve a single, boring, painful problem. He had reasoned himself into believing that their defeat had returned the Germans to rationality. So, along with the relief he felt because he no longer ran the risk of being killed by them, there was the almost as intense relief that he no longer had especially to *think* about them.

Once the war was over, he had advocated reestablishing normal relations with the Germans as quickly as possible, both as good politics and simple humanity. He drank German beer and even bought a Volkswagen, although if it were up to him, given the taste for catastrophe that was latent in the German soul, he would not equip the German Army with the hydrogen bomb. In the course of his business he had very few dealings with Germans and it was only here, in this village in the Graubunden, where their presence was becoming so much more visible each year, that the *idea* of Germans disturbed him any more. But he loved the village and the thought of abandoning his yearly vacation there because of the prevalence of license plates from Munich and Dusseldorf was repugnant to him. Maybe, he thought, from now on he would come at a different time, in January, instead of late in February. Late February and early March was the German season, when the sun was warmer and shone until six o'clock in the evening. The Germans were sun gluttons and could be seen all over the hills, stripped to the waist, sitting on rocks, eating their picnic lunches, greedily absorbing each precious ray of sunlight. It was as though they came from a country perpetually covered in mist, like the planet Venus, and had to soak up as much brightness and life as possible in the short periods of their holidays to be able to endure the harshness and gloom of their homeland and the conduct of the other inhabitants of Venus for the rest of the year.

Robert smiled to himself at this tolerant concept and felt better-disposed toward everyone around him. Maybe, he thought, if I were a single man, I'd find a Bavarian girl and fall in love with her and finish the whole thing off then and there.

"I warn you, Francis," the girl in the lambskin hat was saying, "if you do me to death on this mountain, there are three Juniors at Yale who will track you down to the ends of the earth."

Then he heard the German voice again. "Warum haben die Amerikaner nicht genügend Verstand," the voice said, low but distinctly, near him, the accent clearly Hochdeutsch and not Zurichois or any of the other variations of Schweizerdeutsch, "ihre dummen kleinen Nutten zu Hause zu lassen, wo sie hingehören?"

Now, he knew there was no avoiding looking and there was no avoiding doing something about it. He glanced at Mac first, to see if Mac, who understood a little German, had heard. Mac was huge and could be dangerous, and for all his easy good nature, if he had heard the man say,

THE INHABITANTS OF VENUS

"Why don't the Americans have the sense to leave their silly little whores at home where they belong?" the man was in for a beating. But Mac was still beaming placidly at the Contessa. That was all to the good, Robert thought, relieved. The Swiss police took a dim view of fighting, no matter what the provocation, and Mac, enraged, was likely to wreak terrible damage in a fight, and would more than likely wind up in jail. For an American career soldier on duty in Frankfurt, a brawl like that could have serious consequences. The worst that can happen to me, Robert thought, as he turned to find the man who had spoken, is a few hours in the pokey and a lecture from the magistrate about abusing Swiss hospitality.

Almost automatically, Robert decided that when they got to the top, he would follow the man who had spoken out of the car, tell him quietly, that he, Robert, had understood what had been said about Americans in the car, and swing immediately. I just hope, Robert thought, that whoever it is isn't too damned large.

For a moment, Robert couldn't pick out his opponent-to-be. There was a tall man with his back to Robert, on the other side of the Italian woman, and the voice had come from that direction. Because of the crowd, Robert could only see his head and shoulders, which were bulky and powerful under a black parka. The man had on a white cap of the kind that had been worn by the Afrika Corps during the war. The man was with a plump, hard-faced woman who was whispering earnestly to him, but not loudly enough for Robert to be able to hear what she was saying. Then the man said, crisply, in German, replying to the woman, "I don't care how many of them understand the language. Let them understand," and Robert knew that he had found his man.

An exhilarated tingle of anticipation ran through Robert, making his hands and arms feel tense and jumpy. He regretted that the cabin wouldn't arrive at the top for another five minutes. Now that he had decided the fight was inevitable, he could hardly bear waiting. He stared fixedly at the man's broad, black-nylon back, wishing the fellow would turn around so that he could see his face. He wondered if the man would go down with the first blow, if he would apologize, if he would try to use his ski poles. Robert decided to keep his own poles handy, just in case, although Mac could be depended upon to police matters thoroughly if he saw weapons being used. Deliberately Robert took off his heavy leather mittens and stuck them in his belt. The correction would be more effective with bare knuckles. He wondered, fleetingly, if the man was wearing a ring. He kept his eyes fixed on the back of the man's neck, willing him to turn around. Then the plump woman noticed his stare. She dropped her eyes and whispered something to the man in the black parka and after several seconds, he finally turned around, pretending that it was a casual, unmotivated movement. The man looked squarely at Robert and Robert thought, If you ski long enough you meet every other skier you've ever known. At the same moment, he knew that it wasn't going to be a nice simple little fist fight on the top of the mountain. He knew that somehow he was going to have to kill the man whose icy blue eyes, fringed with pale blond lashes, were staring challengingly at him from under the white peak of the Afrika Corps cap.

It was a long time ago, the winter of 1938, in the French part of Switzerland, and he was fourteen years old and the sun was setting behind another mountain and it was ten below zero and he was lying in the snow, with his foot turned in that funny, unnatural way, although the pain hadn't really begun yet, and the eyes were looking down at him. . . .

He had done something foolish, and at the moment he was more worried about what his parents would say when they found out than about the broken leg. He had gone up, alone, late in the afternoon, when almost everybody else was off the mountain, and even so he hadn't stayed on the normal *piste,* but had started bushwacking through the forest, searching for powder snow that hadn't been tracked by other skiers. One ski had caught on a hidden root and he had fallen forward, hearing the sickening dry cracking sound from his right leg, even as he pitched into the snow.

Trying not to panic, he had sat up, facing in the direction of the *piste,* whose markers he could see some hundred meters away, through the pine forest. If any skiers happened to come by, they might just, with luck, be able to hear him if he shouted. For the moment, he did not try to crawl toward the line of poles, because when he moved a very queer feeling flickered from his ankle up his leg to the pit of his stomach, making him want to throw up.

The shadows were very long now in the forest, and only the highest peaks were rose-colored against a frozen green sky. He was beginning to feel the cold and from time to time he was shaken by acute spasms of shivering.

I'm going to die here, he thought. I'm going to die here tonight. He thought of his parents and his sister probably having tea, comfortably seated this moment in the warm dining room of the chalet two miles down the mountain, and he bit his lips to keep back the tears. They wouldn't start to worry about him for another hour or two yet, and then when they did, and started to do something about finding him, they wouldn't know where to begin. He had known none of the seven or eight people who had been on the lift with him on his last ride up and he hadn't told anybody what run he was going to take. There were three different mountains, with their separate lifts, and their numberless variations of runs, that he might have taken, and finding him in the dark would be an almost hopeless task. He looked up at the sky. There were clouds moving in from the east, slowly, a black high wall, covering the already darkened sky. If it snowed that night, there was a good chance they wouldn't even find his body before spring. He had promised his mother that no matter what happened, he would never ski alone, and he had broken the promise and this was his punishment.

Then he heard the sound of skis, coming fast, making a harsh, metallic noise on the iced snow of the *piste*. Before he could see the skier, he began to shout, with all the strength of his lungs, frantically, *"Au secours! Au secours!"*

A dark shape, going very fast, appeared high up for a second, disappeared behind a clump of trees, then shot into view much lower down, almost on a level with the place where Robert was sitting. Robert shouted wildly, hysterically, not uttering words any more, just a senseless, passionate, throat-bursting claim on the attention of the human race, represented, for this one instant at sunset on this cold mountain, by the dark, expert figure plunging swiftly, with a harsh scraping of steel edges and a *whoosh* of wind, toward the village below.

Then, miraculously, the figure stopped, in a swirl of snow. Robert shouted wordlessly, the sound of his voice echoing hysterically in the forest. For a moment the skier didn't move and Robert shook with the fear that it was all a hallucination, a mirage of sight and sound, that there was no one there on the beaten snow at the edge of the forest, that he was only imagining that he was shouting, that with all the fierce effort of his throat and lungs, he was mute, unheard.

Suddenly, he couldn't see anything any more. He had the sensation of a curtain sinking somewhere within him, of a wall of warm liquid inundating the ducts and canals of his body. He waved his hands weakly and toppled slowly over in a faint.

When he came to, a man was kneeling over him, rubbing his cheeks with snow. "You heard me," Robert said in French to the man. "I was afraid you wouldn't hear me."

"Ich verstehe nicht," the man said. "Nicht parler Französisch."

"I was afraid you wouldn't hear me," Robert repeated, in German.

"You are a stupid little boy," the man said severely, in clipped, educated German. "And very lucky. I am the last man on the mountain." He felt Robert's ankle, his hands hard but deft. "Nice," he said ironically, "very nice. You're going to be in plaster for at least three months. Here—lie still. I am going to take your skis off. You will be more comfortable." He undid the long leather thongs, working swiftly, and stood the skis up in the snow. Then he swept the snow off a stump a few yards away and got around behind Robert and put his hands under Robert's armpits. "Relax," he said. "Do not try to help me." He picked Robert up.

"Luckily," he said, "you weigh nothing. How old are you?—eleven?"

"Fourteen," Robert said.

"What's the matter?" the man said, laughing. "Don't they feed you in Switzerland?"

"I'm French," Robert said.

"Oh," the man's voice went flat. "French." He half-carried, half-dragged Robert over to the stump and sat him down gently on it. "There," he said, "at least you're out of the snow. You won't freeze—for the time being. Now, lis-

THE INHABITANTS OF VENUS

ten carefully. I will take your skis down with me to the ski school and I will tell them where you are and tell them to send a sled for you. They should get to you in less than an hour. Now, whom are you staying with in town?"

"My mother and father. At the Chalet Montana."

"Good." The man nodded. "The Chalet Montana. Do they speak German, too?"

"Yes."

"Excellent," the man said. "I will telephone them and tell them their foolish son has broken his leg and that the patrol is taking him to the hospital. What is your name?"

"Robert."

"Robert what?"

"Robert Rosenthal," Robert said. "Please don't say I'm hurt too badly. They'll be worried enough as it is."

The man didn't answer immediately. He busied himself tying Robert's skis together and slung them over his shoulder. "Do not worry, Robert Rosenthal," he said, "I will not worry them more than is necessary." Abruptly, he started off, sweeping easily through the trees, his poles held in one hand, Robert's skis balanced across his shoulders with his other hand.

His sudden departure took Robert by surprise and it was only when the man was a considerable distance away, already almost lost among the trees, that Robert realized he hadn't thanked the man for saving his life. "Thank you," he shouted into the growing darkness. "Thank you very much."

The man didn't stop and Robert never knew whether he had heard his cry of thanks or not. Because after an hour, when it was completely dark, with the stars covered by the cloud that had been moving in at sunset from the east, the patrol had not yet appeared. Robert had a watch with a radium dial. Timing himself by it, he waited exactly one hour and a half, until ten minutes past seven, and then decided that nobody was coming for him and that if he hoped to live through the night he would somehow have to crawl out of the forest and make his way down to the town by himself.

He was rigid with cold by now, and suffering from shock. His teeth were chattering in a frightening way, as though his jaws were part of an insane machine over which he had no control. There was no feeling in his fingers any more and the pain in his leg came in ever-enlarging waves of metallic throbbing. He had put up the hood of his parka and sunk his head as low down on his chest as he could, and the cloth of the parka was stiff with his frosted breath. He heard a whimpering sound somewhere around him and it was only after what seemed to him several minutes that he realized the whimpering sound was coming from him and that there was nothing he could do to stop it.

Stiffly, with exaggerated care, he tried to lift himself off the tree stump and down into the snow without putting any weight on his injured leg, but at the last moment he slipped and twisted the leg as he went down. He screamed twice and lay with his face in the snow and thought of just staying that way and forgetting the whole thing, the whole intolerable effort of remaining alive. Later on, when he was much older, he came to the conclusion that the one thing that made him keep moving was the thought of his mother and father waiting for him, with anxiety that would soon grow into terror, in the town below him.

He pulled himself along on his belly, digging at the snow in front of his face with his hands, using rocks, low-hanging branches, snow-covered roots, to help him, meter by meter, out of the forest. His watch was torn off somewhere along the way and when he finally reached the line of poles that marked the packed snow and ice of the *piste* he had no notion of whether it had taken him five minutes or five hours to cover the hundred meters from the place he had fallen. He lay, panting, sobbing, staring at the lights of the town far below him, knowing that he could never reach them, knowing that he had to reach them. The effort of crawling through the deep snow had warmed him again and his face was streaming with sweat, and the blood coming back into his numbed hands and feet jabbed him with a thousand needles of pain.

The lights of the town guided him now, and here and there he could see the marker poles outlined against their small, cosy Christmasy glow. It was easier going, too, on the packed snow of the *piste* and from time to time he managed to slide ten or fifteen meters without stopping, tobogganing on his stomach, screaming occasionally when the foot of his broken leg banged loosely against an icy bump or twisted as he went over a steep embankment to crash against a level spot below. Once he couldn't stop

THE INHABITANTS OF VENUS

himself and he fell into a swiftly rushing small stream and pulled himself out of it five minutes later with his gloves and stomach and knees soaked with icy water. And still the lights of the town seemed as far away as ever.

Finally, he felt he couldn't move any more. He was exhausted and he had had to stop twice to vomit and the vomit had been a gush of blood. He tried to sit up, so that if the snow came that night, there would be a chance that somebody would see the top of his head sticking out of the new cover in the morning. As he was struggling to push himself erect, a shadow passed between him and the lights of the town. The shadow was very close and with his last breath he called out. Later on, the peasant who rescued him said that what he called out was "Excuse me."

The peasant was moving hay on a big sled from one of the hill barns down to the valley, and he rolled the hay off and put Robert on instead. Then, carefully braking and taking the sled on a path that cut back and forth across the *piste*, he brought Robert down to the valley and the hospital.

By the time his mother and father had been notified and had reached the hospital, the doctor had given him a shot of morphine and was in the middle of setting the leg. So it wasn't until the next morning, as he lay in the gray hospital room, sweating with pain, with his leg in traction, that he could get out any kind of coherent story and tell his parents what had happened.

"Then I saw this man skiing very fast, all alone," Robert said, trying to speak normally, without showing how much the effort was costing him, trying to take the look of shock and agony from his parent's set faces by pretending that his leg hardly hurt him at all, and that the whole incident was of small importance. "He heard me and came over and took off my skis and made me comfortable on a tree stump and he asked me what my name was and where my parents were staying and he said he'd go to the ski school and tell them where I was and to send a sled for me and then he'd call you at the Chalet and tell you they were bringing me down to the hospital. Then, after more than an hour, it was pitch dark already, nobody came and I decided I'd better not wait any more and I started down and I was lucky and I saw this farmer with a sled and . . ."

"You were very lucky," Robert's mother said flatly. She was a small, neat, plump woman, with bad nerves, who was only at home in cities. She detested the cold, detested the mountains, detested the idea of her loved ones running what seemed to her the senseless risk of injury that skiing involved, and only came on these holidays because Robert and his father and sister were so passionate about the sport. Now she was white with fatigue and worry, and if Robert had not been immobilized in traction she would have had him out of the accursed mountains that morning on the train to Paris.

"Now, Robert," his father said, "is it possible that when you hurt yourself, the pain did things to you, and that you just *imagined* you saw a man, and just imagined he told you he was going to call us and get you a sled from the ski school?"

"I didn't imagine it, Papa," Robert said. The morphine had made him feel hazy and heavy-brained and he was puzzled that his father was talking to him that way. "Why do you think I might have imagined it?"

"Because," said his father, "nobody called us last night until ten o'clock, when the doctor telephoned from the hospital. And nobody called the ski school, either."

"I didn't imagine him," Robert repeated. He was hurt that his father perhaps thought he was lying. "If he came into this room I'd know him right off. He was wearing a white cap, he was a big man with a black anarac, and he had blue eyes, they looked a little funny, because his eyelashes were almost white and from a little way off it looked as though he didn't have any eyelashes at all. . . ."

"How old was he, do you think?" Robert's father asked. "As old as I am?" Robert's father was nearly fifty.

"No," Robert said. "I don't think so."

"Was he as old as your Uncle Jules?" Robert's father asked.

"Yes," Robert said. "Just about." He wished his father and mother would leave him alone. He was all right now. His leg was in plaster and he wasn't dead and in three months, the doctor said, he'd be walking again, and he wanted to forget everything that had happened last night in the forest.

"So," Robert's mother said, "he was a man of about

twenty-five, with a white cap and blue eyes." She picked up the phone and asked for the ski school.

Robert's father lit a cigarette and went over to the window and looked out. It was snowing. It had been snowing since midnight, heavily, and the lifts weren't running today because a driving wind had sprung up with the snow and there was danger of avalanches up on top.

"Did you talk to the farmer who picked me up?" Robert asked.

"Yes," said his father. "He said you were a very brave little boy. He also said that if he hadn't found you, you couldn't have gone on more than another fifty meters. I gave him two hundred francs. Swiss."

"Sssh," Robert's mother said. She had the connection with the ski school now. "This is Mrs. Rosenthal again. Yes, thank you, he's doing as well as can be expected," she said, in her precise, melodious French. "We've been talking to him and there's one aspect of his story that's a little strange. He says a man stopped and helped him take off his skis last night after he'd broken his leg, and promised to go to the ski school and leave the skis there and ask for a sled to be sent to bring him down. We'd like to know if, in fact, the man did come into the office and report the accident. It would have been somewhere around six o'clock." She listened for a moment, her face tense. "I see," she said. She listened again. "No," she said, "we don't know his name. My son says he was about twenty-five years old, with blue eyes and a white cap. Wait a minute, I'll ask." She turned to Robert. "Robert," she said, "what kind of skis did you have? They're going to look and see if they're out front in the rack."

"Attenhoffer's," Robert said. "One meter seventy. And they have my initials in red up on the tips."

"Attenhoffer's," his mother repeated over the phone. "And they have his initials on them. R.R., in red. Thank you. I'll wait."

Robert's father came back from the window, dousing his cigarette in an ashtray. Underneath the holiday tan of his skin, his face looked weary and sick. "Robert," he said, with a rueful smile, "you must learn to be a little more careful. You are my only male heir and there is very little chance that I shall produce another."

"Yes, Papa," Robert said. "I'll be careful."

His mother waved impatiently at them to be quiet and listened again at the telephone. "Thank you," she said. "Please call me if you hear anything." She hung up. "No," she said to Robert's father, "the skis aren't there."

"It can't be possible," Robert's father said, "that a man would leave a little boy to freeze to death just to steal a pair of skis."

"I'd like to get my hands on him," Robert's mother said. "Just for ten minutes. Robert, darling, think hard. Did he seem . . . well . . . did he seem *normal?*"

"He seemed all right," Robert said. "I suppose."

"Was there any other thing about him that you noticed? Think hard. Anything that would help us find him. It's not only for us, Robert. If there's a man in this town who would do something like that to you, it's important that people know about him, before he does something even worse to other boys . . ."

"Mama," Robert said, feeling close to tears under the insistence of his mother's questioning, "I told you just the way it was. Everything. I'm not lying, Mama."

"What did he *sound* like, Robert?" his mother said. "Did he have a low voice, a high voice, did he sound like us, as though he lived in Paris, did he sound like any of your teachers, did he sound like the other people from around here, did he . . . ?"

"Oh . . ." Robert said, remembering.

"What is it? What do you want to say?" his mother said sharply.

"I had to speak German to him," Robert said. Until now, with the pain and the morphine, it hadn't occurred to him to mention that.

"What do you mean you had to speak German to him?"

"I started to speak to him in French and he didn't understand. We spoke in German."

His father and mother exchanged glances. Then his mother said, gently, "Was it real German? Or was it Swiss-German? You know the difference, don't you?"

"Of course," Robert said. One of his father's parlor tricks was giving imitations of Swiss friends in Paris speaking in French and then in Swiss-German. Robert had a good ear for languages, and aside from having heard his Alsatian grandparents speaking German since he was an infant, he was studying German literature in school and knew long passages of Goethe and Schiller and Heine by heart. "It was German, all right," he said.

There was silence in the room. His father went over to the window again and looked out at the snow falling in a soft blurred curtain outside. "I knew," his father said quietly, "that it couldn't just have been for the skis."

* * *

In the end, his father won out. His mother wanted to go to the police and get them to try to find the man, even though his father pointed out that there were perhaps ten thousand skiers in the town for the holidays, a good percentage of them German-speaking and blue-eyed, and trainloads arriving and departing five times a day. Robert's father was sure that the man had left the very night Robert had broken his leg, although all during the rest of his stay in town, Mr. Rosenthal prowled along the snowy streets and in and out of bars searching among the faces for one that answered Robert's description of the man on the mountain. But he said it would do no good to go to the police and might do harm, because once the story got out there would be plenty of people to complain that this was just another hysterical Jewish fantasy of invented injury. "There're plenty of Nazis in Switzerland, of all nationalities," Robert's father told his mother, in the course of an argument that lasted weeks, "and this will just give them more ammunition, they'll be able to say, 'See, wherever the Jews go they start trouble.' "

Robert's mother, who was made of sterner stuff than her husband, and who had relatives in Germany who smuggled out disturbing letters to her, wanted justice at any cost, but after a while even she saw the hopelessness of pushing the matter any further. Four weeks after the accident, when Robert could finally be moved, as she sat beside her son in the ambulance that was to take them both to Geneva and then on to Paris, she said, in a dead voice, holding Robert's hand, "Soon, we must leave Europe. I cannot stand to live any more on a continent where things like this are permitted to happen."

Much later, during the war, after Mr. Rosenthal had died in Occupied France and Robert and his mother and sister were in America, a friend of Robert's, who had also done a lot of skiing in Europe, heard the story of the man in the white cap, and told Robert he was almost sure he recognized the man from the description Robert gave of him. It was a ski instructor from Garmisch, or maybe from Obersdorf or Freudenstadt, who had a couple of rich Austrian clients with whom he toured each winter from one ski station to another. The friend didn't know the man's name, and the one time Robert had been in Garmisch, it had been with French troops in the closing days of the war, and of course nobody was skiing then.

Now the man was standing just three feet from him, his face, on the other side of the pretty Italian woman, framed by straight black lines of skis, his eyes looking coolly, with insolent amusement, but without recognition, at Robert, from under the almost albino eyelashes. He was approaching fifty now and his face was fleshy but hard and healthy, with a thin, set mouth that gave a sense of control and self-discipline to his expression.

Robert hated him. He hated him for the attempted murder of a fourteen-year-old boy in 1938; he hated him for the acts that he must have condoned or collaborated in during the war; he hated him for his father's disappearance and his mother's exile; he hated him for what he had said about the pretty little American girl in the lambskin hat; he hated him for the confident impudence of his glance and the healthy, untouched robustness of his face and neck; he hated him because he could look directly into the eyes of a man he had tried to kill and not recognize him; he hated him because he was here, bringing the idea of death and shamefully unconsummated vengeance into this silvery holiday bubble climbing the placid air of a kindly, welcoming country.

And most of all he hated the man in the white cap because the man betrayed and made a sour joke of the precariously achieved peace that Robert had built for himself, with his wife, his children, his job, his comfortable, easygoing, generously forgetful Americanism, since the war.

The German deprived him of his sense of normalcy. Living with a wife and three children in a clean, cheerful house was not normal; having your name in the telephone directory was not normal; lifting your hat to your neighbor and paying your bills was not normal; obeying the law and depending upon the protection of the police was not nor-

THE INHABITANTS OF VENUS

mal. The German sent him back through the years to an older and truer normality—murder, blood, flight, conspiracy, pillage, and ruins. For a while Robert had deceived himself into believing that the nature of everyday could change. The German in the crowded cabin had now put him to rights. Meeting the German had been an accident, but the accident had revealed what was permanent and non-accidental in his life and the life of the people around him.

Mac was saying something to him, and the girl in the lambskin hat was singing an American song in a soft, small voice, but he didn't hear what Mac was saying and the words of the song made no sense to him. He had turned away from looking at the German and was looking at the steep stone face of the mountain, now almost obscured by a swirling cloud, and he was trying to figure out how he could get rid of Mac, escape the young Americans, follow the German, get him alone, and kill him.

He had no intention of making it a duel. He did not intend to give the man a change to fight for his life. It was punishment he was after, not a symbol of honor. He remembered other stories of men who had been in concentration camps during the war who had suddenly confronted their torturers later on and had turned them in to the authorities and had the satisfaction of witnessing their execution. But whom could he turn the German over to—the Swiss police? For what crime that would fit into what criminal code?

Or he could do what an ex-prisoner had done in Budapest three or four years after the war, when he had met one of his jailers on a bridge over the Danube and had simply picked the man up and thrown him into the water and watched him drown. The ex-prisoner had explained who he was and who the drowned man was and had been let off and had been treated as a hero. But Switzerland was not Hungary, the Danube was far away, the war had finished a long time ago.

No, what he had to do was follow the man, stay with him, surprise him alone somewhere on the slopes, contrive a murder that would look like an accident, be out of the country before anyone asked any questions, divulge nothing to anyone, leave the body, if possible, in an isolated place where the snow would cover it and where it would not be found till the farmers drove their herds high up into the mountains for the summer pasturage. And he had to do it swiftly, before the man realized that he was the object of any special attention on Robert's part, before he started to wonder about the American on his tracks, before the process of memory began its work and the face of the skinny fourteen-year-old boy on the dark mountain in 1938 began to emerge from the avenging face of the grown man.

Robert had never killed a man. During the war, he had been assigned by the American Army as part of a liaison team to a French division, and while he had been shot at often enough, he had never fired a gun after arriving in Europe. When the war was over, he had been secretly thankful that he had been spared the necessity of killing. Now he understood—he was not to be spared; his war was not over.

"Say, Robert . . ." It was Mac's voice finally breaking through into his consciousness. "What's the matter? I've been talking to you for thirty seconds and you haven't heard a word I said. Are you sick? You look awfully queer, lad."

"I'm all right," Robert said. "I have a little headache. That's all. Maybe I'd better eat something, get something warm to drink. You go ahead down by yourself."

"Of course not," Mac said. "I'll wait for you."

"Don't be silly," Robert said, trying to keep his tone natural and friendly. "You'll lose the Contessa. Actually, I don't feel much like skiing any more today. The weather's turned lousy." He gestured at the cloud that was enveloping them. "You can't see a thing. I'll probably take the lift back down. . . ."

"Hey, you're beginning to worry me," Mac said anxiously. "I'll stick with you. You want me to take you to a doctor?"

"Leave me alone, please, Mac," Robert said. He had to get rid of Mac and if it meant hurting his feelings now, he'd make it up to him some way, but later. "When I get one of these headaches I prefer being alone."

"You're sure now?" Mac asked.

"I'm sure."

"Okay. See you at the hotel for tea?"

"Yes," Robert said. After murder, Robert thought, I al-

THE INHABITANTS OF VENUS

ways have a good tea. He prayed that the Italian girl would put her skis on immediately and move off quickly once they got to the top, so that Mac would be gone before Robert had to start off after the man in the white cap.

The cabin was swinging over the last pylon now and slowing down to come into the station. The passengers were stirring a bit, arranging clothes, testing bindings, in preparation for the descent. Robert stole a quick glance at the German. The woman with him was knotting a silk scarf around his throat, with little wifely gestures. She had the face of a cook. Neither she nor the man looked in Robert's direction. I will face the problem of the woman when I come to it, Robert thought.

The cabin came to a stop and the skiers began to disembark. Robert was close to the door and was one of the first people out. Without looking back, he walked swiftly out of the station and into the shifting grayness of the mountaintop. One side of the mountain dropped off in a sheer, rocky face next to the station and Robert went over and stood on the edge, looking out. If the German, for any reason, happened to come over near him to admire the view or to judge the condition of the *piste* of the Kaisergarten, which had to be entered some distance farther on, but which cut back under the cliff much lower down, where the slope became more gradual, there was a possibility that one quick move on Robert's part would send the man crashing down to the rocks some hundred meters below, and the whole thing would be over. Robert turned and faced the exit of the station, searching in the crowd of brightly dressed skiers for the white cap.

He saw Mac come out with the Italian girl. He was talking to her and carrying her skis and the girl was smiling warmly. Mac waved at Robert and then knelt to help the girl put on her skis. Robert took a deep breath. Mac, at least, was out of the way. And the American group had decided to have lunch on top and had gone into the restaurant near the station.

The white cap was not to be seen. The German and the woman had not yet come out. There was nothing unusual about that. People often waxed their skis in the station, where it was warm, or took time to go to the toilets downstairs before setting out on their runs. It was all to the good. The longer the German took, the fewer people there would be hanging around to notice Robert when he set out after him.

Robert waited on the cliff's edge. In the swirling, cold cloud, he felt warm, capable, powerful, curiously lightheaded. For the first time in his life he understood the profound, sensual pleasure of destruction. He waved gaily at Mac and the Italian girl as they moved off together on the traverse to one of the easier runs on the other side of the mountain.

Then the door to the station opened again and the woman who was with the German came out. She had her skis on and Robert realized that they had been so long inside because they had put their skis on in the waiting room. In bad weather people often did that, so that they wouldn't freeze their hands on the icy metal of the bindings in the biting wind outdoors. The woman held the door open and Robert saw the man in the white cap coming through the opening. But he wasn't coming out like everybody else. He was hopping, with great agility, on one leg. The other leg was cut off in mid-thigh and to keep his balance the German had miniature skis fixed on the end of his poles, instead of the usual thonged baskets.

Through the years, Robert had seen other one-legged skiers, veterans of Hitler's armies, who had refused to allow their mutilation to keep them off the mountains they loved, and he had admired their fortitude and skill. But he felt no admiration for the man in the white cap. All he felt was a bitter sense of loss, of having been deprived, at the last moment, of something that had been promised to him and that he had wanted and desperately needed. Because he knew he was not strong enough to murder a cripple, to punish the already punished, and he despised himself for his weakness.

He watched as the man made his way across the snow with crablike cunning, hunched over his poles with their infants' skis on the ends. Two or three times, when the man and the woman came to a rise, the woman got silently behind the man and pushed him up the slope until he could move under his own power again.

The cloud had been swept away and there was a momentary burst of sunlight and in it, Robert could see the man and the woman traverse to the entrance to the run, which was the steepest one on the mountain. Without hesitation, the man plunged into it, skiing skillfully, courageously, overtaking more timid or weaker skiers who were picking their way cautiously down the slope.

Watching the couple, who soon became tiny figures on the white expanse below him, Robert knew there was nothing more to be done, nothing more to wait for, except a cold, hopeless, everlasting forgiveness.

The two figures disappeared out of the sunlight into the solid bank of cloud that cut across the lower part of the mountain. Then Robert went over to where he had left his skis and put them on. He did it clumsily. His hands were cold because he had taken off his mittens in the teleferique cabin, in that hopeful and innocent past, ten minutes ago, when he had thought the German insult could be paid for with a few blows of the bare fist.

He went off, fast, on the run that Mac had taken with the Italian girl, and he caught up with them before they were halfway down. It began to snow when they reached the village and they went into the hotel and had a hilarious lunch with a lot of wine and the girl gave Mac her address and said he should be sure to look her up the next time he came to Rome.

Noises in the City

Weatherby was surprised to see the lights of the restaurant still lit when he turned off Sixth Avenue and started up the street toward the small apartment house in the middle of the block in which he lived. The restaurant was called the Santa Margharita and was more or less Italian, with French overtones. Its main business was at lunchtime and by ten-thirty at night it was usually closed. It was convenient and on nights when they were lazy or when Weatherby had work to do at home, he and his wife sometimes had dinner there. It wasn't expensive, and Giovanni, the bartender, was a friend, and from time to time Weatherby stopped in for a drink on his way home from the office, because the liquor was good and the atmosphere quiet and there was no television.

He nearly passed it, then stopped and decided he could use a whiskey. His wife had told him she was going to a movie and wouldn't be home before eleven-thirty, and he was tired and didn't relish the thought of going into the empty apartment and drinking by himself.

There was only one customer in the restaurant, sitting at the small bar near the entrance. The waiters had already gone home and Giovanni was changing glasses for the man at the bar and pouring him a bourbon. Weatherby sat at the end of the bar, but there were still only two stools between him and the other customer. Giovanni came over to Weatherby and said, "Good evening, Mr. Weatherby," and put out a glass and poured him a big whiskey, without measuring, and opened a soda bottle and allowed Weatherby to fill the glass himself.

Giovanni was a large, non-Italian-looking man, with an unsmiling, square, severe face and a gray, Prussian-cut head of hair. "How's Mrs. Weatherby tonight?" he asked.

"Fine," Weatherby said. "At least she was fine when I talked to her this afternoon. I've just come from the office."

"You work too hard, Mr. Weatherby," Giovanni said.

"That's right." Weatherby took a good long swallow of the whiskey. There is nothing like Scotch, he thought gratefully, and touched the glass with the palm of his hand and rubbed it pleasurably. "You're open late tonight," he said.

"That's all right," Giovanni said. "I'm in no hurry. Drink as much as you want." Although he was talking to Weatherby, Weatherby somehow had the feeling that the words were addressed to the other man at the bar, who was sitting with his elbows on the mahogany, holding his glass in his two hands in front of his face and peering with a small smile into it, like a clairvoyant who sees something undefined and cloudy, but still agreeable, in the crystal ball. The man was slender and graying, with a polite, educated face. His clothes were narrow and modish, in dark gray, and he wore a gay striped bow tie and a button-down oxford white shirt. Weatherby noted a wedding ring on his left hand. He didn't look like the sort of man who sat around alone in bars drinking late at night. The light in the bar was subdued and Weatherby had the impression that in a brighter light he would recognize the man and that he would turn out to be someone he had met briefly once or twice long ago. But New York was like that. After you lived in New York long enough, a great many of the faces seemed tantalizingly familiar to you.

"I suppose," Giovanni said, standing in front of Weatherby, "after it happens, we'll be losing you."

"Oh," Weatherby said, "we'll be dropping in here to eat again and again."

"You know what I mean," Giovanni said. "You plan on moving to the country?"

"Eventually," Weatherby said, "I imagine so. If we find a nice place, not too far out."

"Kids need fresh air," Giovanni said. "It isn't fair to them, growing up in the city."

"No," Weatherby said. Dorothy, his wife, was seven-months pregnant. They had been married five years and this was their first child, and it gave him an absurd primitive pleasure to talk about the country air that his child would breathe as he grew up. "And then, of course, the schools." What joy there was in platitudes about children, once you knew you could have them.

"Mr. Weatherby . . ." It was the other man at the bar. "May I say good evening to you, sir?"

Weatherby turned toward the man, a little reluctantly. He was in no mood for random conversation with strangers. Also, he had had a fleeting impression that Giovanni regretted the man's advance toward him.

"You don't remember me," the man said, smiling nervously. "I met you eight or ten years ago. In my . . . ah . . . in my shop." He made a slight sibilant sound that might have been the beginning of an embarrassed laugh. "In fact, I think you came there two or three times. . . . There was some question of our perhaps doing some work together, if I remember correctly. Then, when I heard Giovanni call you by name. I couldn't help overhearing. I'm . . . ah . . . Sidney Gosden." He let his voice drop as he spoke his name, as people who are celebrated sometimes do when they don't wish to sound immodest. Weatherby glanced across the bar at Giovanni for help, but Giovanni was polishing a glass with a towel, his eyes lowered, consciously keeping aloof from the conversation.

"Oh . . . uh . . . yes," Weatherby said vaguely.

"I had—have—the shop on Third Avenue," Gosden said. "Antiques, interior decoration." Again the soft, hissing, self-deprecating half-laugh. "It was when I was supposed to do over that row of houses off Beekman Place and you had spoken to a friend of mine . . ."

"Of course," Weatherby said heartily. He still didn't remember the man's name, really, but he remembered the incident. It was when he was just starting in, when he still thought he could make a go of it by himself as an architect, and he had heard that four old buildings on the East Side were going to be thrown together and cut up into small studio apartments. Somebody in one of the big firms, which had turned the job down, had suggested it might be worth looking into and had given him Gosden's name. His memory of his conversation with Gosden was shadowy, fifteen or twenty minutes of rather distracted talk in a dark shop with unlit brass lamps and early-American tables piled one on top of another, a sense of time being wasted, a sense of going up one more dead-end street. "Whatever happened?" he asked.

"Nothing," Gosden said. "You know how those things are. In the end, they merely pulled the whole block down and put up one of those monstrous apartment houses nineteen-stories high. It was too bad. I was terribly impressed with your ideas. I do remember, to this day." He sounded like a woman at a cocktail party, talking swiftly to a man in a corner to hold him there, saying anything that came to mind, to try to keep him from escaping to the bar and leaving her there stranded, with no one to talk to for the rest of the evening, for the rest of her life. "I meant to follow your career," Gosden went on hurriedly. "I was sure you were meant for splendid achievements, but a person is kept so frantically busy in this city—with nothing important, of course—the best intentions—" He waved his hand helplessly and let the complicated sentence lapse. "I'm sure I pass buildings you've put up every day, monuments to your talent, without knowing . . ."

"Not really," Weatherby said. "I went in with a big firm." He told the man the name of the firm and Gosden nodded gravely, to show his respect for their works. "I do bits and pieces for them."

"Everything in due time," Gosden said gaily. "So you're one of those young men who are putting us poor New Yorkers into our cold, bright glass cages."

"I'm not so young," Weatherby said, thinking, grimly, *That's* the truth. And, at the most, Gosden could only have been ten years older than he. He drained his drink. Gosden's manner, gushy, importunate, with its hint of effeminacy, made him uncomfortable. "Well," he said, taking out his wallet, "I think I'd better . . ."

"Oh, no, please . . ." Gosden said. There was a surprising note of anguish in his voice. "Giovanni will just lock up the bottle and put me out if you go. Another round, please, Giovanni. Please. And please serve yourself, too. Late at night like this . . ."

"I really must . . ." Weatherby began. Then he saw Giovanni looking at him in a strange, imperative way, as though there were an urgent message he wanted to deliver. Giovanni quickly poured a second Scotch for Weatherby, a bourbon for Gosden and a neat slug of bourbon for himself.

"There," Gosden said, beaming. "*That's* better. And don't think, Mr. Weatherby, that I go around town just offering rounds of drink to *every*body. In fact, I'm parsimonious, unpleasantly parsimonious, my wife used to say, it was the one thing she constantly held against me." He held up his glass ceremoniously. His long narrow hand was shaking minutely, Weatherby noticed, and he wondered if Gosden was a drunkard. "To the cold, beautiful, lonesome glass buildings," Gosden said, "of the city of New York."

They all drank. Giovanni knocked his tot down in one gulp and washed the glass and dried it without changing his expression.

"I do love this place," Gosden said, looking around him fondly at the dim lamps and the gluey paintings of the Ligurian coast that dotted the walls. "It has especial memories for me. I proposed marriage here on a winter night. To my wife," he added hastily, as if afraid that Weatherby would suspect he had proposed marriage to somebody else's wife here. "We never came here often enough after that." He shook his head a little sadly. "I don't know why. Perhaps because we lived on the other side of town." He sipped at his drink and squinted at a painting of sea and mountains at the other end of the bar. "I always intended to take my wife to Nervi. To see the Temple," he said obscurely. "The Golden Bough. As the French would say, Hélas, we did not make the voyage. Foolishly, I thought there would always be time, some other year. And, of course, being parsimonious, the expense always seemed out of proportion . . ." He shrugged and once more took up his clairvoyant position, holding the glass up with his two hands and peering into it. "Tell me, Mr. Weatherby," he said in a flat, ordinary tone of voice, "have you ever killed a man?"

"What?" Weatherby asked, not believing that he had heard correctly.

"Have you ever killed a man?" Gosden for the third time made his little hissing near-laugh. "Actually, it's a question that one might well ask quite frequently, on many different occasions. After all, there must be quite a few people loose in the city who at one time or another have killed a man—policemen on their rounds, rash automobilists, prizefighters, doctors and nurses, with the best will in the world, children with air rifles, bank robbers, thugs, soldiers of the great war . . ."

Weatherby looked doubtfully at Giovanni. Giovanni didn't say anything, but there was something in his face that showed Weatherby the barman wanted him to humor the other man.

"Well," Weatherby said, "I was in the war. . . ."

"In the infantry, with a bayonet, perhaps," Gosden said, in the new, curious, flat, noneffeminate voice.

"I was in the artillery," Weatherby said. "In a battery of 105's. I suppose you could say that . . ."

"A dashing captain," Gosden said, smiling, "peering through binoculars, calling down the fire of the great guns on the enemy headquarters."

"It wasn't exactly like that," Weatherby said. "I was nineteen years old and I was a private and I was one of the loaders. Most of the time I spent digging."

"Still," Gosden persisted, "you could say that you contributed, that by your efforts men had been killed."

"Well," Weatherby said, "we fired off a lot of rounds. Somewhere along the line we probably hit something."

"I used to be a passionate hunter," Gosden said. "When I was a boy. I was brought up in the South. Alabama, to be exact, although I'm proud to say one would never know it from my accent. I once shot a lynx." He sipped thoughtfully at his drink. "It finally became distasteful to me to take the lives of animals. Although I had no feeling about birds. There is something inimical, *prehuman* about birds, don't you think, Mr. Weatherby?"

"I haven't really given it much thought," Weatherby said, sure now the man was drunk and wondering how soon, with decency, he could get out of there and whether he could go without buying Gosden a round.

"There must be a moment of the utmost exaltation when you take a human life," Gosden said, "followed by a wave of the most abject, ineradicable shame. For example, during the war, among your soldier friends, the question must have arisen. . . ."

"I'm afraid," Weatherby said, "that in most cases they

didn't feel as much as you would like them to have felt."

"How about you?" Gosden said. "Even in your humble position as loader, as you put it, as a cog in the machinery—how did you feel, how do you feel now?"

Weatherby hesitated, on the verge of being angry with the man. "Now," he said, "I regret it. While it was happening, I merely wanted to survive."

"Have you given any thought to the institution of capital punishment, Mr. Weatherby?" Gosden spoke without looking in Weatherby's direction, but staring at his own dim reflection above the bottles in the mirror above the bar. "Are you pro or con the taking of life by the State? Have you ever made an effort to have it abolished?"

"I signed a petition once, in college, I think."

"When we are young," Gosden said, speaking to his wavery reflection in the mirror, "we are more conscious of the value of life. I, myself, once walked in a procession protesting the hanging of several young colored boys. I was not in the South, then. I had already moved up North. Still, I walked in the procession. In France, under the guillotine, the theory is that death is instantaneous, although an instant is a variable quantity, as it were. And there is some speculation that the severed head as it rolls into the basket is still capable of feeling and thinking some moments after the act is completed."

"Now, Mr. Gosden," Giovanni said soothingly, "I don't think it helps to talk like this, does it, now?"

"I'm sorry, Giovanni," Gosden said, smiling brightly "I should be ashamed of myself. In a charming bar like this, with a man of sensibility and talent like Mr. Weatherby. Please forgive me. And now, if you'll pardon me, there's a telephone call I have to make." He got off his stool and walked jauntily, his shoulders thrown back in his narrow dark suit, toward the other end of the deserted restaurant and went through the little door that led to the washrooms and the telephone booth.

"My Lord," Weatherby said. "What's *that* all about?"

"Don't you know who he is?" Giovanni said, in a low voice, keeping his eyes on the rear of the restaurant.

"Only what he just told me," Weatherby said. "Why? Are people supposed to know who he is?"

"His name was in all the papers, two, three years ago," Giovanni said. "His wife was raped and murdered. Somewhere on the East Side. He came home for dinner and found the body."

"Good God," said Weatherby softly, with pity.

"They picked up the guy who did it the next day," Giovanni said. "It was a carpenter or a plumber or something like that. A foreigner from Europe, with a wife and three kids in Queens somewhere. No criminal sheet, no complaints on him previous. He had a job to do in the building and he rang the wrong doorbell and there she was in her bathrobe or something."

"What did they do to him?" Weatherby asked.

"Murder in the first degree," Giovanni said. "They're electrocuting him up the river tonight. That's what *he's* calling about now. To find out if it's over or not. Usually, they do it around eleven, eleven-thirty, I think."

Weatherby looked at his watch. It was nearly eleven-fifteen. "Oh, the poor man," he said. If he had been forced to say whether he meant Gosden or the doomed murderer, it would have been almost impossible for him to give a clear answer. "Gosden, Gosden . . ." he said. "I must have been out of town when it happened."

"It made a big splash," Giovanni said. "For a coupla days."

"Does he come in here and talk like this often?" Weatherby asked.

"This is the first time I heard him say a word about it," Giovanni said. "Usually, he comes in here once, twice a month, has one drink at the bar, polite and quiet, and eats by himself in back, early, reading a book You'd never think anything ever happened to him. Tonight's special, I guess. He came in around eight o'clock and he didn't eat anything, just sat up there at the bar, drinking slow all night."

"That's why you're still open," Weatherby said.

"That's why I'm still open. You can't turn a man out on a night like this."

"No," Weatherby said. Once more he looked at the door to the telephone booth. He would have liked to leave. He didn't want to hear what the man would have to say when he came out of the telephone booth. He wanted to leave quickly and be sure to be in his apartment when his wife came home. But he knew he couldn't run out now, no matter how tempting the idea was.

"This is the first time I heard he asked his wife to marry him here," Giovanni said. "I suppose that's why . . ." He left the thought unfinished.

"What was she like?" Weatherby asked. "The wife?"

"A nice, pretty little quiet type of woman," Giovanni said. "You wouldn't notice her much."

The door at the rear of the restaurant opened and Gosden came striding lightly toward the bar. Weatherby watched him, but he didn't see the man look either left or right at any particular table that might have held special memories for him. As he sprang up onto his stool and smiled his quick, apologetic smile, there was no hint on his face of what he had heard over the telephone. "Well," Gosden said briskly, "here we are again."

"Let me offer a round," Weatherby said, raising his finger for Giovanni.

"That is kind, Mr. Weatherby," said Gosden. "Very kind indeed."

They watched Giovanni pour the drinks.

"While I was waiting for the connection," Gosden said, "I remembered an amusing story. About how some people are lucky and some people are unlucky. It's a fishing story. It's quite clean. I never seem to be able to remember risqué stories, no matter how funny they are. I don't know why. My wife used to say that I was a prude and perhaps she was right. I do hope I get the story right. Let me see—" He hesitated and squinted at his reflection in the mirror. "It's about two brothers who decide to go fishing for a week in a lake in the mountains. . . . Perhaps you've heard it, Mr. Weatherby?"

"No," Weatherby said.

"Please don't be polite just for my sake," Gosden said. "I would hate to think that I was boring you."

"No," Weatherby said, "I really haven't heard it."

"It's quite an old story, I'm sure, I must have heard it years ago when I still went to parties and nightclubs and places like that. Well, the two brothers go to the lake and they rent a boat and they go out on the water and no sooner do they put down their lines than one brother has a bite and pulls up the hugest fish. He puts down his line again and once again immediately he pulls up another huge fish. And again and again all day long. And all day long the other brother sits in the boat and never gets the tiniest nibble on his hook. And the next day it is the same. And the day after that, and the day after that. The brother who is catching nothing gets gloomier and gloomier and angrier and angrier with the brother who is catching all the fish. Finally, the brother who is catching all the fish, wanting to keep peace in the family, as it were, tells the other brother that he will stay on shore the next day and let the one who hasn't caught anything have the lake for himself that day. So the next day, bright and early, the unlucky brother goes out by himself with his rod and his line and his most succulent bait and puts his line overboard and waits. For a long time nothing happens. Then there is a splash nearby and a huge fish, the hugest fish of all, jumps out of the water and says, 'Say, Bud, isn't your brother coming out today?' " Gosden looked anxiously over at Weatherby to see what his reaction was. Weatherby made himself pretend to chuckle.

"I do hope I got it right," Gosden said. "It seems to me to have a somewhat deeper meaning than most such anecdotes. About luck and destiny and things like that, if you know what I mean."

"Yes, it does," Weatherby said.

"People usually prefer off-color stories, I notice," Gosden said, "but as I said, I don't seem to be able to remember them." He drank delicately from his glass. "I suppose Giovanni told you something about me while I was telephoning," he said. Once more his voice had taken on its other tone, flat, almost dead, not effeminate.

Weatherby glanced at Giovanni and Giovanni nodded, almost imperceptibly. "Yes," Weatherby said. "A little."

"My wife was a virgin when I married her," Gosden said. "But we had the most passionate and complete relationship right from the beginning. She was one of those rare women who are made simply for marriage, for wifehood, and nothing else. No one could suspect the glory of her beauty or the depths of her feeling merely from looking at her or talking to her. On the surface, she seemed the shyest and least assertive of women, didn't she, Giovanni?"

"Yes, Mr. Gosden," Giovanni said.

"In all the world there were only two men who could have known. Myself and . . ." He stopped. His face twitched. "At eleven-o-eight," he said, "they pulled the switch. The man is dead. I was constantly telling her to leave the chain on the door, but she was thoughtless and she trusted all the world. The city is full of wild beasts, it is ridiculous to say that we are civilized. She screamed. Various people in the building heard her scream, but in the city one pays little attention to the noises that emanate from a neighbor's apartment. Later on, a lady downstairs said that she thought perhaps my wife and I were having an argument, although we never fought in all the years we were married, and another neighbor thought it was a program on a television set, and she was thinking of complaining to the management of the building because she had a headache that morning and was trying to sleep." Gosden tucked his feet under the barstool rung in an almost girlish position and held his glass up again before his eyes with his two hands. "It is good of you to listen to me like this, Mr. Weatherby," he said. "People have been avoiding me in the last three years, old customers hurry past my shop without looking in, old friends are out when I call. I depend upon strangers for trade and conversation these days. At Christmas, I sent a hundred-dollar bill anonymously, in a plain envelope, through the mails to the woman in Queens. It was on impulse, I didn't reason it out, the holiday season perhaps. . . . I contemplated asking for an invitation to the . . . the ceremony at Ossining tonight, I thought quite seriously about it, I suppose it could have been arranged. Then, finally, I thought it wouldn't really do any good, would it. And I came here, instead, to drink with Giovanni." He smiled across the bar at Giovanni. "Italians," he said, "are likely to have gentle and understanding souls. And now, I really must go home. I sleep poorly and on principle I'm opposed to drugs." He got out his wallet and put down some bills.

"Wait a few minutes," Giovanni said, "until I lock up and I'll walk you home and open your door for you."

"Ah," Gosden said, "that would be kind of you, Giovanni. It is the most difficult moment. Opening the door. I am terribly alone. After that, I'm sure I'll be absolutely all right."

Weatherby got off the stool and said to Giovanni, "Put it on the bill, please." He was released now. "Good night," he said to Giovanni. "Good night, Mr. Gosden." He wanted to say more, to proffer some word of consolation or hope, but he knew nothing he could say would be of any help.

"Good night," Gosden said, in his bright, breathy voice now. "It's been a pleasure renewing our acquaintanceship, even so briefly. And please present my respects to your wife."

Weatherby went out of the door onto the street, leaving Giovanni locking the liquor bottles away and Gosden silently and slowly drinking, perched neat and straight-backed on the barstool.

The street was dark and Weatherby hurried up it toward his doorway, making himself keep from running. He used the stairway, because the elevator was too slow. He opened the metal door of his apartment and saw that there was a light on in the bedroom.

"Is that you, darling?" He heard his wife's drowsy voice from the bedroom.

"I'll be right in," Weatherby said. "I'm locking up." He pushed the extra bolt that most of the time they neglected to use and carefully walked, without haste, as on any night, across the carpet of the darkened living room.

Dorothy was in bed, with the lamp beside her lit and a magazine that she had been reading fallen to the floor beside her. She smiled up at him sleepily. "You have a lazy wife," she said, as he began to undress.

"I thought you were going to the movies," he said.

"I went. But I kept falling asleep," she said. "So I came home."

"Do you want anything? A glass of milk. Some crackers?"

"Sleep," she said. She rolled over on her back, the covers up to her throat, her hair loose on the pillow. He put on his pyjamas, turned off the light, and got into bed beside her and she lifted her head to put it on his shoulder.

"Whiskey," she said drowsily. "Why do people have such a prejudice against it? Smells delicious. Did you work hard, darling?"

"Not too bad," he said, with the freshness of her hair against his face.

"Yum," she said, and went to sleep.

He lay awake for a while, holding her gently, listening to the muffled sounds from the street below. God deliver us from accident, he thought, and make us understand the true nature of the noises arising from the city around us.

A Year To Learn the Language

"*La barbe,*" Louise said, "how can you stand the stink?" She was sitting on the floor cross-legged, her bare feet sticking out of her blue jeans, her back against the bookcase. She had on the heavy black tortoise-shell glasses that she used for reading and she was eating miniature éclairs out of a little carton on the floor next to her as she turned the pages of her book. Louise was studying French literature at the Sorbonne for a year, but at the moment was reading *Huckleberry Finn,* in a French translation. French literature was depressing her, she said, and she yearned for a whiff of the Mississippi. She came from St. Louis and at parties she had been heard to say that the Mississippi was the Mother-Water of her life. Roberta wasn't quite sure what this meant, but was secretly impressed by the statement, with its hint of mid-continent mysticism and the liquid boldness of its self-knowledge. Roberta, as far as she knew, had no Mother-Water in her life.

Roberta was at the easel in the middle of the big, dark, cluttered room which she and Louise had shared since they had come to Paris eight months before. Roberta was working on a long thin canvas of Parisian shop windows, trying to overcome the influences of Chagall, Picasso, and Joan Miró, influences that overtook her in disconcerting waves at different periods of the month. She was only nineteen and she worried over her susceptibility to other styles and other people and tried to look at as few paintings as possible.

Louise stood up with a long, swanlike movement, sucking éclair goo off her fingers, shaking her shiny black hair. She went over to the window and threw it open and took several loud, ostentatious breaths of the dank winter afternoon Paris air. "I fear for your health," she said. "I'll bet that if they took a survey, they'd discover that half the painters of history died from silicosis."

"That's a miner's disease," Roberta said, painting placidly. "From the dust. There's no dust in oils."

"I await the result of the survey," Louise said, not giving an inch. She peered out the window down to the street three stories below. "He might even be handsome," she said, "if he ever got a haircut."

"He has beautiful hair," Roberta said, fighting down the almost irresistible impulse to go over to the window and look out. "Anyway, that's the way all the boys wear it these days."

"All the boys," Louise said darkly. She was a year older than Roberta and had already had two affairs, with Frenchmen, that had come out, according to her, disastrously, and she was in an acid and sophisticated period. "Have you got a date with him?" she asked.

"At four o'clock," Roberta said. "He's taking me over to the Right Bank." She poked distractedly at the canvas. The knowledge that Guy was so close made it difficult to concentrate on her work.

Louise looked at her watch. "It's only three-thirty," she said. "What devotion."

Roberta didn't like the ironic tone in Louise's voice but didn't know how to combat it. She wished that Louise would save her sophistication for her own use. Thinking about Guy made Roberta feel trembly and electric and she began to clean her brushes because she couldn't work feeling like that.

"What's he doing?" Roberta asked, trying to sound offhand.

"He's looking yearningly into the window of the butcher shop." Louise said. "They have a specialty today. Rumpsteak. Seven hundred and fifty francs the kilo."

Roberta felt a slight twinge of disappointment. As long as he was there, anyway, it would have been more satisfactory if he had been gazing, yearningly or not, at *her* window. "I think it's perfectly insufferable of Madame Ruffat not to let us have people up here," she said. Madame Ruffat was their landlady. She lived in the same apartment and they shared the kitchen and bathroom with her. She was a little fat woman, stuffed into girdles and grim uplift brassieres, and she had an unpleasant habit of bursting in upon them unannounced and surveying them with a shifty, mistrustful eye, as though she suspected them of being on the verge of despoiling the stained red damask that covered the walls or smuggling in unworthy young men for the night.

"She knows what she's doing," Louise said, still at the window. "Madame Ruffat. She's lived in Paris for fifty years. She understands Frenchmen. You let a Frenchman into your room and you can't get him out until the next war."

"Oh, Louise," Roberta said, "why do you always try to sound so—so disillusioned?"

"Because I *am* disillusioned," Louise said. "And you will be too if you keep going the way you're going."

"I'm not going any way," Roberta said.

"Hah!"

"What does that mean—hah?" Roberta asked.

Louise didn't bother to explain. Instead she peered out the window, with a critical and disapproving expression on her face. "How old does he say he is?" she asked.

"He's twenty-one."

"Has he pounced on you yet?" Louise asked.

"Of course not," Roberta said.

"Then he's not twenty-one." Louise turned away from the window and strode across the room to sink down next to the bookcase again and *Huckleberry Finn* in French and the last éclair.

"Listen, Louise," Roberta said, hoping she was sounding severe and sensible, "I don't interfere with your private life, and I'd appreciate it if you didn't interfere with mine."

"I am merely trying to give you the benefit of my experience," Louise said, her voice a little thick with custard. "My bitter experience. Besides, I promised your mother I'd look after you."

"Forget about my mother, will you? One of the main reasons I came to France was to get away from my mother."

"On your own head," Louise said, turning a page with a

little snap. "There's only so much a friend can do."

The rest of the time Roberta was in the room passed in silence. She checked the water colors in the portfolio she was taking with her and combed her hair and tied a scarf around it and touched her lips with rouge and looked anxiously at herself in the mirror, worrying, as usual, that she looked too young, too blue-eyed, too innocent, too American, too shy, too everlastingly, hopelessly *unready*.

At the door, poised to leave, she said to Louise, who was steadfastly looking down at her book, "I won't be home for dinner."

"One last word," Louise said implacably. "Beware."

Roberta closed the door behind her with a bang and went down the long dark hall, carrying the portfolio. Madame Ruffat was sitting in the salon on a little gilt chair, her back to the window, glaring, above her iron corsets, through the open salon doors into the hallway, playing solitaire and checking on all arrivals and departures. She and Roberta nodded coldly at each other. *Old insufferable witch,* Roberta said under her breath as she manipulated the three locks on the front door with which Madame Ruffat kept the world at bay.

As she descended the dark stairway, with its cavelike odor of underground rivers and cold and forgotten dinners, Roberta felt melancholy and oppressed. When her father, back in Chicago, had told her he'd been able to scrape together enough money for her to paint for twelve months in Paris, saying, "Well, even if nothing else happens, at least you'll have a year to learn the language," Roberta was sure that she was bursting into a new life, a life that would be free, assured, blossoming, open to the fruitful touch of adventure. Instead, what with worrying about everybody's influence on her painting, and the grim surveillance of Madame Ruffat and Louise's constant gloomy warnings, Roberta felt more tied up, uncertain, constrained than ever before.

People had even lied to her about the language. Oh, they had said, in three months, at your age, you'll be speaking like a native. Well, it was eight months, not three, and she had studied the grammar assiduously, and while she could understand most of what was said around her all right, every time she spoke more than five words in French, people replied to her in English. Even Guy, who professed to love her, and whose English sounded like Maurice Chevalier's first movie, insisted upon conducting even the most intimate, the most *French* conversations with her in English.

Sometimes, like this afternoon, she felt as though she would never break the cage of childhood, no matter what she did, that the freedom, the desperate risks and final rewards and punishments of adulthood would forever be beyond her grasp. Stopping for a moment to push the button that buzzed open the door into the street, she had a sickening vision of herself as one of those wispy and virginal old maids, eternally locked in brittle nursery innocence, before whom no one spoke of scandals, death, or passion.

Hugely dissatisfied with herself, she gave a last push to the scarf around her head, hoping for coquetry, and stepped out into the street, where Guy was waiting, in front of the butcher shop, polishing the handlebars of his Vespa. His long, dark, intense Mediterranean face, which Roberta had once, but only once, told Louise looked as though it had been created by Modigliani, broke into a brilliant smile. But this afternoon it didn't have its usual effect on Roberta. "Louise is right," she said cruelly. "You ought to get a haircut."

The smile vanished. In its place appeared a slightly bored, languid, raised-eyebrow expression that at other times had also had a disturbing effect on Roberta, but which did nothing for her, she noted coldly, this afternoon. "Louise," Guy said, wrinkling his nose. "That old bag of tomatoes."

"First of all," Roberta said censoriously, "Louise is my friend and you mustn't talk about my friends like that. Secondly, if you think you're talking American slang, you're way far out. 'Old bag' is possible, if that's what you mean. But nobody's called a girl a 'tomato' in America since before Pearl Harbor. If you must insult my friends, why don't you speak French?"

"*Écoute, mon chou,*" Guy said, in the weary and practically lifeless tone that made him appear so much more grown-up and exciting to Roberta than the breathless and bumbling boys she had known back in Chicago. "I wish to communicate with you and make love to you. Possibly even to marry you. But I do not wish to act as a substitute for the Berlitz School. If you wish to be polite for the rest of the afternoon, you are permitted to climb onto the back seat and I will take you where you wish to go. But if you are going to enervate me you can walk."

This quick and independent harshness, coming from a man who had been waiting patiently for her more than a half-hour in the cold, made Roberta feel deliciously submissive. It gave substance to the statement she had heard (most often from Guy himself), that Frenchmen knew how to treat women and made the boys who had mooned over her on the shores of Lake Michigan seem like debilitated, irresolute children.

"All I said," she said, retreating, "was that maybe you'd look a little better if your hair were shorter."

"Get on," Guy said. He swung onto the saddle of the Vespa and she arranged herself behind him. It was a little awkward, with the huge portfolio which she had to carry under one arm while with the other she gripped Guy around the waist. She wore blue jeans for her expeditions on the machine, because she hadn't liked the swoop of wind under her skirts the one or two times she had worn them, nor the immodest way they sometimes billowed at unexpected moments, which caused pedestrians to look at her with unpleasantly candid appreciation.

She gave Guy the address of the gallery on the Rue Faubourg St. Honoré where she had an appointment with the gallery's director, arranged for by Monsieur Raimond, the painter in whose atelier she studied. "It is a gallery without distinction, Patrini's," M. Raimond had told her, "but the fellow is constantly searching for cheap young people to exploit. And he is amused by Americans. Perhaps, with luck, he will take a water color or two and hang them, provisionally, in a back room, for a few days, and see what happens. Just don't sign anything, not anything at all, and no permanent harm can befall you."

Guy started the Vespa and they dashed off, roaring in and out between cars, buses, bicycles, and pedestrians with doomed looks on their faces. Guy drove at all times with an iron-nerved and debonair disregard of risk. It was an expression of his character, he told Roberta, and a sign of his rebellion against what he called the timid bourgeois love of security of his parents. He lived with his parents because he was still going to school. He was studying to be an engineer and when he was through he was going to build dams in Egypt, railroad bridges in the Andes, roads across India. So he wasn't one of those shaggy and worthless young men who merely hung around St. Germain des Prés all day and all night, sponging off foreigners and damning the future, entwined in indiscriminate sex, like the characters in the *nouvelle vague* movies. He believed in love and fidelity and accomplishment, although he was terribly dashing about it all, and far from having pounced on her, as Louise had so uncouthly put it, in the three months Roberta had known him, he hadn't even kissed her once, except on the cheek when they had said good night. "I'm past all that cheap, adolescent promiscuity. When we are ready for each other we will know it," he had said loftily; and Roberta had adored him for it, sensing that she was getting the best values of Chicago and Paris in the one package. He had never introduced her to his parents. "They're good, solid citizens, *de pauvres mais braves gens,*" he had told Roberta, "but of no interest to anyone but their relatives. One night with them and you'd be bored onto the first boat train back to Le Havre."

They whistled up the Quai d'Orsay, with the Seine below them, and the Louvre looking like a dream of France across the river, and the wind making Guy's bright scarf and long black hair whip back straight from his head and bringing spots of color to Roberta's cheeks and frozen tears to her eyes. She held onto the waist of Guy's smart sheepskin coat, soaringly content with zig-zagging around the city like this through the gray winter afternoon.

Jouncing on the pillion of the noisy little machine, crossing the bridge in front of the Assemblée Nationale, with a portfolio of paintings under her arm and the handsomest boy in Europe speeding her deftly past the obelisk and the stone horses of the Place de la Concorde, on her way to discuss art with a man who had bought and sold twenty thousand pictures in the course of his career, Roberta's doubts left her. She knew that she had been right to leave Chicago, right to come to Paris, right to give her telephone number to Guy three months before when he had asked for it at the party Louise had taken her to at the apartment of her second Frenchman. Omens of happiness and good luck around her head like small, almost visible singing birds, and when she dismounted in front of the little gallery on the Rue Faubourg St. Honoré, she faced the

A YEAR TO LEARN THE LANGUAGE

unwelcoming door with an athlete's spring and confidence.

"*Écoute, Roberta,*" Guy said, patting her cheek, "*je t'assure que va très bien se passer. Pour une femme, tu es un grand peintre, et bientôt tout le monde le saura.*"

She smiled mistily at him, equally grateful for his belief in her and for the delicacy of spirit which had made him declare it in French.

"Now," he said, lapsing into his usual Chevalier English, "I go to do several excruciating errands for Mama. I attend you in a half-hour at Queenie's."

He waved, swung gallantly onto the saddle of the Vespa and, hair and scarf streaming, dodged down the bustling street toward the British embassy. Roberta watched him for a moment, then turned toward the door. In the window of the gallery there was a large painting done in shades of purple that might have represented a washing machine or a nightmare. Roberta scanned it swiftly and thought, It's a cinch I can do better than that, and opened the door and went in.

The gallery was small and plushly carpeted, with many paintings jammed together on the walls, a good many of them by the purple-washing-machine man in the window or his disciples. There was one visitor, a man of about fifty in a coat with a mink collar and a beautiful black Homburg hat. The owner of the gallery, distinguished by a red carnation in his buttonhole and a wary and at the same time predatory expression on a thin, disabused face, stood behind and a little to one side of the man in the fur-trimmed coat. His white hands twitched gently at his sides, as though he were ready instantaneously to produce a blank check or seize the potential client if he showed signs of flight.

Roberta introduced herself to Monsieur Patrini, the owner of the gallery, in her best French, and Patrini said brusquely, in perfect English, "Yes, Raimond says you're not without talent. Here, you can use this easel."

He stood about ten feet away from the easel, frowning slightly, as though he were remembering a dish at lunch that hadn't quite agreed with him, as Roberta took the first watercolor out of her portfolio and placed it on the easel. The sight of the painting did not cause any change in Patrini's expression. He still looked as though he was being mildly haunted by a too-rich sauce or a fish that had been too long in transit from Normandy. He made no comment. Every once in a while his lips twisted minutely, as if in digestive pain, and Roberta took this as a sign of progress and put the next painting on the easel. In the middle of the exhibition, Roberta became conscious that the man in the Homburg hat had given up his examination of the pictures on the walls and was standing off a little to one side, looking at her watercolors as she slid them one by one onto the easel. She was so intent on trying to discover some sign of reaction on Patrini's face that she never even glanced at the man in the Homburg hat throughout the entire performance.

Patrini's lips made a final gaseous twitch.

"There," Roberta said flatly, hating him and resigned to failure, "that's the lot."

"Ummm . . . huh . . . umm," Patrini said. He had a very low bass voice and for a moment Roberta was afraid that he had said something in French and she had been unable to understand it. But then he went on, in English. "There is a certain promise," he said. "Deeply buried."

"Forgive me, *cher ami*," said the man in the Homburg hat. "There is a great deal more than that." His English sounded as if he had lived all his life at Oxford, although he was clearly a Frenchman. "My dear young lady," he went on, taking off his hat and revealing a marvelously barbered head of iron-gray hair, "I wonder if I could bother you further. Would you be good enough to put your paintings all around the gallery so that I might study them and compare them without haste?"

Roberta looked numbly at Patrini. She was sure that she had let her mouth fall open and she shut it with a loud click of teeth. *"Mon cher* Baron," Patrini was saying, his face suddenly transformed by a brilliant, demi-social, demi-commercial smile, "may I present a young American friend of great talent, Miss Roberta James. Miss James, the Baron de Ummhuhzediers."

That was what the name sounded like to Roberta, and she cursed herself again for not having yet gotten the hang of French names, even as she tried to smile graciously at the gray-haired Frenchman. "Of course," she said, her voice an octave too high. "I'd be delighted." She began to grab paintings off the pile on the easel and stand them indiscriminately on the floor against the walls. Patrini, suddenly spry and professional, helped her, and within two minutes, the work of eight months was spread all around the gallery in an impromptu one-woman show.

No word was spoken for a long time. The Baron moved from painting to painting, standing minutes before some of them, passing others quickly, his hands behind his back, a slight, polite smile touching his lips. Occasionally he nodded gently. Roberta stood to one side, anxiously peering at each painting as the Baron approached it, trying to see it anew with those shrewd, experienced eyes. Patrini subtly stood at the window, his back to the room, staring out at the traffic of the busy street outside, the echo of whose passage made a constant *hush-hush* in the carpeted, warm room.

At last the Baron spoke. He was standing in front of a painting Roberta had made at the zoo at Vincennes, of some children in pale blue ski suits looking in at the leopard's cage. "I'm afraid I can't make up my mind," he said, not taking his eyes off the painting. "I can't decide whether I want this one or"—he walked slowly along the wall—"or this one here." He nodded at one of Roberta's latest, one of her shop windows.

"If I may make a suggestion," Patrini said, turning swiftly into the room at the sound of a customer's voice. "Why don't you take them both home for study and make up your mind at your leisure?"

"If the young lady wouldn't mind." The Baron turned deferentially, almost pleadingly, toward Roberta.

"No," Roberta said, struggling to keep from shouting, "I wouldn't mind."

"Excellent," the Baron said crisply. "I'll send my man to pick them up tomorrow morning." He made a little bow, put on his beautiful black hat over his beautiful iron-gray hair and went through the door which Patrini had magically opened for him.

"When the Baron had disappeared, Patrini came back briskly into the shop and picked up the two paintings the Baron had chosen. "Excellent," Patrini said. "It confirms an old belief of mine. In certain cases it is advisable for the client to meet the artist at the very beginning." With the two watercolors under his arm, he peered critically at a monochromatic wash of a nude that Roberta had painted at Raimond's studio. "Perhaps I'll keep that one around for a week or two, also," Patrini said. "If I pass the word around that the Baron is interested in your work, it may stir one or two of my other clients in your direction." He picked up the nude, too. "The Baron has a famous collection, as you know, of course."

"Of course," Roberta lied.

"He has several excellent Soutines, quite a few Matisses, and a really first-class Braque. And, of course, like everybody else, several Picassos. When I hear from him, I'll drop you a line," The telephone rang in the little office at the back of the shop and Patrini hurried away to answer it, carrying the three paintings with him. Soon he was involved in an intense, whispered conversation, the tone of which suggested a communication in code between two intelligence agents.

Roberta stood irresolutely for a while in the middle of the shop, then gathered all her paintings and put them back into the portfolio. Patrini was still whispering into the telephone in the office. Roberta went to the door of the office and stood there until he looked up. *"Au revoir, Mademoiselle,"* he said, waving a white hand at her gently, and lapsed back into his coded mumble.

Roberta would have preferred more ceremony for the occasion. After all, this was the first time anybody had ever expressed even the vaguest intention of buying a painting of hers. But Patrini gave no indication that he might conclude his conversation before midnight, and he had clearly dismissed her. So she smiled uncertainly at him and left.

Outside, in the cold dusk, she walked lightly and gaily past the glowing, jewel-like windows of the expensive shops, her scarf, her short, dun-colored coat, her blue jeans and flat shoes, and the battered green portfolio under her arm setting her puritanically apart from the furred, perfumed, high-heeled women who constituted the natural fauna of the Rue Faubourg St. Honoré. As she walked among them, museum doors swung open before her in a golden trance and she could almost see huge posters, with her name in severe, long letters—*James*—blossoming on the kiosks and on gallery doors. The invisible birds of joy which had sung around her head earlier in the afternoon now sang more loudly and privately than ever as she approached Queenie's, where Guy was waiting for her.

A YEAR TO LEARN THE LANGUAGE

Superstitiously she decided to tell Guy nothing about what had taken place in the gallery. When it had happened, when the painting (whichever of the two it turned out to be) had been bought and paid for and hung on the Baron's walls, there would be time enough to announce and celebrate. Besides, she didn't want to have to admit to Guy that she hadn't caught the Baron's name and had been too shy and flustered to find it out after he'd gone. She would pass by the gallery in the next day or two and find an opportunity to ask Patrini, casually, to spell it out for her.

Guy was sitting in a corner of the large, crowded café, grumpily looking at his watch, a half-finished glass of pineapple juice on the table in front of him. To Roberta's secret disappointment, he never drank any wine or alcohol. "Alcohol is the curse of France," he said again and again. "Wine has made us a second-rate power." On her own, Roberta hardly ever drank anything at all, but she couldn't help feeling a little cheated at being connected with the one man in France who ordered Coca-Cola or lemonade each time the *sommelier* came up to them in a restaurant and offered the wine card. It was uncomfortably like Chicago.

Guy stood up ungraciously as she approached. "What happens?" he said. "I have been waiting forever. I have drunk three juices of pineapples."

"I'm sorry," Roberta said, setting the portfolio down and slipping into a chair beside Guy's. "The man was busy."

Guy sat down, a little mollified. "How did it pass?"

"Not too badly," Roberta said, fighting the temptation to bubble out the news. "He said he'd be interested in seeing my oils."

"They are all fools," Guy said, pressing her hand. "He will bite his nails when you are famous." He waved to a passing waiter. *"Deux jus d'ananas,"* he said. He stared hard at Roberta. "Tell me," he said, "what are your intentions?"

"My intentions?" Roberta said doubtfully. "Do you mean toward you?"

"No." Guy waved rather impatiently. "That will discover itself at the proper time. I mean, in a philosophical sense—your intentions in life."

"Well," Roberta said, speaking hesitantly, because although she had thought about the question for a long time now, she was uncertain about how it would sound put into words. "Well, I want to be a good painter, of course. I want to know exactly what I am doing and why I'm doing it and what I want people to feel when they look at my pictures."

"Good. Very good," Guy said, sounding like an approving teacher to a promising student. "What else?"

"I want my whole life to be like that," Roberta went on. "I don't want to—well—grope. That's what I hate about so many people my age back home—they don't know what they want or how they want to get it. They're—well, they're groping."

Guy looked puzzled. "Grope, groping," he said. "What does that mean?"

"*Tâtonner,*" Roberta said, pleased at this unusual chance to demonstrate her linguistic superiority. "My father is a history student, he specializes in battles, and he's always talking about the fog of war, everybody running around and killing each other and doing the right thing or the wrong thing, winning or losing, without understanding it. . . ."

"Oh, yes," Guy said. "I have heard the phrase."

"My feeling is," Roberta went on, "the fog of war is nothing compared to the fog of youth. The Battle of Gettysburg was crystal clear compared to being nineteen years old. I want to get out of the fog of youth. I want to be *precise.* I don't want anything to be an accident. That's one of the reasons I came to Paris—everybody's always talking about how precise the French are. Maybe I can learn to be like that."

"Do you think I am precise?" Guy asked.

"Enormously. That's one of the things I like best about you."

Guy nodded somberly, agreeing. His eyes, with their heavy fringe of black lashes, glowed darkly. "American," he said, "you are going to be a very superior woman. And you have never been more beautiful." He leaned over and kissed her cheek, still cold from her walk.

"What a lovely afternoon," she said.

They went to see a movie that Guy had heard was very good and after that to a *bistro* on the Left Bank for dinner. Roberta had wanted to go home and leave her portfolio

A YEAR TO LEARN THE LANGUAGE

and change her clothes, but Guy had forbidden it. "Tonight," he said mysteriously, "I do not want you to be exposed to the pronouncements of your friend, Louise."

Roberta hadn't paid much attention to the picture. There were big signs plastered all over the outside of the theater saying that it was forbidden for anyone under eighteen years of age and she had been embarrassed by the ironic stare of the man who took the tickets when they went in. She wished she had her passport with her to prove that she was over eighteen. The picture itself was largely incomprehensible to her, as she had difficulty understanding French when it was reproduced mechanically, either in the movies or over public-address systems. In the movie there were the familiar long scenes of young people chatting away in bed together, all needlessly bare and explicit, to Roberta's way of thinking. She half-closed her eyes through much of the showing, recreating, with certain embellishments, the events of the afternoon, and she was hardly conscious of Guy, at her side, who was raising her hand to his lips and kissing her fingertips in an unusual manner throughout the most dramatic moments of the film.

During dinner, he behaved strangely, too. He remained silent for long periods of time, which wasn't like him at all, and stared across the little table at her with a purposeful directness that made Roberta edgy and uneasy. Finally, with the coffee, Guy cleared his throat oratorically, stretched across the table to take both her hands in his and said, "I have decided. The time is ripe. We have reached the inevitable moment."

"What are you talking about?" Roberta asked nervously, conscious of the barman watching them with interest in the empty little restaurant.

"I speak in an adult manner," Guy said. "Tonight we become lovers."

"Ssssh . . ." Roberta looked worriedly at the barman and drew her hands away and put them out of reach under the table.

"I cannot live any longer without you," Guy said. "I have borrowed the key to the apartment of a friend of mine. He has gone to visit his family in Tours for the night. It is just around the corner."

Roberta could not pretend to be shocked by Guy's proposal. Like all virgins who come to Paris, she was secretly convinced, or resigned, or delighted, by the idea that she would leave the city in a different condition from that in which she had arrived in it. And at almost any other time in the last three months she probably would have been moved by Guy's declaration and been tempted to accept. Even now, she admired what she considered the sobriety and dignity of the offer. But the same superstitious reserve that had prevented her from telling Guy about her two paintings worked again on her now. When the fate of the paintings was known, she would consider Guy's invitation. Not before. Tonight was out of the question for another reason too. However it was fated finally to happen, of one thing she was sure—she was not going to enter the first love affair of her life in blue jeans.

She shook her head, annoyed with herself because of the flush that warmed her cheeks and neck. She looked down at her plate, because looking across at Guy made her blush more intense. "No, please," she whispered. "Not tonight."

"Why not tonight?" Guy demanded.

"It—it's so abrupt," Roberta said.

"Abrupt!" Guy said loudly. "I have seen you nearly every day for three months now. What are you accustomed to?"

"I'm not accustomed to anything. You know that," she said. "Please, let's not talk about it. Not tonight."

"But I have the apartment for tonight," Guy said. "My friend may not go to Tours for another year." His face was sorrowful and hurt and for the first time since she had known him, Roberta had the feeling that he was in need of comforting. She leaned over and patted his hand sympathetically.

"Don't look like that," she said. "Maybe some other time."

"I warn you," he said with dignity, "the next time it will have to be you who will make the advances."

"I will make the advances," she said, relieved and at the same time obscurely annoyed by his quick surrender. "Now pay the check. I have to get up early tomorrow."

Later on, in her narrow, lumpy bed, under the heavy quilt, she was too excited to sleep. What a day, she thought. I am on the verge of being a painter. I am on the verge of being a woman. Then she giggled softly at the solemnity of the phrase and hugged herself. She was favorably impressed by the quality of her own skin. If Louise had been awake, she would have told her everything. But Louise slept sternly in the bed along the opposite wall, her hair in curlers, her face greased against wrinkles that would not appear for another twenty years. Regretfully Roberta closed her eyes. It was not the sort of day you liked to see end.

Two days later, when she came into the room and turned on the light, she saw a *pneumatique* addressed to her on her bed. It was late in the afternoon and the apartment was cold and empty. Louise was out, and for once Madame Ruffat had not been at her post playing solitaire when Roberta had walked down the hall. Roberta opened the *pneumatique*. "Dear Miss James," it read. "Please get in touch with me immediately. I have some important news for you." It was signed "Patrini."

Roberta looked at her watch. It was five o'clock. Patrini would still be in the gallery. Feeling prickly and light headed, she went back along the hall and into the salon, where the telephone was. When Madame Ruffat went out, she locked the dial mechanism with a little padlock, but there was always a chance that for once she had forgotten to do it. But Madame Ruffat had forgotten nothing. The phone was locked. Roberta said, *Insufferable old witch,* three times under her breath, and went into the kitchen to look for the maid. The kitchen was dark and Roberta remembered that it was the maid's day off.

"Oh, damn," Roberta said to herself. "France!" She let herself out of the apartment and hurried down to the café on the corner, where there was a pay telephone. But there was a little damp man with a briefcase in the booth, making notes on a sheet of paper as he talked. From what Roberta could gather over the noise from the bar, the man with the briefcase was involved in a complicated transaction concerning the installation of plumbing fixtures. He gave no sign that he was close to finishing. Paris, Roberta thought unfairly. Everybody's on the phone at all hours of the day and night.

She looked at her watch. It was a quarter past five. Patrini closed the gallery at six. Roberta retreated to the bar and ordered a glass of red wine to soothe her nerves. She would have to chew some gum after to remove the traces of the wine from her breath. She had a date with Guy at seven and it would mean a long lecture if he discovered she'd been drinking. The bar was full of workmen from the quarter, laughing and speaking loudly, obviously not at all concerned with what *their* breaths were going to smell like that evening.

Finally, the plumbing man came out and Roberta leaped into the booth and put in the *jeton*. The line was busy. She remembered the interminable conversation Patrini had engaged in the afternoon she was there and began to get panicky. She tried three times more and each time the line was busy. It was five twenty-five. She rushed out of the booth, paid for her wine and hurried toward the Métro. It was a long trip across the city, but there was nothing else to be done. She couldn't bear the thought of going through the whole night without knowing what Patrini had to say to her.

Even though it was a bitterly cold afternoon, she was perspiring and out of breath from running when she reached the gallery. It was five to six. The lights were still on. The purple man was still represented in the window. Roberta hurled herself through the door. There was nobody in the gallery, but from the office in the back, she heard the secretive whisper of Patrini on the telephone. She had the unreasonable impression that he had been talking like that, in the same position and in the same voice, since the time she had left him two days before. She took a little time to regain her breath, then walked to the rear of the gallery and showed herself at the door to Patrini. He looked up after a while, waved languidly in greeting and continued his conversation. She turned back into the gallery and pretended to be studying a large painting which vaguely reminded her of robins' eggs, magnified thirty times. She was glad for the respite now. It gave her time to compose herself. Patrini, she was sure, was a man who would be adversely affected by signs of excitement or expressions of enthusiasm or gratitude. By the time he came out of the office and approached her, she had frozen her face into lines of mildly amused boredom.

Roberta heard the click of the phone in the office as Patrini hung up. He came up to her like a large soft animal, padding along on the thick carpet. "Good evening, *chère Mademoiselle*," he said. "I called the number you left me this morning, but the lady who answered informed me there was nobody by your name living there."

"That's my landlady," Roberta said. It was an old trick of Madame Ruffat to discourage what she termed the intolerable racket of the telephone bell.

"I wanted to tell you," said Patrini, "that the Baron came by this morning to say that he still couldn't make up his mind which of the two paintings he liked, so he's decided to take them both."

Roberta closed her eyes against the glory of the moment, pretending to be squinting at a painting on the opposite wall. "Really?" she said. "Both of them? He's more intelligent than I thought."

Patrini made a funny sound, as though he were choking, but Roberta forgave him, because at that moment she would have forgiven anybody anything.

"He also asked me to tell you that you're invited to his house for dinner tonight," Patrini went on. "I'm to call his secretary before seven to let him know. *Are* you free for dinner?"

Roberta hesitated. She had the date with Guy at seven and she knew he would appear faithfully at six forty-five and stand waiting on the cold street for her to appear, a gelid victim of Madame Ruffat's detestation of the male sex. For a moment, she hesitated. Then she thought, Artists must be ruthless, or they are not artists. Remember Gauguin. Remember Baudelaire. "Yes," she said offhandedly to Patrini, "I believe I can make it."

"It's number nineteen *bis* Square du Bois de Boulogne," Patrini said. "That's off the Avenue Foch. Eight o'clock. Under no circumstances discuss prices. I will handle that end. Is that understood?"

"I never discuss prices," Roberta said haughtily. She bathed in self-control.

"I will call the Baron's secretary for you," Patrini said. "And tomorrow I will display your nude in the window."

"I may drop by," Roberta said. She knew she had to get out of there fast. She had the feeling that if she had to speak a sentence of more than four words, it would end in a primitive yell of triumph. She started out of the shop.

Unexpectedly Patrini held the door open for her. "Young lady," he said, "it's none of my business, but please be careful."

Roberta nodded in an amused manner. She even forgave him that. It was only when she had floated two hundred yards in a westerly direction that she remembered that she still didn't know the Baron's name. It was while she was passing the bayoneted guards of the Palais Matignon that she realized that there were one or two other problems she had to face. She was dressed as she had been dressed all day—for traveling around on foot on the streets of a wet and wintry Paris. She was wearing a raincoat and a scarf and under it a plaid wool skirt and sweater and dark green wool stockings and after-ski boots. It was hardly the costume for a dinner in a mansion off the Avenue Foch. But if she went home to change, Guy would undoubtedly be there, waiting for her, and she didn't have the courage to tell him that she was ditching him this way to dine with a fifty-year-old member of the French nobility. He would be hurt and at the same time cutting and fierce and certainly would make her cry. He made her cry easily when he wanted to. This was one night she couldn't afford to appear red-eyed and damp. No, she decided, the Baron would have to take her in her green stockings. If you wanted to mingle with artists you had to be ready for certain eccentricities.

But she was uneasy about just leaving Guy standing forlornly outside her door on the cold street. He had weak lungs and suffered from severe attacks of bronchitis every winter. She went into a café on the Avenue Matignon and tried to telephone her apartment. But there was no answer. Louise, Roberta thought angrily. Never around the one time you need her. I bet she's starting on her third Frenchman.

Roberta hung up and got back her *jeton*. She stared at the telephone, considering. She could call Guy's apartment of course, and eventually, in the course of the evening, the message might reach him. But the two or three times she had called his home she had gotten his mother, who had a high, irritated voice and who pretended she couldn't understand Roberta's French. Roberta didn't want to expose herself to that sort of treatment tonight. She tossed the *jeton* thoughtfully in the air once or twice and then left the booth. The problem of Guy would have to be put off until tomorrow. Resolutely, as she walked toward the Champs Elysées, in the ugly dark drizzle she put Guy out of her mind. If you were in love, you had to expect to endure a certain amount of pain.

It was a long walk to the Square du Bois de Boulogne and she had difficulty finding it and it was eight-fifteen and she had made a long unnecessary loop in the black rain before she came upon it. Nineteen *bis* was a large forbidding mansion with a Bentley and several smaller cars and two or three chauffeurs parked in front of it. Roberta was surprised to see these signs that there were to be other guests. Somehow, from the tone in which Patrini had said, "Please be careful," she had been sure that it was going to be a cozy little tête-à-tête dinner that the Baron had arranged for himself and his young protégée. In the course of her long walk, Roberta had pondered this and had decided not to be shocked or alarmed at whatever happened, and to behave in a sophisticated and Parisienne manner. Besides, she was sure she could handle any fifty-year-old man, regardless of how many pictures he bought.

She rang the bell, feeling cold and soaked. A butler in white gloves opened the door and stared at her as though he didn't believe the evidence of his eyes. She stepped into the high-ceilinged, mirrored hallway and took off her sopping coat and scarf and handed it to the man. *"Dites au Baron que Mademoiselle James est là, s'il vous plaît,"* she said. But when the man just stood there, gaping at her, holding her coat and scarf at arm's length, she added sharply, *"Je suis invitée à dîner."*

"Oui, mademoiselle," the man said. He hung up her coat on a rack, at a noncontaminating distance from a half-dozen or so mink coats that were ranged there, and disappeared through a door which he carefully closed behind him.

Roberta looked at herself in one of the mirrors in the hallway and quickly attacked the dismal wet tangle of her hair with a comb. She had just succeeded in imposing a rough kind of order on her dank curls when the hallway door opened and the Baron came out. He was dressed in a dinner jacket and he stopped for just the briefest part of a second when he saw her, but then a warm smile broke over his face and he said, "Charming, charming. I'm delighted you could come." He bent over her hand ceremoniously and kissed it, and said, with the quickest edge of a glance at her after-ski boots, "I hope the invitation wasn't at too short notice."

"Well," Roberta said honestly, "I certainly would have changed my shoes if I'd known it was going to be a party."

The Baron laughed as though she had said something immensely witty and squeezed her hand and said, "Nonsense, you're absolutely perfect as you are. Now," he said, taking her arm conspiratorially, "I want to show you something before we join the other guests." He led her down the hall into a sitting room with pink walls, in which a small fire was glowing in the grate. On the wall opposite the fireplace were her two watercolors, handsomely framed, separated by a glorious pencil drawing by Matisse. On another wall there was, indeed, a Soutine.

"How do you like them?" the Baron asked anxiously.

If Roberta had told the Baron how she *really* liked seeing her pictures hanging amid this glorious company, she would have sounded like the last movement of the Ninth Symphony. "OK," she said flatly. "I think they're OK."

The Baron's face was twisted by an almost invisible quick grimace, as though not smiling was causing him considerable pain. He reached into his pocket and took out a check, folded in half, which he pushed into Roberta's hand. "Here," he said. "I hope this strikes you as being enough. I've discussed it with Patrini. Don't worry about his commission. It's all arranged for."

Taking her eyes away from her pictures with difficulty, Roberta unfolded the check and looked at it. The first thing she tried to make out was the Baron's signature, so that she would finally know his name. But the signature was in a wild, spiky French script and there was no deciphering it. Then she looked at the figure. It was for 2500 new francs. More than five hundred dollars, her mind registered automatically. Her father sent her one hundred and eighty dollars a month to live on. I will be able to live in France forever, she thought. My God!

She felt herself grow pale and the check shook in her hands. The Baron looked at her, alarmed. "What's the trouble?" he asked. "Isn't it enough?"

A YEAR TO LEARN THE LANGUAGE 87

"Not at all," Roberta said. "I mean—well, what I mean is, I never dreamed it would be so much. . . ."

The Baron gestured generously. "Buy yourself a new dress," he said. Then, after an involuntary glance at her plaid skirt and old sweater, and obviously fearing that she might feel he was criticizing her taste in clothes, he added, "I mean, do anything you want with it." He took her elbow again. "Now," he said, "I'm afraid we must really join the others. Just remember, whenever you wish to come and look at your work, all you have to do is call me."

He led her gently out of the pink room and across the hall into the salon. It was an enormous room with paintings by Braque and Rouault and Segonzac on the walls and was populated by an orderly mob of Frenchmen in dinner jackets and bare-shouldered and bejeweled Frenchwomen who, moving gracefully between the pieces of gilt and brocade furniture, gave off that high, self-satisfied, musical tone which is educated Parisian conversation at the peak moment of propriety and contentment which that particular society reaches five minutes before dinner is announced.

The Baron introduced her to a great many of the guests, none of whose names Roberta could catch, but who smiled amiably at her or kissed her hand, in the case of the men, as though it were the most natural thing in the world to dine in a house like that with an American girl in green wool stockings and after-ski boots. Two or three of the more elderly gentlemen said complimentary things about her paintings, in English, of course, and one lady said, "It *is* reassuring to see Americans painting like that again," which had an ambiguous note to it, but which Roberta finally decided to consider as praise.

Then, suddenly, she was alone in a corner of the room, with a glass containing an almost colorless liquid in her hand. The Baron had had to go meet some new guests and the last group of people he had introduced her to had melted into other groups in different sections of the room. Roberta kept her eyes rigidly fixed forward, with the idea that if she never looked down once during the evening, she might be able to forget the way she was dressed. Maybe, she thought, if I drink enough, I will finally feel as though I'm wearing something from Dior. She took a sip from her glass. She had never tasted the drink before, but some profound racial knowledge informed her that she had just entered the world of martini drinkers. She didn't like the taste, but she drained the glass. It gave her something to do. A waiter passed with another tray of drinks and she took a second glass and drank it down swiftly and without coughing. The after-ski boots on her feet were rapidly being transformed into shoes by Mancini, and she was sure by now that all the elegant people in the room, although they seemed to have their backs turned to her, were talking about her admiringly.

Before she had time to seek out the waiter and get a third glass, dinner was announced. She made her way among the undulating bare shoulders and the diamond earrings into the dining room. It was lighted by candles and the long table, with its batteries of wineglasses, was covered by an immense pink lace tablecloth. I must write Mother about *this,* Roberta thought, as she looked for her name on its place card. I am in French Society. Like Proust.

She was seated at the very end of the table, next to a bald man, who smiled mechanically at her once, then never looked at her again. Across from her sat another bald man, who was engrossed throughout the dinner by the large blond woman on his left. The Baron was four places down, in the center of the table, as the host, but after one quick friendly glance in her direction, there was no further communication from that quarter. Since the people around her were not speaking to Roberta, they were talking French. They spoke swiftly and elliptically, with their heads turned away from Roberta a good part of the time, and that, combined with the fact that the two martinis had somewhat loosened her control over the language, made the conversation only fitfully comprehensible to her and began to give her a sensation of exile.

She was surprised by the wine waiter, who whispered into her ear as he leaned over and poured her a glass of white wine. She couldn't quite make out what he was saying, but for a moment she thought he was trying to give her his telephone number. *"Comment?"* she said loudly, ready to embarrass him.

"Montrachet, *mil neuf cent cinquante-cinq,"* he whispered again, and she realized that he was merely announcing the wine. It was delicious, besides, and she had two more glasses of it with the cold lobster that was served as the first course. She ate enormously, because she had never tasted food as good, but with a growing sense of hostility toward everybody else at the table, because they paid no more attention to her than if she had been dining alone in the middle of the Bois de Boulogne.

As soup followed lobster, and pheasant followed soup, as Château Lafitte 1928 followed Montrachet 1955, Roberta began to look with misty disdain at her fellow guests. First of all, there was nobody at the table, she was sure, under forty. What am I doing in this old people's home? she thought as she took a second helping of pheasant and a large gob of currant jelly. The food only stoked the fires of her anger. These tottering Gallic Babbitts, these stockbrokers and their overdressed, high-pitched women didn't deserve the company of artists if all they did was sit them at the bottom of the table and feed them like charity cases at a soup kitchen and ignore them. Somehow, during the course of the dinner, she had become convinced that all the men present were stockbrokers. She munched on pheasant breast, now bitterly conscious again of her green stockings and tangled hair. She made a forceful attempt to understand what was being said around her and, her linguistic sense sharpened by contempt, she began to get the drift of the several conversations going on within earshot. Somebody said that the rainy summer had been disastrous for the shooting. Somebody said that a strong stand had to be taken in Algeria. Somebody spoke about a play that Roberta hadn't heard of and complained that the second act was outrageous. A lady in a white dress said she had heard from an American friend that President Kennedy had surrounded himself with Communists.

"What nonsense," Roberta said, quite loudly, but nobody even turned his head.

She ate some more pheasant, drank some more wine, and brooded. She began to suffer from a suspicion that she didn't exist. She wondered what she could say to get anyone there to acknowledge the fact that she was alive. It would have to be fairly shocking. She played with various opening statements. "I heard someone mention President Kennedy. I happen to be very close to the family. I wonder if it would interest anyone here to know that the President plans to remove all American troops from France by August." *That*'d make them look up from their plates for a few seconds, she thought grimly.

Or perhaps a more personal attack would serve better. Something like, "I must apologize for having been late this evening, but I was speaking over the cable to the Museum of Modern Art in New York. They want to buy four of my oils, but my agent wants me to wait until my one-man show this autumn."

Snobs, she thought, looking around her fiercely, I'll bet that'd swing the conversation around a bit.

But she sat dumbly, knowing she would never say anything, ignominiously trapped in her youth, her outlandish clothes, her ignorance, her infuriating shyness. Proust, she thought with huge self-scorn. French society!

Belligerence stirred within her. As she glared around her, over the crystal lip of her glass, the other people there seemed frivolous and false, with their talk of a bad season for pheasants, and their outrageous second acts, and their Communists surrounding the President. She glared at the Baron, so vainly barbered and foppishly perfect, and began to hate him most of all. I know what *he's* after, she muttered to herself, into the wineglass, and he's not going to get it.

She ate some more, heartily.

Her hatred for the Baron grew tropically. He'd invited her as a freak, to amuse his friends, she decided, and he hung her paintings in the same room with the Matisse and the Soutine as a joke, because he knew as well as she did that they didn't belong there. The minute she left, after he'd made his pass and failed, he'd have one of the butlers in white gloves take the paintings down and put them in the basement or the attic or the cook's bathroom, where they belonged.

Suddenly the vision of Guy, standing, faithful and frozen, outside her window in the winter night, swam before her. Tears welled in her eyes at the thought of how heartless she'd been to him and how much better he was than all these chattering gluttons at the table. She remembered how much he loved her and how he respected her and how pure he was and how happy she could make him just by lifting her little finger, so to speak. Sitting there with her plate heaped with breast of pheasant and purée of marrons, and her glass filled once more with a 1928 Bordeaux, she felt that it was intolerable that she wasn't with Guy at that moment and she could feel her immortal soul being corrupted second by second within her.

Abruptly, she stood up. Her chair would have fallen if one of the men in white gloves hadn't leaped and caught it. She stood very straight, wondering if she was as pale as she felt. All conversation ceased and every eye was turned upon her.

"I'm terribly sorry," she said, addressing the Baron. "I have a very important telephone call to make."

"Of course, my dear," the Baron said. He stood, but with a sharp little gesture kept the other men seated. "Henri will show you where the telephone is."

A waiter stepped forward, wooden-faced, from his station against the wall. Walking erectly, keeping her head high, her after-ski boots making a curious but not unmusical noise on the polished floor, she followed the waiter out of the silent room. The door closed behind her. I will never enter that room again, she thought. I will never see any of those people again. I have made my choice. My eternal choice.

Her knees felt cloudy and she was not conscious of the effort of walking as she followed Henri across the hall and into the pink salon.

"Voilà, Mademoiselle," Henri said, pointing to a phone on an inlaid table. *"Désirez-vous que je compose le numèro pour vous?"*

"Non," she said coldly. "Je le composerai moi-même, merci." She waited until he had left the room, then, sat down on the couch next to the phone. She dialed the number of Guy's home. While she listened to the buzzing in her ear, she stared at her paintings on the opposite wall. They looked pallid and ordinary and influenced by everybody. She remembered how exalted she had been when the Baron had led her into the room to show her the pictures so short a time ago. I am a pendulum, she thought, I am a classic manic-depressive. If I came from a rich family they would send me to a psychiatrist. I am not a painter. I must give up wearing blue jeans. I must devote myself to being a good woman and making a man happy. I must never drink again.

"*Allô! Allô!*" a woman's irritated voice said over the phone. It was Guy's mother.

Speaking as clearly as possible, Roberta asked if Guy was home. Guy's mother pretended not to understand Roberta at first and made her repeat the question twice. Then, sounding enraged, Guy's mother said yes, her son was home, but was sick in bed with a fever, and could talk to no one. Guy's mother seemed dangerously ready to hang up at any moment, and Roberta spoke urgently, in an attempt to get a message through before the phone went dead.

Guy's mother kept saying, "*Comment? Comment? Qu'est-ce que vous avez dit?*" in a shrill crescendo of annoyance.

Roberta was trying to say that she would be home in an hour, and that, if Guy felt well enough to get out of bed, she would like him to call her, when there was the sound of male shouts over the phone, and then thumping noises, as though there was a struggle going on for the instrument. Then she heard Guy's voice, panting. "Roberta? Where are you? Are you all right? What happened?"

"I'm a bitch," Roberta whispered. "Forgive me."

"Never mind that," Guy said. "Where are you?"

"I'm surrounded by the most terrible people," Roberta said. "It serves me right. I behaved like an idiot. . . ."

"Where are you?" Guy shouted. "What's the address?"

"Nineteen *bis* Square du Bois de Boulogne," Roberta said. "I'm awfully sorry you're sick. I wanted to see you and tell you—"

"Don't move," Guy said. "I'll be there in ten minutes."

There was an off-instrument cascade of French from Guy's mother, and then the click as Guy hung up. Roberta sat there a moment, the pain of her wounds beginning to vanish, soothed by the swift, dependable voice of love on the telephone. I must deserve him, she thought religiously. I must deserve him.

She stood up and went over and stared at her paintings. She would have liked to be able to scratch out her signature, but the paintings were covered with glass, and it wasn't possible.

She went out into the hall and put on her coat and tied her scarf around her head. The house seemed silent and empty. None of the men in white gloves were to be seen and whatever the guests were saying about her in the dining room was mercifully muffled by distance and a series of closed doors. She took a last look around, at the mirrors, the marble, the mink. This is not for me, she thought without regret. Tomorrow she would find out the Baron's name from Patrini and send him a dozen roses with a note of apology for her bad manners. Otherwise, she would never be able to face her mother again. She wondered if her mother had ever gone through a night like this when she was nineteen.

She opened the door softly and slipped out. The Bentley and the other cars were still there, and the chauffeurs standing in the cold, sad attendants of the rich, were grouped in the mist under a lamppost. Roberta leaned against the iron fence of the Baron's house, feeling her head clearing in the cold night air. Soon she was chilled to the bone, but doing penance for the hours Guy had spent outside her window, she didn't move or try to keep warm. Sooner than she had dared to hope she heard the roar of the Vespa and saw the familiar figure of Guy, dangerously angled, as he sped through the narrow passage into the square. She went out under the lamppost so he could see her and when he skidded to a halt in front of her, she threw her arms around him, not caring that the chauffeurs were all watching. "Thank you, thank you," she whispered. "Now take me away from here. Quick!"

Guy kissed her cheek briefly, and squeezed her. She got on the pillion behind him and held him tight as he started the Vespa. They surged out between the dark buildings and into the Avenue Foch. For a moment, that was enough—the speed, the fresh cold wind, the crisp feel of his coat between her arms, the sense of escape, as they crossed the Avenue Foch and headed down the empty boulevard toward the Arc, shimmering insubstantially under its floodlights in the thin mist.

She held Guy closely, whispering into the fleece collar of his coat, too low for him to hear, "I love you, I love you." She felt holy and clean, as though she had been delivered from the danger of mortal sin.

As they approached the Étoile, Guy slowed down and

turned his head. His face looked drawn and tense. "Where to?" he said.

She hesitated. Then she said, "Do you still have the key to your friend's apartment? The one who went to Tours?"

Guy started violently and the Vespa skidded and they only recovered their balance at the very last moment.

He pulled the Vespa over to the curb and stopped. He twisted around to face her. For a fleeting instant she had the feeling that he looked frightened. "Are you drunk?" he asked.

"Not any more. *Do* you have the key?"

"No," Guy said. He shook his head in despair. "He came back from Tours two days ago. What are we going to do?"

"We can go to a hotel," Roberta said. She was surprised to hear the words come out of her mouth. "Can't we?"

"What hotel?"

"Any hotel that will let us in," Roberta said.

Guy gripped her arm above the elbow, hard. "Are you sure you know what you are doing?"

"Of course." She smiled at him. She was enjoying doing this wicked planning for them. Somehow, it helped wipe out the memory of all the gaucheries she had committed that night. "Didn't I tell you I would make all the advances? I'm now making the advances."

Guy's lips trembled. "American," he said, "you are magnificent." Roberta thought he was going to kiss her, but he didn't seem to trust himself to go that far yet. He turned again on the saddle and started the Vespa. Now he drove with the care of a man transporting a load of precious porcelain on a rough mountain road.

They wound through the eighth arrondissement, passing hotel after hotel, but none of them seemed to attract Guy. He would hesitate as he saw one ahead of him, then shake his head and mumble something to himself and keep the Vespa at cruising speed. Roberta had never realized there were so many hotels in Paris. She was beginning to feel terribly cold, but she said nothing. This was Guy's town and she had had no experience in these matters. If he had some perfect image of a hotel for this occasion and would be satisfied with nothing less, she would ride half across the city behind him without complaint.

A YEAR TO LEARN THE LANGUAGE 95

They crossed the Pont Alexandre III and swept up and around the Invalides into the Faubourg St. Germain, through dark, discreet streets, where huge mansions reared behind high walls. Even here, there were a surprising number of hotels, large ones, small ones, luxurious ones, modest ones, hotels brightly lit and hotels that seemed to be dozing in low lamplight. Still, Guy kept on.

Finally, in a section of the city that Roberta had never visited before, near the Avenue des Gobelins, on a street that seemed on the verge of becoming a slum, Guy came to a halt. A dim light illuminated a sign that read Hôtel du Cardinal, Tout Confort. There was no indication which Cardinal was being commemorated here and the paint was chipped and flaky on the lettering of Tout Confort.

"I have found it," Guy said. "I have heard about this place from a friend. It is very welcoming, he said."

Roberta dismounted stiffly. "It looks very nice," she said hypocritically.

"If you will stay here and guard the machine," Guy said. "I will go in and make the arrangements." He seemed distracted and avoided looking Roberta in the eye. He was feeling for his wallet as he went into the hotel, like a man in a crowd at a sporting event who is worried about pickpockets.

Roberta stood with her hand possessively on the saddle of the Vespa, trying to put herself into the proper frame of mind for what lay ahead of her. She wished she had had a third martini. She wondered if there were going to be mirrors on the ceiling, and Watteau-like paintings of nymphs. She hadn't heard about much in Paris, but she had heard about *that*.

I must behave with grace, gaiety and beauty, she thought. This must be a lyrical experience.

She wished Guy would come out. Standing out there alone in the dark protecting the Vespa made her nervous. It wasn't the *idea* of making love that bothered her, she told herself, it was the practical details, like what expression to put on her face when she passed the clerk in the lobby. In the movies that Guy took her to see, the girls, even though they were only seventeen or eighteen years old, never seemed to be bothered by these problems. They were graceful as panthers, sensual as Cleopatra, and they slipped into bed as naturally as eating lunch. Of course, they were French, and that helped. Well, Guy was French. She was comforted by this thought. Still, for the first time in some months, she wished Louise were at her side for a moment or two, and she regretted the questions she hadn't asked on those nights when Louise had come home late and eager to talk.

Guy came out of the hotel. "It's all right," he said. "The man is permitting me to station the Vespa in the lobby." Guy took the Vespa by the handle bars and trundled it up the steps and through the door into the lobby of the hotel. Roberta followed him, wondering if she ought to help him with the machine, because he seemed to be panting with the effort of getting it up the steps.

The lobby was narrow and dark, with only one light over the clerk at the desk. The clerk was an old man with thin gray hair. He looked at her with a dead, all-knowing eye. *"Soixante-deux,"* he said. He gave Guy the key and went back to reading a newspaper that he had spread out on his desk.

There was no elevator and Roberta followed Guy up three flights of a narrow staircase. The carpet on the staircase was scuffed and smelled dusty. Guy had some trouble getting the key into the lock of the door of Number 62, and muttered under his breath as he struggled with it. Then the lock gave way and Guy opened the door and turned on the light. He squeezed Roberta's arm as she went past him into the room.

There were no mirrors on the ceiling and no nymphs on the walls. It was a small, plain room with a narrow brass bed, a yellow wooden armchair, a table with a scruffy piece of blotting paper on it, and a tattered screen in one corner concealing a bidet, all under the blue glare of the single bare bulb hanging on a braided wire from the ceiling. And it was bitterly cold, with the cold of many unforgiving winters concentrated between the stained walls.

"Oh," Roberta said in a small, desolate whisper.

Guy put his arms around her from behind. "Forgive me," he said. "I forgot to take any money with me, and all I had in my pocket was seven hundred francs. Ancient francs."

"That's all right," Roberta said. She turned and tried to smile at him. "I don't mind."

Guy took off his coat and threw it over the chair. "After all," he said, "it is only a *place*. There is no sense in being sentimental about *places*, is there?" He avoided looking at her and kept blowing on his knuckles, which were red with cold. "Well," he said, "I suppose you ought to undress."

"You first," Roberta said, almost automatically.

"My dear Roberta," Guy said, blowing assiduously on his knuckles, "everybody knows that in a situation like this, the girl always undresses first."

"Not this girl," Roberta said. She sat down in the armchair, crushing Guy's coat. It was going to be difficult, she realized, to behave with grace and gaiety.

Guy stood over her, breathing hard. His lips were blue with cold. "Very well," he said, "I will give in to you. This once. But you must promise not to look."

"I have no desire to look," Roberta said with dignity.

"Go to the window and keep your back turned," Guy said.

Roberta stood up and went to the window. The curtains were threadbare and smelled like the carpet on the staircase. Behind her, she heard the sounds of Guy's undressing. Oh, God, she thought, I never imagined it was going to be like this. Twenty seconds later, she heard the creak of the bed. "All right," he said, "you can look now."

He was under the covers, his face dark and gaunt on the grayish pillow. "Now you," he said.

"Turn your head to the wall," Roberta said. She waited until Guy turned his head to the wall. Then she undressed swiftly, laying her clothes neatly over the disorderly pile Guy had left on the chair. Icy, she hurried under the covers. Guy was clamped along the wall on the other side of the bed and she didn't touch him. He was trembling, making the bedclothes quiver.

With a violent movement he turned toward her. He still didn't touch her. *"Zut,"* he said, "the light is still on."

They both looked up at the light. The bulb stared down at them, like the night clerk's eye.

"You forgot to turn it off," Guy said accusingly.

"I know," she said.

"Well, turn it off."

"I'm not budging from this bed," said Roberta.

"You were the last one up," Guy said plaintively.

"I don't care," she said.

"That is absolutely unfair," said Guy.

"Unfair or not," Roberta said, "I'm staying right here." Even as she spoke, she had the impression that she had had a conversation very much like this somewhere before in her life. Then she remembered. It had been with her brother, who was two years younger than she, and it had been in a cottage in a summer resort, when she was six years old. The echo disturbed her.

"But you're on the outside," Guy said. "I'll have to climb over you."

Roberta thought this over for a moment. She knew she couldn't bear the thought of his touching her, even accidentally, with the light still on. "Stay where you are," she said. With a convulsive movement she threw back the covers, leaped out of bed and fled across the room. She switched off the light and hurled herself back into bed, pulling the covers up around her neck.

Guy was trembling more than ever. "You are *exquise*," he said. "I cannot bear it." This time he hadn't turned his face away. He reached out his hand and touched her. Involuntarily, she gasped and gave a little jump. His hand was like a fistful of ice. Disastrously, he began to weep. Roberta lay rigid and alarmed on her side of the bed, as Guy sobbed heartbrokenly.

"It is awful," he said, between sobs. "I do not blame you for pulling away. It is not the way it should be at all. I am too clumsy, too stupid. I do not know anything. It serves me right. I have been lying to you for three months. . . ."

"Lying?" Roberta asked, remaining absolutely still. "What do you mean?"

"I have been playing a role," Guy said brokenly. "I have no experience. I am not studying to be an engineer. I am still in the *lycée*. I am not twenty-one years old. I am only sixteen."

"Oh." Roberta closed her eyes slowly, blotting out the night. "Why did you do that?"

"Because you would not have looked at me otherwise," he said. "Is that not true?"

"Yes," Roberta said, "it is true." She opened her eyes, because you couldn't keep your eyes closed forever.

"If only it had not been so cold," Guy wept, "if only I had more than seven hundred francs, you would never have known."

"Well, I know now," Roberta said. No wonder he only drank pineapple juice, she thought. How can I be so inaccurate? Will I ever change?

Guy sat up. "I suppose I ought to take you home," he said. His voice was broken, dead, devoid of hope.

She wanted to go home. She thought of her single bed with longing. She wanted to retreat and stay hidden and start everything, her whole life, all over again. But there was no starting all over again with the echo of that forlorn, childish voice to haunt her. She put out her hand and touched his shoulder. "Lie down," she said gently.

After a moment, Guy slid down and lay motionless, away from her, on his side of the bed. She moved toward him and took him in her arms. He put his head high on her shoulder, his lips touching her throat. He sobbed once. She held him and after a while they were both warm under the covers. He sighed and fell asleep.

She dozed fitfully during the night and woke each time to feel the warm, slender, adolescent body curled trustingly against her. She kissed the top of Guy's head with modesty and pity and affection.

In the morning, she got out of bed without waking him and dressed quickly. She drew back the curtains. It was a sunny day. Guy was sleeping, flat on his back, under the covers, his face defenseless and happy. She went over to him and touched his forehead with her fingertips. He woke and stared up at her.

"It's morning," she whispered. "You'd better get up. It's time for you to go to school." She smiled at him and after a while he smiled gravely up at her. He sprang out of bed and began to get dressed. She watched him candidly.

They went down to the lobby. The night clerk was still on duty. He regarded them dully, thinking a night clerk's thoughts. Roberta nodded to him without shame or embarrassment, and helped Guy trundle the Vespa out of the lobby and down the steps to the street. They mounted the Vespa and sped through the morning traffic, and in ten minutes were at the entrance to the building in which Roberta lived. Guy stopped the Vespa and they both got off. Guy seemed to have trouble speaking. He started several sentences with, "Well, I . . ." and, "Someday I suppose I should . . ." In the morning light his face looked very very young. Finally, playing nervously with the brake handle, his eyes downcast, he said, "Do you hate me?"

"Of course not," Roberta said. "It was the most wonderful night of my life." At last, she thought exultantly, I'm learning to be accurate.

Guy looked up uncertainly, searching her face for signs of mockery. "Will I ever see you again?" he asked.

"Of course," she said lightly. "Tonight. As usual."

"Oh, God," he said. "If I do not get out of here I am going to cry again."

Roberta leaned over and kissed his cheek. He swung back onto the saddle of the Vespa and spurted down the street, swift and showy and careless of danger.

She watched him disappear, then entered the building, moving serenely, womanly, amused, innocent, pleased with herself. She climbed the dark stairway and put her keys into the locks of Madame Ruffat's door. But she hesitated a moment before turning the last key. She made a firm resolve. Never, NEVER would she tell Louise that Guy was only sixteen years old.

She chuckled, turned the key and went in.

Love on a Dark Street

The night is the time for calls across the ocean. Alone in the hours past midnight in a foreign city, a man's thoughts center on another continent, he remembers loved voices far away, he calculates differences in time zones *(it is eight o'clock in New York, the taxis are bumper to bumper, all the lights are lit)*, he promises himself that there will be a general saving on such things as cigarettes, liquor, and restaurants to make up for the sweet extravagance of several moments of conversation across the three thousand miles of space.

In his apartment on the narrow street behind the Boulevard Montparnasse, Nicholas Tibbell sat, holding a book in his hand, but not reading. He was too restless to sleep, and although he was thirsty and would have liked a beer, he was not resolute enough to go out once more and find a bar that was still open. There was no beer on ice in the apartment because he had neglected to buy any. The apartment, which he had rented from a German photographer for six months, was an ugly, small place, with only two badly furnished rooms, the walls of which were covered by blown-up photographs of emaciated nude women whom the German had posed in what Tibbell considered rather extreme positions. Tibbell spent as little time and thought on the apartment as possible. At the end of six months, the company for which he worked, a large organization which dealt in chemicals on both sides of the Atlantic, would decide whether he was to be kept in Paris or sent somewhere else. If his base was to be permanently in Paris, he would have to find more comfortable quarters for himself. In the meantime, he used the apartment merely for sleeping and for changing his clothes, and tried to keep down the waves of self-pity and homesickness which assailed him at moments like this, late at night, trapped among the unfleshed contortionists of the German's living room.

From the stories he had heard from other young Americans in Paris, it had never occurred to Tibbell that he would have to face so many nights of loneliness and vague, unformed yearning once he had established himself in the city. But he was shy with girls and clumsy with men and he saw now that shyness and clumsiness were exportable articles that passed from country to country without tax or quota restrictions and that a solitary man was as likely to find himself alone and unremarked in Paris as in New York. Each night, after a silent dinner with only a book for companion, Tibbell, with his neat American haircut, his uncreased, neat Dacron suit, his naïve, questing, blue, polite American eyes, would go from one crowded *terrasse* of St. Germain des Prés to another, drinking as little as he dared, waiting for the one brilliant night when he would be noticed by some glorious, laughing band of young people who, with the legendary freedom of the capital, would seize upon him, appreciate him, sweep him along with them in their expeditions among the joyous tables of the Flore, the Epi Club, the Brasserie Lipp and out to the gay and slightly sinful inns in the smiling green countryside beyond Paris.

But the one brilliant night never arrived. The summer was nearly over and he was as alone as ever, trying to read a book, near the open window, through which the warm night breeze carried an erratic distant hum from the traffic of the surrounding city and a thin fragrance of river water and dusty September foliage. The thought of sleep, even though it was after midnight, was intolerable.

Tibbell put down the book (it was *Madame Bovary*, to improve his French) and went over to the window and looked out. He found himself looking out the window a good deal of the time when he was in the apartment. There wasn't much to see. The apartment was one floor up, confronted by tightly locked shutters and flaky soot-grey stone

LOVE ON A DARK STREET

walls. The street was narrow and looked as though it was waiting to be bombed or torn down to make way for a modern prison and at the busiest of times carried very little traffic. Tonight it was silent, and deserted except for two lovers who made a single, unmoving shadow in a doorway diagonally across from him.

Tibbell peered at the lovers with envy and admiration. What a thing it was to be French, he thought, and experience no shame in the face of desire and be able to display it so honestly, on a public thoroughfare. If only he had gone to Paris during his formative years instead of to Exeter!

Tibbell turned away from the window. The lovers kissing in the arch of the doorway across the street disturbed him.

He tried to read, but he kept going over the same lines again and again—"Une exhalaison s'échappait de ce grand amour embaumé et qui, passant à travers tout, parfumait de tendresse l'atmosphère d'immaculation où elle voulait vivre."

He put the book down. He felt much sorrier for himself than for Emma Bovary. He would have to improve his French some other night.

"The hell with it," he said aloud, making a decision, and picked up the phone from its cradle on the bookcase full of German books. He dialed the overseas operator and asked for Betty's number in New York, in his careful, accurate, though unimproved French, which he had learned in two years in Exeter and four at Swarthmore. The operator told him to hold on, saying that there was a possibility that she could put the call through immediately. He began to sweat a little, pleasurably, at the thought of talking to Betty within the next two minutes. He had a premonition that he was likely to say something original and historic tonight and he turned out the light because he felt he could express himself more freely in the dark.

But then the operator came on the line again to say that the call would take some time to put through. Tibbell looked at the radium dial of his watch and told her to try anyway. He pushed the phone to one side and leaned back in his chair with his eyes half-closed, and thought of what Betty's voice would sound like from the other side of the ocean, and how she would look, curled on the sofa of her tiny apartment, twelve stories above the streets of New York, as she spoke into the telephone. He smiled as he remembered the familiar, lovely, small image. He had only known Betty eight months and if the Paris trip hadn't come up two months before, he was sure that a propitious moment would have presented itself in which to ask her to marry him. He was nearly thirty and if he was ever going to get married it would have to be soon.

Leaving Betty behind had been a sorrowful experience and it had only been by the exercise of the stoniest self-control that he had managed to get through their last evening together without risking everything then and there and asking her to follow him on the next plane. But he prided himself on being a sensible man and arriving to take up a new and perhaps temporary job in a new country with a new wife at his side was not his idea of how a sensible man should act. Still, the combination of pleasure and longing with which, hour after hour, he thought of her, was something he had never experienced before and tonight he wanted to make powerful and naked statements to her that until now he had been too timid to voice. Up to now Tibbell had contented himself with writing a letter a day, plus a call on Betty's birthday. But tonight he was irresistibly moved to indulge himself in the sound of her voice and in his own avowal of love.

He waited, impatiently, for the phone to ring, trying to make the time seem shorter by imagining what it would be like if Betty were beside him now, and what they would be saying to each other if they were hand in hand in the same room instead of divided by three thousand miles of humming wire. He had closed his eyes, his head leaning back against the chair, a little smile on his lips as he remembered old whispers of conversation and imagined new exchanges, when he heard voices, harsh and excited, coming through the open window. The voices were passionate, insistent. Tibbell stood up and went to the window and looked down.

Below him, outlined in the light of the street lamp stood three people, tensely together, arguing, their voices sometimes hushed, as though they were trying to keep their quarrel to themselves, and sometimes, in bursts of anger, carelessly loud and brutal. There was a man of about sixty, with gray hair and a bald spot, clearly visible from Tibbell's post at the window, and a young woman who was sobbing into a handkerchief, and a young man in a windjacket. The young woman had on a gay, flowered-cotton dress and her hair was blond and piled high on her head in the inevitable Brigitte Bardot style of the season, the ensemble making her look like a stuffed, cleansed little piglet. The old man looked like a respectable engineer or government official, robust and vaguely intellectual at the same time. They were grouped around a Vespa that was parked in front of the building. During the most heated exchanges the young man kept stroking the machine, as though reassuring himself that *in extremis* a means of escape was still available to him.

"I repeat, *Monsieur*," the old man was saying loudly, "you are a *salaud*." His speech had a rotund, self-important ring to it, almost oratorical, as if he were accustomed to addressing large audiences.

"I repeat once more to you, Monsieur Banary-Cointal," the young man said, equally loudly, "I am not a *salaud*." His speech was street-Parisian, rasping, rough, formed by twenty-five years of constant argument with the fellow citizens of his city, but his overall air suggested the student or laboratory assistant or pharmacist's clerk.

The young woman wept, her hands trembling on a large patent-leather purse she was carrying.

"But you are," the old man said, his face close to the other man's face. "The worst kind. Do you wish proof?" It was an oratorical question. "I will give you proof. My daughter is pregnant. Due to your attentions. And what do you do now that she is in this condition? You abandon her. Like a serpent. And to add to the injury, you propose to get married tomorrow. To another woman."

Undoubtedly, the conversation would have had a different ring to it for a Frenchman who happened to overhear it, but to Tibbell's Exeter-cum-Swarthmore ear all spoken French was translated automatically into English that was constructed like a schoolboy's version of excerpts from Racine and Cicero. To Tibbell, all Frenchmen seemed to have a slightly archaic and elevated vocabulary and they always sounded to him as though they were making a speech to a group of senators in the forum or exhorting the Athenians to kill Socrates. Far from annoying Tibbell, it gave an added, mysterious charm to his contacts with the inhabitants of the country, and on the rare occasions when he understood accurately a few words of argot it supplied a piquancy to his relations with the language, as though he had discovered a phrase of Damon Runyon's in Act Three of *Le Cid*.

"I will leave it to the opinion of the most neutral observer," M. Banary-Cointal was saying, "if that is not the action of a man who deserves to be termed a *salaud*."

The young woman, standing stiffly upright, not yet looking pregnant, wept more loudly.

In the shadow of their doorway, the lovers shifted a little; a bare arm moved, a kiss was planted on an ear rather than on lips, a muscular arm took a new hold—but whether that was due to the commotion around the Vespa or to the natural fatigue and need for variation of prolonged *amour* Tibbell could not tell.

Farther down the street a car approached, with bright lights and an Italian roar of motor, but it stopped near the corner, swinging in to park in front of a closed laundry shop, and the lights were extinguished. The street was left to the disputants.

"If I'm getting married tomorrow," the young man said, "it's her fault." He pointed accusingly at the girl.

"I forbid you to go on," said M. Banary-Cointal with dignity.

"I tried," the young man shouted. "I did everything I could. I lived with her for a year, didn't I?" He said this righteously, with pride and self-pity, as if he expected congratulations all around for his sacrifice. "At the end of the year it became clear to me—if I ever wanted a worthy home for any children I might have, I would never get it from your daughter. It is time to speak frankly, Monsieur. Your daughter conducts herself in an impossible manner. Impossible. In addition, her character is abominable."

"Be careful in your choice of words, young man," the father said.

"Abominable," the young man repeated. He waved his arms in emphasis and his long black hair fell over his forehead into his eyes, adding to the effect of blind and uncontrollable rage. "As her father, I will spare you the details, but I will permit myself to say that never has a man had to bear such treatment from a woman who in theory shared his home for twelve months. Even the phrase makes me laugh," Raoul said, without laughing. "When you say 'share a home,' you imagine that it means that a woman is occasionally physically present in the foyer—for example, when a man comes home to lunch or when he returns for an evening of peace and relaxation after a hard day's work. But if you imagine that in the case of your daughter, M. Banary-Cointal, you are sadly mistaken. In the last year, M. Banary-Cointal, I assure you I have seen more of my mother, of my maiden aunt in Toulouse, of the woman who sells newspapers opposite the Madeleine, than I have seen of your daughter. Ask for her at any hour of the day or night—winter or summer—and where was she? Absent!"

"Raoul," the girl sobbed, "how can you talk like that? I was faithful from the first day to the last."

"Faithful!" Raoul snorted contemptuously. "What difference does that make? A woman says she is faithful and believes that excuses everything from arson to matricide. What good did your fidelity do me? You were never home. At the hairdresser, at the cinema, at the Galéries Lafayette, at the Zoo, at the tennis matches, at the swimming pool, at the dressmaker, at the Deux Magots, on the Champs Élysées, at the home of a girl friend in St.-Cloud —but never home. Monsieur"—Raoul turned to the father —"I do not know what it was in her childhood that formed your daughter's character, but I speak only of the results. Your daughter is a woman who has only the most lively detestation of a home."

"A home is one thing, Monsieur," the old man said, his voice trembling with parental emotion, "and a clandestine and illicit ménage is another. It is the difference between a church and a . . . a . . ." The old man hesitated, searching for the proper crushing comparison. "The difference between a church and a racecourse." He permitted himself a wild smile at the brilliance of his rhetoric.

"I swear to you, Raoul," the girl said, "if you marry me I will not *budge* from the kitchen."

"A woman will promise anything," Raoul said, "on the night before a man is due to marry somebody else." He turned brutally to the father. "I will give you my final judgment on your daughter. I pity the man who marries her, and if I were a good citizen and a good Christian, I would send such a man an anonymous letter of warning before he took the fatal step."

The young woman cried out as though she had been struck and threw herself against her father heartbrokenly, to sob against his shoulder. Her father patted her distractedly, saying, "There, there, Moumou," while the girl brokenly repeated, "I love him, I love him, I can't live without him. If he leaves me I'm going to throw myself in the river."

"You see," the father said accusingly, over his daughter's bent, tragic head, "you serpent of ingratitude, she can't live without you."

"That's just too bad," Raoul said, his voice high with exasperation. "Because I can't live *with* her."

"I warn you," the father said, speaking loudly, to be heard above the thunder of his daughter's sobs, "I hold you personally responsible if she throws herself in the river. I, her father, am saying this. Solemnly."

"The river!" Raoul laughed in harsh disbelief. "Call me when it happens. I will personally accompany her. Anyway, she swims like a fish. I'm surprised that a man your age can be innocent enough to be taken in by female guff like that."

Somehow, this last statement enraged Moumou more than anything else Raoul had said. With a sound that was a kind of mixture of growl and air-raid siren, Moumou leapt from the shelter of her father's arms and flung herself on Raoul, hurling him out into the middle of the street whacking him ferociously with the huge leather bag, holding it by the handle, swinging it again and again like an Olympic hammer-thrower. From the noise it made as it smashed against Raoul's head and shoulders Tibbell calculated that it weighed about ten pounds and was filled with glass and metalware. Raoul raised his arms to protect himself, shouting, dancing backwards, "Moumou, Moumou, you're losing control of yourself!"

To halt the brutal, arching blows of the bag, which were coming in at all angles, he lunged forward and grappled with Moumou, but she continued her attack with her sharply pointed shoes, kicking him pitilessly in the shins and grinding her high, needle-sharp heels into the soft suede of his moccasins. To Tibbell, watching bemused from his window, the couple seemed to be performing some eccentric tribal dance, with their shadows, thrown by the nearby lamppost, whirling around them and up and down the face of the buildings opposite in an elongated African pattern.

"Moumou, Moumou," Raoul shouted hoarsely, as he clutched her and at the same time kept up his painful, jigging dance, to try to avoid the cruel pert heels that dug into his toes. "What good does this do? It solves none of our problems. Moumou, stop it!"

But Moumou, now that she had started, had no mind to stop it. All the indignities, deceptions, and false hopes of her life were welling up in her, finding ecstatic expression in the blows and kicks with which she was belaboring her defaulting partner. The grunts and muffled growls that accompanied her efforts had a note of triumph and wild, orgiastic release in them, hardly fitting, Tibbell thought, for a public performance on a public street. Foreign and American as he was, he was uneasy at the thought of intervention. In New York City, if he had been the witness of a fight between a man and a woman, he would have rushed to part the combatants. But here, in the strange land of France, where the code of behavior between the sexes was at best a titillating mystery to him, he could only wait and hope for the best. Besides, by any system of scoring, the woman was clearly winning by a large margin, delivering all the blows, gaining many points for what is approvingly called aggressiveness in the prize ring and only suffering such incidental damage as came her way when Raoul's head bumped her forehead as she tried to bite him.

The father, who might have been expected to be disturbed by the spectacle of his pregnant daughter locked in hand-to-hand combat with her faithless lover at this odd hour of the morning, never made a move to stop the action. He merely moved along the street with the struggle, circling it warily, keeping a keen eye on the principals, like a referee who is loath to interfere in a good fight so long as the clinching is not too obvious and the low blows unintentional.

The noise, however, had awakened sleepers, and here and there along the street, shutters opened a crack on dark windows and heads appeared briefly, with that French combination of impartiality, curiosity and caution which would lock the shutters fast on the scene of violence with the approach of the first gendarme.

By this time, Moumou had stamped and hammered

Raoul some fifteen yards away from the point of the original attack and they were swaying and panting in front of the lovers who had been tranquilly kissing all this time in the shadow of the doorway on the other side of the street. But now, with the noise of battle on their very doorstep, as it were, and the contestants threatening invasion at any moment, the lovers separated, and the man stepped out protectively in front of the figure of the girl he had been crushing so cosily and for so long against the stone doorway. Tibbell saw that the man was short and burly and dressed in a sports jacket and an open-necked shirt. "Here, here," the man in the sports jacket said authoritatively, seizing Raoul by the shoulders and pulling at him, "that's enough of that. Go home and go to sleep."

His appearance distracted Moumou for an instant. "Go back to your doorway fornication, Monsieur!" she said. "We don't need your advice." At that moment, Raoul slid away from her and pounded up the street. "Coward," Moumou shouted, and took off after him, swinging her bag menacingly, running with surprising speed and agility in her high-heeled, pointed shoes. She seemed actually to be gaining on Raoul when he came to the corner and ducked around it, closely followed by Moumou.

The street seemed strangely quiet now and Tibbell could hear the discreet clicking of shutters being closed, now that the principals had departed the scene.

But the father was still there, staring with melancholy, weary eyes at the corner around which he had last seen his daughter disappear, brandishing the patent-leather handbag. He turned his glance on the young man in the sports jacket, who was saying to his girl, "Well, there's a pair for you. Barbarians."

"Monsieur," the father said gravely, "who asked you to meddle in other peoples' affairs? It is the same all over this poor country. Nobody minds his own business any more. Privacy is a thing of the past. No wonder we are on the edge of anarchy. They were on the point of agreement when you destroyed everything."

"Listen, Monsieur," the man in the sports jacket said belligerently, "I am by nature a simple, honorable man. I do not stand by idly while a man and a woman beat each other in my presence. It was my duty to separate them and, if you were not old enough to be my grandfather, I would say that you should be ashamed of yourself for not having separated them sooner."

M. Banary-Cointal examined the simple, honorable man with scientific detachment, as though he were weighing the last statement judiciously, without prejudice. But instead of answering, he turned to the girl, still discreetly in shadow and arranging her ruffled hair with little pats of her hand. "Young woman," the old man said loudly, "you see what's ahead of you? The same thing will happen to you as happened to my daughter. Mark my words, you'll find yourself pregnant and that one"—the old man pointed like a prosecuting attorney at the sports coat—"that one will disappear like a hare in a cornfield."

"Simone," the man in the sports coat said, before the girl had a chance to reply, "we have better ways of spending our time than listening to this old windbag." He pushed a button on the wall next to him and the door against which he and the girl had been leaning opened with an electric buzzing. With dignity, he took the girl's arm and escorted her into the deeper shadow of the inner court. The old man shrugged, his duty done, his warning to a careless generation delivered, as the huge wooden door clicked shut behind the interrupted lovers. Now the old man seemed to be looking around for another audience for his views on life, but the street was deserted, and Tibbell pulled back a bit from the window, fearful of being harangued.

Deprived of further targets for his wisdom, M. Banary-Cointal sighed, then walked slowly toward the corner around which his daughter had vanished in pursuit of Raoul. Tibbell could see him standing there, caught in the dark stone geometry of the city crossroads, a solitary and baffled figure, peering off in the distance, searching the lonely street for survivors.

Now there was the click of shutters again below Tibbell and old women's voices, seeming to rise from some underground of the night, made themselves heard, from window to window.

"Ah," one voice said, "this city is becoming unbearable. People will do anything on the street at any hour. Did you hear what I heard, Madame Harrahs?"

"Every word," a second old voice spoke in a loud, hoarse, accusing, concierge's whisper. "He was a thief. He tried to snatch her purse. Since De Gaulle a woman isn't safe after dark any more in Paris. And the police have the nerve to demand a rise in pay."

"Not at all, Madame," the first voice said irritably. "I saw with my own eyes. She hit him. With her bag. Thirty or forty of the best. He was bleeding like a pig. He's lucky to be alive. Though he only got what's coming to him. She's pregnant."

"Ah," said Madame Harrahs, "the *salaud*."

"Though to tell the truth," said the first voice, "she didn't seem any better than she should be. Never at home, flitting around, only thinking about marriage when it was too late, after the rabbit test."

"Young girls these days," said Madame Harrahs. "They deserve what they get."

"You can say that again," said the first concierge. "If I told you some of the things that go on in this very house."

"You don't have to tell me," said Madame Harrahs. "It's the same on both sides of the street. When I think of some of the people I have to open the door to and say Monsieur Blanchard lives on the third, to the right, it's a wonder I still have the courage to go to Mass at Easter."

"The one I feel sorry for is the old man," said the first concierge. "The father."

"Don't waste your pity," said Madame Harrahs. "It's probably all his fault. He is obviously lacking in authority. And if a man hasn't authority, he has to expect the worst from his children. Besides, I wouldn't be a bit surprised if he didn't have a little thing on the side himself, a little *poupette* in the Sixteenth, like that disgusting lawyer in Geneva. I got a good look at him. I know the type."

"Ah, the dirty old man," the first voice said.

Now Tibbell heard footsteps approaching from the corner and he turned to see the dirty old man approaching. The shutters clicked tight again and the old ladies subsided after their choric irruption, leaving the street to the weary sound of the old man's shoes on the uneven concrete and the asthmatic sighs he emitted with every other step. He stopped below Tibbell's window, looking sorrowfully at the Vespa, shaking his head, then sat down uncomfortably on the curb, his feet in the gutter, his hands dangling loose and helpless between his knees. Tibbell would have liked to go down and comfort him, but was uncertain whether M. Banary-Cointal was in any condition that night to be consoled by foreigners.

Tibbell was on the verge of closing his own shutters, like the two concierges, and leaving the old man to his problems on the street below, when he saw Moumou appear at the corner, sobbing exhaustedly, walking unsteadily on her high heels, the bag with which she had so vigorously attacked Raoul now hanging like a dead weight from her hand. The father saw her too and stood up, with a rheumatic effort, to greet her. When she saw the old man, Moumou sobbed more loudly. The old man opened his arms and she plunged onto his shoulder, weeping and clutching him, while he patted her back clumsily.

"He got away," Moumou wept. "I'll never see him again."

"Perhaps it is for the best," the old man said. "He is far from dependable, that fellow."

"I love him, I love him," the girl said wetly. "I'm going to kill him."

"Now, now, Moumou . . ." The father looked around him uneasily, conscious of witnesses behind the shuttered windows.

"I'll show him," the girl said wildly. She broke away from her father and stood accusingly in front of the parked Vespa, glaring at it. "He took me out to the Marne on this the first time we went out together," she said in a throbbing voice, meant to carry the memory of ancient tenderness, betrayed promises, to unseen and guilty ears. "I'll show him." With a swift movement, before her father could do anything to stop her, she took off her right shoe. Violently, holding the shoe by the pointed toe, she smashed the sharp heel into the headlight of the scooter. There was the crash of breaking glass and a tinkling on the pavement, closely followed by a shriek of pain from Moumou.

"What is it? What is it?" The old man asked anxiously.

"I cut myself. I opened a vein." Moumou held out her hands, like Lady Macbeth. Tibbell could see blood spurting from several cuts on her hand and wrist.

"Oh, my poor child," the old man said distractedly. "Hold your hand still. Let me see. . . ."

But Moumou pulled her hand away and danced unevenly on her one shoe around the Vespa, waving her arm over the machine, spattering the wheels, the handle bars, the saddle, the black pillion, with the blood that sprayed from her wounds. "There!" she shouted. "You wanted my blood, take it! I hope it brings you good luck!"

"Moumou, don't be so impetuous," the old man implored her. "You will do yourself a permanent harm." Finally he managed to grab his daughter's arm and inspect the cuts. "Oh, oh," he said. "This is dolorous. Stand still." He took out a handkerchief and bound her wrist tight. "Now," he said, "I will take you home and you will get a good night's sleep and you will forget about that serpent."

"No," Moumou said. She backed against the wall of the building on the opposite side of the street and stood there stubbornly. "He will come back for his Vespa. Then I will kill him. And after that I will kill myself."

"Moumou . . ." the old man wailed.

"Go home, Papa."

"How can I go home and leave you like this?"

"I will wait for him if I have to stand here in this place all night," Moumou said, her words awash with tears. She gripped the wall behind her with her hands, as if to keep her father from taking her away by force. "He has to come here sometime before the church. He won't get married without his scooter. You go home. I will handle him myself."

"I can't leave you here alone in this condition," the old man said, sighing. Beaten, he sat down again on the curb to rest.

"I want to die," Moumou said.

The street was quiet again, but not for long. The door behind which the two lovers had taken refuge opened and the man in the sports jacket came out, his arm around his girl. They passed slowly beneath Tibbell's window, ostentatiously ignoring Moumou and her father. The old man looked balefully up at the linked couple. "Young lady," he said, "remember my warning ofit by the events you have witnessed tonight. If it is not too late already. Reenter into your home, I speak as a friend."

"See here, old man," the man in the sports jacket pulled away from his companion and stood threateningly in front of Moumou's father, "that's enough out of you. I do not permit anybody to speak like that in front of . . ."

"Come on, Edouard," the girl said, pulling the man in the sports jacket away. "It is too late at night to become enraged."

"I ignore you, Monsieur," Edouard said, then let the girl lead him away.

"Permit, permit. . . ." M. Banary-Cointal said loudly, getting in the last word, as the couple rounded the corner and disappeared.

Tibbell watched the old man and his daughter for another moment, wishing that the two of them would move away from their stations of affliction on his doorstep. It would be difficult to sleep, Tibbell felt, knowing that those two grieving, dissatisfied, vengeful figures were still outside his window, waiting for some horrid, violent last act of their drama.

He was just about to turn away when he heard a car door slam far down the street. He looked and saw a woman in a green dress striding swiftly toward him, away from the car that he had earlier noticed being parked near the far corner. Now the car lights switched on, very bright, and the car followed the woman as she half-walked, half-ran, in the direction of Moumou and her father. She was obviously in flight. Her dress shone a violent, electric lime color in the headlights of the pursuing car. The car, which was a bright red, new Alfa Romeo Giulietta, stopped abruptly just before it reached the old man, who was still sitting on the curb, but with his head turned suspiciously in the direction of the woman bearing swiftly down on him, as though he feared that she was bringing with her, stranger though she was, a new burden of trouble to load onto his bowed and tortured shoulders. The woman darted toward a doorway, but before she could press the button for entry, a man in a black suit leaped out of the car and seized her wrist.

Tibbell watched without surprise. By now he felt that the street below him was a preordained scene of conflict, like Agincourt or the pass of Thermopylae, and that clash would follow clash there continually, like the performances in a twenty-four-hour-a-day movie house.

"No, you don't!" the man in the black suit was saying, pulling the woman away from the door. "You don't get away that easily."

"Let me go," the woman said, trying to escape. She was

breathless and she sounded frightened and Tibbell wondered if now, finally, was the time for him to run down the stairs and enter into the night life of the street in front of his window, a tardy Spartan, a belated recruit for Henry's army.

"I'll let you go when you give me my three hundred francs," the man in the black suit said loudly. He was young and slender and Tibbell could see, by the light of the automobile headlights, that he had a small mustache and long, carefully brushed hair that fell over the back of his high, white collar. He reminded Tibbell of certain young men he had seen lounging in various bars in the neighborhood of Pigalle, and he had the kind of face which looks fitting in newspaper photographs that accompany the stories of the arrest of suspects after particularly well-planned jewel robberies and pay-roll thefts.

"I don't owe you any three hundred francs," the woman said. Now Tibbell heard that she had an accent in French, probably Spanish. She looked Spanish, too, with luxuriant black hair swooping down over her exposed shoulders, and a wide, shiny black leather belt around a very narrow waist. Her skirt was short and showed her knees every time she moved.

"Don't lie to me," the man in the dark suit said, still holding the woman's wrist and shaking her arm angrily. "It was never my intention to buy them."

"And it was never my intention to let you follow me to my home," the woman snapped back at him, trying to pull away. "Let me go, you've annoyed me enough tonight!"

"Not until I get my three hundred francs," the man said, gripping her more firmly.

"Unless you let me go," the woman said, "I'll call for the police."

The man glared at her and dropped her wrist. Then he slapped her hard across the face.

"Here, here!" said Moumou's father, who had been watching the affair with mournful interest. He stood up. Moumou, lost in the egotism of her own unhappiness, took no notice of what was happening.

The man in the dark suit and the Spanish woman stood close to each other, breathing heavily, looking curiously undecided, as though the slap had brought some new and unexpected problem into their relationship which for the moment confused them and made them uncertain about further action. Then the young man, his white teeth gleaming under his mustache, slowly raised his hand again.

"Once is enough," the woman said and ran over to Moumou's father for protection. "Monsieur," she said, "you have seen him strike me."

"The light is bad," the old man said, even in his sorrow instinctively extricating himself from possible formal involvement with the police. "And at the moment, I happened to be looking the other way. Still," he said to the young man, who was advancing menacingly on the Spanish woman, "let me remind you that striking a woman is considered in certain quarters to be a most serious offense."

"I throw myself on your protection, Monsieur," the woman said, stepping behind M. Banary-Cointal.

"Don't worry," the man with the mustache said contemptuously. "I won't hit her again. She is not worth the emotion. All I want is my three hundred francs."

"What do you think of a man," the woman said, from the shelter of the old man's bulk, "who buys a lady flowers and then demands to be reimbursed?"

"To keep the record clear," the man with the mustache said, "let me say once and for all that I never bought her any flowers. When I went to the toilet she took the violets from the basket and when I came back the woman asked me for three hundred francs and rather than make a scene I . . ."

"Please," the old man said, interested now despite himself, "this is all very confusing. If you would be good enough to start from the beginning, perhaps I can be of service."

Tibbell was grateful to the old man for this request for clarification, since without it he was sure he would be kept awake most of the night trying to figure out just what the sequence of events had been which had resulted in this midnight chase and punishment. Tibbell had never hit a woman in his life and could not imagine ever doing so, and certainly never for three hundred francs, which was, after all, worth just about sixty cents.

"Let me reconstruct," the man in the dark suit said immediately, presenting his side quickly, before the Spanish woman could roil the crystal waters of truth. "I saw her sitting at a bar, waiting to be picked up."

"I was not waiting to be picked up," the woman said hotly. "I was on my way home from the cinema and I stopped in to have a glass of beer, before going to bed."

"Enfin," the man in the dark suit said impatiently, "you allowed yourself to be picked up. If we are going to quibble about terms, we will be here all night."

"I allowed you to pay for one glass of beer," the woman said. "I am not responsible for any sordid interpretation you choose to put on it."

"You also allowed me to pay for three hundred francs' worth of violets," the man in the dark suit said.

"I allowed it as a small gesture of gallantry," the woman said haughtily. "In Spain one is used to gentlemen."

"You also allowed yourself to get into my car," the man in the dark suit said, "and you furthermore allowed yourself to inflame the emotions by kissing on the lips."

"That, now," the woman said dramatically to Moumou's father, "is a superb lie."

"If it's a lie," said the man in the dark suit, "what about this?" Violently, he seized the point of his white collar and pulled it away from his neck to show M. Banary-Cointal.

The old man peered at it nearsightedly, bending close to the man in the dark suit. "What is it?" the old man asked. "It's awfully dark here. I can't see anything."

"Lipstick," said the man in the dark suit. "Look." He took the old man's arm and pulled him over in front of the headlights. Both men leaned over low so that the old man could inspect the collar. M. Banary-Cointal stood up. "There's no doubt about it," he said. "Lipstick."

"Aha," said the man in the dark suit, casting a look of angry triumph at the Spanish woman.

"It is not mine," she said coldly. "Who knows where this gentleman has been spending his time and who knows how many times a week he changes his shirt?"

"I warn you," said the man in the dark suit, his voice thick with rage, "I regard that as insulting."

"What difference does it make whose lipstick it is?" the woman said. "You do not please me. All I want is to be allowed to go home alone."

"Ah," said Moumou, her attention finally caught, "if that were only possible—to go home alone."

Everybody, including Moumou's father, looked puzzledly for a moment at the somber figure against the wall, as though it had been a statue that had given cryptic utterance.

"My dear man," said M. Banary-Cointal reasonably, addressing the man in the dark suit, "certainly this lady has made herself very clear." He made a slight bow in the direction of the Spanish woman, who nodded politely in answer. "She doesn't demand very much. Just to go to her own home in peace. Surely, this is not too much to ask."

"She can go wherever she damn pleases," said the man in the dark suit, "as soon as she gives me my three hundred francs."

A look of censure creased the old man's face. "Monsieur," he said, with some asperity, "I am a little surprised that a man like you, the possessor of an automobile of this quality and price"—he touched the gleaming hood of the little Italian car—"could really need three hundred francs enough to make such a . . ."

"It is not a question of three hundred francs," said the man in the dark suit, his voice beginning to be edged, too, at this imputation of miserliness. "It would not even be a question if the sum were fifty thousand francs. It is a question of principle. I have been led on, I have been inflamed, as I mentioned before, I have been induced to spend my money—the amount has nothing to do with the matter, I assure you, Monsieur—all corruptly and under false pretenses. I am a generous and reasonable man but I do not like to be cynically made a fool of by a *putain!*"

"Here, now," the old man said sternly.

"What's more, look at her hand!" The man in the dark suit seized the woman's hand and held it in front of M. Banary-Cointal's eyes. "Do you see that? The wedding ring? By a *putain*, who, on top of everything else, is married!"

Tibbell, listening, fascinated, could not discover why the girl's marital condition added so powerfully to the rage of the man in the dark suit, and concluded that perhaps it was something in the man's past, some painful disappointment with some other married woman that had left him tender on the subject and which now served to pour fuel on the fire of his wrath.

"There is nothing more disgraceful than a Spanish whore with a wedding band," the man in the dark suit shouted.

"Here, that's enough of that," M. Banary-Cointal said

with authority, as the woman unexpectedly began to sob. The old man had had enough of women's tears for the night, and this new flood made him testy. "I will not allow you to talk in such terms in front of ladies, one of whom happens to be my daughter," he said to the man in the dark suit. "I suggest you leave immediately."

"I will leave when I get my three hundred francs," the man said stubbornly, crossing his arms.

"Here!" M. Banary-Cointal dug angrily in his pocket and pulled out some coins. "Here are your three hundred francs!" He threw them at the man in the dark suit. They bounced off his chest and onto the pavement. With great agility, the man in the dark suit bent and scooped up the coins and threw them back into M. Banary-Cointal's face. "If you're not careful, Monsieur," the old man said with dignity, "you are going to get a punch in the nose."

The man in the dark suit raised his fists and stood there, in the pose of a bare-knuckle English fighter of the early part of the eighteenth century. "I await your attack, Monsieur," he said formally.

Both women now wept more loudly.

"I warn you, Monsieur," M. Banary-Cointal said, taking a step backwards, "that I am sixty-three years of age, with a faulty heart, and besides, I wear glasses, as you can see. The police will be inclined to ask you some very searching questions in the event of an accident."

"The police!" said the man in the dark suit. "Good. It is the first sensible suggestion of the evening. I invite you all to get into my car and accompany me to the commissariat."

"I am not getting into that car again," said the Spanish woman.

"I am not budging from here," Moumou said, "until Raoul gets back."

There was a ringing behind Tibbell, and he suddenly became conscious that it had been going on for some time, and that it was the telephone. He stumbled across the dark room and picked up the instrument, the voices outside his window becoming a blurred buzzing on the night air. He wondered who could be calling him at this time of the night.

"Hello," he said, into the mouthpiece.

"Is this Littré 2576?" an impatient female voice crackled through the receiver.

"Yes," Tibbell said.

"On your call to New York," the operator said, "we are ready now."

"Oh, yes," Tibbell said. He had forgotten completely that he had put the call in for Betty. He tried to compose himself and put himself back into the tender and rosy mood that had swept over him an hour before, when he had decided to call her. "I'm waiting."

"Just a minute, please." There were some Atlantic, electric howls on the wire and Tibbell pulled the telephone away from his ear. He tried to hear what was being said outside, but all he could distinguish was the noise of a car starting up and surging down the street.

He stood next to the German's bookcase, the telephone held loosely along his cheek, remembering that he had wanted to tell Betty how much he loved her and missed her, and perhaps, if the conversation turned irrevocably in that direction, as indeed it might in the three allotted minutes, to tell her that he wanted to marry her. He found himself breathing heavily, and the ideas churned confusedly in his head, and when he tried to think of a proper opening phrase, all he could think of was, "There is nothing more disgraceful than a Spanish whore with a wedding band."

"Just a moment, please," said an American voice. "We are ringing."

There was some more electrical scratching and Tibbell switched the phone to his other ear and tried to make out what was being said downstairs and at the same time to push from his mind the remark about the wedding band.

"Miss Thompson is not home," the American voice said, with great crispness and authority. "She has left word she will come back in an hour. Do you wish us to put the call in then?"

"I . . . I . . ." Tibbell hesitated. He remembered the old man's admonition to the girl who had been kissing in the doorway—"Profit by the events you have witnessed tonight."

"Can you hear me, sir?" the crisp New World voice was saying. "Miss Thompson will be back within an hour. Do you wish to place the call then?"

"I . . . no," Tibbell said. "Cancel the call, please. I'll make it some other time."

"Thank you." America clicked off.

Tibbell put the phone down slowly. After a moment, he walked across to the window, and looked down. The street was empty and silent. Thermopylae had been cleared of corpses. Agincourt lay waiting for the plow. Unfinished, unfinishable, unresolved, unresolvable, the conflict, the inextricable opponents, had moved off into the darkness, and now there were only fleeting admonitory echoes, ghosts with warning fingers raised to vanishing lips.

Then Tibbell saw a figure stealing furtively down the other side of the street, keeping close to the walls. It was Raoul. He came out into the light of the lamppost to inspect the scooter. He kicked once at the broken glass on the pavement. Then he waved at the corner. A girl came running out toward him, her white dress gay and dancing and bridal on the dark street. As she sat on the pillion behind Raoul and put her arms lovingly around his waist, she laughed softly. Her laughter rose lightly and provocatively to Tibbell's window. Raoul started the Vespa, with the usual loud, underpowered, falsely important snarl. The Vespa, without headlight, sped down the street, the white dress dancing in the wind, slanting out of sight at the far corner. Tibbell sighed and silently wished the bride luck.

Downstairs, there was the creak of a shutter.

"Spaniards," the night voice said, "what can you expect from Spaniards?"

The shutter creaked again and the voice ceased.

Tibbell closed his own shutters. As he stepped back into the dark room he was thankful for the first time that he had gone to Exeter and Swarthmore for his education.

Once, in Aleppo

This is a story of the old days, the days between Prohibition and Alcoholics Anonymous, the days when it still took weeks to get anyplace, the days before jets reached everywhere in time for dinner, the days when you were rather surprised to hear that a friend had been in Arles or Siberia or Djibouti, the days when Colonialism was the White Man's Burden and not a dirty word, when we thought it was our duty to bring the Word to the Heathen and before the Heathen started pushing the Word back down our throats.

The main avenue of Aleppo was shining in the sun. The afternoon siesta was just over and in the cafes men in fezzes were sipping tiny cups of syrupy coffee. A fat Turk with a moustache, half-awake, sat and sleepily pulled at a hookah from time to time. When three or more flies congregated around his mouth, he would raise a sleepy hand and whisk them away unmaliciously with a fly whisk.

A barefooted woman in black shuffled past, on her head a cane-slatted rectangular basket with five sorrowful live chickens in it, all topped by a heap of roses and bougainvillaea.

Stanford Lovejoy, in his pressed white suit and sun helmet, strolled slowly down the shady side of the street, smiling gently at the flickering life of the desert city. He was a small, quiet man, and every time he walked through the town, among the swift, dirty children, the tiny dancer-hoofed donkeys under their burdens of alfalfa and watermelons, the tall, slender Arabs with their shining white burnooses, striped with black braid, looking like charioteers and pirates from a forgotten world, a pleasant little tingle of adventure rang through his blood. *How far*, the song sounded subconsciously in the back of his brain, *how far I have come from Vermont.*

He had just finished a year of teaching English to Arab children at the Mission School and he couldn't help feeling a decent thrill of accomplishment each time he opened a class and looked at the polite and eager faces, heard the low Eastern voices say "How do you do, Mr. Lovejoy?" with the ineradicable granite twang of his own Vermont caught forever in them. He never had any trouble in class, such as you might expect in young boys' classes back home. He was small, but he had a deep, impressive voice, and a high-domed and impressive forehead, full of authority. He looked as Samuel Johnson might have looked as a young man, but secretly hoped that one day he would look like Sir Walter Raleigh.

A camel carrying great porous jugs swung slowly past him, not changing its path for the heavily loaded old motorbus which creaked around the corner and waited for the camel to get on its way. A farmer, turned merchant for the day, and selling rabbits to the townspeople, held a buck up by the ears to display its fine points to a rug dealer, who decided to buy it. The farmer bent the rabbit's head back and slit its throat, dropping it on the sidewalk to allow the blood to flow freely. The rug dealer paid him and after the rabbit had kicked to its end, picked it up and took it inside his shop for dinner.

How different from Vermont, the chant went at the back of Lovejoy's head. When he had finished taking his MA, a relative in California had offered Lovejoy a job in his cement plant, with a good salary to begin with, and large chances of swift advancement. Lovejoy had nearly accepted, but the opportunity to come to Aleppo had presented itself, and he had written his cousin a graceful note, declining the kind offer.

"I have known two or three Arabs," his cousin had written, "and they are dirty, diseased people who have no

ONCE, IN ALEPPO

desire to learn English. They have gotten along without you in filth and ignorance for five thousand years and they can get along without you for another five thousand in exactly the same state. I may as well tell you that it was only at the representations of your Aunt Sarah, who told me that you were a poor, helpless boy with small chances of succeeding unaided in the world, that I offered you a position in the Plant, which, incidentally, is one of the fastest-growing organizations in one of the fastest-growing industries it the country.

"Any man who prefers Syria to California and Bedouins to Californians has forfeited all claims on my sympathies. I will not repeat the offer. Yours truly . . ."

The letter had shaken Lovejoy a little, but since coming to Aleppo, he had never regretted his decision. He was learning Arabic, and the mysterious and complex ways of the Middle East. Around him stretched the old fields of history, cultivated by men dead thousands of years; in timeless circles spread the desert, the Persian mountains, the miraculous valley of the Nile. To the East lay India. . . . Great events were brewing and there would be a great place for a man who knew the language, the silent and inscrutable people of the Arabic-speaking world. Lawrence had started with no more. Two more years to finish his contract here, learn all there was to be learned, then back to America. He could almost see the large, dark car draw up to his door in Vermont, the swift, secret trip through the night, the flight by chartered plane to Washington, the room with blinds drawn, the electric light yellow on important and famous faces. "Mr. Lovejoy, there is no need to remind you that this is a delicate mission. You know the problem better than we do. . . ."

Two small boys spurted out of a shop. They stopped suddenly as they nearly ran into him, smiled shyly at him, holding each other's hand. They were students of his, not as clean now as they were in class.

"Good evening, Mr. Lovejoy," they chanted in unison in their Vermont-Arab English. "Our health is very good, thank you very much." Then they giggled and dashed off among a flock of fat-tailed sheep, marked with red for Ramadan.

Lovejoy turned into a little bookshop. On sale were old copies of *Life, Look, Click,* and the *Saturday Evening*

Post, two raveled sets of Dickens, a great many books by H. G. Wells. Victor Hugo, Colette, and Michelet were available in large quantities in French, besides endless secondhand paper-covered copies of recent French novels. A large pile of Arabic magazines filled one corner of the little store and six copies of *The Spoon River Anthology* and one of *Death in the Afternoon,* were lying between two small plaster casts of Beethoven, also for sale. *Das Kapital* and a dog-eared library of books on physiology and surgery, in German, were intermingled with biographies of Napoleon, Shelley, and John D. Rockefeller. Lenin and Tolstoy, in Russian, and a copy of the *Best British Short Stories of 1927,* were also in evidence.

Alabaster reproductions of statuettes from the Pyramids and small blue and red clay vases were also for sale, as was a piece of the True Cross, in a velvet-lined box.

On the wall hung seven rugs which could be bought for a reasonable price.

Irina was there, too.

She was in a corner, her pale blond head bent over an account book. Each time he looked at her, Irina's frailty, her demure and troubled beauty, struck at Lovejoy's heart all over again. He walked softly up behind her, engrossed in her accounts, took her hand and pressed it to his lips.

Irina jumped back hurriedly. "Stanford," she said, her voice small and musical and Russian among the dusty literature of six languages. "It is not to be done!"

"There's nobody here," Lovejoy said, smiling softly at her.

"Somebody might make an entrance." Irina looked fearfully at the door.

"What if they did?"

"I knew it would happen," she wailed softly, turning away, hiding her face. "You do not respect me any more. I don't blame you. A man is not to be blamed."

"I respect you," Lovejoy said fervently, "from the bottom of my heart."

"Words," Irma said. "Words. I knew it would happen. I blame only myself. But we must part."

"Irina," Lovejoy said seriously, although not too worried. She suffered from these attacks of delicacy and regret several times a week and went to church to confess regularly. Her doubts and maidenly accesses of sensitivity

ONCE, IN ALEPPO

made her all the more desirable in Lovejoy's eyes, as he was not the man to approve of wanton conduct. He had known Irina for more than eight months before he had as much as held her hand, and she had wept for three solid hours after he had made love to her the first time. "Irina," he said, "I respect you as though you were my mother."

Irina turned and gave him a tremulous, clouded smile. "It is so difficult," she said, "to be a woman."

Lovejoy smiled back at her and she permitted him to touch her hand lightly. He took out his wallet and gave her the money he had brought with him.

"It tears my heart to shreds," Irina said, tucking the money into her small, exquisite bosom, "to take your money, Stanford. But my poor father . . ."

"Delighted," Lovejoy mumbled. Irina's father was a White Russian who had remained in Russia when Irina and her mother had fled the Revolution. He was too upright and determined a man to work for the Reds and it was necessary for Irina to send him money every month to keep him from proudly starving. "Delighted," Lovejoy repeated, although he was scraping the bottom of his savings account by now. "Will you call on me at nine o'clock, darling?"

"It tears my heart to shreds," Irina whispered, "if anyone sees, suspects . . ."

"No one will see."

"Nine-thirty, dear Stanford," Irina said, giving him a sad, Slavic, surrendering smile, delicate, but with the promise of unbearable voluptuousness. "It is darker then."

Lovejoy looked hurriedly around him and ducked his head and brushed her cheek with his lips.

"God forgive me," Irina said mournfully, "you are a wild boy. . . ."

"Nine-thirty." Lovejoy waved and went out of the den of literature to the brilliant street beyond. He thought of nine-thirty that night and smiled and whistled merrily to himself as he walked more quickly among the beggers and mango sellers, the drovers and date merchants. At the end of the street, where it bloomed into a little square lined with cafes, Lovejoy noticed a crowd gathered in a wide semicircle opposite the most impressive cafe. Curiously, he quickened his step. Perhaps an accident, an American, or one of his students . . .

He stopped when he reached the crowd and smiled. It was a street entertainment. But it was like no street entertainment he had ever seen. Two immense, burly men with bare knees, dressed in shorts and football jerseys, were doing intricate tricks on shining bicycles. A third man, rather small, but also in a football jersey, with a small, mangy monkey perched on his shoulder, stood to one side holding a third glittering bicycle. On the backs of all the jerseys, which were deep green, was written, in gold letters, "Café Anatole France, 9 Place Pigalle." On the front of the jerseys of one of the giants, was a large number 95, such as football players wear. On the other large man's jersey was the number 96. The man with the monkey wore a simple 0 on his chest. And the heads of all three men were shaven absolutely clean, their heads shining like light globes in the brilliant sun.

The two performers circled tightly around in front of the cafe, their front wheels revolving double-jointedly in their sockets, the spectators sighing politely and admiringly. The sweat poured down the cyclists' faces and stood out like sickle-pears on their bald white heads as they pumped away widely and good-humoredly.

Number 95 leaped off his bicycle, whipping it debonairly at the third little man with the monkey. It crashed with a light scraping sound against the little man's shin and he winced in pain, but held on and smiled mechanically at the audience. The monkey gripped his ear for better purchase.

Number 96 kept circling easily over the flagstones, his bare knees and the chromium of the bicycle flashing dizzily in the sun.

"*Allez!*" called Number 95, in a strong, booming voice. He stood with arms outstretched, wide, rippling and powerful in his green jersey against the background of slender Arabs.

Number Zero adjusted the monkey on his shoulder and tossed 95 a resin bag. Elaborately 95 dusted his hands, while 96 circled easily and continuously, and the audience watched with kindled interest.

Lovejoy took it all in with puzzlement and delight. The East, he felt, full of rich surprise.

Finally 95 finished powdering his hands, carelessly tossed the resin bag in a graceful arc over his shoulder, calling, once more, in the booming deep voice, "*Allez!*"

Number Zero had to lunge quickly to catch the bag and a pedal of one of the bicycles he was holding scraped loudly against his ankle and the monkey grabbed his nose frightenedly to keep from being unseated. A short, reproachful look of pain creased Number Zero's dark face, but he caught the resin bag, stood up, tore the monkey's paw away from his nose, and watched the show impassively.

"Ready, Saint Clair?" shouted Number 95, as though his partner was hard of hearing and a quarter of a mile off.

"Ready, Roland!" hoarsely bellowed Number 96, putting on a burst of speed.

"*Allez!*" called 95, like a steamboat whistle on a bad night.

"*Allez,*" replied 96, racing wildly past the shrinking Arabs, dazed by the speed and sound of the Occident.

Number 95 tensed himself and suddenly was hurtling through the air, outlined against the white stone of the mosque across the square like an icebox, painted green, in flight. He landed with a surprisingly light thud on 96's shoulders, his arms spread, swan-like and triumphant, a wide, appealing grin on his sweating, powerful face.

"For Christ's sake, Roland," said 96 loudly, pedalling fiercely to keep the curvetting bicycle from tilting over. "My ear!"

Number 95 said nothing. He merely stood there, proud, erect, foursquare, a whirling great block of green and pink, flashing against the white of stone and burnoose, his teeth gleaming whiter than either in the strong rosy jaws.

The audience broke into applause and three little seminaked children danced dangerously close to the rushing bicycle before they were pulled back by their elders.

"*Allez!*" called 96 in the fog-piercing, prairie-covering voice.

"*Allez!*" replied 95, and almost quicker than the eye could follow, he had made a desperate and amazing reversal and was standing on his head on 96's head, his huge, meaty legs arched and rigid, pointing beautifully toward the brazen blue desert sky.

At the same time 96 took his hands off the handlebars and they rolled swiftly and perilously around the square, a quivering bulky monument to Man's daring and purpose.

"Bravo!" called Number Zero coolly. "Bravo!"

The crowd rustled with approval and Lovejoy applauded loudly, smiling at the whirling acrobats. Number 95, still rigid and head down, with his feet describing a dashing arc against the Syrian sky, looked at Lovejoy, grinned, winked, and on the next trip around the square, called to him. "Hi, bud. See you right after the show at the Franco-Syrian Bar."

Lovejoy smiled shyly, pleased and embarrassed to be noticed by one of the artists. A moment later, with an amazing leap, 95 hurtled to the ground, arriving there upright, resilient, smiling; 96 vaulted off his bicycle and they both stood there, bowing. Then, with wide, friendly grins, they went through the crowd passing out postcard-size photographs of themselves.

Number 96 gave one to Lovejoy, patting him heavily on the shoulder as he did so. Lovejoy looked at the photograph. It was one which had caught the two daredevils at the very apex of their performance, 96 standing on his head on 95's head, with a background of large cumulus clouds. "Roland and Saint Clair Calonius," the legend read. "Around the World on Two Wheels. Ambassadors of Good Will. Daring!!! Extraordinary!!!"

While he was looking at the photograph, the Calonius brothers mounted their bicycles, took the third bicycle between them, with the monkey riding on the empty saddle, and sped dashingly down the street.

"Four piastres, pleassse," Lovejoy heard a voice say. He looked around. Number Zero was standing there, a worried look on his face, hand outstretched. "Four piastres, Pleassse," Number Zero repeated.

"For what?" Lovejoy asked.

"For the photograph of the daring Calonius Brothers, pleassse." Number Zero had a liquid Balkan accent and a harrowed Balkan face, full of the sorrows of a land that had known only wars, famines, and disloyal kings for fifteen hundred years.

"I don't want a photograph of the Calonius Brothers," Lovejoy said, trying to hand the postcard back.

"Impossible, pleassse." A further shade of sorrow flitted across Number Zero's face, like the flicker of a bat's wing, and he put his hands behind his back so that by no accident could Lovejoy place the photograph in his hand. "Once accepted—finished. Four piastres, pleassse. . . ." His face was stubborn, despairing, dark, under the shining bald scalp.

Lovejoy took out four piastres and paid him and put the photograph neatly in his wallet, as Number Zero went on to the next customer. There was a slight argument, Lovejoy noticed, but Number Zero got his four piastres there, too. But across the square, at the café tables, a sulky and violent look was coming over certain powerfully built possessors of photographs of the Calonius brothers and Lovejoy moved on down the street, not wishing to become embroiled in what he recognized as an inevitable clash between East and West, with the West heavily outgunned.

"Four piastres, pleassse," he heard the hissing little persistent voice as he walked toward the Franco-Syrian Café.

The three bicycles were leaning against a table and the two Calonius brothers were seated, still sweating, drinking beer.

"Saint Clair," Roland was booming, "you step on my ear once more, I break your ankle."

"Hazards of the trade," Saint Clair shouted angrily.

"Don't give me hazards of the trade!" Roland leaned across and stared bitterly into his brother's eyes. "Watch where you put your goddamn feet!" The monkey pulled at his leg and Roland tilted his glass over and drenched it with beer. The monkey scrambled miserably back to the bicycle saddle, and both brothers roared good-humoredly and ordered more beer.

"Pardon me, gentlemen . . ." Lovejoy began.

"If you're an American," 96 said, "sit down."

"I'm an American."

"Sit down!" Number 96 waved for more beer. "That's what I thought when I saw you. Though it's a little hard to tell, upside down." He laughed heartily and nudged Lovejoy as though he had told a dirty joke.

"What do you think of our act?" demanded 95.

"Extremely . . ."

"Never was a wheel act like it," 95 said. "We absolutely defy the laws of . . . Where's that beer?" he bawled in French at the small, dark waiter, who ran off hurriedly.

"Nice little town you got here," 96 said. "What's the name of it again?"

"Aleppo," Lovejoy said.

"Aleppo," 95 said. "Is that much out of our way?"

"Where're you going?" Lovejoy asked.

"China," both Calonius brothers answered. "Where's that beer?" Their voices clanged along the tables and through the cafe and all the waiters moved faster than they had moved in fifteen years.

"Well . . ." Lovejoy began.

"My name's Saint Clair," 96 said. "Saint Clair Calonius. This is Roland."

The handshakes were numbing. "My name is Stanford Lovejoy."

"What the hell're you doing here?" Saint Clair asked.

"I'm at the Mission."

"A lot of bint in this town?" Roland looked hungrily around.

"Uh?"

"Bint. *Bint*."

"Oh," Lovejoy said. "There are some young ladies. But the mothers're rather strict. French style."

"We never should've left Cairo," Roland said.

"That Greek dame's husband was coming back, anyway," Saint Clair said. "I like this town. What'd you say the name was?"

"Lovejoy."

"The town, Stanford."

"Oh, excuse me." Lovejoy felt himself getting a little rattled in the high fire of roaring conversation. "Aleppo."

"Anything ever happen here?"

"Well, during the Crusades, there was . . ."

"I mean at night."

"Well," said Lovejoy, "I lead a rather quiet . . ."

"Put the beer here," Roland said to the waiter, in approximate French, "and get three more."

They raised their glasses. "To good will," Saint Clair said, as though it was a ritual, and both brothers laughed loudly and drank half their glasses off.

"Syrian beer," Saint Clair said. "Drinkable. But everyone connected with Egyptian beer should be executed."

"Where is that sonofabitch Ladszlo?" Roland peered down the street. "I told you the first time I looked at him I didn't trust him."

"He's slow," Saint Clair said. "He's honest, but he's slow."

Lovejoy thought of the dark frail man trying to get four

ONCE, IN ALEPPO   133

piastres by force from the descendants of unconquered tribesmen at the café tables and nearly said something, but thought better of it and drank some more beer.

"Listen, Stanford," Roland said, "you don't know how good it is to see an honest American face again."

"Thanks," Lovejoy said, "glad to be of . . ."

"The hotels in this part of the world," Saint Clair said, bewilderingly, " 're full of bugs. You wouldn't believe it."

"You probably have a villa, haven't you, Stanford?" Roland said. "Land is cheap in these parts. The rate of exchange is wonderful, too.'"

"Yes," Lovejoy said, not knowing quite what he was saying yes to.

"It'll be wonderful staying in an American house again," Saint Clair said. "Even for one night."

"You're perfectly . . ." Lovejoy said.

"Ah, there you are, you sonofabitch," Roland said.

Lovejoy looked up. Ladszlo was standing there, bleeding. One eye was already swelling, the green jersey was torn; on the spindly calf of the right leg there were two ragged blunt wounds. The dark face was a little darker, a little more sorrowful. There was a sour little zoolike smell, Lovejoy noticed, hanging over the small, torn figure. Without a word Ladszlo extended his hand. Roland and Saint Clair leaped up and seized the money in it, counted it hurriedly.

"Forty-four piastres!" Roland roared.

Saint Clair reached over and cuffed Ladszlo lightly across the face. Ladszlo fell back into a chair, stunned.

"Goodness," Lovejoy said.

"We could get five hundred dollars a week for the Calonius brothers in Radio City," Saint Clair yelled.

"Thiss iss not Radio City, gentlemen," Ladszlo mumbled humbly. "Thiss iss Aleppo, a small Oriental city, full of savage, poverty-stricken Arabs."

"We gave out fifty pictures of the Calonius brothers," Roland leaned over and grabbed Ladszlo's chin and held his head up stiffly. "That means two hundred piastres."

"Pardon me, Gentlemen," Ladszlo said. "It doesss not mean two hundred piastres."

"How many times," Saint Clair roared, "have I told you not to take back any pictures?"

"I do not take back any pictures, gentlemen."

"Insist!" Roland shouted. "How many times do I have to tell you? Insist!"

A small sour smile played for a fraction of a second over the corner of the bruised lips. "Gentlemen," the humble dark voice murmured. "I inssisst. Two dogs bit me and a large young Arab hit me wiss a large copper vessel. Gentlemen, let uss face it, it iss impractical sysstem, inssissting."

"Are you trying to tell us our business?" Saint Clair lifted his hand threateningly.

"Gentlemen," said Ladszlo, wiping a little blood off his chin, "I am merely saying I will be dead by Bagdad if the sysstem iss not improved somewhat."

Saint Clair started to hit him again, but the waiter arrived with fresh beers. Saint Clair put one into Lovejoy's hand, and the brothers raised their glasses. They smiled good-humoredly at each other. "To good will," they said. They drained their glasses and laughed heartily.

"Stan," Roland said, "can you ride a bicycle?"

"Yes, but . . ."

"Get on Ladszlo's wheel and lead the way." He left some money for the beer. "Ladszlo, you carry Mrs. Buchanan and follow us."

"Yes, gentlemen," Ladszlo said, picking up the monkey.

Lovejoy looked surreptitiously at Ladszlo as he mounted the bicycle. Ladszlo stood there, head bowed in the attitude of universal suffering, his eyes fixed on Lovejoy, without reproach. Lovejoy turned guiltily and started down the street. The Calonius brothers rode by his side, scattering pedestrians, rug merchants, children, donkeys, and Coptic priests all along the street. Ladszlo trotted behind, the monkey clinging grimly to his head.

"This is damned hospitable of you, Stan," Saint Clair roared.

"Think nothing of . . ."

"That's the great thing about traveling," Roland roared. "Americans stick together."

"Well," Lovejoy said, "we're all far from home and the least . . ."

"Can you get steak for dinner?" Roland asked.

"I think so," Stanford slowed down as much as he dared, to give Ladszlo, whose tongue was hanging out, a chance to catch up.

"One thing I miss," Saint Clair said, "is good American steak."

"We should've stayed in Cairo," Roland said.

"Will you for the love of God stop saying we should've stayed in Cairo?" Saint Clair bellowed.

"This is where I live," Lovejoy said, hurriedly, as they wheeled into the Mission grounds.

"Like a king!" Saint Clair said enthusiastically, looking around him at the draggled little Mission buildings. "Roland, maybe we ought to stay a couple of days in Aleppo."

"Maybe," Roland said. He flung himself gracefully off his bicycle as Lovejoy stopped in front of his house. "Maybe."

Ladszlo came trotting up, his face slightly green from the exercise in the blazing sun.

"Ladszlo," Roland said. "Bring the wheels in."

"Yess, gentlemen," Ladszlo panted, shifting the monkey away from the bare sweating skin of his neck.

"But I live upstairs," Lovejoy pointed up the outside flight of narrow steps that it was necessary to climb to get to his apartment.

"That's all right," Saint Clair said. "Ladszlo'll get 'em up. Lead the way, Stan, old boy."

Lovejoy looked sidelong at Ladszlo, then led the way up the steps.

"This is really like home," Roland said happily, sinking into the one easy chair and looking at the photograph of Herbert Hoover on the wall. Lovejoy secretly was an admirer of Rossevelt, but the President of the school had a frigid Republican air about him, and the photograph of the statesman in the high starched collar had been hanging on the wall when Lovejoy arrived and he had wisely not moved it.

"The one thing that would make life complete," Saint Clair murmured from the floor, lying comfortably, "is a drink."

"Stanford, you old dog," Roland waved his hand jovially, "I'll bet you've got some stashed away."

"Well," said Lovejoy worriedly, "this is a Mission School, and they rather frown on . . ."

"You old dog," Saint Clair boomed, as Ladzlo, sweating more than ever, brought the first bicycle through the door, "bring it out."

"We'll have to drink it in coffee cups, in case the president happens to . . ."

"I'll drink whiskey out of coconut gourds and chamber-pots if I have to." Roland got up and clapped Lovejoy good-naturedly on the back. "Bring it out, you old dog. Ladszlo, you are the worst-smelling Hungarian I've ever met." Roland sniffed heavily, grimacing.

"It's Mrs. Buchanan," Ladszlo said humbly. "She pisses all over me." He went out to get the second bicycle.

Lovejoy went over to the huge Italian cabinet in which he kept all his meager belongings. Saint Clair stood behind him and watched with interest as Lovejoy threw the doors open, and dug down under the heavy winter woolen underwear.

"Roland," Saint Clair said. "Come over here." Roland came over and also stood behind Lovejoy.

"Look at that underwear," Saint Clair said. "We could use that in China in the winter."

"Just what the doctor ordered." Roland leaned over and took the top piece and measured it consideringly against his immense shoulders.

"Wool stretches," Saint Clair said. "Remember that."

"That's true," Roland put the underwear back thoughtfully.

"Johnny Walker!" Saint Clair said merrily.

"Three bottles! You old dog!"

"In case of sickness," Lovejoy said. "Or special occasions. I am not much of a drinking . . ."

"I'll open it," Roland took the bottle and ripped away the paper. Lovejoy carefully placed the winter underwear over the other two bottles and closed the cabinet. By this time Roland had poured three tremendous drinks into coffee cups.

"To good will," chanted the Calonius brothers, holding the cups high. Lovejoy looked at them, strange, exciting visitors from another world. Only in the East would your life hold such surprises. "To good will," he said strongly, and drank a long draught of Johnny Walker.

"Ladszlo," called Saint Clair to the puffing Hungarian, "be careful for the paint on that bicycle! That's a very expensive bicycle."

"Yes, gentlemen," Ladszlo said, finally putting the third

bicycle away and leaning palely against a wall to recover his strength!

"Perhaps," Lovejoy whispered, "Ladszlo would like a . . ."

"Ladszlo never drinks," Saint Clair said, pouring himself another large cupful of Johnny Walker. "He's a Greek Catholic."

"If you'll excuse me," Lovejoy said, "I'll go into the kitchen and tell the servant to prepare dinner for tonight."

"Go right ahead, Stan," Roland waved a large, gracious hand. "We're fine here. You've really made us feel as though this was our home."

"Thank you very much," Lovejoy said, feeling a slight warm flush of gratitude. He ordinarily lived a quiet, secluded life, and he had few friends.

"There should be more like you," Roland said.

"Thank you again."

"For dessert," Saint Clair said, "I like raisins and walnuts. They contain valuable minerals."

"I'll see what I can do," Lovejoy said, squeezing apologetically past Ladszlo, still leaning, drained and tattered and dark, against the wall in the passageway, with the monkey once more on his shoulder, and the sour little zoo-smell more noticeable than ever.

When he got back after a bitter half-hour in the kitchen, in which Ahmed, the cook, a eunuch who had been castrated by the Turks in 1903, had burst into tears twice in a frenzy of misunderstanding, the living room was roaring with argument.

"I did not rape any waitress in Tel Aviv!" Saint Clair was screaming. A second bottle of Johnny Walker, Lovejoy noticed, was standing on the table. "After the first half-hour you never saw so much cooperation in your whole life."

"Tell that to the police," Roland stood up and waved the empty Scotch bottle for emphasis. "You're going to get us all hung with that damned strong-man act of yours. . . ."

"Gentlemen," said Lovejoy, his head rather vague with the beer and Scotch and sudden company, "it is impossible to get walnuts."

"That's all right," Saint Clair smiled at him cheerfully. "Tomorrow's soon enough. Have a drink."

"Thank you," Lovejoy said, feeling, for the first time in

his life, a genuine craving for alcohol, "I think I will."

While waiting for dinner, they worked on the second bottle and the Calonius brothers talked about themselves.

"Bakersfield, California," Saint Clair said, "is all right for cowboys."

"That's where we were born," Roland said.

"It lacks romance. Same thing, day in, day out. Beef and grapefruit. Have a drink." Saint Clair poured all around. "A man's got to see the world. . . ."

"That's exactly what I . . ." said Lovejoy.

"George Buchanan would've killed you if you'd stayed in Bakersfield another twenty-four hours," Roland said. "The only trouble was it was Sunday and he had to wait till the stores opened on Monday to buy a shotgun." Roland laughed merrily, remembering. "We named the monkey after Madame Buchanan. Amazing resemblance."

"George Buchanan," Saint Clair shouted, "was absolutely mistaken about that oil lease. Any court of law . . ."

"Anyway," Roland said comfortably, "the money got us to Paris."

"What a city, Paris!" Saint Clair said dreamily.

"Paris . . ." murmured Lovejoy. "How did you happen to leave?"

"You can only stay so long in any one place," Saint Clair said. "Then it's the call of the open. . . ."

" 'Messieurs,' the Captain of the Sûreté said," Roland chuckled in retrospect, " 'you have exactly thirty-six hours.' He spoke excellent English."

"The trouble with Americans," Saint Clair said, "is that the rest of the world mistrusts them. The wrong type of people represent America throughout the world. Diplomats, school teachers on vacation, retired merchants. Now, if ever," Roland said sonorously, "America has to be represented by its best types. Young, virile, friendly, *plain* people. Good will. Understand?"

"Yes," said Lovejoy, vaguely and happily, sipping on his third triple Scotch.

"And on a bicycle," Saint Clair said, "you really get to see a country. The plain people. You entertain them. You amuse them. You impress them with the fact that Americans are not decadent."

"Americans," Roland said proudly, "are a race who can stand on their heads on a moving bicycle."

"Berlin, Munich, Vienna," Saint Clair said. "We were sensational. Don't believe what you hear about the Germans. They have absolutely no desire to fight anyone. You can have my guarantee."

"That's very reassuring," Lovejoy said.

"That's the thing about traveling by bicycle," Roland said. "You feel the pulse."

"Yes," Lovejoy said.

"Rome, Florence, Naples . . ." Saint Clair went on. "Spaghetti, wine, fat Italian girls. You have no idea the amount of good will . . ."

"Unique," said Roland. "This is an absolutely unique tour. Do you think anyone ever bicycled around China before?" he asked anxiously.

"I hardly . . ."

"Hungary was at our feet," Saint Clair said. "We picked up Ladszlo in Budapest."

Lovejoy glanced dreamily at Ladszlo, who was sitting in a corner on the floor, combing Mrs. Buchanan's back for fleas.

"He seems like a very nice . . ." Lovejoy said.

"For a Hungarian," Roland said, "he's not bad."

"You've got to watch Hungarians," said Saint Clair. "That's another thing about traveling the way we do. You become a student of national character."

"I can readily understand . . ."

"Istanbul, Alexandria, Cairo," chanted Roland.

"They did everything but throw roses at us in Cairo. Although their taste in entertainment is low."

"Belly dancers," Roland complained darkly. "If it isn't a belly dancer throw it out. A man on a bicycle might just as well lay down and die."

"Jerusalem is an improvement," Saint Clair said. "Jews like bicycles."

"How can you bear just to sit in one little place all your life?" Roland asked suddenly.

"It never occurred to me before," said Lovejoy reflectively. "Though I can see now that perhaps I . . ."

"Baghdad, Calcutta," chanted Roland. "And we intend to make a thorough job of Japan. The long-established bonds of friendship between America and . . . Cherry trees in Washington. It will be sensational. Have a drink."

He poured the Johnny Walker generously. At the wet,

rippling sound, Ladszlo looked up from his corner a moment and his tongue licked drily at the corner of his mouth. Then he went back to Mrs. Buchanan.

"Where do we sleep?" Saint Clair stood up and yawned, stretching widely.

Lovejoy stood up too, and led the way into the other room. "I'm sorry," he said, "there are only two beds. Ladszlo . . ."

"Perfectly all right, old man," Roland said. "He'll sleep on the floor in your room. Hungarians love floors."

"This'll do." Saint Clair stretched enormously on one of the beds.

"Dinner, thank you." The eunuch slipped into the room and out. Saint Clair leaped up lightly. "By God," he said, "dinner."

Lovejoy led the way into the dining room. Somehow, the third bottle of Johnny Walker was on the table. As they sat down, Ladszlo slid in and sat down at the foot of the table.

"Good American cooking," Roland said happily, pouring some whiskey. "Can't be beat."

The eunuch brought the steaks, which had cost Lovejoy three days' salary.

"Tomorrow, old boy," Roland said, "let's have some red wine with the meat."

"France," Saint Clair explained. "You develop the taste."

"Yes," Lovejoy said.

Ladszlo, sitting in front of the steak with his knife and fork poised, for the first time had a light of life and excitement in his eyes. His mouth worked a little, expectantly, as he cut into the rare red meat.

"Ladszlo," Saint Clair sniffed strongly, wrinkling his nose in distaste.

"Yess, gentlemen?" The fork was poised delicately over the first slice.

"My God, Ladszlo, you stink!"

Ladszlo put his fork down quietly. "Yess, gentlemen," he said. "Mrs. Buchanan pisses all . . ."

"Go take a bath," Saint Clair said.

"Yess, gentlemen. Ass soon ass I have taken a little nourish . . ."

"Now!"

ONCE, IN ALEPPO 141

Ladszlo swallowed drily, sighed a small Balkan sigh, stood up. "Yess, gentlemen." He left the room.

"Hungarians," Roland said. "They're living in the seventeenth century." He took an immense bite of steak.

By now the unaccustomed liquor had taken full effect and Lovejoy remembered nothing more of the meal except that the Calonius brothers talked rather disjointedly of various cities throughout the world they had visited, in all of which certain misunderstandings had arisen, although of no very grave dimensions. Ladszlo, Lovejoy also noticed, did not return.

Just as they were finishing their coffee, there was a light knock on the door.

"Permit me," Saint Clair said, as Lovejoy struggled slowly to his feet. Saint Clair sprang across the room and threw the door open.

"Oh!" Irina stood there, her head wrapped in a black silk shawl.

Lovejoy shook his head a trifle dazedly and stood up. In the excitement he had forgotten all about her.

"Excellent!" Saint Clair was saying loudly, looking at Irina. "Excellent!"

"Stanford . . ." Irina lifted a shy, slightly accusing small hand toward Lovejoy.

"Forgive me," Lovejoy said, walking carefully toward her. "Unexpected . . ."

"Excellent," Saint Clair said. "Excellent."

"I'm afraid I'd better leave." Irina turned, doelike, to go.

"I'll walk you to the gate," Lovejoy said hurriedly, taking her arm.

"A vision," Roland boomed from the table. He stood up and bowed in Irina's direction. "A beautiful Russian vision."

"Perhaps," Lovejoy said, "I'd better take you to your . . ."

"How did you know I was Russian?" Irina turned back and her voice was sidelong and musical, although still shy and ladylike, as she spoke to Roland.

"Only in the cold snows," Roland boomed, advancing. "Only in the immense pine forests . . ."

"Wouldn't you like to come in and have a drink?" Saint Clair asked.

"A certain pure, cold, blond beauty . . ." Roland smiled widely down at the small, demure figure in the black scarf.

"We're drinking Scotch tonight," Saint Clair said.

"Irina doesn't drink," Lovejoy said, worriedly, fearing that Irina would be angry with him because of his blunt American friends.

"Perhaps," said Irina, taking a small, hesitant, White Russian step into the room, "perhaps just a little at the bottom of the glass."

Lovejoy closed the door behind her.

At the third drink, Saint Clair was making pertinent comments on the Russians. "No other race," he said oratorically, "would have the vision, the courage. . . . The Revolution. My God, the greatest step forward since . . ."

"They liquidated fourteen members of my family," Irina said, "and burnt down three country houses." She began to cry.

"No one will deny, of course," said Saint Clair, tenderly giving her a handkerchief, "that the old regime was better. The Church. Ikons. Candles burning. The Czarina. The ballet. The hope of the world . . ." He waved his arms magniloquently and Irina sobbed in gratitude.

"It's getting late," Lovejoy said vaguely, his ears roaring with Johnny Walker and conversation. "Perhaps I'd better see you home. . . ."

"Just to the gate, Stanford, you wild boy." Irina stood up, swept the scarf around her, gave her hands to the Calonius brothers, who kissed them, each muttering something that Lovejoy couldn't hear. Irina hesitated a moment, pulled her hands away, slipped out, graceful, doelike.

"Don't come home late, wild boy," Roland said.

Lovejoy followed Irina into the darkness. He walked beside her in the still, clear desert night.

"Irina, darling," he said troubledly to the silent shade at his side. "It was unavoidable. Certain Americans have a tendency to be boisterous. They mean no harm. They'll be gone tomorrow. Do you forgive me, darling?"

There was a silence. Irina reached the gate and turned toward him, her face undecipherable in the starlit night. "I forgive you, Stanford," she said softly, and allowed him to kiss her good night, although they were only a hundred yards from the president's home, and there was a dreadful chance of being observed.

Lovejoy watched her disappear light-footedly into the darkness, and turned and went back to his house.

From the bedroom came loud snores. The Calonius brothers were sleeping off the strains and stresses of a normal day.

Lovejoy looked around him at the empty bottles and the bicycles and Mrs. Buchanan sitting scratchily in the corner. He sighed, undressed, and put out the light. It had been an exciting day. The Calonius brothers had brought a deep breath of the wide world into his life, full of pageantry, adventure, and hearty laughter. In his youth, as a boy on the stone hills of Vermont, he had dreamed of becoming just such a man, footloose, easy, at home at the four corners of the world, a man whom you'd remember even if you saw him only once. As he looked at it now, teaching dark children English every day in the same room, seemed intolerably quiet and monotonous. . . . The Johnny Walker sang through his skull. Somewhere in the room, a cushion gave out a little of the fragrance of Irina's perfume. There was the strange small jungle sound of the monkey scratching herself sleepily.

In the next room Roland and Saint Clair Calonius snored.

Lovejoy smiled a little to himself in the darkness and fell asleep.

He did not sleep well. Through the wall of slumber, sometime in the late, dark hours, half-awake, half-dreaming, he seemed to hear a woman's soft giggle nearby, sensual and abandoned, and he twisted uneasily on his hard bed, almost opened his eyes, was claimed once more by oblivion.

The moon came up and shone through the open window into his eyes, and he woke sharply, certain that someone was in his room, something was happening. . . .

The moon shone on a narrow figure crouched in the corner, bent over, its arms moving fiercely and jerkily, as though it were tying up a bundle. The figure stood up and Lovejoy saw that it was Ladszlo.

"Ladszlo," he said in relief. "Where have you been?" Ladszlo wheeled around. His eyes flashed wildly in the glint of the moon. He strode over to the bed.

"You!" he said harshly. "Keep quiet, pleasse!"

"Lad . . ." Lovejoy stopped. A long cold blade shone in Ladszlo's fist.

"Do not think, gentlemen," Ladszlo's voice scraped against his eardrums, "I will hessitate to usse it."

"What . . ." Lovejoy sat up warily, feeling the sheet grow clammy over his legs. "What're you doing?"

"Gentlemen." Ladszlo brought the knife very close, the memory of all the assassins who ever roamed the Balkans clamoring in his blood. "Gentlemen, be quiet."

Lovejoy sat up, quiet.

Ladszlo turned back to his work in the corner, and for the first time, Lovejoy saw what the Hungarian had been doing. Mrs. Buchanan was lying there, a maniac look on her cranky, brute face, her mouth gagged with strips of towel, her hands and ankles securely bound with twine. Ladszlo stood over her, menacing, triumphant.

"What . . . ?" Lovejoy began.

"Quiet!" Ladszlo snarled. He got out some more twine, and by the bright light of the moon at the window, he made an intricate and perfect hangman's knot. Lovejoy felt the sweat start out all over his body and his throat go wooden and salty. He blinked disbelievingly when Ladszlo put the noose around the monkey's thin neck and threw the other end of the rope over a tall bridge lamp.

"You're not really . . ." he said under his breath.

Ladszlo ignored him and pulled on the rope. Lovejoy closed his eyes. This was the first time he had ever seen a monkey hanged and he didn't feel he was up to the strain of watching. He kept his eyes closed until he heard Ladszlo's voice, thin and trumpet-like. "Well," Ladszlo was saying, "that's the last time you'll piss on me."

Lovejoy felt it was safe to look. Mrs. Buchanan hung limp, like a dead monkey. Ladszlo stood before her, revenge incarnate.

"Ladszlo," Lovejoy whispered cautiously. "How could you do it?"

Ladszlo whirled on him, strode over to his bed.

"Gentlemen," he said, leaning over dramatically, "I warn you. Leave while there iss still time."

"What're you talking about?"

"Inside there . . ." Ladszlo's finger shot out, stiff with warning. "Inside there you have two devilss."

"Why, Ladszlo," Lovejoy even managed to laugh a little. "They're just two simple high-spirited American boys."

"In that case," Ladszlo said, "spare me America. Devilss! I hate them, all three of them, the Calonius brothers most of all, and then Mrs. Buchanan. Unfortunately, it is not possible to hang the Calonius brothers." With somber gratification he looked at the monkey's corpse, swinging gently in the night wind. "I tell you. If you know what's good for you, you will get away from them, if you have to walk."

"It's true," Lovejoy said, "they don't treat you very well."

Ladszlo laughed a horrible laugh, like broken glass, at the understatement. "I had a good job," he said, "in Budapest. I sold lace. I was preparing to marry. Then I met the Calonius brothers. In two days they had sold me the bicycle . . . forty pounds. Later I found out, a man they had picked up in Strasbourg had deserted them. He could not stand it any more. They told me we were going to America. They painted a bright picture. Five hundred dollars a week in Radio City. I would be an American citizen. I could forget Hungary. I could forget the lace business. I brought wiss me one hundred pounds, in cash. Farewell. And every town we visited. Riots, husbands with guns, police. Customs officials. Pregnant women. It is like going through Europe with a shipload of pirates. Now, I have no more money, I have no job, I am in the middle of the desert, but when they told me to leave my dinner and go take a bath, I knew it wass the end. . . ."

There was a rustling in the next room and Ladszlo jumped back into the shadows fearfully. "I warn you," he whispered bleakly, and vanished.

Lovejoy looked at Mrs. Buchanan, stiffening noticeably at the bridge lamp. He put his face to the wall, but he did not sleep.

When Lovejoy rose in the morning and had his coffee and started off to school, the snores, regular and peaceful, were still coming out of the bedroom in which the Calonius brothers slept undisturbed.

Lovejoy was not feeling very well. His head occasionally expanded and contracted spasmodically; two or three times during the morning he saw double, and the shrill voices of the young Arab children for the first time made a nerve-racking clangor in his ears.

And when President Swenker came into his classroom in the middle of a lesson in advanced English composition and asked Lovejoy to have lunch with him, an uneasy tremor of anticipation ran down Lovejoy's spine. President Swenker's long and angular face was cold and forbidding, and Lovejoy was sure he had heard about the drinking the night before.

The last two hours of the morning Lovejoy hardly heard what was going on in the classroom, as he tried to invent explanations and to phrase apologies in his throbbing brain.

But over the bean salad and canned pineapple of President Swenker's severe lunch (the president was a vegetarian), with Mrs. Swenker and young Carlton Swenker sitting in decorous, lettuce-crunching silence, the president merely outlined a plan for a new Bible Class, "The New Testament in terms of Modern American Life, or Jesus Through the Eyes of an American Taxpayer." This was to be an evening class for adults and in his relief that the interview was not about liquor, Lovejoy was effusively enthusiastic, even though it meant two precious evenings a week away from Irina, and long hours of preparation.

An angular smile of satisfaction lit the president's face as he saw the genuine pleasure in his subordinate's eyes. "Well," the president said, patting Lovejoy bonily on the wrist, "this may make educational history in Aleppo. Have some more bean salad."

Lovejoy had to go directly to his afternoon classes from the president's lunch table, and he did not get home until nearly six o'clock.

He stopped at the foot of the steps leading up to his apartment and looked up the stairs, a nervous little tic of apprehension pulling somewhere inside his breast. All was quiet, except for a strange thudding noise that occasionally came through the windows, and a slight shaking of the thick mud walls. Lovejoy swallowed and climbed the steps slowly and opened the door.

Roland and Saint Clair Calonius were on the floor, half-naked, locked in gigantic combat. Saint Clair was on top and was beating his brother's head against the floor, which accounted for the dull thuds.

ONCE, IN ALEPPO 147

The entire place smelled like a steam-heated gymnasium after a closely contested basketball game. The eunuch Ahmed stood at the door, his eyes gleaming with excitement.

"Gentlemen. . ." Lovejoy said forlornly.

Suddenly, with a violent, twisting motion, Roland heaved himself up and a second later Saint Clair was hurling through the air, only to crash, with a house-shaking noise, against the wall. Ahmed fled, Saint Clair dropped dazedly to his knees for a moment, then stood up and smiled.

"That was very clever, Roland," he said.

"Gentlemen," Lovejoy said.

Both Calonius brothers looked at him strangely for a moment, as though they couldn't quite place him. Then a smile lit Saint Clair's face. "He lives here," he explained to Roland.

Roland smiled then, too. "You old dog," he said.

"Just keeping in condition," Saint Clair said. "Roland and me. Wrestling exercises every muscle of the body. Also good for the appetite. Have a drink. We're going to take a shower." They disappeared, sweating, their muscles rippling under steaming skin.

Lovejoy sat down and looked around him. The appearance of the room had changed completely. The two beds from the other room had been dragged in. His own couch, he could see through the doorway, was in the other room. Also the bicycles. Mrs. Buchanan, fortunately, had disappeared. Four bottles of Cuban rum stood on the table and three dozen lemons. A handsome Persian jug, ancient and valuable, which he suddenly realized he had seen before in the home of the Danish professor of mathematics, stood next to the lemons. He went over and smelled it. It had been recently used for mixing cocktails.

He heard a step behind him and wheeled nervously. It was the eunuch, with a bowl full of ice cubes. With sinking heart, Lovejoy remembered that the only electric refrigerator in town capable of making ice cubes was in the home of President Swenker.

"Ahmed . . ." he began, but the eunuch merely put the bowl down and shuffled out.

Lovejoy sank into a chair. His eyes roamed the disordered room. Something else had changed, something was missing, a small nagging voice told him. . . . He couldn't remember. He closed his eyes, ran his hands over them, opened them again. Then he saw. The *Encyclopaedia Britannica*. All the volumes from AA to PRU.

There must be, he told himself, some perfectly natural explanation.

Roland entered, huge and naked, drying himself with a towel. "Ah," he said. "More ice."

"Pardon me, Mr. Calonius," Lovejoy said. "I wonder if you could tell me how the ice . . ."

"You may have noticed, old man," Roland slapped himself vigorously on his bare pink chest, "that we've made certain small rearrangements."

"Yes," Lovejoy said. "Later we can . . ."

"Saint Clair has weak kidneys," Roland said. "And he didn't want to disturb you going through your room to the bathroom all night. Daiquiri?"

"Thank you, I . . ."

"You wouldn't think, looking at this town," Roland squeezed four lemons, bare-handed, "that you'd be able to get ice cubes like this."

"If I might ask," Lovejoy said, "how is it that you . . . ?"

"In this climate," Roland said, "rum is the only drink."

Saint Clair came in, also naked, slapping himself with one of Lovejoy's Turkish towels. "I suppose you know," he said, "Mrs. Buchanan was hanged here last night."

"Yes, I . . ."

"We're having her stuffed," Roland said, measuring the rum. "As a memento for you."

"Thank you very much. You're very kind, but . . ."

"Only a Hungarian," Saint Clair said, "would think of hanging a monkey. How would you like to buy a bicycle, old man?"

"At the moment I don't think I can afford . . ."

"Maleish," Saint Clair said.

"I wonder if you gentlemen know anything about several copies of the *Encyclo* . . ."

"Not too much sugar, Roland," Saint Clair warned.

"Mind your own goddamn business," Roland said calmly; he put his hand over the top of the ancient and valuable Persian jug, the property of the Danish professor of mathematics, and began to shake the cocktail vigorously, the ice clanking brightly against the precious glazed sides.

"The copies from AA to PRU," Lovejoy said stubbornly. "They seem to be missing. Perhaps you know something about . . ."

"Not a thing, old man," Saint Clair said carelessly. "They'll probably turn up. You know how people are about books."

The door was flung lightly open and Irina danced in.

"Irina!" Lovejoy said, shocked. It was the first time she had visited his house before dark. "They're not quite dressed."

"Hello, boys," Irina said gaily.

"Just in time," Saint Clair said, negligently wrapping the towel about the ridged muscles of his abdomen. "Have a drink."

Roland poured the frothy, freezing Daiquiris into coffee cups.

Irina lifted her drink. "To good will," she said charmingly and the Calonius brothers laughed loudly and Roland slapped her playfully on the behind.

Lovejoy watched incredulously for a moment, the demure figure now in a blazing yellow dress, tight and shiny, and the two immense, almost naked men, drinking swiftly.

He lifted his cup and drained it. "I think I'd like another," he said firmly.

"That's it, Wild Boy," Roland said, and poured him a big one.

The rest of the night was something of a blur for Lovejoy. There was a heavy dinner, steak again, and Burgundy, and Irina's hair coming undone and hanging loose and wild over one shoulder and Irina's teeth flashing in mirth and all of them singing Russian songs and Irina dancing, with flashing eyes and twitching hips, while the Calonius brothers sang and kept tremendous time with their hands. Vaguely, Lovejoy remembered, there was some talk about money, and he was sure he saw Irina take many bills out of her exquisite bosom and give them with both hands, in a bold, generous, Mother-of-Earth kind of gesture to Roland and Saint Clair Calonius. There was talk, too, of a *real* party the next night, and Roland saying, "Wild Boy, you're a good fellow. Wild Boy, we're glad we came to Aleppo. Wild Boy, you're an American. . . ."

In a curious way, Lovejoy had never had a better time in his whole life, although at the back of his mind throughout the entire evening, a voice kept calling, "All this is very expensive, all this is costing you a great deal of money." But he was very sorry when the ninth Daiquiri brought long periods of whirling blackness, and Saint Clair had to pick him up in his arms and carry him to his bed.

"Saint Clair," he kept mumbling, "breath of the wide world. Friends for life . . . Nothing like this would ever happen in Vermont. Friends for life . . ."

During the night he awoke to a stabbing sharp clarity, at about 3 A.M. In the next room, he heard a woman's sighs, then a moment later, low laughter, sensual and intimate in the quiet house. His mind puzzled over the sounds for a moment. Then he fell asleep again.

The next morning he stumbled dazedly out of the house, all shadowy and hushed, with pulled blinds against the glare of the morning sun. The classes had a tendency to whiten and disappear from time to time, and when President Swenker came in about eleven o'clock his face seemed to rise and fall in a white froth, like waves against rocks.

"Lovejoy," he said coldly, "I would like to see you at the noon hour."

"Yes, sir," said Lovejoy.

"I'm a broad-minded man," President Swenker said at noon, "and I know the debilitating effects of this climate on white men, but I have heard certain rumors about some guests of yours. . . ."

"Yes, sir," said Lovejoy faintly.

"I think it would be wise," said President Swenker, "if they left immediately."

"Yes, sir," Lovejoy said more faintly.

President Swenker patted Lovejoy more tolerantly on the shoulder, "Of course," he said, "I do not believe the rumors about the monkey and the Russian lady."

"Yes, sir," Lovejoy whispered, and hurried back to his apartment. The rooms were empty. Maybe, Lovejoy thought, maybe they've picked up and gone. . . .

But when he returned after class in the afternoon, he stood at the foot of the steps and looked up at the once hospitable and welcoming door of his home and he felt as a man must feel before going for the first time into a cage full of young tigers of unknown temper and dependability.

"Well," he said to himself, "no use standing down here all night."

ONCE, IN ALEPPO 151

He walked decisively up the steps and threw the door open.

Irina was lying relaxedly on the couch, with Saint Clair calmly and rather impersonally stroking her thigh. And in the center of the room stood Carlton Swenker, in earnest conversation with Roland.

"He's liable to kill me," Carlton was saying. Even as his blood froze at the boy's words, something in Lovejoy noticed that the rest of the *Encyclopaedia* was gone, from PRU to ZZ. Also the bridge lamp from which at another time Mrs. Buchanan had hung, and a large silver samovar and eight silver cups that had come with the house.

"Nobody will kill you," Roland said impatiently. "Just follow instructions. God almighty, Carlton, how old are you?"

"Eleven."

"You ought to be ashamed of yourself."

"Carlton," Lovejoy said in a loud, clear voice, "I think you'd better go home."

Carlton stopped at the door. "I'll be seeing you," he said, waving at the Calonius brothers. On the couch, Saint Clair raised his hand lazily from Irina's slender, exquisite thigh and waved to Carlton. "Give my regards to your old man," he said. Then he went back to stroking the thigh, this time under the skirt. Irina comfortably lighted a cigarette and leaned over and picked up a Daiquiri that was resting on the table beside her.

Lovejoy closed the door firmly. "Gentlemen," he said loudly, "I have some bad news for you."

"Have a drink, Wild Boy," Saint Clair said.

"Gentlemen," Lovejoy said, "I'm afraid I must tell you to leave."

There was a long silence. Saint Clair took his hand out from under Irina's skirt.

"I am under orders, gentlemen," Lovejoy said, because he could no longer tolerate the hush.

"It's an awful thing," Roland said quietly, "when Americans twelve thousand miles from home can't . . ." He didn't finish.

"Do you want us to go now?" Saint Clair asked. Lovejoy considered. They were being surprisingly reasonable. He remembered the vague glorious evening the night before.

"I can't see that it'll do any harm if you stay till morning," he said.

"Have a drink, Stanford," Roland boomed, turning toward him and clapping him heavily on the base of the neck.

"Sorry, old man," Saint Clair said, disentangling himself entirely from Irina and standing up to help with the liquor, "if we've caused you any inconvenience. . . ."

"I think," Irina sat up and pushed her hair back angrily, "I think you are behaving like mud, Stanford."

"Now, now," Roland said. "Let's forget it and have our last evening together as though nothing had happened." And he poured the drinks, frothy and tropic-fragrant, and beaded with the cold of President Swenker's ice cubes.

There were four drinks before dinner, and somehow, during dinner, Saint Clair was saying, "Wild Boy, I like you. Wild Boy, you're a great American. Wild Boy, you're just the sort of man we need on a trip like this. The Plain American with Brains."

"The Chinese," Roland said, "will be crazy about him."

"Also," said Saint Clair, "you're a master of tongues. College graduate. You can introduce us to consuls, speak the language. You will be a sensation in Jodphur."

"He's wiry," Roland said. "He's as wiry as they come. He'll make a great trick rider."

"He's not so wiry," Irina said.

"For fifty pounds you can have Ladszlo's bicycle," Saint Clair said. "The Calonius Brothers and Wild Boy. Daring!!! Extra . . ."

"Don't call me Wild Boy," said Lovejoy looking his eighth drink straight in the eye.

"How can a young man like you, with your talents, stand this town?" Roland marveled. "Year in, year out . . ."

"It's true," said Lovejoy, "that I sometimes . . ."

"The romantic East," chanted Saint Clair. "Crowded. Unknowable."

"We will send for Irina," Roland said, "as soon as we get some place where we can buy a small bicycle."

Irina clapped her hands. "I am everybody's good friend," she said gaily.

"You're too fine to be a schoolteacher," Saint Clair was saying earnestly. "You got fire, Stan. Dash."

"He's damned wiry," Roland said feeling Lovejoy's arm.

"Absolutely unique," Saint Clair kept on. "You can look back and say I have lived an absolutely unique life."

Lovejoy sat and stared silently into the depths of an empty Burgundy bottle. India, the ancient hills of China. Free, unfettered. He could just picture his uncle's face when he passed through San Jose on a bicycle.

"All right," he said suddenly.

They clapped him on the back and offered him a drink and Irina threw off her blouse and skirt and danced charmingly on the table in black lace panties and brassiere. From the brassiere, Lovejoy noticed vaguely, the corners of five pound notes peeped out.

Lovejoy opened his shirt and from a money belt he wore next to his skin he took out his last fifty pounds. Saint Clair put the money away gravely. Roland left the room, and reappeared a moment later with a towel, a bowl of hot water, some soap, and a straight-edge razor. While Lovejoy was pouring himself another drink, Roland came up behind him and tied the towel around his neck.

"Say," asked Lovejoy mildly, "what are you doing?"

Roland started to lather the top of Lovejoy's head. "In our act, everyone but Irina gets their head shaved." He got up a good thick lather. "It gives a better impression."

"You'll look more wiry, Stan," said Saint Clair.

For one moment, Lovejoy hesitated. *"Allez,"* he said.

Swiftly and expertly, as Lovejoy worked slowly on his tenth Daiquiri, Roland began to shave his head. One-half the job was done, the left side of the scalp lying clean and pink as a baby's bottom, when the door was thrown open. Lovejoy looked up.

President Swenker stood there, his face slowly clouding over, like a Dakota winter. His eyes left the shining semi-egg of Lovejoy's scalp and took in the slender and exquisite, black-laced figure of Irina studiously practicing entrechats on the dining table, among the bottles.

Lovejoy sighed.

"Goodness," said President Swenker.

"Hi, buster," Roland said cheerfully.

"Mr. Lovejoy," President Swenker said, "I shall speak to you in the morning, under more . . . more formal circumstances."

He closed the door carefully behind him. Lovejoy sighed again and Roland started to work on the right side of his head.

When he awoke the next morning, Lovejoy's head was very large, but he vaguely remembered that he'd an exhilarating evening. He remembered that he'd told the Calonius brothers that they must move on, and how gentlemanly they'd been about it. After that, it was a cloud of rum, song, and dance. He smiled a little, although his head ached enormously. With all their faults, he had to admit, as he lay there, in the darkened guest room, the Calonius brothers had given him the most exciting three days of his life. Now they were going, and it probably would cost him thirty or forty pounds to make final payments on everything, but joy came dear in this world, and it was worth it.

He got out of bed, holding on to the wall for support. He had never realized he could learn to like liquor so well. He looked at his watch. Lord, he thought, I'll be late for class.

He walked as quickly as he was able toward the bathroom. In the main room, the two beds were pulled together and Irina was lying rather athwart the two Calonius brothers. All three were asleep. Irina, Lovejoy noticed, was no longer wearing lace panties.

He made his way painfully into the bathroom and began to wash his teeth. Suddenly, his hand poised with toothbrush in midair, he caught sight of a strange gleam in the mirror. He looked hard at the glass. "My God," he said, the toothbrush still halfway up, the mouth still frothing with dental cream. He was as bald as a stone egg. He looked, disbelieving. Then slowly it all came back. He put the toothbrush down and sat down slowly on the edge of the tub.

India, China, Japan . . . He had paid off fifty pounds for the bicycle, the last money he had in the world; his head was shaven; he had incurred huge debts in town he could never pay. He could never appear before a class of children with his head like this. And it would take at least two months for a decent covering to grow back.

Then he remembered President Swenker's face as the president had stood at the doorway and looked at Irina dancing in black lace underwear on the dinner table. "Oh, my," he said weakly and stumbled back toward his room.

ONCE, IN ALEPPO

In the main room the three sleepers slept calmly on, with Irina favoring Saint Clair slightly, one exquisite leg thrown carelessly over his knee. Lovejoy stopped and looked down dazedly.

At one time he had toyed with the idea of marrying Irina. At least he had been warned off *that*.

He put a sheet over the entwined figures and stumbled into the guest room. He lay down and stared at the ceiling, the white froth of the toothpaste still on his lips. It began to sting and he licked it off. In a moment he had a severe case of heartburn.

There was no doubt about it now. Only one thing remained to be done. For good or ill, his lot was thrown with the Calonius brothers. When they awoke, he would pack quietly a few things in a small bag, start on a new, nomadic life. As he thought about it, even in the clear light of morning, there still were certain advantages.

Suddenly he fell asleep.

He was awakened by the pad of footsteps in his room. He opened his eyes slowly. His landlady, for some unaccountable reason, was in his room, her back to him, with a pencil and a pad of paper in her hand, on which she frequently made notations. She was a small, fat old lady, with a face designed for lamentation. At the moment, Lovejoy saw as she turned around, her mouth was working with some indescribable emotion.

"Madam," he said, sitting up, having trouble with his French, "what are you doing in my room?"

"Aha!" the landlady said.

Lovejoy shook his head to clear it.

"Madam, I'll thank you to . . ."

"The rug!" The landlady jabbed at her notebook. "Aha!" she scuttled out suddenly.

From the next room he heard a high, excited, man's voice in Arab-French, "Come out or we shoot!"

Lovejoy swallowed uncomfortably. He wondered if the Calonius brothers were going to be shot in his house.

"I will give you five," the excited voice called. *"Un . . . deux . . . trois . . .* Monsieur Lovejoy, I repeat, I will give you *cinq . . ."*

Like lightning, Lovejoy realized . . . whoever it was, was addressing him. By *quatre* he was out in the main room.

Two policemen were standing there, facing the door. One of them had a gun in his hand and the landlady was standing excitedly behind him. Irina and the two Calonius brothers still slept on.

"What . . . ?" began Lovejoy.

"Don't ask any questions," said the policeman with the gun. "Come on."

The two policemen had dangerous expressions on their faces, especially for so early in the morning. "If you'll permit me," Lovejoy said, "I'd like to put on a pair of trousers."

They came in and watched him put on trousers and shoes, still with the gun drawn.

"I wish," said Lovejoy, "you'd tell me what I've done. . . ."

"*Bouge!*" said the policeman with the gun.

Lovejoy went out between them. His landlady followed at a safe distance. Irina and the Calonius brothers slept on. As he left the building, Carlton Swenker ran past him, up the steps.

The police did not take him far, merely to the office of President Swenker. As they drew near, Lovejoy heard a mumbling and buzzing inside. He hesitated at the door.

"In!" said the policeman with the gun, kicking open the door.

Lovejoy stepped in, only to be met with such a blast of shouts and murmurs and oaths that, if it weren't for the policemen at his back, he would have turned and run. A third of the population of Aleppo seemed to be crammed into the office, with President Swenker in a corner, behind his desk, standing, spreading his hands, trying to maintain order. The Danish professor of mathematics was there, the small Englishman who taught history was there, the owner of the bookshop, Irina's boss, was there, the local taxidermist, a liquor merchant, two rug merchants, a butcher, and two maiden ladies who taught knitting and sewing and cooking, were all there. And Lovejoy's landlady crowded in and looked over the room proudly and malevolently.

"Ladies and gentlemen," the President kept saying, "ladies and gentlemen."

The excited tide of Oriental conversation welled higher than ever.

"Mr. Lovejoy," the president said loudly and bitterly,

ONCE, IN ALEPPO

"what in the name of God have you been doing?"

Suddenly the room fell quiet. All eyes stared with equal wrath at Lovejoy, liquor-eyed and seedy between the policemen at the door.

"I . . . I . . . I really don't know what you mean," Lovejoy said.

"Don't think for a moment you're going to make good your escape, young man," the president said.

"No, sir," said Lovejoy.

"If it weren't for me, you would even now be at the mercy of Syrian justice."

Lovejoy shuddered a little. "Please," he whispered, "may I sit down?"

"What the hell has happened to your hair?" the president asked irritably.

Involuntarily, Lovejoy's hand went up to his head. Then he remembered.

"I . . . I . . . uh . . . shaved it," he said.

"God almighty, Lovejoy," the president shouted, "I'm going to have a thing or two to say to the University of Vermont!"

Suddenly the door was thrust open and Lovejoy's cook, the eunuch Ahmed, was flung into the room, followed by another policeman. The eunuch took one look around him, then lay down on the floor and wept. Sweat started on Lovejoy's forehead.

"Tell the truth, young man," the landlady barked at him, "weren't you intending to leave Aleppo today?"

Lovejoy took a deep breath. "Yes," he said.

A fierce murmur ran through the room.

"We would have shot you down on the road," the policeman with the gun said. "From behind."

"Please," Lovejoy begged. "Please explain . . ."

Then, bit by bit, with many interruptions by various impassioned townspeople, it came out. It all started when the landlady saw her bridge lamp in a furniture shop. Then she saw her silver samovar being melted in the rear of a jewelry shop. Then, feverish and hysterical, in four different shops, she had seen six rugs from various houses which she had rented to members of the school faculty. She wailed, in time with Ahmed, weeping on the floor, as she described seeing various bedcovers, cushions, small tables, silver vases, with which she had furnished her houses, in cotton-goods stores, junkshops, butcher shops. She had run hysterically to the police, who had traced everything to Ahmed.

"He said Mr. Lovejoy wanted to borrow some blankets for unexpected guests," one of the sewing-and-cooking ladies said shrilly, "and naturally, it never occurred to me . . ."

Ahmed, shattered and damp on the floor, was too broken to say a coherent word. "They are pleasant gentlemen," he kept murmuring incomprehensibly, "very pleasant gentlemen. They like to eat and drink. They sing to me in the kitchen. They give me five piastres extra a day. They sing to me in the kitchen."

Lovejoy looked down horrified at the faithless servant, bribed by a song in the scullery, and twenty cents every twenty-four hours. He passed his hand wearily over his eyes as the taxidermist demanded payment for stuffing a monkey.

"A particularly horrible case," the taxidermist was saying. "The monkey was hanged, I assure you. Hanged by the neck."

With his eyes closed, Lovejoy felt the shudder of revulsion sweep the room.

"For God's sake, Lovejoy!" He heard President Swenker's high, biblical voice. "This is monstrous!"

Lovejoy opened his eyes just in time to see Mrs. Swenker come streaming in, tears roaring down her cheeks.

"Walter," she sobbed, "Walter!" and heaved herself onto her husband's bosom.

"What's the matter with you?" President Swenker asked.

"Carlton . . ."

Lovejoy felt his stomach contract sickly over the name.

"What's wrong with *him?*" President Swenker shouted.

"Your son Carlton," Mrs. Swenker's voice rang out dramatically, "has stolen fifty pounds from your wall safe."

President Swenker sank into a chair, put his head in his hands. "Oh Lord, how much more," he roared, this time out of the Old Testament, "do I have to endure?"

"I think, sir," Lovejoy said timidly, "I know where I can get your money back."

"God almighty, Lovejoy!" President Swenker looked up. "Are you mixed up in this, too?"

ONCE, IN ALEPPO

"Perhaps if you'll come with me, we can clear up a lot of things at once," Lovejoy said with dignity.

"One move," said the policeman with the gun, "and I shoot. To kill."

"Where do you want to take us?" President Swenker asked. "Oh, for God's sake, Corinne, stop bawling!"

Mrs. Swenker fled the room, stifling sobs.

"To my house, sir," Lovejoy said. "There are two gentlemen there who might throw some light on several subjects."

"They like to eat and drink," Ahmed sobbed on the floor, "and sing to me in the kitchen."

"All right," President Swenker said shortly. "Come on."

The policeman pressed the muzzle of the gun into Lovejoy's ribs, and the procession wound its way to the house which late had seen so much revelry. On the way across the yard, President Swenker said, snarling, "this is going to cost you a pretty penny, Lovejoy."

Lovejoy swallowed drily. "I don't have any, sir."

"You'll work it out," President Swenker said, "if it takes twenty years."

Lovejoy swallowed once more.

"Also," President Swenker said, "you've got to get a wig."

"A *what*, Sir?"

"A wig! A wig! What's wrong with you? Are you deaf? A wig. A toupé."

"Oh."

"The boys would laugh you out of the city looking like that. Discipline would be ruined for six months."

"Yes, sir. Only, sir . . . I have no money to buy a toupé."

"Uh." The President paused. "I'll advance it to you. You'll work it out with interest."

"Thank you, sir."

Just as they got to the foot of the stairs leading to Lovejoy's apartment, Carlton Swenker came sailing around the corner on a bright, shiny bicycle, much too large for him.

"Carlton!" thundered the president. Carlton stopped. The entire procession stopped.

"Carlton," shouted President Swenker, "where did you get that bicycle?"

"I bought it, Daddy," said Carlton.

President Swenker swung. Carlton dropped senseless to the ground. Then the president started up the steps, followed by the procession, all careful to avoid treading on the slight young figure lying in the dust.

The president threw open the door and strode in. Everyone strode in after him. Lovejoy looked at the two beds. They were empty. The room was torn as though several cavalry charges had been conducted in it, and there were bottles strewn around like a brewers' picnic, and the landlady was whimpering painfully as she jotted down new damage on her pad of paper, but the room was empty.

"Well," President Swenker turned on Lovejoy. "Where are the two gentlemen?"

"Watch him, André!" the landlady cried to the policeman. "It's a trick."

"Perhaps in the next room," Lovejoy said without hope.

Silently the entire party went into the next room. The same dismal and complete desolation, but no Calonius brothers. The party went back into the main room. Lovejoy walked over to the large Italian cabinet. "They took all the woolen underwear," he said aimlessly.

"All right," President Swenker said, "Now we can get down to cases. You have two alternatives. You can stand trial before Syrian justice or you can guarantee to stay in this town and work out all damages, down to the last penny, no matter how long it takes. How long," the President addressed the policeman with the gun, "do you think they'd be likely to give him in jail?"

"Thirty years," the policeman said promptly.

"I'll pay," Lovejoy said.

It took until three-thirty that afternoon before all the claims were in and added up, the vases, silverware, rugs, steaks, wines, linen, bridge lamps, tables, monkey-stuffing, books. There was also the fifty pounds that Carlton had stolen from the wall safe and the estimated ten pounds for a toupé. All in all, it came to 374 pounds, 27. At this present rate of pay, eating only twice a day, Lovejoy figured that he might be able to pay off his debt and be released to go home to America in seven more years.

He signed an agreement all around, for which a lawyer was called in, making it 377, 27. The policeman with the gun gave him a cigar and suddenly he was left alone, in the wreckage of his home, the wreckage of his life.

ONCE, IN ALEPPO   161

He looked out the window. President Swenker was picking up the still limp and senseless body of Carlton and carrying it home.

Lovejoy sat down and sighed. He lit the cigar the policeman had given him and stared at the empty bottles.

Month followed month after that, and the horrible episode of the Calonius brothers began to seem to Lovejoy like an aimless and sudden visitation, a senseless plague, a purge by evil, outside the control of man. His hair grew back and he sold back the toupé at a loss of only one pound fifty, and except for a little fright with Irina, who imagined for several days that she was pregnant with twins, Lovejoy went along as before, although every hour was tempered by bitter poverty and the knowledge that his deliverance might take as long as Jacob's.

By the time he could part his hair again, he had almost completely forgotten the Californians on the bicycles.

Then one day . . .

He was reading *The Seven Pillars of Wisdom*, with Lawrence in the hands of the Turks, when, in the distance, he heard his name shouted faintly. He put the book down. "Stanford . . ." the voice quavered. "Stan . . ."

No, it couldn't be. . . . He stood up, feeling his upper lip curl back into an atavistic snarl.

"Stanford . . ." came the voice.

He hurried down the steps, his legs almost buckling under him. There, in the main road, was a strange caravan. Astride a donkey, wavering from heat, starvation, thirst, exhaustion, supported on both sides by strong men, was Saint Clair Calonius, his eyes sunken, his lips pale and bloodless. And behind him, on another donkey, in exactly the same state, was Roland Calonius.

"Found him in the desert," the driver nearest Lovejoy said. "Just lying there. Nearly dead. Found *him*" —with a jerk of the thumb for Roland,—"down at the bottom of a well, nearly dead."

Saint Clair smiled horribly at Lovejoy. "Stanford, old boy . . ." he whispered hoarsely through cracked lips. "Delighted. See you soon as we get out of the hospital. Old boy . . ."

Lovejoy's heart sank and the tears came to his eyes. He walked unsteadily back to Roland.

"Stanford, old boy . . ." Roland put out a frail hand, held Lovejoy's shoulder. "Glad to see you. Soon as we get out of the hospital." He leaned over drunkenly, whispered into Lovejoy's ear. "Gotta do me a favor . . ."

"Not in a million . . ."

"Gotta. That sonofabitch threw me into a well. Can't get away with it. Stanford, old man, go into town and buy me the biggest, sharpest spring-knife you can find, five-inch blade. Leave it in that cabinet in your house. Top drawer. When we get out of hospital. First move he makes . . . the throat . . ." Roland made a horrible, murderous noise. "Show sonofabitch can't throw me into any well. Stanford, old boy, don't shake your head. . . ."

Suddenly Lovejoy stopped shaking his head. A slow, ecstatic look came into his eye, then died. "I can't buy you anything," he said. "I haven't got a penny."

Roland pushed drunkenly into a pocket, brought out a handful of notes, stuffed them into Lovejoy's hand. "Money no object . . ." He swooned and the two strong men held him up. Lovejoy put the money carefully into his wallet and walked up to Saint Clair.

"Anything I can do for you?" he asked in a clear, vibrant voice.

Saint Clair looked around him with lunatic caution. "One thing, old boy," he said. "That sonofabitch Roland thinks I threw him into well. Wants to kill me. Nobody can do that to me." He fished wearily in a pocket, brought out a fistful of bills, peered around him warily. "Go down, old boy, and buy me one .45 revolver with seven bullets. Leave it in that cabinet where you kept the Johnny Walker. Top drawer. Then when we get back from hospital . . . first move sonofabitch makes. Seven slugs."

Stanford gravely put the money in his wallet.

"Listen, Stanford," Saint Clair leaned anxiously and crazily off the donkey, "you'll do this little thing for me, won't you . . . ?"

"Gladly," Lovejoy said in an even, firm voice.

"Good old Stan . . ." Saint Clair collapsed and the two drovers had to hold him up, as the caravan wound its way toward the hospital.

Lovejoy watched the donkeys disappear down the street, then walked swiftly into town and bought the best spring-

ONCE, IN ALEPPO

knife he could find and an excellent, brand-new .45 revolver with seven cartridges.

There was considerable money left over and he bought three bottles of Johnny Walker.

He went back to his home and emptied the top drawer of the cabinet and placed the gun and knife neatly side by side. Then he soaped the drawer, so that no one would have any difficulty in opening it, even in a great hurry.

Then he sat down and waited for the Calonius brothers to come out of the hospital. He poured himself a large drink. He took a good swig of the whisky and smiled a little.

Circle of Light

There was mist lying low along the ground and the headlights made a milky thin soup in every dip of the road. It was nearly one o'clock in the morning and they didn't pass any other cars as they wound along the narrow road up the hill toward the house. There were only four other houses between the main highway and the Willards' house, and they were all dark.

They were sitting in the front seat, Martin and his sister and her husband. Linda had the radio on and was singing softly, accompanying the orchestra, singing, "It's the wrong time, and the wrong place . . ."

John Willard sat comfortably at the wheel, driving fast, smiling when Linda leaned over and sang into his ear, burlesquing passion in the style of a nightclub singer, "Though it's such a pretty fa-aaace . . ."

"Be careful," Willard said. "You're tickling the ear of the driver."

"There were more fatalities on the roads last year," Martin said, "from tickling the ear of the driver than from drunkenness, national holidays, and faulty brakes."

"Who said that?" Linda asked aggressively.

"It's a well-known statistic," Martin said.

"I don't care," Linda said. "I'm crazy about the ear of the driver."

Willard chuckled.

"Wipe that complacent grin off your face, soldier," Linda said.

Willard chuckled again and Linda went back to finishing

the song, her head leaning against Martin's arm, her face lit dimly by the dashboard glow, looking gay and young, framed by her loose dark hair.

Ten years after *I* get married, Martin thought, glancing sideways at his sister, I hope my wife and I feel like that on the way home after a night in the city.

Martin had arrived from California late that afternoon, after sending a telegram that he was giving up his job and was on his way to Europe and could he count on a bed and meal enroute. Linda had met him at the airport, looking the same, he thought, after the two years of separation, and they had picked up Willard at his office and had had a couple of drinks and a good dinner and an extravagant bottle of wine to celebrate Martin's arrival. It was Friday and Willard didn't have to work the next day, so they had gone to a nightclub and listened to a girl in a white dress singing French songs. Martin and Willard had taken turns dancing with Linda, and Linda had said, "Isn't this nice? If you had given me more warning I'd have felt I'd have had to find a girl for you for the evening and there would've been four of us and the whole thing would've been ruined. Don't you hate the number four?"

Martin was seven years younger than Linda, and her favorite brother. When he was still in college he had spent his summers with Linda and Willard, acting as spare man at parties, playing tennis with Willard, and endangering the lives of their two small sons, as Linda put it, teaching them how to swim and dive and ride bicycles and catch a baseball and fall out of trees.

"Oh, God," Linda said as the car swung through an overgrown stone gate, "two years are too long, Martin. What're we going to do without you when you're in Europe?"

"Come and visit me," Martin said.

"Listen to that," Linda said.

"It's only overnight by plane."

"You know anybody wants to give us a free ride?" She waved her hand at the dark woods outside the car window. "It'll take ten years before we get through paying off Gruesome Acres."

"It looks very nice." Martin peered through the misted window at the dripping black woods. "Very rural."

"It's rural all right," Linda said. "Seventeen acres of impenetrable underbrush."

"Can't you clear part of it," Martin asked, "and grow something on it?"

"Taxes," Willard said briefly, swinging out of the woods and into the circular driveway in front of a large brick house with white pillars, rising dimly out of the mist.

There were no lights showing downstairs, only a pale glimmer coming from a curtained window on the upper storey, and the house bulked impressively in the darkness.

"There ought to be at least one light left on at the entrance, Linda," Willard said.

"It's the new maid," Linda said. "I tell her all the time, but she's a demon for economy."

Willard stopped the car and they all got out, Martin taking his bag off the back seat.

"Notice the exquisite architecture," Linda said, as they climbed the steps and went between the pillars to the front door. "Spectral Greek."

"Wait till you see the inside, though," Willard said, opening the door and turning on the light. "It makes up for the whole thing. And the land around it is great for the kids."

"It has one other glorious advantage," Linda said, taking off her coat and throwing it across a chair in the wall-papered front hall. "The television reception is horrible."

They went into the living room and Linda switched on the lamps and Willard poured them some whiskeys for Martin to admire the house on. The living room was big and airy and pleasant, with a clutter of paintings on the walls and a lot of books and magazines and small semiuseful objects not quite in place. Martin smiled, looking at it and recognizing his sister's undisciplined, cheerful touch in the bright choice of colors, the profusion of vases, flowers, antique odds and ends, and in the air of comfortable disorder that the room presented now, at one o'clock in the morning, after it had been empty and unused all evening.

Linda took her shoes off and sat with her legs up in the corner of the big couch, holding her whiskey glass in two hands and the two men sat facing her, sleepy, but reluctant to end the night of reunion. "Now, really, Martin," Linda said, "you can't possibly mean it when you say you're not going to stay at least a week."

"I have to go up to Boston on Monday," Martin said. "And I'm taking the plane for Paris from there on Wednesday."

"The boys're going to be black with disappointment," Linda said. "Maybe you'll meet somebody over the weekend here and you'll change your mind. We're invited to three parties."

Martin laughed. "It's a lucky thing I have to go to Boston," he said. "I can recover in Boston."

Linda swished the whiskey around in her glass. "John," she said, "don't you think this is as good a time as any to give him the lecture?"

"It's awfully late, you know, Linda," Willard said, a little uncomfortably.

"What lecture?" Martin asked suspiciously, beginning to feel, in advance, like a younger brother.

"Well," Willard began, "Linda and I were talking on the phone after you sent the telegram, and we began to add up — What's this, the third job you've given up since you left college?"

"Fourth," Martin said.

"First in New York," Willard said, doing his duty as a brother-in-law and as a friend and as a solid citizen who was still with the same firm he had joined when he finished law school fifteen years before. "Then in Chicago. Then California. Now Europe. You're not a kid any more and maybe a little stability would . . ."

"Don't lay it on too thick, now," Linda said, worried by the way Martin's face was closing up as he sat there, listening, playing with his glass. "I mean, don't make it sound like a commencement address at M.I.T. or General Patton addressing the troops, John. What we were talking about to each other," she said, addressing Martin, "was that all of a sudden one day you're liable to find out you're thirty and your life is sliding away. . . ."

Willard grinned at her. "Have you found out you're thirty and your life is sliding away?"

"Like sand through the fingers," Linda said. Then she giggled, and Martin's face began to open up again.

"But it *is* important," Linda said, grave once more. "It's so easy for the good-looking ones to wind up bums. Especially in France."

"I don't know enough French to wind up as a bum,"

Martin said cheerfully. He got up and touched the top of his sister's hair and then went over to the low table in front of the window which they used as a bar, to put some ice into his drink.

"The idea was, Martin," Linda said, "just to give you a carefully modulated warning. We don't want to . . ."

"Say," Martin said, staring out the window, "are you expecting guests?"

"Guests?" Willard asked, surprised. "At this hour?"

"There's a man out there, looking in," Martin said. He twisted his neck to look toward the corner of the house. "And there's a ladder up against the balcony. . . . Now he's gone. . . ."

"A ladder!" Linda sprang up. "The children!" she ran out of the room and up the staircase, with the two men racing after her.

There was a lamp in the hall outside the children's bedroom and by its light Martin could see the two small boys sleeping quietly in their beds, ranged against the walls on opposite sides of the room. Through the half-opened door which led into the next room came the steady snoring of the maid. While Linda and Willard reassured themselves about the children, Martin went to the windows. They were open, but the room was closed off from the balcony by full-length shutters, still hooked in place. Martin undid the shutters and stepped out onto the balcony, which ran along the front of the floor of the house, supported by the porch columns. The night was raw and dark and the mist had grown thicker and the light from the downstairs windows reflected back confusingly. Martin went to the edge of the balcony and peered down. He heard a sound to his left, off to the side of the house, and looked in that direction. He got a glimpse of a patch of white moving swiftly against the dark background of tree trunks and he turned and ran back through the boys' room, whispering to Willard, "He's down there. On that side."

Willard came after him as he took the steps four at a time and flung open the front door and ran across the driveway gravel, and around the side of the house, past the ladder. Willard had picked up a flashlight in the front hall, but it wasn't a strong one, and its beam flickered meaninglessly across the sloping, overgrown wet lawn and the tangled mass of shrubs and trees into which the intruder had disappeared.

Without much hope of success, Martin and Willard pushed their way some distance through the woods, scratching themselves on bushes and ploughing through drifts of soaked dead leaves, flicking the searchlight beam around them in sudden, prying movements. They were silent and angry and if they had found the man he would have had to be armed and ready to use his weapon to get away from them. But they saw nothing, heard nothing.

After five minutes, Willard gave up. "Ah, it's no use," he said. "Let's get back."

They walked back to the house in silence. When they reached the edge of the lawn they saw Linda out on the corner of the balcony with the light from the now opened shutters of the children's room outlining her form in the darkness. She was leaning over and pushing at the ladder and finally it teetered and fell to the ground.

"Did you find him?" she called to Martin and Willard.

"No," Willard said.

"Nothing's been touched in any of the rooms," Linda said. "He never got in. It's our ladder. The gardener was using it this afternoon and he must have left it out."

"Get inside," Willard called to her. "You'll freeze up there."

Martin and Willard took one last look at the dark lawn and the looming black wall of the woods. They waited until Linda had stepped back into the children's room and locked the shutters. Then they went into the house. Martin stayed downstairs while Willard went up to look at the children once more. The living room didn't look as gay and pleasant to Martin as it had before.

When Willard and Linda came down again Martin was standing at the window from which he had seen the man on the lawn outside, and the ladder.

"What an idiot," he said. " 'Are you expecting guests?' " He shook his head ruefully. "At this hour of the morning."

"Well, remember," Linda said, "you've just come from California."

They laughed then and everybody felt better and Willard poured them some more whiskey.

"What I should've done," Martin said, "was pretend I hadn't seen him and just acted natural and gone out a side door. . . ."

"People are only as clever as that in the movies," Willard said. "In real life they say, 'Are you expecting guests?.'"

"You know something," Martin said, remembering, "I think I'd recognize that fellow if I saw him again. After all, he was only five feet away from me and the light from the window was right on him."

"Did he look like a criminal?" Linda asked.

"Everybody looks like a criminal at one o'clock in the morning," Martin said.

"I'm going to call the police and report this," Willard said and got up and started toward the telephone, which was in the hall.

"Oh, Johnny," Linda said, putting out her hand and stopping him. "Wait till morning. If you call, they'll just come over and keep us up all night."

"Well, you can't let people climb all over your house and try to break in and do nothing about it, can you?" Willard said.

"It won't do any good. They'll never find him out there tonight," Linda said.

"That's true enough," said Martin.

"And they'll want to go up and look at the children's room and they'll wake them up and scare them. . . ." Linda was talking rapidly and nervously. She had been calm enough before but the reaction had set in and she didn't seem to be able to sit still or talk at a normal speed now. "What's the sense in it? Don't be pig-headed."

"Who's being pig-headed?" Willard asked, surprised. "All I said was that I thought we ought to call the police. Did I sound pig-headed to you, Martin?"

"Well," Martin began judicially, wanting to placate his sister. "I think . . ."

But Linda interrupted. "He didn't do anything, anyway, did he? After all, he just looked in the window. There's no sense in losing a night's sleep just because a man happened to look in the window. I bet he wasn't a robber, at all. . . ."

"What do you mean?" Willard asked sharply.

"Well, what've we got to rob here? I don't have any jewels and the one fur coat I own is seven years old and any thief in his right mind . . ."

"Then what was he doing here with his damn ladder?" Willard asked.

"Maybe he was just a peeping Tom," Linda said.

"Just!" Willard gulped down his drink. "If you wouldn't walk around naked with all the blinds up all the time . . ."

"Oh, don't be such a prude." Linda said. "Who's going to see me in this house? The chipmunks?"

"Not only this house," Willard said. "Wherever we live. Women these days." He turned bitterly toward Martin. "When you get married you'll find you're spending half your time pulling down blinds to keep the American public from admiring your wife dressing and undressing."

"Don't be stuffy, John," Linda said, her voice rising. "Who'd ever think in the middle of the woods like this . . ."

"I'd think," Willard said. "And that guy with the ladder obviously thought, didn't he?"

"Who knows what he thought?" Linda said. "All right, you win. From now on, I'll pull every blind in the house. But it's so awful. To have to live like that in your own house. All closed in."

"It's not being all closed in to put on a bathrobe once in a while," Willard said.

"John," Linda said, her voice sharp, "you have a terrible tendency to turn stuffy in a crisis."

"Boys, boys," Martin said. "I'm here on a holiday."

"Sorry," Willard said shortly, and Linda laughed, strainedly.

"You ought to buy a dog," Martin said.

"He hates dogs," said Linda, starting to turn the lamps out. "He prefers to live in a vault."

They left it at that and went up to bed, leaving an extra light on in the downstairs hall, for security, although it was certain that the prowler, whoever he was, and for whatever reason he had come, would not come back that night, at least.

Willard called the police in the morning and they promised to come over. Linda had to invent an elaborate reason to take the children away until lunchtime, because she didn't want them to see the policeman and ask questions and begin to feel insecure in their own house. It was difficult to get the children out of the house because they wanted to spend the morning with their uncle and they couldn't understand why Martin wouldn't come with them and he couldn't tell them that he had to stay and try to give the police a description of a man who had prowled outside their window while they slept.

The children were out of the way when the police car drove up. The two policemen walked soberly over the grounds, looking professionally at the ladder and the balcony and the woods and taking notes. When they asked Martin what the man looked like he was a little embarrassed by the vagueness of the description he could offer and had the feeling that the policemen were disappointed in him.

"I'm pretty sure I could recognize him, if I saw him again," Martin said, "but there wasn't anything particularly special about him to latch onto. I mean, he didn't have a big scar or a patch over one eye or a broken nose or anything like that."

"How old was he?" Madden, the older of the policemen, asked.

"Sort of middle-aged, Sergeant," Martin said. "Somewhere between thirty and forty-five, I guess."

Willard smiled and Martin saw that Madden was trying not to smile.

"You know what I mean," Martin said. "In between."

"What kind of complexion did he have, Mr. Brackett?" Madden asked.

"Well, in that light, in the mist . . ." Martin hesitated, digging into his memory. "He looked pale."

"Was he bald?" Madden made an entry in his book. "Did he have a lot of hair?"

Again Martin hesitated. "I guess he was wearing a kind of hat," he said.

"What kind of hat?"

Martin shrugged. "A hat."

"A cap, would you say?" Madden suggested.

"No, I guess not. Just a hat."

"What sort of shape was he, would you say?" Madden went on methodically, putting everything down. "Tall, stocky, what?"

Martin shook his head embarrassedly. "I'm afraid I'm

CIRCLE OF LIGHT 173

not much help," he said. "He was standing there with the light just hitting his head, below the window, and I . . . I really couldn't say. He looked . . . well, if I had to make up my mind about it . . . solid."

"Have you any notions about who it might be, Sergeant?" Willard asked.

The two policemen looked at each other judiciously. "Well, Mr. Willard," Madden said, "there're bound to be two or three cases of people walking around at night in any town. We'll check. They're building that new shopping center near the bank and there're a lot of workmen in from New Haven. All sorts of people," he said, making a heavy judgment on foreigners from New Haven. He closed his book and put it in his pocket. "We'll let you know if anything comes up."

"I'm pretty sure I'd know him if I saw him," Martin repeated, trying to reestablish himself with the policemen.

"If we get any ideas," said Madden, "maybe we'll ask you to come with us and look over a suspect or two."

"I'm leaving tomorrow night," Martin said. "For France."

The two policemen exchanged glances again, bleakly eloquent about the civic attitude of Americans who witnessed crimes and then fled to France.

"Well," Madden said heavily, without optimism, "we'll see what we can do."

Martin and Willard watched the police car drive off. "Isn't it funny," Willard said, "how easy it is for a policeman to make you feel guilty?"

Then they went into the house and Willard used the telephone to call Linda and tell her it was all right to bring the children home, the police had gone.

They had been invited to a friend's house for cocktails that evening and after that to another friend's for dinner and at first Linda said she wouldn't go, she couldn't dream of leaving the children alone in the house after what had happened. But Willard asked her what she intended to do —stay home every night until the children were twenty years old? Anyway, Willard said, whoever it was had had a real scare and would keep as far away from the house as possible. Then Linda decided that he was right, but now she'd have to tell the maid. It wouldn't be moral, she said, to go out and leave the maid in ignorance. But, she warned her husband, there was a good chance that the maid would pack her bags and leave. The maid had only been with them for six weeks and was getting on in years and was not a calm type. So Linda went into the kitchen while Willard paced the living room jumpily, saying to Martin, "One thing I couldn't stand is going through finding a new maid. We've had five since we moved in here."

But Linda came out of the kitchen smiling and saying the maid was a calmer type than she appeared and was taking the news placidly. "She's too old to be raped," Linda said, "and she loves the children, so she'll stay."

Willard put the ladder in the garage and locked the garage and made sure the shutters were hooked from the inside in the children's room and in Linda's bedroom and in his own bedroom and in the bathroom in between, because all those rooms gave on the balcony against which the ladder had been propped the night before.

At the cocktail party, which was a replica of a thousand other cocktail parties being given on that particular Saturday night within a radius of one hundred miles from New York City, Willard and Linda told about the prowler and Martin had to describe what he looked like, feeling once more, as he had with the policemen, that it was a sign of low intelligence on his part that he couldn't be more accurate. "He had this hat over his eyes and he didn't have any expression on his face and he was rather pale, as I told the sergeant, and intense-looking. . . ." Even as he spoke, Martin realized that he was adding to the portrait of the man on the other side of the window in the misty night, that the intensity of the man's expression was a new discovery, dredged from his memory, that the remembered face was being simplified, intensified, becoming heraldic, symbolic, a racial, dangerous apparition staring out of dark and dripping forests at the frail safety of the sheltered circle of light.

The Willards' visitor started everyone off on their own stories of burglars, prowlers, kidnappers.

". . . so there was this fellow suddenly staring down the skylight, it was summer and the skylight was open, on West 23rd Street, and my friend ran up to the roof and chased him across the roofs and cornered him and the fellow whipped out a knife and it took five transfusions before he was out of danger. Of course, the police never found him."

". . . a loaded .45. Right next to my bed, at all times. These days, with all these crazy kids. Anybody who tries anything in my house is in for a hot welcome. And don't think I wouldn't shoot to kill."

". . . the chain on the door and everything from every single drawer and cupboard piled in a heap on the rug. And I can't tell you what else they did, in mixed company, but you can imagine. The police told them it was quite common, especially when they were disappointed in their haul. But of course, they were asking for it, living surrounded by all those Puerto Ricans."

". . . this was a long time ago, of course, when he had this Great Dane kennel, but the day after the Lindbergh kidnapping he sold every single dog he had in the place. At three times what he'd been asking before."

Glass in hand, Martin listened politely, realizing with some surprise that all these solid, comfortable people, in their cosy and orderly community, shared a general fear, a widespread uneasiness, and that the face outside the Willard window had made them all remember that there were obscure and unpredictable forces always ready to descend upon them in their warm homes and that, with all their locked doors and all their police and all their loaded .45's, they were exposed and vulnerable to attack.

"You've sent a delicious shiver down every spine," Linda said, coming over to Martin.

"Not so delicious," he said thoughtfully, looking around him at the serious home-owning faces. Linda, he saw, had made up her mind to take the whole thing lightly, after the rattled nerves of the night before and the fuss about the police. He admired her for it, but it worried him, and he didn't like the idea of leaving her out there in that pillared, echoing house surrounded by acres of wilderness, especially since Willard worked late in the city several times a week and didn't get home until midnight. After all, uncaught and unsuspected, there was nothing to stop the man from coming back a week from now, a month, two months. . . . On another rainy night, with no moon.

"We'd better be going now," Linda said. "We're expected for dinner at eight-thirty." She glanced slyly around the room. "Anybody you want to take? The Charles's said if you wanted to bring anybody, it's only a buffet supper, really...."

"No, thanks," Martin said, smiling. "They're all very nice, but..." Then he stopped. A tall, blond woman in a blue dress had just come into the room and was making her excuses to the hostess for being late. Her hair was done in a low bun on the back of her neck, making her look stately and old-fashioned. Her voice, as she made her explanations to the hostess, was murmuring and melodious, and she was by far the prettiest woman in the place. "Well," Martin said to Linda, grinning, "maybe that one. Give me ten minutes."

Linda shook her head. "No go, Brother," she said. "Her name is Anne Bowman, and she's married. And there's her husband at the door."

Linda gestured with her glass toward the door and Martin saw a tall man in a well-tailored dark suit, with his back to him, talking to Willard and the host.

"In that case," Martin said, taking a last look at the beautiful Mrs. Bowman, "we might as well leave now."

"You'll see her tomorrow," Linda said, as they made their way to the door. "I think Willard arranged a tennis game at their house tomorrow morning."

They pushed unobtrusively toward the door to pick up Willard, who was still talking to their host. Bowman had moved off several steps and was talking to a group nearby.

"We're going?" Willard said, when Linda and Martin came up to him. "Good, it's about time." He reached over and tapped Bowman on the shoulder. "Harry," he said, "I want you to meet my brother-in-law. He's coming over with me tomorrow to play tennis."

Bowman had his back to them, finishing a story, and it was a moment before he turned around, on a burst of laughter that the story had provoked from his listeners. He had a smile on his pale, well-kept face and he put out his hand to Martin. "This is a pleasure," he said, "I've heard so much about you. Your sister tells me all. Is it true, as she says, that you once nearly took a set from Herb Flam?"

"We were both twelve years old at the time," Martin said, keeping his face straight and trying to act naturally, like anybody else leaving a cocktail party and responding in the ordinary way to an ordinary and casual introduction. It wasn't easy, because after ten seconds of looking at the candid, healthy, successful face in front of him, he was sure that Bowman was the man he had seen outside the window the night before.

"Get a good night's sleep," Bowman was saying to Willard. "We'll have a hot doubles." He leaned over and kissed Linda goodbye, familiarly, on the cheek. "You can bring your boys," he said to her. "They can play with our kids. They won't be in the way." He waved and turned back to the people he had been talking to, mannerly, well-dressed, at home, surrounded by friends, the sort of man, pushing a robust forty, you might see at the reunions of a good college or behind a vice-president's desk of one of those polite businesses where everybody has a deep rug on the floor and where money is only mentioned in quiet tones and behind closed doors.

Martin walked silently out of the house behind Willard and his sister, not responding when Willard said, "He plays a damn good game, especially doubles. He doesn't like to run too much any more." And he was still silent in the car going over to the dinner party, trying to piece everything together and wanting solitude and reflection for it, remembering Bowman's open and untouched smile as he shook hands, remembering the hard feel of Bowman's dry, tennis-player's hand, remembering the familiar, habitual way Bowman had kissed Linda good night.

"Linda," Willard was saying, at the wheel of the car, as they bumped along the narrow country road toward the dinner party, "you must promise me one thing."

"What's that?" Linda asked.

"You must promise to announce, each time we set out for a cocktail party, 'Willard, you are too old for gin.'"

At the dinner party Martin had to repeat, for the benefit of the guests who had not been at the Slocums' for cocktails, his description of the man he had seen outside the window. This time he made it as vague as possible. It was not easy. Bowman's face and figure (aged nearly forty, blue eyes, sandy hair cut close, wide, smiling mouth, white, even teeth, height nearly six feet, weight probably about one seventy-five, complexion fair, shoulders broad, general impression—good citizen, father of family, responsible businessman) kept crowding in, the statistics, recognizable, damaging, on the tip of his tongue, making it difficult to recall the hazy generalities by which he had described the man until then. But there was no sense, Martin decided, in damning the man so soon and it would only lead to trouble if even a random word of his cast suspicion on Bowman before he made absolutely certain that Bowman was the man he had seen.

On the way home with Linda and Willard, and over a nightcap before going up to bed, he decided not to say anything to them yet, either. Staring at his sister, he remembered how anxious she had been not to call the police, how she had fought Willard about it and won, how she had leaned over to be kissed by Bowman at the door as they were leaving the cocktail party. She and Willard slept in separate rooms, he remembered, both giving on the balcony, and Willard stayed in town late two or three times a week. . . . Martin was ashamed of himself for the speculation, but he couldn't help it. Linda was his sister and he loved her, but how well did he know her, after all these years? He remembered his own sensuality and the regrettable things he had done, himself, because of it. She was his sister, however innocent and wifely and delightful she seemed, and the same blood ran in both of them. No, he thought, wait.

They were on the tennis court at eleven o'clock the next morning, Willard and Martin playing against Bowman and a man called Spencer, who had a big service but nothing much beyond that. Bowman turned out to be agile and crafty and played with a good-humored enjoyment of the game, whether he was winning or losing.

Martin and Willard had brought over the two boys and they played at the edge of the court with the Bowman's three children, two boys and a girl, ranging in age from six to eleven, all three of them rather pale and subdued, too polite and reserved, Martin thought, for children their age.

After the second set, Mrs. Bowman, looking surprisingly formal in a dark cotton dress with a white collar under her heavy bun of rich, dark blond hair, came out of the house with a tray with orangeade in a pitcher and some glasses. She stayed for some time, watching the game, and while she was there Martin made more errors than usual, because he kept glancing over at her, studying her, trying, almost unconsciously, to catch an exchange of looks between her and her husband, a sign, an indication. . . . But she sat there quietly, not saying anything, not applauding the good shots or commenting on the bad ones. She seemed to pay no attention, either, to the five children playing around her, and after a while, she got up, in the middle of a point, and wandered back toward the house, tall, curiously elegant, unattached, a silent and decorative figure on the sweeping green lawn which led up to the big, white, pleasant house.

The wind sprang up during the third set and made lobbing and overheads difficult and they decided to quit. They all shook hands and went over to the side of the court and drank their orangeade. The two Willard boys climbed all over their father, clamoring for a drink, but the Bowman children stood off at a little distance, silently, watching their father, and only coming over when he had poured a glass of the orangeade for each of them and called to them to come and drink it. They said, "Thank you," in hushed voices and retired again to sip their drinks.

"It's too bad you won't be here all summer," Bowman said to Martin, as they sat at the edge of the court with their drinks. "You'd raise the level of the tennis around here considerably. You might even get your poor old brother-in-law up to the net once in a while." He chuckled good-naturedly, winking at Martin and wiping the sweat off his forehead with a towel.

"I have to be in Paris by the end of the week," Martin said, watching Bowman's face for a change of expression, a flicker of relief.

But Bowman merely kept wiping his face with the towel, placidly, smiling. "We'll miss you," he said, "especially on weekends. But, anyway, you're coming to dinner this evening, aren't you?"

"He's set on catching the six o'clock to New York," Willard said.

"Oh, that's silly," said Bowman. "We're having a barbecue in the garden. If it doesn't rain. Stay another night. New York is dead on Sunday, anyway." He sounded friendly, hospitable.

"Well," said Martin, deciding suddenly, "maybe I will."

"That's the boy," Bowman said heartily, as Willard

looked at Martin, mildly surprised. "We'll try to make it worth your while. I'll warn the dull country folk they have to put their best foot forward. All right, children," he called. "Ready for lunch."

On the way home, Willard looked over from the wheel. "What made you change your mind, Martin?" he asked. "Mrs. Bowman?"

"She is beautiful, isn't she?" Martin said, going along with his brother-in-law.

"Every one of the local Don Juan's has tried his luck," Willard said, grinning. "Zero."

"Daddy," asked the older boy from the back seat, "what's a Don Juan?"

"He was a man who lived a long time ago," Willard said briskly.

During the afternoon, Martin asked as many questions as he dared about the Bowmans. He found out that they had been married fourteen years, that they were rich (Mrs. Bowman's family owned cotton mills and Bowman himself ran the New York office), that they gave many parties, that they were liked by everybody, that the Willards saw them two or three times a week, that Bowman, unlike some of the other husbands of the community, never seemed the least bit interested in other women.

While he was dressing for the evening, Martin felt himself growing more and more baffled. When he had first seen Bowman at the party the night before, Martin had been sure Bowman was the man who had stared up at him from outside the living-room window, and when he had first seen him that morning on the tennis court the certainty had grown. But the house, the wife, the children, the things that Willard and Linda had said about Bowman, above all, the candid and relaxed manner in which Bowman had greeted him and pressed him to come to dinner, the transparent good humor, with no hint of any shadow beneath it, all conspired to shake Martin. If it really had been Bowman, he must surely have recognized Martin and been almost certain that Martin had recognized him. After all, they had stared at each other, both of them in a strong light, for a full ten seconds, at a distance of five feet. And if it had been Bowman, it would have been so easy for him to have called off the tennis game, to have telephoned and said he had a hangover, or there was too much wind, or with a dozen other excuses.

"Oh, hell," Martin said to himself, knotting his tie in front of the mirror, knowing he had to do something and do it that night, but feeling rushed, isolated, unsure of himself, on the verge of acts which might have grotesque, perhaps tragic consequences. When he went downstairs, Willard was alone in the living room reading the Sunday papers and Martin was tempted to tell him everything and get some of the load of responsibility off his own shoulders. But just as he was about to talk, Linda came in, ready for the party, and he had to keep quiet. He went out to the car with them, still carrying the whole thing himself, wishing he had two weeks more, a month, to observe, to move carefully, to act discreetly and with decision. But he didn't have two weeks. He had one night. For the first time since he had decided to quit his job in California he bitterly regretted that he was going to France.

The party was a big one, with more than twenty people. The night was warm enough and they were all outside on the lawn, which was set with tables and hurricane lamps in which candles burned, throwing a soft, generous light on the guests grouped around them, while two waiters the Bowmans had hired for the occasion hurried back and forth from the big barbecue at the end of the garden at which Bowman, dressed in a chef's apron and pink with the heat of the fire, was broiling steaks.

Martin sat at the same table with Mrs. Bowman, between her and a pretty young woman by the name of Winters who kept flirting with a man at the next table. In the middle of the meal, Martin was surprised to learn that the man Mrs. Winters was flirting with was her own husband. Mrs. Bowman talked to Martin about France, where she had been, as a girl, before the war, and once again, some five years before. It turned out that she was interested in tapestries and told Martin he must go to Bayeux to see the great ones in the cathedral there and to the Museum of Modern Art in Paris, where there were examples of some of the work that contemporary artists had done in the same field. Her voice was soft, gentle, rather flat and uninflected and you felt that even on other, more intimate subjects, she probably would speak in the same melodious, murmuring, impersonal, changeless tone, like a song in a minor key, restricted arbitrarily to one low octave.

"Do you plan to go to France again, soon?" Martin asked.

"No," she said. "I don't travel any more."

She turned to the neighbor on her right and Martin didn't get a chance to ask her why she didn't travel any more, and the sentence stood like that, flat, definite, a statement of policy. For the rest of the meal the conversation was general at the table and Martin joined in it sporadically, his eyes from time to time straying over to the table at which Bowman presided, in his white apron, flushed, speaking a little loudly, busy with the wine bottle, laughing easily at his guests' jokes, never looking in the direction of the table at which his wife sat, next to Martin.

It was nearly midnight and some of the guests had already left when Martin finally got a chance to talk to Bowman alone. Bowman was standing at a table that had been put alongside the wall of the house to serve as a bar and was pouring himself a brandy. He had taken his apron off and after he had poured the brandy he stood there staring down at it, his face pale once more and suddenly fatigued and remote, as though for the moment he had forgotten the party, his role as host, his departing guests. Martin came up to him, ready to use the opening he had been planning for the last half-hour.

"Mr. Bowman," he said.

For a second or two Bowman didn't seem to hear him. Then he shook himself, almost imperceptibly, and raised his head and put on the easy, friendly smile he had been using all evening.

"Harry, boy," Bowman said, "Harry."

"Harry," Martin said dutifully.

"Your glass is empty, boy," Bowman said, reaching for the brandy bottle.

"No, thank you," Martin said. "I've had enough."

"You're right," said Bowman. "Brandy keeps you from sleeping at night."

"I've been thinking," Martin said, "about your problem."

"Uh . . . what's that?" Bowman squinted at him.

"About your tennis court," Martin said quickly. "I mean about the fact that it's on a rise and as soon as a wind comes up, like today . . ."

"Oh, yes," Bowman said. "It's a nuisance, isn't it? I guess we put it in the wrong place, exposed to the north, but the builder insisted. I don't know, something about drainage. . . ." He waved his hand vaguely, then sipped his brandy.

"You know," Martin said, "I think I could show you how to fix it."

"Oh, you could? Good. Very kind of you."

Bowman was speaking a little thickly now. "You must come over some day and we'll . . ."

"Well," Martin said, "I'm leaving tomorrow and . . ."

"Oh, yes, of course." Bowman shook his head as though irritated with himself for his lapse of memory. "France. The city of light. I forgot. Lucky boy. At your age."

"I thought," Martin said, "if you wanted to come with me now, it would only take a minute or two. . . ."

Bowman put his glass down thoughtfully, then peered into Martin's face, blinking a little.

"Of course," he said. "Very good of you."

They started through the garden, among the tables, in the direction of the tennis court, whose fence made a distant, spikey tracery of iron poles and wire against the starlit sky some hundred yards away.

"Martin," Linda called, "where're you two off to? It's time to go home."

"I'll be back in a minute," Martin said.

He and Bowman walked up the gentle slope toward the tennis court, their footsteps silent in the dewy grass.

"I hope it wasn't too boring for you," Bowman said. "The party. I'm afraid there weren't enough young people. There're never enough young people. . . ."

"It wasn't boring at all," Martin said. "It was a wonderful party."

"Was it?" Bowman shrugged. "Well, you have to do something," he said, obscurely.

They were at the tennis court now, and the quarter moon made a shadowy pattern of the base lines. There was no wind and it was very still up there and the sounds of the dying party among the candles a hundred yards away were small but clear in the distance.

"A friend of mine had the same problem," Martin said, watching Bowman closely, "on a court he built outside Santa Barbara and he put up a row of box-hedge along the north side. You don't get a shadow on the court that way. In a couple of years it was about eight feet high, and except for lobs, you could play a normal game, even when the wind was really bad. And you put it back about two feet from the fence, so it doesn't stick through and the balls don't get lost in it. Right about there, I'd say," Martin said, pointing.

"Ah, yes. Good idea." Bowman said. "I'll talk to the gardener this week." He was fiddling with his trouser zipper. "Join me?" he said. "One of the most satisfactory of pleasures. Adding to the dew in the moonlight in this over-mechanized age."

Martin waited silently until Bowman had zipped up his trousers again and said, brightly, "There we are," like a child after a small praiseworthy achievement. "Now, I'd better get back to my guests."

Martin put out his hand and held Bowman's arm. "Bowman," he said.

"Huh?" Bowman stopped, sounding surprised.

"What were you doing outside my sister's window Friday night?"

Bowman pulled away a little and turned and faced Martin, his head to one side, looking puzzledly at Martin. "What's that?" He laughed. "Oh, it's a joke. Your sister never told me you were a joker. In fact, I got the impression from her that you were rather a solemn young man. It worried her, she told me once, now I remember. . . ."

"What were you doing outside the window?" Martin repeated.

"Boy, I'm afraid you'd better go home now," Bowman said.

"All right," said Martin. "I'll go home. But I'll tell my sister and Willard it was you, and I'll call the police and I'll tell them."

"You're becoming something of a pest, boy," Bowman said lightly, smiling in the moonlight. "You'll just embarrass everybody. Yourself, most of all. Nobody'll believe you, you know."

"My sister'll believe me. And Willard." Martin started back toward the candlelit garden. "We'll see about the rest." He heard Bowman's steps behind him.

"Wait a minute," Bowman said.

Martin stopped and the two men faced each other in silence.

Then Bowman chuckled drily. "Is that why you decided to stay another night, boy?"

"Yes."

Bowman nodded. "I thought so." He rubbed his face with the back of his hand, making a little dry, unshaven sound. "All right," he said in a flat voice. "Supposing it was me. What do you want?"

"I want to know what you were doing there." Martin said.

"What's the difference?" Bowman said. Now he sounded like a stubborn and unreasonable child and his voice had taken on a whining, high tone. "Was anything stolen? Was anything broken? Let's put it this way—I was paying a visit."

"With a ladder?" Martin said. "That's a hell of a visit."

"People shouldn't leave ladders lying around." Bowman said wearily. "Why don't you leave me alone? Why don't you go to France and leave me alone?"

"What were you doing there?" Martin persisted.

Bowman waved both his hands, clumsily, in a broken gesture. "I was on my rounds," he said.

"For the last time," Martin said, "I tell you I'm going to go to the police."

Bowman sighed. "All I ever do is watch," he said, whispering. "I never hurt anyone. Why don't you leave me alone, boy?"

"What do you mean, watch?"

Bowman chuckled, almost soundlessly. "I watch the happy ones," he said. Now he sounded coquettish, like a young girl, and Martin, for the first time, began to wonder about the sanity of the man standing beside him on the moonlit dewy grass. "You'd be surprised," Bowman said, as though imparting a secret, "how many happy people there seem to be around here. All ages, all sizes, all religions. . . . They go around with big smiles on their faces, they shake each other's hands, they go to work in the morning and kiss their wives at the station when they come home, they sing at parties, they put money in the collection box at church, they make speeches at the parent-teachers' association meetings about how to bring up the younger generation, they go off together on vacations, they invite their friends in, they make love, they deposit money in the bank and buy insurance, they make deals, they tell each other how successful they are, they buy new houses, they greet their in-laws and baptize their children, they get checked for cancer every twelve months, they all seem to know what they're doing, what they want, where they're going. . . . Like me." He chuckled again, the same rasping chuckle. "The major question is, who're they fooling? Who am I fooling? Look at me." He came close to Martin, his breath, freighted with gin and wine and brandy, hot in Martin's face. "The biggest house in the neighborhood, the prettiest wife. I'm proud to say ten men around here've made passes at her and she's never as much as blinked an eye. Three children who say 'Yes sir, no sir,' and recite their prayers at night, if I die before I wake, and remember Mommy and Daddy. And it's all a show. Don't believe a minute of it. Sometimes I make love to my wife and it doesn't mean anything. One animal falling on another animal in the jungle. One driven, the other—what shall I say —resigned. No more than that. I get up from her bed and I go to my bed and I'm ashamed of myself, I don't feel like a human being. Can you understand that? I'm drunk, I'm drunk, but if I ever was honest when I was sober, I'd say the same thing. And what does it mean to my wife? She's more interested in whether she's going to buy green curtains next year for the dining room than whether I live or die. I have the feeling when I go to work in the morning, she has to stop and think hard three times a day to remember my name. And my children—they're a separate state, behind frontiers, waiting for the appropriate time to declare war. Surprise—drop the bomb and kill daddy. It's normal. Read the papers. Children kill their fathers every day. To say nothing of abandoning them and letting them die. Look at the populations of the old peoples' homes. The incurable wards. I sit in an office all day, I hire people and fire them, I make important, business-like gestures, and right behind me all the time, what is there—a blank, a big blank."

Martin stepped back a little, feeling smothered by the alcoholic breath, by the sudden, racing spill-over of language from this man who until that moment had sounded more or less like everyone else Martin had met during the weekend. "Still," he said, wondering if Bowman was cunningly sidetracking him with this incoherent, rambling, pitiable confession, "what's that got to do with climbing balconies and looking in at windows?"

"I'm looking for an answer." Bowman grinned slyly. "I'm an explorer, looking for an oasis in the middle of the great American desert. I'm an optimist. I believe there's an answer. I believe that some people aren't fooling. They seem happy and they *are* happy. Only you have to catch them by surprise, boy, when they don't know you're watching them, to find out the secret. Anybody puts a smile on his face when he knows you're watching him, like getting your picture taken in front of a monument on vacation. The beast in his natural habitat. Preferably at a significant moment, as the photographers say, when the secret is laid bare. Sitting having a cup of coffee late at night in the kitchen talking over what his life is like with his wife. Is there love on his face, hate, boredom? Is he thinking of going off to Florida with another woman? Helping his ten-year-old son with his homework. What does his face reveal? Does he have any hope? Making love. Do they show the tenderness of human beings, do they touch each other with benevolence and gratitude, or is it one animal falling on another animal, like my wife and myself?"

"You mean to say," Martin asked incredulously, "that you try to watch at times like that?"

"Of course," Bowman said calmly.

"You're crazy," Martin said.

"Well, if you're going to talk like that . . ." Bowman shrugged, sounding aggrieved and misunderstood. "There's no sense in trying to explain to you. What's crazier—living the way I do, year after year, not feeling anything, thinking, Somebody has the secret, it's there, I just have to find out, and doing something about it. Or just giving up, surrendering. . . . What is it? Is the whole thing a blank? For everybody? Do you know? Maybe you ought to watch outside a couple of windows yourself sometime," Bowman said contemptuously. "With that honest, eager California face of yours. Stay here—I'll take you around with me. *You*'ll get the inside dope on some of the people right there now—" He gestured toward the candlelit garden. "That pretty one who was on your right during dinner. Mrs. Winters. The one that's hanging all over her husband all the time and laughing at his jokes as though he made a million dollars a year on television and holding his hands at parties as though they're going to be married three days later. I've been there, I've been there. . . . You know what they do when they get home at night?"

"I don't want to hear," Martin said. He had liked Mrs. Winters.

"That's all right," Bowman said mockingly. "It won't offend your pristine sense of modesty. They never say a word. She goes upstairs and takes a handful of pills and greases her face and puts a mask over her face to sleep and he sits downstairs by himself, with one light on, drinking whiskey straight. And after he's knocked off half a bottle he lies down on the couch with his shoes on and sleeps. I've been there four times and it's been the same each time. Pills, whiskey, silence. The public lovebirds. God, it makes me laugh. And the others . . . even when they're alone. You don't know our minister, do you, the Right Reverend Fenwick?"

"No," Martin said.

"No, of course not. We played tennis today instead of worshipping." Bowman chuckled. "I made a call on the man of God a few Sundays ago. His bedroom is on the ground floor. He's a marvelous-looking gray-haired gentleman. If you were casting somebody to play the Pope in a movie, he'd get the job in five minutes. Always with a soft humble smile on his face, and divine forgiveness radiating out from him all over the state of Connecticut. And what do you think he was doing when I looked in on him? He was standing in front of a full-length mirror with only his shorts on, pulling his gut in, looking at himself critically and approvingly in profile. You'd've been surprised what good condition he's in, he must do fifty pushups a day. Standing there, pushing his hair forward in little dabs, like a woman making up, to get that effect of other-worldly carelessness he's famous for. He always looks as though he's too busy communicating with God to pay attention to mundane things like combing his hair. And he was making faces at himself and raising his hands in holy benediction, practicing for next Sunday's performance, just about naked in his shorts, with legs like an old fullback. The old faker. I don't know what I hoped for. Maybe to find him on his knees, praying, in communion with God, with some secret happiness showing on his face that never is quite there in church. For the joys of the flesh," Bowman said, switching abruptly, speaking in a confidential whisper, leaning toward Martin in the darkness. "I tried our African cousins. . . ."

"What're you talking about?" Martin asked, puzzled.

"Our colored population," Bowman said. "Closer to the primeval push. Simpler, I thought, less inhibited. The Slocums have a colored couple. You saw them passing drinks last night. About thirty-five years old, both of them. The man's huge, he looks as though he could move walls with his bare hands. And the woman's beautiful. Oversized, black, with great big breasts and a fantastic behind. I've sat behind them in the movies and when they laugh it's like cannon going off in a twenty-one-gun salute. You'd think that if you saw them in bed together you'd shrivel with shame at your own white, niggling, sin-haunted, worn-out, puritanical gropings. Well, I saw them once. They have a room back of the kitchen at the Slocums' and you can get up real close. I saw them, and they were in bed together all right, only all they were doing was reading. And do you know what she was reading?" Bowman laughed breathlessly. "She was reading *The Second Sex*. That's that French book about how badly women have been treated since the Pleistocene Age. And he was reading the Bible. The first page. Genesis. In the beginning, there was the Word." Bowman laughed again, sounding delighted with his story. "I went back a couple of times, but they had the curtains drawn, so I don't know what they're reading these days. . . ."

"Harry! Harry!" It was Mrs. Bowman's voice, calling. She was standing, a white blur in the moonlight, about thirty yards from them. "What're you doing out there? People're going home."

"Yes, dear," Bowman called. "We're coming right away. I'm just coming to the tag line of a joke with young Martin, here. I'll be right along."

"Well, hurry. It's late." Mrs. Bowman turned and walked through the moonlight back toward the house. Bowman watched his wife silently, his eyes brooding and puzzled.

"What did you want from my sister and Willard?"

Martin asked, shaken by everything he had heard, no more certain now about what he should do than when he had arrived that evening.

"They were my last hope," Bowman said in a low voice. "We'd better get back to the party." He started across the lawn, Martin walking at his side.

"If ever two people seemed"— Bowman hesitated. —"*connected*—dear to each other, *pleasurable* to each other . . . I've come home on the same train with Willard in the evening and the wives're waiting, and your sister always seems to be a little apart, preparing herself, almost, and something happens to her face when she sees him. . . . They're not all over each other, of course, like the Winters, but once in a while they touch each other with their fingertips. And with their boys . . . They know something, they've found something, that I don't know and I haven't found. When I see them, I have the feeling that I'm on the verge. It's almost there, I almost have it. That's why you nearly caught me the other night. God, I've been doing this for years and nobody's ever come close. I'm careful as a cat. But that night, watching all three of you in the living room, late at night, I forgot where I was. When you came to the window, I . . . I wanted to smile, to say . . . to say, yes, good for you . . . Ah, maybe I'm wrong about them, too."

"No," Martin said, thoughtfully, "you're not wrong."

They were close to the candlelit tables by now and somebody had turned on the radio inside the house and from a loudspeaker on the terrace music was playing and several couples were dancing. Willard and Linda were dancing together, lightly, not close to each other, barely holding each other. Martin stopped and put his hand on Bowman's arm to halt him. Bowman was trembling and Martin could feel the little shudders, as though the man were freezing, through the cloth of his sleeve.

"Listen," Martin said, watching his sister and her husband dance, "I ought to tell them. And I ought to tell the police. Even if nobody could prove anything, you know what that would mean to you around here, don't you?"

"Yes," Bowman said, his eyes on the Willards, longing, baffled, despairing. "Ah, do whatever you want," he said flatly. "It doesn't make any difference to me."

"I'm not going to say anything now," Martin said, sounding harsher than he felt, trying, for Bowman's sake, to keep the pity out of his voice. "But my sister writes me every week. If I hear that anybody has seen a man outside a window—once—just once . . ."

Bowman shrugged, still watching the dancers. "You won't hear anything," he said. "I'll stay home at night. I'm never going to learn anything. Why'm I kidding myself?"

He walked away from Martin, robust and demented, a spy lost in a dark country, his pocket crammed with confused intelligence, impossible to decipher. He walked slowly among the dancers, and a moment later, Martin heard his laughter, loud, genial, from the table that was being used as a bar and around which three or four of the guests were standing, including Mr. and Mrs. Winters, who had their arms around each other's waists.

Martin turned from the group at the bar and looked at his sister and her husband, dancing together on the flagstone terrace to the soft, late-at-night music, that sounded faraway and uninsistent in the open garden. Looking at them with new understanding, he had the feeling that Willard did not feel the need of leading, or Linda of following, that they moved gently and irresistibly together, mysteriously enclosed, beyond danger.

Poor Harry, he thought. But even so, he thought, starting over to Linda to tell her he was ready to go home, even so, tomorrow I'm buying them a dog.

Wistful, Delicately Gay

The phone rang, and Miss Drake answered it. Miss Drake is my secretary. She was presented to me on Christmas, when I was made a junior partner in Ronaldson, Ronaldson, Jones and Muller. She has her desk in my office. My office is only nine by eight feet and it does not have a window of its own, but she is a sign that I am advancing in life, and I still find myself looking over at her with the same gloating sense of ownership and achievement that a yachtsman has in looking at the first cup he won in a big regatta.

"Mr. Royal," Miss Drake said, "it's for you. A Miss Hunt." She has a provocative, half-scolding, half-indulgent way of talking to me whenever a woman asks for me on the telephone, even when it's my wife.

A Miss Hunt.

I hesitated a moment, weighing dangers.

Miss Drake waited. She was new to the firm, and Carol Hunt on the telephone was only a Miss Hunt to her. She was not yet well enough established in the office hierarchy to have heard all the gossip. Or perhaps the gossip was so old that even the most malicious or most loose-tongued of the secretaries had forgotten it or at least considered it so worn it would only be trotted out when everything else had been exhausted. After all, it was almost two years ago....

Pain has its own rules, and those people who tell you the human race seeks to avoid it do not, of course, know what they're talking about.

"Shall I tell her you're busy?" Miss Drake asked, holding her hand over the phone. She is one of those girls who eventually have to be fired because they do too much thinking for their employers.

"No," I said, hoping my face was my usual weekday business face. "I'll speak to her."

Miss Drake flipped a lever and I picked up the phone, and there was Carol's voice, after two years. "Peter," she said, "I hope you don't mind my calling you."

"No," I said. Whatever I felt, "mind" was not the word to describe it.

"I've debated with myself for weeks," she said, "and I've put it off and put it off, and today's the last day and I just had to talk to you." Her voice was the same—low, trained, musical, sensual, and I turned in my chair so Miss Drake couldn't see my face. I closed my eyes, listening, and the two years, slippery, lost, painful, slid dangerously away, and Carol Hunt was calling me to tell me to meet her at the bar near her house on Second Avenue, calling me to remind me we were expected for lunch on Sunday in Westport, calling me to tell me she loved me. . . .

"I'm leaving this afternoon, Peter," the voice went on, flowing, grave, with its sunny echoes of childhood that had once given me so much pleasure, "and if it isn't too much bother for you, I'd love to see you. Just for a few minutes. There's something I want to tell you."

"Leaving?" I wished Miss Drake would get out of the office. "Where to?"

"I'm going home, Peter," Carol said.

"Home?" I asked stupidly. Somehow, it had always seemed to me Carol's only home was New York City.

"San Francisco," she said. "My train leaves at three-thirty."

I looked at the clock on my desk. It was eleven-fifteen.

"Look," I said, "I'll take you to lunch." As I said it, I decided I wouldn't tell Doris. After six and a half months of marriage, a man is entitled to one lie.

"I can't make lunch," Carol said.

There was no point in arguing with her. Whatever other changes the two years had made in her, I was sure that hadn't changed.

"When?" I said. "When and where do you want me to meet you?"

"Well, the train leaves from Pennsylvania Station," she said. "Do you want to meet me across the street, in the Statler bar, at"— She hesitated, as though she were going over in her mind exactly what she had to say to me, and timing it, like the director of a radio program with a stop watch. —"At say, two thirty?"

"Two thirty," I said. Then I made one of those jokes that wake you up at night and make you squirm in your bed. "What'll you be wearing?" I asked. "In case I don't recognize you." I suppose I wanted to prove the two years hadn't damaged me as much as they had damaged me. Or maybe was just trying to sound brainlessly hard-boiled because that was the style; everybody we know tries, as much as possible, to sound brainlessly hard-boiled.

There was a silence on the phone, and for a moment I was afraid she had hung up.

Then she spoke. Her voice was flat and controlled and not affectionate. "I'll be wearing a smile," she said. "A wide, girlish, demolished smile. See you at two-thirty."

I put the phone down and I tried to work for another half-hour, but of course I couldn't work. Finally I stood up and put on my hat and coat and told Miss Drake I wouldn't be in till around four o'clock that afternoon. One advantage of being a junior partner at Ronaldson, Ronaldson, Jones and Muller is that you can occasionally take an afternoon or part of an afternoon off for private tragedy or celebration, if the tragedies and celebrations do not crowd each other with unbusinesslike frequency.

I walked aimlessly around the city, waiting for two-thirty. It was a clear, cold, sunny day, and New York had a winter glitter, a brilliance of light reflected off a million windows, a deep richness of northern shadow which made the city seem bold, busy, and entertaining. I wondered how Carol felt at that moment, knowing that in three hours she would be leaving the city.

I met her at a theatrical cocktail party in an apartment on Fifty-fourth Street. I was still new enough to New York so that I went to every party I was invited to. Harold Sinclair, who worked in the office with me, had a brother, Charley, who was an actor and who occasionally took us along with him when he was invited out. I liked theatrical parties. The girls were pretty, the drinks plentiful, and the people seemed bright, generous, and amusing, especially after a day spent among lawyers.

She was standing against a wall talking to an elderly woman with bluish hair who was, I later found out, the widow of a producer. I had never seen Carol Hunt before, on or off the stage, and she had not yet played any part important enough so that people would remember her name or point her out. I looked at her, and I was sure she was the most beautiful girl I had ever seen. Maybe I still think so.

She was not spectacular-looking, but she seemed to shine, in the corner of the crowded, smoky room, with a scrubbed, springtime health. She was small, blond, with a neat-brushed head and deep-blue eyes, and her movements were plain and unaffected, and as she talked to the producer's widow her eyes did not flicker hungrily over the room, as did the eyes of most of the other women there. She had a slender throat that rose out of the high collar of her dress, and her mouth, which had only a light touch of lipstick on it, seemed almost childish and delicately gay.

She gave the impression of being frail, innocent, and very young, and even though we were at a place in which almost all the people were connected in one way or another with the theater, I felt she was, like me, an outsider. I also felt that, because of the delicacy of her structure and coloring, I was the only one who realized how beautiful she was. I was, of course, wrong.

Three months later, I asked her to marry me.

In those three months, I met her almost every night, waiting for her at the stage door of the theater in which she was playing and taking her out, with a miser's wisdom, to supper in small, quiet restaurants. I watched her in her play six or seven times, and although she had only a small and undistinguished part, I came away each time with the feeling she was a superlatively talented actress.

Lovers become biographers, and in those three months of quiet midnights I ransacked her past, feeling, I suppose, that in discovering the modest details of her childhood and adolescence and the exact nature of her ambitions I was somehow making her more completely my own. The more

I learned about her the more I became convinced she was not only a beautiful girl but an extraordinary and valuable one.

Since the war I had had the uneasy impression that a good many of my friends, men and women alike, had allowed themselves to become soft, to drift, to limit their aspiration. While it was easy to find excuses in the unsteady climate of our times, I could not help feeling that quite a few of the people I liked best and was most attached to were, finally, useless and unworthy. So it was almost a sense of relief that, finding myself irrevocably in love with Carol Hunt, I found her at the same time to be so full of merit.

She had arrived in New York five years before, along with four thousand or forty thousand other girls. She was just out of college, and she had firmly told a young man who ran the eight-eighty faster than any other young man on the Pacific Coast that year, that she would not marry him. His name was Dean and he looked more like a movie star than a runner, Carol said, and his family owned a chain of hotels on the West Coast. As far as she could tell, carefully taking into account her youth and her inexperience and the natural pride that came with being offered a man who was the target for all the other girls she knew, she was in love with him. She had only five hundred dollars to her name and her father was dead and her mother had married a man who worked, not very prosperously, in an engineer's office, but she said no.

She said no because she wanted to go to New York and be an actress. She was aware of the banality of the ambition, aware, too, of the four thousand other girls who would descend upon the city that year with the same ambition and who would, along with the survivors and victors of previous years, compete with her in that dwindling arena for the few prizes of the season. She was aware of the size of the gamble, the stake she was risking (her youth; the fleet, well-loved young man; the chain of hotels, with everything that went along with it); she was aware of the role of luck in the profession, the waste of talent, the probability and pain of failure.

She had figured it all out, logically and hardheadedly, because she was a logical and intelligent girl and capable of thought, an attribute that, she knew, made her superior to almost all the other four thousand girls, and that, given the nature of the theater, would not help her to succeed over them. And after figuring it all out, she had taken her five hundred dollars out of the bank, kissed the mournful runner good-by, and sat up three days and four nights in a steamy coach and arrived in New York.

She did all this not because she was stagestruck or had any false notions about the gaiety of backstage life, or because she was adventurous and wanted to live in a strange, great city or meet the kind of men she would never be able to meet in San Francisco. She did it because she possessed, she was sure, great talent, because there was nothing else in the whole world she wished to do. She did it with the hard, sexless obsessiveness of an artist cleaving to his art.

She had figured it all out, logically and hardheadedly, small parts and did them acceptably or better or even did them as well as they could be done. But the satisfaction she derived from all this was tantalizing and incomplete. The necessity of subduing her powers, of which she was by now more confident than ever, to the modest, supporting tones of a bit-part actress left her with a sense of time wasted, opportunities lost, energies dissipated.

Three or four times she was called back for audition after audition for leading parts in plays in which other girls finally made great successes. But each time something happened—a star telegraphed from Hollywood that she would be available for the season; a girl who, in the eyes of the director, was a more likely match for the leading man, was discovered; an actress who had received rave reviews the season before suddenly closed on the road and stepped in.

Each time she disciplined her disappointment and impatience, accepted smaller roles, and did them with hidden fury, smeared, as she put it, with ingénue charm. Carefully, she made no enemies, displayed no grudges. When her chance came, when the jumble of events finally fell into the one, glittering pattern that would send her climbing upwards, she would have no offended director; no half-guilty, half-angry producer; no jealous character actress, unexpectedly standing in her way.

In the meantime, she tried television, but after she had been in three different programs, she turned down all other offers for jobs in that medium. She could have used the money, but the three programs had convinced her the damage she was doing herself was more than the money was worth. She had an accurate conception of how she worked best, and she knew she was one of those actresses who feel their way into a part, who need long rehearsals and weeks of reflection to master a role. It was not modesty but pride and reliance on her own powers of criticism that made her realize that, with the short days of rehearsal that were all the television people could afford, she played inadequately, even if the inadequacy, for the moment, was noted only by herself.

When, like almost every pretty girl around the theater, she was offered a screen test, she worked hard on it and was not displeased with the result when she saw it on the screen. The man who had arranged the test and who sat in the projection room with her when it was shown, was impressed, too. But he was an old man who had been in the business a long time and he had seen many pretty and talented girls.

"Very good," he said, "very good, indeed, Miss Hunt." He had a soft, polite voice and courtly manners, and he was used to discouraging hungry young people in the gentlest, most assuaging way. "But there would be objections on the Coast to the present nose."

"What?" Carol asked, surprised and a little hurt. She was proud of her nose and thought in some ways it was her best feature. It was quite long and a little arched, with tense, nervous-looking nostrils, and an artistic young man who had been attached to her had once told her it was like the noses of the great English beauties of the portraits of the eighteenth century. By a trifle, a shadow, it seemed to deviate to one side, but one had to study her face to realize this, and the slight irregularity gave, she was sure, an added note of interest to her face. "What's wrong with the nose?" she asked.

"It's a little long for film, my dear," the old man said gently, "and you and I know, don't we, that it is not plumb straight. It is a lovely nose and one you could be proud of all the days of your life," the old man went on, smiling, honeying the harsh, official impersonal truth with his own sweet-tempered, but personal and therefore finally valueless truth, "but the American public is not quite used to seeing young girls on film with noses of that particular quality."

"I could name you six stars," Carol said stubbornly, "with noses a lot funnier-looking than mine."

The old man smiled and shrugged. "Of course, my dear," he said. "But they are stars. They are personalities. The public accepts a personality all in one lump. If you were a star, we would assign publicity men to write poems to your nose. In a little while, it would be a priceless asset. When an unknown girl came into the office, we would say, 'Look, she has the Hunt nose. Let's hire her at once.'"

He smiled at her again, and she couldn't help smiling back, warmed, even at the moment of disappointment, by his absurd, gentle manner.

"Well," she said, getting up, "you've been very kind."

But the old man did not rise. He sat in the big leather chair, his hand absently touching the controls of the box that communicated with the operator in the projection booth, staring thoughtfully at her, doing the job he was paid to do. "Of course," he said, "something could be done."

"What do you mean?" Carol asked.

"Noses," the old man said, "while works of God, are susceptible to the intervention of man."

Now Carol saw he was embarrassed by what he was forced by his position to say, and was using this high-flown and rhetorical fashion of speaking to show her he was embarrassed. She was certain there were few actors or actresses who could embarrass this hard, gentle old man, and she was flattered by it.

"A plastic surgeon," the old man was saying, "a little snip here, a little scraping of bone there, and in three weeks you could almost be guaranteed a nose that would meet with anyone's approval."

"You mean," Carol said, "in three weeks I could have the standard, regulation-issue starlet's nose."

The old man smiled sadly. "More or less," he said.

"And what would you do then?"

"I would sign you to a contract," the old man said, "and I would predict quite a promising future for you on the Coast."

Quite, Carol noticed. *Quite a promising. He refuses to*

lie, even in his predictions. Almost as if the old man had put it into words, she could sense the images that were going through his head. The pretty girl on a contract, with her acceptable bobbed nose, being used for bathing-suit publicity stills, small parts, perhaps after a while for unimportant leads in unimportant pictures, for two, three, four years, then being let out to make room for other, newer, more acceptable pretty girls.

"No, thank you," Carol said. "I'm terribly attached to my present crooked long nose."

The old man stood up now, nodding, as though he was pleased, on his own, if not on the company's account, by her decision. "For the stage," he said, "it is faultless. Better than faultless."

"I'm going to confess something," Carol said candidly, more open with this old man than she had permitted herself to be with anyone else in the city. "The only reason I'm up here is that if you make a name for yourself in the movies, it's easier to go where you want to go in the theater. I've planned myself for the stage."

The old man stared at her, rewarding her candor with surprise, then approval. "So much the better for the stage," he said gallantly. "I'll call you again."

"When?" Carol asked.

"When you're a great star," he said lightly, "to offer you all the money in the world to work for us."

He put out his hand, and Carol shook it. He held her hand in both his for a moment, his face saddened, mischievous, regretful, touched by the memory of all the lovely, ambitious, courageous girls he had seen in the last thirty years. "Isn't it hell?" he said, grinning, patting her hand in his rosy hands.

"I too," I said, when she told me this story, "am attached to your present nose. And to your present hair. And to your lips. And to your—"

"Careful," she said. "Remember, one of the reasons I like you so much is that you're so restrained and legal."

So, for a little while longer, I remained restrained and legal.

With all her devotion to her talent, Carol was careful to keep it almost completely to herself. Obsessions, she explained one night, especially the obsession with one's own abilities and ultimate triumph, could very easily give a woman a reputation for harshness and egotism, and arouse resentment in the people one might eventually depend on for the big chance. And her quality, which she judged coolly and without conceit, was one of frailty, wistfulness, pathos, adolescence, romance. These were good things to have and great careers had been made in the theater with just such weapons, but there would be little chance to display them on stage if off stage she spoke with the assurance of a general in command of a victorious army or an evangelist preaching the certainty of hell.

So she carried her ambition with her as undeclared baggage, as a curious kind of magic, hidden food that nourished her only so long as no one suspected its existence. Actually, there was little strain in hiding it. Because her vanity was concerned only with her final full expression of herself on the stage, Carol sought no intermediate, meaningless social triumphs. At parties she never pressed for the center of attention, was kindly in her criticisms, made no attempt to steal away from other girls the occasional playwrights and directors whom they appeared with and who might be useful in obtaining parts. She was wary and fastidious with men and was, in male company, frail, wistful, pathetic, delicately gay, adolescent, romantic. And only part of this was cynical.

The three months of revelations served a double purpose. I am methodical by inclination and training, and I felt I was learning all there was to know about the girl I was going to ask, when the time was ripe, to marry me. What's more, everything I learned about her made her seem more valuable. The sobriety and purity of her purpose put her far above the aimless young women I had until then traveled with, and the courage and intelligence with which she handled herself would be, I felt, reassuring foundations for a marriage. And the combination of these rather austere virtues with her delicacy and youth I found charming and deeply touching.

As for her, the discovery, after five years of reticence, of a confidant who would not compete with her or betray her and who so plainly admired the very qualities she had to dissemble everywhere else, seemed to slacken a nervous tension in her and lift a burden from her shoulders. At first she was suspicious of my curiosity, then amused and grateful; and finally, I think, it seemed, as much as anything else, to bring her to the point where she told me she loved me.

We were sitting in my car in front of her apartment building on East Fifty-eighth Street when I asked her to marry me. It was a Sunday night, and I had picked her up at the theater in which she was rehearsing a play that was due to open in Boston in twenty days. Charley Sinclair was in the same play, and we had stopped off for a drink with him before driving on home across town from the theater. It was about eleven-thirty at night, in the autumn, and the street was dark and deserted and I felt, Well, this is as good a time as any.

I asked her, and she didn't say anything. She just sat neatly, in her big cloth coat, on her side of the front seat, looking straight ahead through the windshield at the dark street and the rows of lampposts.

It was the first time I had ever asked a girl to marry me and I wasn't quite sure of procedure, and it didn't look as though Carol was going to be any help at all.

"I'm doing this as a health measure," I said, smiling erratically to take the taint of ceremony off the moment and make it easier for her to say no if that was what she wanted to say. "I have to get up at seven o'clock in the morning to get to the office on time, and if I have to meet you for supper at eleven-thirty every night for a couple of more months I'm going to run down like a pitiful old 1925 Ford. I'm just not durable enough," I said, "to be a lovelorn young lawyer who keeps a lovelorn young actor's hours."

Carol sat there silently, looking through the windshield, her profile outlined by the lamplights.

"Give me a minute," she said at last. "I have something solemn to say."

"Take an hour," I said. "Take the whole blessed, beautiful night."

"I was waiting for you to say it," Carol said. "I wanted you to say it."

"What?" I said. "That my health was failing because of night work?"

"No. That you wanted to marry me."

"I have a brilliant idea," I said, moving toward her. "Let's get married next week, before you find out about my past or another war starts, and let's go someplace that's warm and lawyerless for our honeymoon. I can get six weeks since it's my first honeymoon."

"I can't get six weeks," Carol said. "That's part of the solemn thing I have to say."

"Oh," I sighed. "The theater. I forgot. Maybe," I said hopefully, "it'll be a turkey and close in Boston and we can fly to Sicily the day after—"

"It's not going to be a turkey," she said. "I think it's going to be a success. But even if it isn't I wouldn't leave New York for six weeks in the middle of the season."

"Okay," I said, "we'll have our honeymoon on Forty-fourth Street."

"You must listen," Carol said. "I want you to know now what it would be like if we got married."

"I know how it would be if we got married," I said. "Smashing."

"I want you to remember something. I mean to be a great actress."

"Hell," I said, "I'm not going to complain about that. I'm modern. If it was up to me, I'd throw open all the harems." I hadn't known how I was going to behave the first time I asked a girl to marry me, but I certainly never expected I'd be making one jittery joke after another.

"What I'm trying to say," Carol went on stubbornly, "is that if I get married it has to be on certain terms. Just as though I were a man—"

"Now, darling," I said, "nobody here is opposed to female suffrage or—"

"What I mean," Carol said, "is that I'm not going to be one of those girls who hang around the theater for a couple of years and then get married and have babies and move to the suburbs and talk about how they were actresses in New York for the rest of their lives—"

"Now, wait a minute, darling," I said. "Nobody's moving to the suburbs—"

"The main thing in my life," Carol said, "is not going to be my husband. It's going to be my work, just as the main thing in a man's life is, finally, his work. Is that okay with you?" she asked harshly.

"Dandy," I said. "I love it."

"It hasn't happened yet," Carol said, "but it's going to happen. My chance. And when it comes, I'm going to be there to jump at it. I'm not going to be off on vacations or tending babies or giving bridge parties. And if I have to go on the road with a play for a year at a time, because that's what I have to do—"

"Oh, lady," I groaned, "not tonight."

She had to laugh then and we kissed, and for a while we just sat there, close together, half-forgetting what she had been talking about, and when I said, "It'll work out all right," she nodded and kissed me again, and then we went to a bar to celebrate and we decided to get married sometime in June, at which time her play would probably have finished its run, anyhow.

When I left her at her door, I kissed her good night, and then, holding her, I said, very seriously, "One question, Carol . . ."

"Yes?"

"What happens," I asked, "if *nothing* happens? If your chance never comes?"

She hesitated a moment. Then she said soberly, "I'll be disappointed for the rest of my life."

The chance came a little more than three weeks later, in Boston, and it came in a way nobody predicted and it finished us.

We spoke over the phone almost every night, and the next to the last time I called her it was nearly one o'clock in the morning and she was in her hotel room. The play had opened two nights before, and she told me she had gotten a nice little notice in one of the evening papers, that Eileen Munsing, the star who had come back from the movies to play the lead, had received very good reviews and was no longer growing hysterical during rehearsals. She also told me she loved me and she was looking forward to Saturday, when I was coming up on the morning train for the weekend.

Twelve hours later, when I left my office to go out to lunch, I bought a newspaper and there, on the front page, was Carol's picture. The photograph of a man by the name of Samuel Borensen was next to it, and the reason the two pictures were together was that at four-thirty that morning Samuel Borensen had been found lying dead on the bed in Carol Hunt's hotel room in Boston.

Samuel Borensen's photo had been on the front pages of

the newspapers a good many times during his life—smiling, from airplane ramps on the way to conferences in Europe; patriotic, addressing banquets of leaders of industry; solemn, receiving honorary degrees from universities at commencement exercises. He was one of those people you think of as moving publicly from place to place, making pronouncements and running things. I had never met him and I hadn't known Carol knew him.

I looked carefully at his photograph. He looked fleshy, handsome, robust, and conscious of his own value. I read the account that went with the photograph and discovered he was fifty years old and he had a wife and two almost grown children in Palm Beach. Carol, according to the newspaper, was an attractive, youthful blond, at the moment appearing in *Mrs. Howard,* which was scheduled to open in two weeks in New York.

I threw the paper away and went back to my apartment and called Boston.

I was surprised I was put through immediately to Carol's room. Somehow I had the feeling that now Carol had made the front page of the newspapers she would be very hard to reach.

"Yes?" Her voice was calm, musical.

"Carol, this is Peter."

"Oh."

"Do you want me to come up there?" I asked. I tried to keep my voice free of accusation or judgment.

"No," she said.

"Do you want to explain anything?"

"No," she said.

"Well," I said, "good-by."

"Good-by, Peter."

I hung up. I took a drink, then called my office and told them I was going out of town for ten days. I had told people about our engagement, and they had read the newspapers down at the office by then and they said, "Sure, go ahead."

Then I got into the car and drove into Connecticut, to a little town where there was a pleasant hotel I had stopped at, the summer before, for lunch. I was the only guest, and I spent my time reading, taking walks, and looking out at the bare trees and the dead winter landscape.

I thought about Carol a good deal of the time. I went over our three months together, searching for clues I might have missed out of stupidity or infatuation, and I couldn't find a single one. Borensen's name hadn't come up once, I was sure, and whatever attachments she might have had with other men she must have broken off as soon as she met me, because I couldn't remember any time she hadn't been able to see me when I asked for a date.

Curiously, I wasn't angry. I was hurt, of course, and shaken, and for a time I thought of leaving New York and starting over somewhere else, but I found myself worrying more for her sake than for my own. The vision of Carol, frail, girlish, proper, caught up with doctors, policemen, reporters, and forced to come onto a stage to be devoured by the gossiping eyes of a new audience every evening kept me from sleeping at night. As for her career, I was sure it was finished. After five days alone in the empty hotel, I was thinking almost exclusively of Carol, and trying to figure out ways I could help her.

Love, I was finding out, does not stop conveniently, just because one day, on the way to lunch, you pick up a newspaper and see a girl's picture on the front page.

I was on the point of getting into the car and driving up to Boston to see for myself if there was anything I could do for Carol, when I remembered Charley Sinclair was in the same play. I called Harold Sinclair at the office for Charley's telephone number, and then I put in a person-to-person call for Charley in Boston. Before appearing there, it would help if I found out just what was happening to Carol and in just what way I could help her most. There was no question in my mind, of course, of going through with the marriage. I was going on a rescue mission, I told myself grimly, not as a garlanded sacrifice.

"Hi, Peter," Charley said when they finally put the connection through. "What's the good word?" He sounded surprised to hear from me.

"I'm all right," I said. "How is it up in Boston?"

"Standing room only for the last two nights," Charley said.

"I don't mean that," I said impatiently. Charley Sinclair is a kind of lightweight, and he has a knack for saying the wrong thing. I suppose that's why he became an actor. "How's Carol?"

"Blooming," Charley said. "She's being so brave and bereaved she'd make a statue weep gin."

I had always thought Charley liked her. I suddenly realized why Carol had always been so quiet about herself around theatrical people.

"How are they treating her?" I asked, forcing myself to be patient with him. "The people in the play, I mean?"

"Everybody's being so damned considerate," Charley said, "you'd think her father just died."

"Have they asked her to give notice?"

"Hell, no," Charley said. "They're just kicking themselves they didn't put her name up in lights. Why do you think we're selling out every night?"

"Are you kidding?" I still didn't believe him. I know strange things happen in the theater, but this was too much.

"Kidding?" he asked. "When she comes out on the stage, they make a funny little gurgling sound, and then it gets so quiet you'd think they'd all been strangled in their seats. And you can *feel* them following every move she makes, as though she had a private spotlight on her all night. And she brings down the house when she goes off. Eileen Munsing is ready to blow."

"I don't care about that," I said. "How is *she* taking it?"

"Who knows," Charley said coolly, "how that girl takes anything? If you're interested, the director says she's twenty times better than she ever was before."

"Well," I said lamely, "that's fine."

"Why?" Charley asked.

"One more question," I said, ignoring the "Why?" "Do you think people will hire her after this?"

"They'll fall all over themselves," Charley said. "Two agents have been up from New York already. You coming up?"

"No," I said.

"People die every day," Charley said. "Some give their bodies to science, some to art. Do you want me to pass on any word?"

"No," I said. "Thanks, Charley."

"You're a fine friend," Charley said. "You didn't ask me once how *I* was doing."

"How're you doing, Charley?"

"Lousy," he said. He chuckled coldly. You'd never think

he and his brother are in the same family. "See you in New York."

He hung up.

After that, there didn't seem to be any sense in hanging around an empty little hotel in Connecticut in the middle of the winter, and I drove to the city and went back to work. The first few days were not easy, and every time I came into a room I had the feeling people had been telling each other about me. Even now, two years after it happened, I still get suspicious if people break off their conversations when I approach them, and I find myself searching their faces for hidden signs of amusement or pity.

I hadn't intended to see Carol again, but on the opening night of her play, I was in the balcony, alone, hunching into myself a little, I suppose, hoping no one would recognize me. I paid very little attention to the play itself. I was waiting for Carol's entrance, and when it came I saw Charley Sinclair had been telling the truth. There was a rippling, hushing sound, and then a kind of riveted silence. And I saw what Charley meant when he said it was as though Carol had a private spotlight on her which followed her wherever she moved and sucked the attention of the audience to her, making even the plainest of her lines and least important of her movements take on a significance out of all proportion to her role.

And it was true, too, she was better than she had ever been. She looked beautiful, and she played with a new certainty and serenity, as though this sudden, intense focusing on her had deepened her talent.

At the curtain, she received almost as much applause as the star of the show, Eileen Munsing, and as I made my way out of the theater, I heard her name on people's lips again and again.

I bought all the papers the next day and saw she had received a great deal of notice, more than her part deserved. The critics, who were gentlemen and not gossip writers, said nothing about what had happened in Boston, and two of them went all the way about her, predicting stardom. And one critic, who, I was sure, Carol must have thought was the most perceptive man in New York that morning, even used the words *frail, wistful, romantic*, and *gay*.

My own reaction was one of neither pain nor pleasure.

WISTFUL, DELICATELY GAY

I was numb and I was curious, and I think I was searching, both at the theater and in the papers the next day, for a key to where I had gone so wrong.

I didn't see Carol after that, but I followed her on the theatrical pages, and I was not surprised when I read she was leaving the cast of *Mrs. Howard* to take the leading part in a new play. I went to the opening of that play, too, and I had a feeling first of surprise, then of gratification, at seeing Carol's name so large on the billboards. Even though we were completely broken apart, I suppose I was still being influenced by the faith I had put in her talent and was pleased to see it justified so soon.

The producers had cast her shrewdly. She played a young girl who was sweet and pathetic for two and a half acts and turned out at the end to be a bitch. They had cast not only her qualities but her reputation, and she couldn't have been shown off to a better advantage.

The curious thing was she didn't quite come off. I don't know why, but although she seemed to be doing everything right and performed with an assurance and confidence you rarely see in a girl that young, the final result was disappointing. The audience was polite enough and the reviews the next day were not bad, but the man who played opposite her and a middle-aged character woman who came on only in the second act received more attention than Carol.

I thought all this would do her no harm and that in her next play or the one after, she would finally come into her own. But Charley Sinclair told me I was wrong.

"She's had it," Charley said. "She had her chance and she muffed it."

"I didn't think she was that bad," I said.

"She wasn't bad," Charley said, "she just wasn't good enough to carry a play. And now everybody knows it. Farewell."

"What will happen to her?" I asked.

"This play will flop in three weeks," he said, "and then, if she's smart, she'll go back, quick, to playing supporting parts. If she can get them. Only she won't be that smart, because nobody is, and she'll hang around waiting for a lead again, and some fool will give it to her and then they'll really take off her hide and pin it to the wall and she'd better learn how to type and take shorthand or find some man and marry him."

The fact that everything worked out as Charley said it would, made me think more highly of his intelligence, although it didn't make me like him any better. Carol did go into another play the following season and she did get mercilessly criticized. I didn't go to see her in the play, because I had met Doris by then and I felt there was no sense in looking for trouble.

I never saw her, even by accident, and I didn't come across her name again in the theatrical news and I stopped seeing Charley Sinclair, so that by the time Carol called me that morning in my office, I had no notion of what she had been doing with herself. When I happened to think of her, I recognized there was still a painful and dangerous spot on my memory, and I deliberately turned to other things.

I got to the Statler a little early and ordered a drink and watched the door. She came in exactly at two-thirty. She wore a beaver coat she hadn't had when I used to see her every night, and a neat and rather expensive-looking blue suit. She looked exactly as beautiful as I remembered her, and I noticed that as she walked through the room toward my table, most of the other men in the room looked longingly at her.

I didn't kiss her or even shake her hand. I suppose I smiled and said hello, but all I remember is that I kept thinking she hadn't changed as I awkwardly helped her take off her coat.

We sat side by side, facing out to the room, and she ordered a cup of coffee. She never drank very much, and whatever the experiences of the past two years had done to her, they hadn't pushed her to liquor. I turned on the banquette to look at her, and she smiled at me a little, knowing what I was doing, knowing I was searching her face for the marks of failure and regret.

"Well," she said. "How do you like it?"

"The same," I said.

"The same." She laughed a little, soundlessly. "Poor Peter."

I didn't want to get started on that. "What're you going to do in San Francisco?" I asked.

She shrugged, carelessly. That, at least, was something new, that gesture. "I don't know," she said. "Look for some kind of job. Hunt a husband. Reflect on my mistakes."

"I'm sorry it turned out this way," I said.

She shrugged again. "Hazards of the trade," she said. She looked at her watch, and we both thought of the train that was waiting to take her away from the city after seven years. "I didn't come here to cry on your shoulder," she said. "There's something I have to tell you about that night in Boston, to keep the record straight, and I haven't much time."

I sat, sipping at my drink, not looking at her, as she talked. She talked swiftly and without emotion, and never hesitated for a moment, as though every detail of what had happened that night would be clear in her memory, in its proper place, for the rest of her life.

She had been alone in her room, she told me, when I called her from New York, and after she had spoken to me she had looked over some changes in her part. Then she had gone to sleep.

When the knocking on the door awakened her, she lay still for a moment, first thinking she had been dreaming, then thinking that whoever it was must have mistaken her room for someone else's and would go away. But the knocking came again, light, guarded, persistent, unmistakable.

She switched on the light and sat up in her bed. "Who is it?" she called.

"Open the door, please, Carol." It was a woman's voice, low and urgent and muffled by the door. "It's me. Eileen."

Eileen, Eileen, Carol thought stupidly. I don't know any Eileens.

"Who?" she asked, still dulled by sleep.

"Eileen Munsing," came the whisper through the door.

"Oh," Carol said. "Miss Munsing." She jumped out of bed, and barefooted, in her nightgown, with the curlers in her hair, she went over to the door and threw it open. Eileen Munsing brushed past her, knocking against her in her hurry.

Carol closed the door and turned to face Eileen Munsing, standing next to the rumpled bed in the little room, her face blocked out in sharp light and shadow by the single bedside lamp. She was a handsome woman of thirty-five who looked like a handsome woman of thirty on the stage and a handsome woman of forty off the stage. The on-stage subtraction of five years was due to the bold modeling of the bones of her face and head and an almost visible reservoir of animal energy. The offstage addition of five years was due to drink, the bite of ambition, and according to report, a good deal of handling by men.

She was dressed in the black jersey skirt and sweater Carol had observed on her when they came up in the elevator together after the show and said good night to each other in the corridor. The door to Eileen Munsing's suite was about thirty feet away, across the corridor from Carol's room, on the front side of the hotel. Almost automatically Carol noticed Eileen Munsing was not drunk, her stockings were slightly twisted on her legs, a ruby pin she had been wearing on her shoulder earlier was no longer there. Also, her lipstick had just been put on, too lavishly and not quite accurately, and her wide mouth, almost black in the harsh light, seemed to be sliding unsteadily off to one side of her face.

"What is it?" Carol asked, trying to make her voice calm and soothing. "What's the matter, Miss Munsing?"

"I'm in trouble," the woman whispered. Her voice was hoarse and frightened. "Bad, bad trouble. . . . Who's in the next room?" She turned her head suspiciously toward the wall next to the bed.

"I don't know," said Carol.

"Anybody from the company?"

"No, Miss Munsing," Carol said. "We're the only ones from the company on this floor."

"Cut the Miss Munsing. I'm not your grandmother."

"Eileen," Carol said.

"That's better," said Eileen Munsing. She stood there, swaying slightly, staring at Carol as though she were slowly approaching a decision about her. Carol kept close to the door, feeling the knob in her back.

"I need a friend," Eileen said. "I need help."

"Anything I can do . . ."

"Don't be so sweet," said Eileen. "I need *real* help."

Carol felt very cold now, in her bare feet and thin gown, and she shivered. She wished the woman would go away.

"Put on something," Eileen Munsing said, as though she had made her decision. "And come back with me to my room, please."

"It's awfully late, Miss Munsing. . . ."

"Eileen."

"—Eileen. And I have to get up early tomorrow morning and—"

"What're you frightened of?" Eileen Munsing asked harshly.

"I'm not frightened," Carol said, lying. "It's just that there doesn't seem to be any reason—"

"There's a reason," said Eileen Munsing. "There's a very good reason. There's a dead man in my bed."

The man lay on the wide bed, on top of the blankets, his head turned a little on the pillow toward the door, his eyes open, an expression of almost smiling surprise on his face. His shirt and jacket were off, hung, with a solid navy-blue necktie, over the back of a chair, and one foot was bare. The other foot still had a sock on it, dribbled around the ankle, with a garter dangling from it. A pair of black shoes, neatly arranged, stood on the floor, half under the bed. He was an enormous man, with a fat, swelling diaphragm and oysterish skin, and he seemed too large, even for the big double bed.

He was about fifty years old, with stiff gray hair, and even though he was dead and half-naked, he looked like a successful and important man who was used to ordering people around.

Then Carol recognized him. Samuel Borensen. She had seen his photograph in the newspapers, and he had been pointed out to her in the lobby of the hotel two days before.

"He was starting to get undressed," Eileen Munsing said, staring bitterly at the bed, "and he said, 'I feel a little funny. I think I'll just lie down for a minute,' and then he died."

Carol turned her back to the bed. She didn't want to look at the flabby, domineering corpse any more. She had put on a negligee over her nightgown and fleece-lined slippers, but she was colder than ever. She wanted to get out of the room and back into her own bed and pull the covers up, warm, and not remember any more that anyone had ever knocked on her door. But Eileen Munsing barred the way, standing before the open door that led into the brightly lit living room of the large, two-room suite, filled with flowers, bottles, baskets of fruit, telegrams, because she was a star opening in a play everybody thought was going to be a hit.

"I've known him for ten years," Eileen Munsing was saying, glaring past Carol at the bed. "We've been friends for ten years, and then he goes and does something like that."

"Maybe he's not dead," Carol said. "Have you called the doctor?"

"A doctor!" Eileen Munsing laughed harshly. "That's just what we need. What do you think would happen if I called a doctor at three o'clock in the morning and he found Sam Borensen dead in Eileen Munsing's bedroom? What do you think the papers would be like tomorrow?"

"I'm sorry," Carol said, keeping her eyes resolutely turned away from the body. "But I think I'd better just go back to my room. I won't say anything and—"

"You can't leave me alone," Eileen Munsing said. "I'll jump out the window if you leave me alone."

"I'd love to help, if I could," Carol said, having difficulty, because her throat was dry and seemed to be contracting in little, sharp spasms when she tried to talk. "But I don't know what I could do. . . ."

"You can help me dress him," Eileen Munsing said flatly, "and get him back to his room."

"Miss Munsing?"

"He's too big for me to handle," Miss Munsing said. "I tried and I couldn't even get his shirt on. He must weigh two hundred pounds. He ate too much," she said fiercely, reproaching the still figure on the bed for all the appetites that had brought him to this place and left him there, intractable. "But between the two of us . . ."

"Where's his room?" Carol asked, fighting the spasms in her throat.

"On the ninth floor."

"Miss Munsing," Carol said, noticing she was still gasping. "We're on the fifth floor. That's four stories. Even if I *did* help, what could we do? We couldn't take him in the elevator—"

"I wasn't thinking of the elevator," Eileen Munsing said. "We could carry him up the fire-escape stairs."

Carol made herself turn and look at the dead man. He bulked on the blankets, looking huge, immovable, making the bed sag in the middle. If she had to get mixed up in something like this, Carol thought, why couldn't she pick a normal-size man.

"Not a chance," Carol said through the constricted throat. "The fire-escape stairs are way down at the other side of the building, and we never could carry him, we'd have to drag him." Even as she spoke she was surprised at herself for working so naturally on the problem, making herself responsible for joining, even in that limited way, the conspiracy. "We'd have to pass twenty rooms, dragging him, and somebody would be bound to hear or the night watchman would come by. And even if we got to the stairs, we'd never get him up even one flight—"

"We could leave him on the stairs," Eileen Munsing said. "They wouldn't find him until morning."

"You mustn't talk like that."

"Well, *what?*" Eileen Munsing said wildly. "Don't stand there grinning, telling me all the things I *can't* do."

Carol touched her face, surprised, as though to test, with her fingers, the quality of the expression. The effort of trying to talk through her fright and the dry spasms in her throat had contorted her mouth, and she supposed to Miss Munsing, in her state, it had looked like a smile.

"Is there anybody else from the company on this floor?" Eileen Munsing asked. "Any men?"

"No," Carol said. Seward, the producer, had gone down to New York for two days, and the other men were at another hotel. "Mr. Moss," Carol said, hopefully, remembering, "is staying here, though." Mr. Moss was playing the male lead opposite Miss Munsing.

"He hates me," Eileen Munsing said. "He's up on the tenth floor. Anyway, he's with his wife."

Carol looked at the traveling clock on the bed table, next to the pale, half-smiling twisted face. It was nearly four o'clock. "I'll tell you what," she said, falsely, beginning to sidle away. "I'll go into my room and think, and if anything occurs to me I'll—"

She moved suddenly, and catching Eileen Munsing by surprise, fled past her into the living room. She was at the door, fumbling with the knob, when Eileen Munsing caught her, clamping her fingers over Carol's wrist.

"Wait a minute. Please," the woman begged. "You can't leave me alone like this."

"I don't know what I can possibly do, Miss Munsing," Carol said, panting as though she had been running for a long time, although here, in the brightly lit living room with the bowls of flowers and the baskets of fruit, she was in better control of herself. "I would really like to help, if I could. But I—"

"Listen," Eileen Munsing whispered, holding her. "Don't get hysterical. There's plenty to do. Come on over here," she said soothingly, leading Carol to the couch. "Sit down. Be sensible. There's plenty of time. We don't have to lose our heads."

Carol let herself be guided to the couch. She wanted to say she was sorry but it was none of her business, *she* hadn't invited a famous man with a bad heart to her bedroom at three in the morning, *she* hadn't been friends for ten years with a man who had a wife and two children in Palm Beach. But she was both frightened of Eileen Munsing and sorry for her, and she couldn't bring herself to leave her alone in the welter of flowers, telegrams, ruin, scandal.

"Do you want a drink?" Eileen Munsing asked. "I think we can both use a drink."

"Yes, please."

The actress poured two stiff whiskeys and gave one to Carol. I am a very good friend of Eileen Munsing's, Carol thought foolishly, we often sit in her room after the show to all hours, drinking and talking about theatrical problems, I owe a great deal of my present success to the hints I . . .

"Listen, Carol," Eileen Munsing said, sitting beside her, "there's one thing for sure—he can't be found here."

"No," Carol said stupidly, for a confused moment *being* Eileen Munsing and realizing the impossibility of having Samuel Borensen found dead in her room. "But—"

"I can't stand it," Eileen Munsing said. "This would finish me. There was enough of a stink about my second divorce."

Vaguely, Carol remembered newspaper stories about detectives, a diary, pictures taken with telephoto lens and shown in court, and the automobile accident a few years before that, on the highway from Mexico, and the laborer who had been run over coming out of a dirt road and the police finding out the man driving the car was drunk and not Eileen Munsing's husband at all (the first, the second, the third?) although they had spent three days and nights under a name that belonged to neither of them in a hotel at Ensenada.

"They had to hold up releasing my pictures for more than a year," Eileen Munsing was saying, drinking in gulps, her hand working bonily on the glass, "and it looked as though they'd never take me back. If this comes out," she said bitterly, "every woman's club in the country will vote to have me burned. Lord," she said, overcome with self-pity, "every time I make a move it blows up in my face. I've used it all up," she said. "I've used up everybody's forgiveness. Everything happens at the wrong time." She drank thirstily, mechanically.

"If something like this had happened when I was just starting, it would have been all right. It would've been better than all right—it would have helped. If I were a young girl starting in," Eileen Munsing went on, her bitter, hoarse voice whispering in the large, plush room, "people'd say, 'Well, you can't blame her too much—she's just a young girl on her own. Naturally, a man like that could talk her into anything.' And they'd be interested in me, they'd be curious about me, they'd talk about me, they'd want to see me. Lord," she said extravagantly, "if it had happened fifteen years ago, it would have been better than a trunkful of rave reviews."

Carol stood up. She wasn't cold any more, and the spasms in her throat had stopped. She looked down calmly at Eileen Munsing, sympathetic, linked, sisterly, understanding.

"Eileen," she said, the name for the first time coming naturally to her lips, thinking, This is the moment. Who would have ever thought it was going to come like this? "Eileen," she said, putting her drink down and taking the older woman's hands, soothing, sisterly, in hers, "don't worry. I think there's something that can be done."

Eileen Munsing looked up at her, suspicious, not understanding. "What?" she said, her hands cold and limp in Carol's.

"I think," Carol said, her voice steady, reassuring, "we'd better get started if we want to get him into my room before daylight."

The calm, remembering, melodious voice stopped. Once more we were back in the Statler bar, two years past the remembered night. We sat in silence for a moment, I because I was too confused and shaken to speak, Carol because the story, as far as she was concerned, was complete.

"The truth is," she said, after the pause, "everything worked out exactly as we planned. The only trouble was I miscalculated. I thought I was better than I was, that's all. Well, who doesn't make a mistake now and then?" She looked at her watch and stood up. "I have to go."

I helped her on with her coat, and walked to the door with her.

"One thing," I said. "Why did you finally tell me this?"

She looked at me candidly, sweetly, standing there at the open door with the traffic of the city behind her. "We probably will never see each other again," she said, "and I wanted to let you know I hadn't been unfaithful to you. I wanted you to be left with a good opinion of me."

She leaned over and kissed my cheek and started across the avenue, youthful, delicate, beautiful, demented-looking, with her pretty suit and soft fur coat and her shining fresh blond hair, as though she were setting out to conquer the city.

Tune Every Heart and Every Voice

"How goes it?" Webel said, standing at the bar.

"Nighttime, nighttime," Eddie said, mournfully, serving Webel a cup of black coffee.

It was two-thirty in the morning, but there were still more than a dozen people in the bar. There were a few couples in the booths; near the beer spigots a tall, youngish man sat talking in a low voice to a girl with chopped black hair and green wool stockings; two or three industrious drinkers stared into their glasses, hunched into their overcoats over the damp mahogany; John McCool, wearing a wrinkled corduroy jacket and a lumberjack's red-and-black-checked shirt, sat alone at the small table near the entrance, drunk and doodling on the menu. Webel had said hello to McCool when he came in and had looked at the doodle. It was a picture of a football player with three legs and seven or eight arms, like a statue in an Indian temple. "The best elements of East and West," McCool had said thickly. "Ambition, speed, brutality, and fair play, allied to multiplicity of means and the denial of the material and degrading of the natural world."

Webel had given McCool back his doodle, without further investigation. McCool was a good scene-designer and a bad painter, and after a few drinks his conversation was likely to be gloomy, oblique, and difficult to follow.

"Nobody ever goes to sleep in this town," Eddie said. He surveyed his customers with loathing. He had to stay open until four every morning anyway, but he lived in the hope that one night his bar would be empty by two o'clock and he could close early with a calm conscience and go home and sleep. He had the face of a man who worried more about sleep than about the Russians, the Bomb, the Democratic Party, death or love. The bar was on West Forty-sixth Street and was a hangout for actors and theatrical people in general, who didn't have to go to work until eight o'clock at night, if they had to go to work at all, and who shared the profession's enduring revulsion to daylight.

"How many cups a coffee you drink a day, Mr. Webel?" Eddie asked.

"Twenty, thirty a day," Webel said.

"Why?"

"I don't like the taste of alcohol."

"Do you like the taste of coffee?"

"Not much," Webel said, lifting the cup.

"There you are," Eddie said. He swabbed the bar to one side of Webel sorrowfully. "Nobody makes any sense these days."

"Eddie," called the man who was sitting on the stool next to the girl in green stockinges. "Two Gibsons, please, if it's not too much of an imposition."

"Imposition," Eddie muttered, still swabbing the bar. "Do you get the sarcasm? Gibsons at two-thirty in the morning. Who drinks Gibsons after midnight? Fairies, alcoholics, and exhibitionists. I tell them to their faces." Without looking at the man who had ordered, he poured the gin and vermouth into the glass, shoveled in the ice and stirred savagely.

"Glacial, if you don't mind, Eddie," the man said. He had a lofty, good Eastern-school accent that was sometimes hard for Webel to bear, especially this late at night. The man's clothes, narrow and proper, matched the accent, and Webel, who looked like a dressed-up truck driver or a Marine top sergeant on furlough, no matter what tailor he used, found himself disliking the man's clothes, too.

"Eddie," the barman muttered, whirling the drink around in the glass. "Everybody thinks he has the right to call me Eddie."

"Who is he?" Webel asked in a low voice.

"Some television jerk," Eddie said, plopping in onions. "Madison Avenue. They're invading the West Side now. It's chic, some dame mentioned the joint in *Vogue*. Or maybe it's just the population explosion. The baby boom is driving th'upper classes into the Hudson." Gloomily, he moved down the bar and served the Gibsons.

"Excellent, Eddie," the man said, tasting his drink.

Eddie grunted, accepting no largesse. He rang up the charge on the cash register and stuck the slip in a puddle on the bar under the elbow of the girl with the green stockings.

"Terence," the girl was saying, "you should have seen Dominguín at Santander. He cut four ears. The *faena* with the second bull was absolutely chilling. And he killed *recibiendo*."

My Dear Holy Lord, Webel thought, is there no escape. He drank his coffee in one gulp and burned his tongue.

"Mr. Holstein," John McCool called to Eddie from his table, "another whiskey please, and two more menus."

Eddie served McCool and gave him his menus and glowered at the couple in booth Number Three, who had been holding hands over two bottles of beer since one o'clock. Eddie came back to Webel with a fresh cup of coffee, steaming hot. He watched Webel sip at it, the expression on his face a mixture of fascination, disbelief, and disgust. "You mean to say," Eddie said, "you can go home and go to sleep after all that coffee?"

"Yes," Webel said.

"Without pills?"

"Without pills."

Eddie shook his head wonderingly. "You must have the constitution of a infant," he said. "Of course, you got a hit running on Forty-fourth Street, I guess anybody can sleep with a hit."

"It helps," Webel said. He was the company manager for a musical that had opened two weeks ago and that looked good for a run of three years.

"You know, Edgar Wallace," Eddie said, "he killed himself with tea. The writer, Edgar Wallace. His doctor said, "You are tanning the interior of your intestines, Mr. Wallace, with all that tea, you are drinking yourself to death, but he kept on, like you with your coffee, if you don't mind my saying so."

"I don't mind at all, Eddie," Webel said.

"Maybe you ought to get married, Mr. Webel," Eddie said. "A man who drinks all that coffee."

"I have been married," Webel said.

"Me, too," Eddie said. "Three times. What am I saying? This hour of the night, a man says the godamndest things. I take it back."

"Oh, Eddie." It was old Narrow Shoulders again, the man the girl had addressed as Terence, lifting a long white hand. "Have you got two bottles of drinkable Chablis I can take with me?"

Webel watched Eddie's face with interest. The greenish midnight pallor vanished and in its place rose a hearty, ruddy, flamelike glow, giving Eddie, for the moment, the complexion of an English gentleman farmer who rode to the hounds three times a week. Webel had never seen Eddie looking so healthy.

"What was that, Mister?" Eddie asked, keeping his voice under control with some difficulty.

"I wondered if you had a couple of bottles of white wine I could take home with me," Terence said. "I'm going down to New Haven tomorrow for the game and we're picnicking near the Bowl and it'll be a bore scrambling around looking for a wineshop in the morning."

"I got some Christian Brothers white," Eddie said. "I don't guarantee it's drinkable. I ain't tasted it."

"Throw them into a bag, like a good fellow," the man said. "We'll just have to make do."

Webel burned his tongue again on his coffee, as he watched Eddie scowl down into the refrigerator chests and come up with two bottles, which he put in a large brown paper bag, and set on the bar in front of the man and his girl.

"By the way, Eddie," the man said, "who do you think is going to win tomorrow?"

"Who do *you* think?" Eddie asked, his voice edgy.

"Princeton," the man said. He laughed easily. "Of course I'm prejudiced, dear . . ." He turned to the girl and touched her arm lightly. "I'm a Princeton man, myself."

What a surprise, Webel thought.

"*I* think Yale," Eddie said.

"*Lux et Veritas,*" John McCool said, from his table near the entrance, but nobody paid any attention to him.

"You think Yale," the Princeton man said, mimicking Eddie's proletarian Third Avenue accent just enough to make Webel think with fleeting approval of revolution and the overthrow of all established orders. "I'll tell you what I'll do with you, Eddie, since you think Yale. I'll make a little wager. I'll wager the price of these two bottles of wine that Princeton wins."

"I don't gamble my liquor," Eddie said. "I buy it and I sell it."

"You mean you're not prepared to back your opinion," the Princeton man said.

"I mean what I said," Eddie turned his back on the man and rearranged some bottles of Scotch behind the bar.

"If you're that eager to bet," Webel said, "I might be able to oblige." He hadn't thought about the game and he didn't follow football very closely and he was not a gambling man, but at the moment he would have bet on the Republicans if the Princeton man had said he was a Democrat, on Patterson if the man had come out for Liston, on Peru against Russia, if the man had expressed his preference for the Red Army.

"Oh," the man said coolly, "you might be able to oblige. That's interesting. Up to what amount, might I ask?"

"Any amount you like," Webel said, grateful for the musical on Forty-fourth Street that permitted him gestures like this.

"I suppose a hundred dollars would be too steep for you," Terence said, smiling gently.

"Actually not," Webel said. "Actually I find it rather piddling." Hit or no hit, he didn't really feel like losing a hundred dollars, but the man's voice, assured and supercilious, drove him blindly on into extravagance. "I was thinking of something more important than that."

"Well," Terence said, "let's keep it on a small, friendly basis. Let's say a hundred dollars. What odds do you offer?"

"Odds?" Webel asked, surprised. "It's an even-money game."

"Oh, my dear fellow," said the Princeton man, pretending to be amused. "I'm loyal to the old school and all that, but not to *that* extent. I'll take two and a half to one."

"All the papers make it an even-money game," Webel said.

"Not the papers I read," the Princeton man said, inferring by his tone that Webel undoubtedly read only crooked tip sheets, true-confession magazines, and pornographic tabloids. Terence took out his wallet and dug into it and brought out two twenty-dollar bills, which he laid on the bar. "Here's my money," he said. "Forty dollars to your hundred."

"Eddie," Webel said, "have you got an evening paper here? Let's show this fellow."

"I am not interested in what some poor hack of a sportswriter dreams up in a drunken stupor," Terence said. "I know the teams. Both coaches are friends of mine. I assure you, my dear fellow, I am being most generous in taking two and a half to one."

"Eddie," Webel said, "do you know a bookie we can get hold of at this hour to quote the odds?"

"Sure," Eddie said. "But it's a waste of time. It's been the same all week. Six to five, take your choice. That's even money, Mister."

"I never have any truck with bookies," Terence said. He started to put his money back in his wallet. "If you didn't intend to bet," he said frostily to Webel, "it would have been wiser to keep quiet in the first place." He turned ostentatiously toward the girl, presenting his back to Webel. "Would you like another drink, dear?"

At this moment, McCool, who had been bent over his drawing, seeming to pay no attention to the conversation, looked up and said in a loud, clear, carrying voice. "Look here, Brother Tiger," he said, "I'm a Princeton man myself, and I say that no gentleman would ask for two and a half to one on this game. The odds are even money."

Silence enfolded the bar, frigid and palpable. Terence put his wallet away deliberately and turned slowly to regard McCool at his table near the entrance. McCool had his head down again and was placidly drawing on the menu. The expression on Terence's face was shocked, mildly disbelieving, amused, and tolerant, all at the same time. It was the sort of expression that you might find on the face of a liberal clergyman who had been invited to dinner by a group of his parishioners only to discover that a striptease was in progress in the center of the room.

"Excuse me, dear," Terence said to the girl in the green stockings. Then he walked slowly, with dignity toward McCool. He stopped a good four feet away from McCool's table, making his halt look like a prophylactic measure, keeping him safely out of the invisible aura that only he was fine enough to sense as it emanated from the region inhabited at the moment by McCool.

McCool drew contentedly, his head down. He was almost completely bald on top and he had a fringe of red hair about the ears and a long, aggressive jaw covered with a russet stubble. For the first time Webel realized that McCool looked just like the picture of the Irish laborers who had been brought over in the 1860's to build the Union Pacific Railroad. Webel didn't blame Terence for being surprised. It took a bold leap of the imagination to conceive of McCool at Princeton.

"Did I hear you correctly, sir?" Terence asked.

"I don't know," McCool said, without looking up.

"Did you or did you not say you were a Princeton man?"

"I did." Now McCool looked up belligerently and drunkenly at Terence. "I also said no gen'l'man would ask for odds. Just in case you didn't hear *that* correctly."

Terence made a slow semicircle in front of McCool, examining him with scientific interest. "So," Terence said, his voice edged with aristocratic skepticism, "you say you're a Princeton man?"

"I say," said McCool.

Terence turned toward the girl at the bar. "Did you hear that, dear?" Without waiting for an answer, he wheeled back to face McCool. His voice now was rich with the scorn of a prince of the blood in the presence of a plebeian impostor caught in the act of trying to crash the Royal Enclosure at Ascot. "Why, sir," he said, "you're no more of a Princeton man than . . . than . . . than . . ." He looked around him, searching for the most extreme, the most ludicrously impossible comparison. "Why you're no more of a Princeton man than Eddie here."

"Hey, wait a minute, mister," Eddie said, displeased, behind the bar. "Don't make any more enemies than is absolutely necessary."

Terence ignored Eddie and concentrated on McCool. "I'm interested in your case, Mr. . . . Mr. . . . I'm afraid I didn't catch your name."

"McCool," said McCool.

"McCool," Terence said. He made the name sound like a newly discovered skin disease. "I'm afraid I don't know any family by that name."

"My father was a wandering tinker," McCool said. "Going up and down the bogs, with a song in his heart. It was the family business. It kept us in luxury since the eleventh century, I'm surprised you haven't heard of us." He began to sing "The Harp That Once Through Tara's Halls," off key.

Webel watched with pleasure. He was delighted that he had decided to come into Eddie's bar instead of going home to sleep.

"You still insist," Terence said, breaking into McCool's musical croaking, "that you went to Princeton?"

"What do you want me to do?" McCool said irritably, "Strip and show you my black and orange tattooing?"

"Let me ask you a question, Mr. McCool," Terence said smoothly, with false friendliness. "What club did you belong to?"

"I didn't belong to any club," McCool said.

"Aha," said Terence.

"I have never recovered from the blow," McCool said. He began to sing "The Harp That Once Through Tara's Halls" again.

"I can understand your not having belonged to a club," Terence said genially. "But even so, I imagine, you could tell me where the Ivy is or Cannon. Couldn't you, Mr. McCool?" He leaned slightly toward McCool's table, inquisitive and sure of himself.

"Lemme see . . . lemme see," McCool mumbled. He stared down at the table and scratched his bald head.

"Say in relation to the Pyne Library," Terence said. "Or Holder Hall."

"I'll be goddamned," McCool said. "I forgot. I got out before the war."

Now Webel was annoyed with McCool. The Princeton Dramatic Club invited McCool down to lecture to their members almost every year, and even drunk as he was McCool should have been able to remember where Prospect Street was.

Terence was smiling loftily now, pleased with his brilliant cross-examination. "Let's skip that for the moment," he said magnanimously. "Let's try something else. Let's try 'Old Nassau,' for example. You've heard of 'Old Nassau,' I imagine?"

"Sure I've heard of 'Old Nassau,' " McCool said doggedly. Plainly, he was ashamed of his performance on the examination about the clubs.

"That's the song that starts, 'Tune every heart and every voice, Let every care withdraw . . .' Does that ring a bell, Mr. McCool?"

"I know it," McCool said sullenly.

"I'd be interested to hear you try to sing it," Terence said. "That is, if the other patrons of the bar don't mind?" He turned and smiled, mannerly as a butler, in the direction of the bar.

"Just keep it low," Eddie said. "I don't have an intertainment license."

"Now, Mr. McCool," Terence said kindly. "We're waiting." Helpfully, he hummed a few bars of the song.

"Tune every heart and every voice, Let every car withdraw," McCool began, droning tunelessly, "uh . . . Let . . . something . . . uh . . . with something . . . uh . . ." He shook his head disgustedly. "Hell, I haven't sung it for twenty years."

"You mean you don't know it?" Terence asked with false amazement.

"I forgot it," McCool admitted. "I'm loaded. So what?"

Terence smiled widely. "I'm going to tell you something, Mr. McCool," he said. "In all my experience, I have never known a Princeton man who couldn't sing every word of 'Old Nassau' right up to the day he died."

"Well," said McCool, "now you know one."

"You're a faker, sir," Terence said. "I'll bet one thousand dollars that you're no Princeton man and never were one." The last part of the challenge was addressed to the room at large. Terence, certain that he was on sure ground now, was making up for the embarrassment he had suffered in front of his girl in the discussion about the odds on the football game. He stared triumphantly at Webel.

Webel took a deep breath. This is too good to be true, he thought deliciously. It's a dirty trick to play, but this sonofabitch is asking for it. Webel took his checkbook out of his pocket and put it down on the bar, with a smart little slapping sound. "Terence, old friend," he said, "you've got yourself a bet. One thousand dollars that says John McCool is a graduate of Princeton."

Terence glared at Webel, surprised, immediately shaken. He took a new tack. "What school did *you* go to?"

"I'm an outcast and a social leper," Webel said. "I went to Lehigh. But I'm writing out my check for a thousand dollars. If you haven't your checkbook on you, you can use mine, Eddie here'll hold the bets. Won't you, Eddie?"

"With pleasure," Eddie said.

Webel took out his fountain pen and opened it and held it poised over the checkbook ceremoniously. "Well?" he asked Terence.

Terence was beginning to pale. Webel's promptness and something in the tone with which Eddie had said "With pleasure," had unnerved him. He looked uncertainly at McCool again and his thought processes were easy to follow as he felt the trap closing in on him. McCool did not look, sound or smell like any Princeton man that Terence would like to acknowledge as a collegiate brother of his, and the fact that McCool had not come up with the name of a Club and didn't know the location of Club Street or the words of "Old Nassau," should have been, by all ordinary standards, crushing proof that McCool was lying. But times were changing; a Democrat had been elected to the White House, society was in flux; this was after all a low theatrical bar, little bettter than a slum saloon, where he, Terence, had no business coming in the first place and whose patrons might turn out to be *anybody*, including graduates of Princeton. And a thousand dollars was a lot of money, even on Madison Avenue.

"Well, Terence," Webel said cruelly, "I don't see you writing out your check."

"Put your pen away, old man," Terence said. The words were meant to be offhand and dismissive, but the voice was shaky. "I'm not betting. This is not the sort of thing one bets on." Ignoring McCool, he strode past Webel to the girl at the bar. "I think it's time for another drink, don't you, dear?" he said loudly.

"I think everybody in this bar heard you offer to bet a thousand dollars on a simple question of fact," Webel said, determined to make the man suffer. "What's changed your mind, Terence?"

"It was just a rhetorical turn of phrase, actually, old man," Terence said. "Two more Gibsons, please, Eddie."

Eddie didn't move. "Mister," he said, "I been listening carefully. You caused a disturbance in this bar. You embarrassed a old customer. You offered to bet and you welshed. Now you order two Gibsons." Eddie made this sound like the worst charge in the litany. "Let us make a suggestion. A gentleman in your position right now would do one of two things. Either he would cover this gentleman's check here"—Eddie waved, indicating Webel, like an announcer introducing a prizefighter in the ring—"or," Eddie went on loudly, "he would apologize."

"Apologize?" Terence said, sounding disagreeably surprised. "To whom?"

"To the gentleman whose word you doubted," Eddie said. "To Mr. McCool."

Terence looked over at McCool, who was happily doodling away on his third menu.

"Oh, come now, Eddie," Terence said crisply, "let's have our drinks and forget it."

"You don't get any drinks in this bar until you do like I said," Eddie said.

"See here, Eddie," Terence said, "this is a public bar and . . ."

"Terence." The girl laid her hand soothingly on his arm, but her voice was cool. "Don't be any stuffier than you usually are."

"Listen to the lady, mister," Eddie said grimly.

Terence lifted one of the bottles of wine out of the bag on the bar in front of him. He looked at the label and grimaced and let the bottle slide back into the bag again. Nobody said anything. "Oh, well," Terence said offhandedly, "if everybody's taking a little matter like this so big . . ." He lit a cigarette deliberately and sauntered over to McCool's table. He stopped his prophylactic four feet away. "By the way," he said to McCool's bent head, "I'm sorry if I inadvertently offended you."

"Huh?" McCool lifted his head, squinting. "What did you say? Come closer, I can't hear you."

Terence went up to the table. "I said I'm sorry," he said, his face working under the strain of cowardice, embarrassment and lifelong bad faith.

"Tell him you take it all back," Eddie said mercilessly,

from behind the bar. "Tell him you agree he's a Princeton man."

"Don't put words into my mouth, Eddie," Terence said snappishly, sounding suddenly like an old maid. "I'm perfectly capable of expressing myself."

"What'd you say, mister?" McCool asked, looking blearily up at him.

"I was wrong," Terence said. "I'm now convinced that you're a Princeton man."

"You are?" McCool said, surprised.

"Yes, I am!" Terence was leaning close to McCool now, shouting into his face.

"Screw Princeton," McCool said. He reached up with both hands and grabbed Terence's lapels and shook the man vigorously. "And screw you, too, brother." He shook him again.

Terence pushed violently against McCool's arms and only the fact that McCool's chair was backed against the wall prevented McCool from falling to the floor.

Webel started to move, but the girl in the green stockings was faster. After all those Gibsons, Webel thought, surprised. She flicked in front of him and did something he couldn't quite follow, with her foot. Suddenly, Terence was on the floor, among the cigarette butts and spilled beer. "Now, Terence," the girl said gently. "Gentlemen don't hit drunks where I come from."

Terence looked up at her with hatred. On the floor, his narrow impeccable clothes looked shabby and out of style.

She helped Terence up.

"You tripped me," he said accusingly.

"Yes, indeed I did, Terence," the girl said calmly, brushing him off a little.

"I think we'd better go home," Terence said, glowering at the quiet faces around him. "This place has lost its charm."

"Not for me," the girl said. "You go home. Give me a ring, sometime."

Terence started to get out his wallet, but the girl pushed at his hand. "I'll pay," she said. She was smiling, but the smile came direct from Alaska.

Terence looked around him once more. Eddie was knocking the top off a glass of beer, paying a great deal of attention to the job. Webel was standing four feet away, with the disappointed expression of a man who had been cheated of a fight. The couple in the booth had gone back to holding hands over the two beers they had bought at one A.M. McCool was shading in the left leg of Brigitte Bardot.

"Well," Terence said, making it sound like an important political announcement. He turned and closed the door loudly behind him.

The girl went back to the stool at the bar and Webel went back to his corner. There was a silence for a moment. The girl kicked off her ballet slippers and stripped off first one green wool stocking, then the other, Webel couldn't help but look surprised.

"I hate these things," the girl said. "But Terence says he likes Bohemian girls. That's his idea of Bohemian—green stockings. Also"—she took a sip of her drink—"don't believe that stuff about Dominguín at Santander. I've never been within three thousand miles of Santander and I've never seen a bullfight in my whole life. I picked up all that guff in a magazine. Terence was in Spain three summers ago and he won't look at a girl if she doesn't talk about *manoletinas* and the day José Whatever took his *alternativa* against Miura's in Vittoria. *Olé.*" She laughed harshly. "I was in Far Rockaway all last summer. Girls're jerks. You know why girls're jerks?"

She addressed this directly to Webel, so he had to say something. "Why?" he asked.

"Because they go out with jerks," the girl said. "Anything to keep the dire, damn telephone ringing." She then, unexpectedly, sang the entire set of verses of "Old Nassau," sweetly and with feeling. When she had finished, she said, to no one in particular, "I told him I went to Antioch College. Hah! I never even graduated from James Madison High School."

"I'd like to offer you a drink, miss," Eddie said. "You're helping stop the invasion. You struck a blow for Democracy."

"No, thank you, Mr. Holstein," the girl said, rolling up the green stockings and putting them into her bag. "This little girl has had enough gin for one night. Beddy-bye, *recibiendo*, Mr. Holstein."

She put some money down on the bar.

Eddie touched the paper bag with the two bottles of wine in it. "I don't suppose you'll be wanting this," he said.

"Oh yes, I do, Mr. Holstein," the girl said. She took the bag. "I will drink this drinkable almost-Chablis with my picnic lunch on West Seventy-fourth Street tomorrow. I am only sixty-five miles, as the crow flies, from the Yale Bowl."

Barefoot, she started out. "Tune every heart," she said, womanly and encompassing, as she went though the door.

"Nighttime," Eddie said, after a while, shaking his head. He turned to Webel. "Anything else you want?"

"Coffee, Eddie," Webel said.

"Coffee?" Eddie's face grew mournful. "Remember Edgar Wallace," he said. Then he went to get some fresh coffee.

Goldilocks at Graveside

She was surprised to see him in the church. She hadn't known he was in Los Angeles. And there had only been the one notice in the one newspaper—"Ex-State Dept. Officer Dies. William MacPherson Bryant died last night at the Santa Monica Hospital, after a long illness. Entering the foreign service in 1935, he held posts in Washington, Geneva, Italy, Brazil and Spain, before resigning for reasons of health in 1952. The couple were childless and he is survived only by his widow, who, under her maiden name, Victoria Simmons, is the editress of the Women's Page of this newspaper."

The church was almost empty, as Bryant had made no friends since they moved West, and there was just a scattering of people from the paper, who came as a matter of courtesy to the widow, so Victoria saw Borden almost immediately. It was a dark, rainy day, and he was sitting alone, in the rear of the church, near the door, but his blond head was unmistakable. Irrelevantly, while paying only half-attention to what the minister was saying, Victoria remembered the secret nickname by which, among the three of them, Borden had been called—Goldilocks.

There were only two cars in the cortege to the cemetery, but Borden found room in the second car and stood bareheaded in the rain during the ceremony at the grave. Victoria observed that he was now dyeing his hair and that, although at a distance there was still an appearance of boyish good looks about him, up close his face was lined by fine wrinkles and seemed dusted over by uncertainty and fatigue.

As she walked away from the grave, an erect, veiled, middle-aged, slender woman, tearless behind the black cloth, Borden asked her if he could drive back with her. Since she had come out to the cemetery with only the minister and there was plenty of room, she said yes. Borden's voice had changed, too. Like his dyed hair, it pretended to a youthfulness and energy that she remembered and that was no longer there.

The minister was silent most of the way back to town. Victoria had only met him for the first time the day before, when she was making the arrangements for the funeral. Neither she nor her husband had been members of the congregation and the minister had that slightly aggrieved expression that one remarks on the faces of the representatives of religion when they know they are only being used out of necessity and not out of faith.

Among the three of them they spoke no more than thirty words on the way back into town. The minister got off at the church and after his embarrassed little handshake, Borden asked Victoria if he could accompany her home. She was in perfect control of herself—all her tears had been shed years before—and she told him she didn't need any help. In fact, she had planned to sit down directly at her desk when she got home and start working on the full page for the Sunday issue, both because it needed doing and as a remedy against melancholy. But Borden persisted, with the same light good manners and concern for the welfare of others that had made him so popular in the years of their friendship.

With the minister gone, Victoria asked for a cigarette. She threw back her veil as Borden offered her a cigarette from a flat gold case and lighted both hers and his own with a flat gold lighter. There was something a little displeasing to Victoria in the action of his hands. She would have been hard put to explain why. They seemed, for lack of a better word, *exaggerated*.

They drove in silence for a minute or two. "Was he happy," Borden asked, "those last few years?"

"No," she said.

"What a waste," Borden sighed. The sigh, she was sure,

was not only for her husband. "He was an able man, an able man." The tone was pompous. For that moment he might have been a politician making a speech at the dedication of a statue, much delayed, to the dead of a half-forgotten war.

"What did he do after he retired?" Borden asked.

"He read," she said.

"Read?" Borden sounded puzzled. "Is that all?"

"Yes. My job on the paper supported us well enough."

"I didn't know you were any kind of writer," Borden said.

"Necessity," she said. "I used to get A's in English courses in college." They both smiled.

"Is Clare here with you?" Victoria asked.

Borden looked at Victoria strangely, as though he suspected her of sarcasm. "Didn't you hear?"

"Hear what?"

"We were divorced six years ago. She married an Italian. He owns race horses. She won't come to America."

"I'm sorry," she said.

He shrugged. "It wasn't much of a marriage." His voice was flat and careless. "We put on a good show for a few years, while it still did any good. After that—*Adieu, Chérie.* . . ."

"What are you doing out here?" Victoria asked.

"Well," he said, "after the debacle, Clare and I wandered around Europe for awhile, but it never was the same. The jobs I might have had I didn't want and we had enough money so that I didn't *have* to work—and there was always that little whispering when we came into a room. Maybe we only imagined it, but . . ."

"You didn't imagine it," Victoria said.

They drove in silence for awhile. Then he asked her for her telephone number and wrote it down, with exaggeratedly neat little strokes of a small gold pencil in a handsome leather notebook.

"When you feel like," he said, "please call me and we can have dinner." He gave her his card. "Borden Staines," it read. "Bottega del Mezzogiorno—Styles for Men."

"I'm there every day," he said, "after eleven o'clock."

She had passed the shop many times. The name on the window had always struck her as pretentious and foolish. After all, in English, it only meant "The South Shop." The place was elegant, expensive, and displayed gaudy shirts and ties and Italian sweaters and things like that, all a little too showy for her taste. She had never gone in.

"I bought it five years ago," Borden said. "I decided I had to do *something*." He smiled a little apologetically. "It's amazing how well it's done. I must say it never occurred to me that I would wind up as a Beverly Hills haberdasher. Anyway, it keeps me busy."

The car stopped in front of the apartment house in which Victoria lived. It was still raining, but Borden hurried out to open the door for her and sent the driver on his way, saying that he preferred to walk a bit. "You're sure you don't mind being alone?" he said. "You know, I'd be delighted to come up and . . ."

"Thank you, no," she said.

"Well . . ." he said, uncertainly, "I felt I just had to come. After all, we had so many good times together, all of us . . ." His voice trailed off.

"It was very good of you to come, Borden," she said.

"I have a confession to make," Borden said. He looked uneasily around him, as though fearful of being overheard. "I did see you that afternoon, Vicky. When you smiled and I turned away. I've always felt foolish about it and guilty and I . . ."

"What afternoon?" Victoria said. She turned and opened the lobby door.

"You don't remember . . . ?" He stared at her, his eyes suspicious and searching.

"What afternoon, Borden?" she repeated, standing with her hand on the doorknob.

"I guess I was mistaken," he said. "It isn't important." He smiled at her, with his almost-perfect imitation of boyishness and kissed her lightly on the cheek, good-bye now, probably good-bye forever, and walked off, very trim and young-looking in his smart raincoat, with his blond hair glistening with rain.

She went upstairs and unlocked the door. She threw off her hat and veil and walked aimlessly around the empty apartment. The apartment was nondescript. Nobody ever comes here, the apartment said, this is merely a place where two people once took shelter. Temporarily. Reduced now. To one.

Without emotion, Victoria looked at a photograph of

her husband in a silver frame. It had been taken more than ten years ago. It was a sober portrait, posed carefully in a studio, and her husband looked serious and responsible, the sort of man who gets elected, young, to the board of trustees of the university from which he was graduated. You could not imagine his ever wearing any of the clothes displayed in the window of a California shop called "Bottega del Mezzogiorno."

There was work laid out all over the desk, but she couldn't get herself to sit down and finish it. The meeting with Borden had started too many memories. It was so unexpected that it had unsettled her in a way that her husband's death, long awaited, had not.

She went to the closet where she kept her files and pulled down a carton. The carton had "1953" written in large numerals on its label. She leafed through the pages until she came upon what she was looking for. It was a folder, neatly held together by clasps, with about twenty-five typewritten pages in it.

She sat down in a chair near the window, which was still streaming with rain, and put on her glasses and started to read. It was the first time in at least ten years that she had even glanced at the folder.

"From the Desert," she read. "A short story by V. Simmons."

She made a little grimace and reached over and picked up a pencil and blacked out the V. Simmons. Then she settled back and started to read.

Naturally, *she read,* I am not going to sign my real name to this. If the reader persists to the end, the reason will be plain to him.

If I am ever successful in the attempt to become a writer, it will be quite easy for me to keep my identity hidden. I have never written anything before and in all the years since I have been married, I have put down in answer to all questionnaires and official requests, *Occupation: Housewife.* I am still making beds and cooking three meals a day and going into town twice a week to do the shopping and we have no neighbors and we have made no friends who might see the typewriter on my desk or the ream of cheap paper which I was sensible enough to buy in C——, the large city which is fifty miles away from where we live. I have taken the precaution, also, of renting a postal box in the same city under the pseudonym which I intend to use and all communications from publishers and editors will be delivered to me there. When I have to send any of the things I plan to write through the mails, I shall make the trip to the city and mail the manuscripts in an ordinary envelope at a time when the traffic in the post office is at its peak and a rather plain, modestly dressed, middle-aged woman standing momentarily before the outgoing slot in the wall can most probably pass unnoticed.

All these measures must seem rather excessive to the reader, but until recently my husband and I have been leading our lives in an atmosphere of surveillance, of rumors, of hidden microphones, intercepted mail and confidential reports of private conversations with friends. While I am sure the rumors were more lurid than the facts, there was never any means of discovering just how lurid they were and I have become accustomed to a permanent quiver of uneasiness. Even living as we do now, on the bare face of the desert, with no servants and not another house in sight, and no telephone for the curious, the malicious, or the inquiring to listen in on, I cannot rid myself of the posture of suspicion.

Our habit of isolation has been accepted on strange terms in the town in which I do our shopping. My husband never goes into town and the people of the town know, of course, that we receive no visitors. Somehow, the shopkeepers, and the postmistress, who are my only points of contact with the town, have decided my husband is suffering from consumption and has come here to take advantage of the dryness of the climate and the tranquillity of the desert. Naturally, we have said nothing to disabuse them. John, my husband (that is not his real name, of course), was never well known enough to have his name in the newspapers, and the events leading to his retirement were handled, largely by luck, with circumspection.

My decision to try to write came slowly and from a variety of reasons. I found myself with a great deal of time on my hands, as the work of the house, which is a small and simple one, can be done in three or four hours a day. Since his arrival here, my husband has become less and less communicative and spends the greater part of his time reading in a corner of the patio, protected by the wall from the

GOLDILOCKS AT GRAVESIDE 239

wind, or staring, for hours on end, at the mountains which rim our desert to the north and east. The question of money will begin to be of importance within the next year and I have reached the conclusion that my husband, at the age of forty-five, will never work again.

When we first came here, I supposed that our retreat was only to be temporary, while my husband came to terms with his defeat and gathered his forces for an effort in a new direction. In the beginning he sent out several letters a week to old friends and acquaintances with the suggestion that, after a prolonged vacation of perhaps six months, he would be ready to work again. He understood that in the field of public service his usefulness was probably at an end, at least in the foreseeable future, but he felt that a man of his education and experience, especially abroad, could be of considerable value in a variety of private enterprises. The tone and quality of the responses to his letters, especially from men who had been his friends since his college days, proved disillusioning, although in this instance, as always, he showed nothing, on the surface, of his disappointment. For three months now he had not written a letter to anyone.

My husband has never told me that he has given up hope but I know him too well to require direct statements from him. I spy on him. I read his letters. I covertly watch his expression every moment I am with him. When we eat a new dish I scan his face minutely for signs of approval. When we still had friends I could tell, almost to the second, when a friendship was beginning to bore him, and I would take steps immediately to bring the relationship painlessly to an end. In matters that are secret between a man and wife and which, as a writer, despite the present style, I do not intend to discuss, I have made myself a connoisseur of his pleasure. When he reads a book, I read it immediately after. I am a dossier of his likes and dislikes, his moods, his satisfactions. I do not do all this out of jealousy or a sick, female love of possession. I do it so that at all times I can amuse and interest him and I do it for him and not for myself and I do it out of gratitude.

My husband is an extraordinary man, with an appearance that is studiedly ordinary. He wears the correct, unobtrusive clothes of his caste and he has his hair cut short and brushed straight back, although he has a long, bony face and a bold nose and the shortness of hair above it makes the proportions somehow unpleasing. Once, when he and I spent a vacation alone on an island in the Caribbean, he permitted his hair to grow and he developed a full, thick black moustache. Suddenly, his face assumed its proper proportions and character. With the deep tan that he acquired on the beach and on a small sailing vessel that we rented, he looked like the photographs of the young men, dedicated and spirited, who go on expeditions to climb the Himalayas. But when the time came to return to his post, he shaved the moustache and clipped his hair, so that his face assumed once more the unremarkable expression and not quite harmonious proportions behind which he protects himself.

His manner, like his appearance, is designed, too, for disguise rather than display. He is a snob who is unfailingly polite to his inferiors and carefully disinterested in the presence of people whom he admires. He is subject to fierce and sudden tempers which he controls, with an exhausting expense of will, by forcing himself, at the moment when he is under the greatest stress, to speak slightly more slowly and with a hesitant and lowered voice. He is perfectly confident of his intelligence and has a deep contempt for the powers of most of the men with whom he has had to work, but he has spent endless hours listening to their ramblings and pretending to take their proposals into consideration. He is a man tortured by ambition without limit and he has unfailingly refrained from using all the hundred expedients by which his less gifted colleagues have won advancement. Racked, as I know, by passion, he has hardly even reached for my hand in public or allowed himself even the most casual expression of interest in the presence of the beautiful women who frequented the society in which we moved for so long a time. Avid for the touch of destiny, he has not moved a step in its direction.

This is the man who sits now day after day, reading in the silent desert sunlight, wearing, even here, the neat collar and tie and gray jacket of his working days, protected by the patio wall from the constant wind.

If he wishes to remain here, alone with me, for the rest of his life, I am content. Since, situated as we are, there is no other way to earn money, and both our families having long since succumbed into the economic morass so that there is no help to be hoped for from them, I have taken to the typewriter. We do not need much to keep us going in this remote place and while I have had no experience in the field of letters I am encouraged by the dismal quality of the writing which is published daily in this country. Certainly, a person of education, and one who has been close to the center of important affairs, as I have for nearly twenty years, should, with such pitiful standards to meet, be able to sustain a modest existence on almost the barest level of literacy.

I admit that I look forward to the experience with pleasure. I am a plain and vindictive woman who has had to remain silent in the company of fools and self-seekers for a long time and in the process of paying them off, I feel there should be profit both for me and whatever readers I may attract who have not been irremediably numbed by the floods of sentimentality, violence and hyprocrisy which pour forth from our presses.

Writers of the first class, I have read somewhere, are invariably men or women with an obsession. While I do not deceive myself about my merits or the grandeur of the heights I might ultimately reach, I share that one thing with them. I have an obsession. That obsession is my husband and it is of him that I shall write.

My husband came of a family that, in another country or other times, might fairly be called aristocratic. The family fortune held out long enough so that he went to the proper schools and was graduated from the proper college, in the same class with a surprising number of men who have since done extremely well in business and in government. Unsympathetic to commerce and springing from a family which has a long tradition of public office, my husband applied for the Foreign Service. This was at a time when the other departments of the government were being thrown open to hordes of noisy and unpleasant careerists, of doubtful origin, painful manners, and the most imperfect education. The Service, because of its rigid system of selection and its frank prejudice in favor of intellectual and conservative young men of good family, was the one enclave in a welter of shallow egalitarianism in which a gentleman might serve his country without compromise.

My husband, who never spared himself when there was

a question of work, was given one good post after another. He was never popular, but he was always respected and at the time he married me, four years after his first appointment, we both could reasonably suppose that in time he would rise to the most important positions in the Service. During the war he was given a mission of the utmost danger and delicacy, and performed it so well that he was told, personally, by the Secretary, that he was responsible for saving the lives of a considerable number of Americans.

Just after the war, he was appointed to the Embassy at X——. (Forgive me for the old-fashioned symbols. At this moment in our country's history candor is foolhardy, reprisals devastating.) I did not accompany my husband to X——. It was at that time that I found it necessary to undergo an operation which turned out to be not so simple as my doctor had hoped. A second operation was considered advisable, complications developed, and it was six months before I could join my husband. In those six months of living alone in a turbulent city, my husband became involved with the two people who, it turned out, were to destroy him. The first was Munder (the name, like all others I shall use, is an invention, of course), who at that time was making a brilliant record for himself as first secretary of the embassy. John and he had been friendly at college and the friendship was renewed and strengthened in the embassy, helped in great part by their recognition in each other of similar ambitions, equal devotion to their jobs, and complementary temperaments. The ambassador at that time was an amiable and lazy man who was pleased to turn over the real work of the embassy to his subordinates, and between them, Munder and my husband were, in an appreciable degree, responsible for the carrying-out of directives from Washington and the formulation of local policy. It was at that period that the Communists were profiting most, throughout Europe, from the post-armistice confusions, and the success of the Embassy at X—— in tactfully shoring up a government favorable to the interests of the United States was in no small measure due to the efforts of Munder and my husband. In fact, it was because of this that some time later Munder was recalled to Washington, where he played, for several years, a leading part in the formulation of policy. His prominence, as it so often does, finally resulted in his downfall. When the time came to offer up a sacrifice to the exasperation and disappointments of the electorate, Munder, because of his earlier distinction, was treated in such a manner that he decided to resign. While they did not understand it at the time, his friends and aides in the Service were also marked for eventual degradation, or, what is almost as bad, stagnation in humiliatingly unimportant posts.

The other person my husband became involved with was a woman. She was the wife of a diplomat from another country, a distinguished idiot who foolishly permitted himself to be sent off on distant missions for months at a time. She was that most dangerous of combinations—beautiful, talkative, and sentimental; and it was only a question of time before she blundered into a scandal. It was my husband's misfortune that her luck ran out during his tenure as her lover. As it later turned out, it might just as well have been any one of three or four other gentlemen, all within the diplomatic community, which the lady favored exclusively for her activities.

I knew, of course, almost from the beginning, although I was four thousand miles away, of what was going on. Friends, as they always do, saw to that. I will not pretend that I was either happy with the news or surprised by it. In marriages like mine, in which the partners are separated for months on end and the woman is, like me, rather drab and no longer young, it would take a fool to expect perfect fidelity from a passionate and attractive man. I do not know of a single marriage within the circle of my friends and acquaintances which has not required, at one point or another, a painful act of forgiveness on the part of one or both of the partners, to ensure the survival of the marriage. I had no intention of allowing the central foundations of my life to be laid in ruins for the fleeting pleasure of recrimination or to satisfy the busy hypocrisy of my friends. I did not hurry my convalescence, confident that when I appeared on the scene a workable *modus vivendi* would gradually be achieved.

Unhappily, when my husband told the lady of my impending arrival and announced to her that that would mean the end of their relationship, she made one of those half-hearted attempts at suicide with which silly and frivolous women try to prove to themselves and their lovers that they are not silly and frivolous. The lady telephoned my husband just after she took the pills, and was unconscious, in negligee, in her apartment, when he arrived. He did what was necessary and stayed with her at the hospital until he was assured by the doctors that she was out of danger. Luckily, the people at the hospital were civilized and sympathetic, and my husband managed, with a minimum of bribery, to keep the entire matter out of the newspapers. There was a wave of rumor, of course, in certain circles of the city, and there was no doubt a quite accurate estimate of the situation current for a week or two; but in Europe present scandal blends easily into centuries of anecdote, and when the lady appeared two weeks later, looking as pretty as ever, on her husband's arm at a diplomatic reception, the event seemed safely in the past.

My husband recounted the entire story to me on the first afternoon after my arrival. I listened and told him I would say no more about it and we have not mentioned the matter again to this day. I think I can honestly say that I have not permitted the incident to change, in the smallest particular, our relations with each other.

It is at this point in my story that I begin to perceive some of the problems that a writer faces. To make understandable what has happened it has been necessary to explain, as fully as I have, the background and personality of my husband, the kind of marriage we enjoy, and the stages and accidents of his career. But none of these things has its proper meaning unless it is viewed in relationship to the climate in which he worked and in which we lived and the pressures to which he was subjected. A more skillful writer would no doubt manage to include as much information of this nature as was necessary in a well-contrived series of dramatic scenes, so that the reader, while being held in suspense and amused by the brisk conflict of personalities, would be brought, almost without his realizing it, adequately prepared, to the climax of the story. There are two reasons why I have not attempted to do this. In the first place, I find it beyond my still undeveloped powers. And secondly, in my reading, I have found, for my own tastes, that the writers who did this particular thing most deftly were the ones I finally could not stomach.

There are crucial days in the lives of men and women, as in the lives of governments and armies; days which may

GOLDILOCKS AT GRAVESIDE

begin like all other days, ordinary and routine, with no warning of the crises ahead and which end with cabinets fallen, battles lost, careers brought to a sudden and catastrophic halt.

The crucial day for my husband was clear and warm, in late spring, when the waters of the harbor of the port in which he was serving as vice-consul were blue and calm. At breakfast we decided the season was well enough advanced so that we could dine thereafter on the terrace of our apartment and I told my husband that I would search in the shops that day for a pair of hurricane lamps to shield the candles on our table in the evening. Two friends were coming in after dinner for bridge, and I asked my husband to bring home with him a bottle of whiskey. He left the apartment, as usual, neat, brushed, deliberate, unmistakably American, despite his many years abroad, among the lively pedestrian traffic of our quarter.

My husband is a methodical man, with a trained memory, and when I asked him, later on, for my own purposes, exactly what took place that morning he was able to tell me, almost word for word. The consul had gone north for several days and my husband was serving temporarily as chief of the office. When he reached the office he read the mail and despatches, none of which was of immediate importance.

Just as he had finished reading, Michael Laborde came into the office. (Remember, please, that all names used here are fictitious.) Michael had the office next to my husband's and he wandered in and out through a connecting door, almost at will. He was no more than thirty years old and held a junior post in the commercial side of the consulate. He was personable, though weak, and my husband considered him intelligent. He was lonely in the city and we had him to dinner at least once a week. He had a quick, jumpy mind and he was always full of gossip and my husband has confessed that he enjoyed the five-minute breaks in the day's routine which Laborde's visits afforded. This morning, Michael came into the office, smoking a cigarette, looking disturbed.

"Holy God," he said, "that Washington."

"What is it now?" my husband asked.

"I got a letter last night," Michael said. "Friend of mine works in the Latin-American section. They're howling in anguish. People're getting dumped by the dozen, every day."

"A certain amount of deadwood . . ." my husband began. He is always very correct in questions like this, even with good friends.

"Deadwood, hell!" Michael said. "They're cutting the living flesh. And they're going crazy on the pansy hunt. My friend says he heard they have microphones in half the hotels and bars in Washington and they've caught twenty of them already, right out of their own mouths. And no nonsense about it. No looking at the record for commendations, no fooling around about length of service or anything. A five-minute interview and then out—as of close of business that day."

"Well," my husband said, smiling, "I don't imagine you have to worry about that too much." Michael had something of a reputation locally as a ladies' man, being a bachelor, and, as I have said, quite personable.

"I'm not worried about myself—not about that, anyway," Michael said. "But I'm not so sure about the principle. Official purity. Once people declare for purity they're not satisfied until they nail you to the wood. And my friend wrote me to be careful what I say in my letters. My last letter had scotch tape on it. And I never use scotch tape."

"Your friend is too nervous," my husband said.

"He says Il Blanko has ninety paid spies in Europe," said Michael. Il Blanko was Michael's epithet for the senator who was freezing the Foreign Service into a permanent attitude of terror. "My friend says the damndest people are reporting back all the time. He says they sit next to you in restaurants and write down the jokes when you're not looking."

"Eat at home," my husband said. "Like me."

"And he says he's heard of a new wrinkle," Michael went on. "Some crank you never heard of decides he doesn't like you and he sends an anonymous letter to the FBI saying he saw you flying the flag upside down on the Fourth of July or that you're living with two eleven-year-old Arab boys and then he sends a copy to some hot-eyed congressman and a couple of days later the congressman gets up waving the letter and saying, 'I have here a copy of information that is at this moment resting in the files of the

FBI,' and the next thing you know you're in the soup."

"Do you believe that?" my husband asked.

"How the hell do I know what to believe? I'm waiting for the rumor they they've discovered a sane man on F Street," Michael said. "Then I'm going to apply for home leave to see for myself." He doused his cigarette and went back into his own office.

My husband sat at his desk, feeling, as he told me later, annoyed with Michael for having brought up matters which, to tell the truth, had been lying close to the surface of John's consciousness for some time. John had been passed over for promotion twice and his present appointment, even when the most optimistic face had been put upon it, could only be regarded as a sign that, at the very least, he was out of favor in certain influential quarters in the Service. For more than a year he had had moments of uneasiness about his own mail and had, without specifically admitting it to himself, taken to keeping the tone and contents of his letters, even to intimate friends, mildly noncommittal. As he sat there, he remembered, disquietingly, that several personal letters among those he had received in the last few months had had scotch tape on the flaps of the envelopes. And in the course of his duties in the visa and passport sections he had received information through intelligence channels on various applicants, of a surprisingly intimate nature, information which must have been gathered, he realized, in the most unorthodox manner. And in recent months he had been visited, with annoying frequency, by investigators, persistent and humorless young men, who had questioned him closely for derogatory information about colleagues of his, going back in time as far as 1933. Since all this, as the investigators always pointed out, was merely routine, my husband was conscious of the fact that the very same young men must certainly be making the same inquiries about himself.

My husband is a realist and was not one of those who considered these activities merely wanton persecution of the department. An actor in it himself, he realized better than most the obscure and fearful nature of the struggle which was taking place in the world and the necessity for measures of defense; treachery existed, and he regarded as ingenuous those of his friends and acquaintances who pretended it did not. It was only in the current vagueness of definition and limits of the term that he was uneasy. Trained to assess guilt and innocence by definite standards, and, as a result of his extended service in Europe, having grown into a habit of tolerance of political diversity, he could not help but feel that perhaps he would be considered old-fashioned and not sufficiently severe by his superiors. The custom he had fallen into of discussing with me all invitations, with a view to avoiding being associated, even in the most casual way, with anyone who might conceivably descredit him, was, while necessary, increasingly irksome. The pleasure of society, to be truly enjoyed, must have a certain automatic and spontaneous quality, and in the last year or so all that had vanished. To judge, professionally, the virtue of colleagues and applicants, is one thing—it is quite another to be forced, on the most innocent occasions, to speculate on the politics, the discretion, the potential future disgrace, of dinner companions and tourists to whom one is introduced, by chance, in a bar.

John's speculation was interrupted by the arrival of Trent. Trent was an executive of an American oil company which had an office in the city. He was a large, soft-spoken man, from Illinois, a little older than my husband. John occasionally played golf with him and considered him a friend. My husband rose and shook Trent's hand and offered him a chair. They talked for several moments about inconsequential matters before Trent settled down to the business that had brought him to the consulate.

"There's something I want your advice about," Trent said. He looked uncomfortable and uncharacteristically ill-at-ease. "You're mixed up in this particular line and you know what's going on better than I do. I've been over here a long time. I read the magazines from home every week, but it's hard to tell from them just how serious something like this would be. I have a problem, John."

"What is it?" my husband asked.

Trent hesitated, and took out a cigar and bit the end off without lighting it. "Well," he said, finally, laughing sheepishly, "I was once asked to join the Communist Party."

"What?" my husband asked, surprised. Trent is a large, expensively dressed man with carefully brushed gray hair and he looks the perfect image of what, in fact, he is—an ambitious, successful business executive. "What did you say?"

GOLDILOCKS AT GRAVESIDE

"I said I was asked to join the Communist Party," Trent repeated.

"When?" my husband asked.

"In 1932," Trent said. "When I was in college. The University of Chicago."

"Yes?" my husband said, puzzled, not understanding what Trent wanted from him.

"What am I supposed to do about it?" Trent asked.

"*Did* you join?" my husband asked.

"No." Trent said. "Though I'll admit to you that I thought about it for a long time."

"Then I don't quite see what the problem is," my husband said.

"The man who asked me to join," Trent said, "was an instructor. In the Economics Department. He was one of those young ones, in tweed jackets, who'd been to Russia. He'd have the bright boys up to his apartment for beer and a bull session once a week and we'd talk about sex and God and politics and feel pretty damned intelligent about everything. In those days he seemed like one hell of a guy. . . ."

"Yes?" my husband was still puzzled.

"Well," Trent said, "I see they're going after the colleges now, the committees, I mean, and I wonder if I oughtn't to send in his name."

At that moment, my husband decided to be careful. He realized then that he didn't know Trent very well, despite the afternoons on the golf course. He picked up a pencil and pulled a pad over toward him. "What's the man's name?" he asked.

"No," Trent said, "I don't want to get you mixed up in it. And I'm not sure yet that I want to get mixed up in it myself."

"Where's the man now?" my husband asked.

"I don't know," said Trent. "He's not at Chicago any more. I used to correspond with him for a few years and then it petered out. For all I know he's dead now or he's taken up yoga."

"What, exactly," my husband asked, a little sharply, "is it that you want from me?"

"I just wanted your opinion," said Trent. "To sort of help me make up my mind."

"Send in his name."

"Well . . ." Trent said uncertainly. "I'll see. We used to be pretty good frineds and I thought a lot of him and something like this could do a man a lot of harm and it's more than twenty years ago. . . ."

"You asked me for advice," my husband said. "My advice is send in his name."

At this moment, the door opened and the consul came in, without knocking. He hadn't been expected back for two days and my husband was surprised to see him.

"Oh, I didn't realize you had someone with you," the consul said. "As soon as you're through, I'd like to see you in my office, please."

"I'm just going," Trent said, standing up. "Thanks. Thanks for everything." He shook hands and went out.

The consul closed the door carefully behind him and turned toward my husband. "Sit down, John," he said. "I have some very grave news for you."

The consul was a young man, not much older then Michael. He was one of those fortunate young men who appear to swim upward, in any organization, without any apparent effort on their own part. He had clever, slender good looks and he always seemed to manage to be evenly and healthily tanned. He had been married, within the last year, to a very pretty girl, the only daughter of a wealthy family, and the two of them together had the valuable reputation of being an amusing couple, and were much in demand for parties and long weekends at famous houses. He was a young man whose career his elders delighted to advance and he had been clearly singled out almost from the very beginning of his service, for high position. My husband, from whom he differed in luck and temperament so markedly, shared the common attitude toward him, and willingly and almost with pleasure took on the extra duties that the consul's full social schedule prevented the consul from fulfilling. That is not to say that my husband was not deeply envious of him. My husband was too conscious of his own worth and his solid achievements in the service not to feel a sense of injustice when he contemplated their comparative positions and their probable futures. And besides, while they were both attached to the embassy at X———, my husband had occupied a position of considerably greater importance and no man takes easily to seeing a younger man moved over his head into authority. But an attitude of envy, affection, and devotion, all mingled together, is less rare in a hierarchy than is generally thought possible.

Alone among his fellow workers, Michael Laborde did not think much of the consul, and called him slightingly, because of his light blond hair and his unfailing luck, Goldilocks. I must admit that I, too, was not so completely charmed by the consul as my husband. There was something that I found vaguely unpleasant and false about him, although I was careful not to give any intimation of this to my husband. I also kept to myself a curious little incident in which the consul and I were the only participants. I was out shopping one afternoon by myself and had stopped in front of a window for a moment, when I looked up to see the consul coming out of a doorway just a few feet away. He looked, as always, neat and beautifully dressed. He was not wearing a hat and his hair was wet and newly brushed, as though he had just taken a shower. He took a step in my direction and I began to smile in greeting, when he suddenly turned, without giving any sign of recognition, and walked swiftly away. I was certain he had seen me and there was in his whole performance a sense of embarrassment which was unusual for him. I watched him turn the corner and started on my own way, puzzled. Then, out of curiosity, I stopped and retraced my steps and went to the doorway from which the consul had emerged. The names of the six occupants of the building were on the side of the door and I recognized only one. It was the name of a young American, who was reputed to have a large independent income and who had settled, in the last three months, in our city. I had met him once or twice at parties, and even if his reputation had not preceded him, I would have been able, from his manner of walking and talking, to judge him immediately for what he was. Of course, if the consul had merely nodded to me and said Hello in the normal manner it would never have occurred to me to look at the names on the doorplates.

"I came down from the embassy earlier than I expected," the consul said, when my husband had seated himself, "because I had to tell you this myself. You're suspended, John, as of close of business this day."

My husband has told me, speaking of that moment, that he experienced a curious sense of relief. Subconsciously and without apparent reason, for almost two years, he had been living in expectation of hearing just those words. Now that they had been finally said, it was almost as though a burden had been lifted from his shoulders. Certainty, even of so disastrous a nature, was, for a flicker in time, more comfortable to bear than continuing doubt.

"Repeat that, please," my husband said.

"You're suspended," the consul said, "and I advise you to resign immediately."

"I'm permitted to resign?" my husband asked.

"Yes," said the consul. "Friends of yours have been working for you behind the scenes and they've managed that."

"What's the complaint against me?" my husband asked. Curiously enough, despite his premonitions of the last two years, he had, up until that moment, no inkling of what the complaint would be.

"It's a morals charge, John," the consul said. "And if you fight it, that much is bound to get out and you know what people will think."

"They'll think that I've been kicked out for homosexuality," my husband said.

"Well, not the people who really know you," said the consul. "But everyone else . . ."

"And if I fight it and win?"

"That's not possible, John," the consul said. "They've had people after you and they know all about the lady who tried to commit suicide. They have statements from the doctor, from the porter at the lady's apartment, from somebody at the embassy who went out and did some detective work on his own and then tipped them off."

"Who was that?" my husband asked.

"I can't say," the consul said, "and you'll never find out."

"But it happened more than five years ago," my husband said.

"That makes no difference," said the consul. "It happened."

"If I resign suddenly, like this," my husband said, "the people who don't think it's because of homosexuality will think it's because I'm a security risk—or disloyal."

"I told you," the consul said, "that everybody concerned has agreed to keep it as quiet as possible."

"Still," my husband said, "these things always leak a little."

"A little," the consul admitted. "Perhaps the best thing would be for you to leave as quietly as possible and go to some place where you're not known for a year or so and let it blow over."

"What if I were to go to all the people I've worked for in the Service," my husband said, "and got statements from them about the value of my work for those periods while I was with them—that is, a defense of my record to balance against this one extra-curricular offense—"

"There are no extracurricular offenses any more," the consul said.

"Still," my husband persisted. "What if I got the statements—some of them from people very high in the government by now—"

"It wouldn't do any good," the consul said.

"Even so," my husband said, "perhaps I'd like to try. Would you make such a statement for me?"

The consul hesitated for a moment. "No," he said.

"Why not?" my husband asked.

"For several reasons," the consul said. "Remember, you're being treated leniently. You're being permitted to resign and people have agreed to do their best to keep it quiet. If you oppose them, you're bound to anger someone who'll talk and you'll find yourself all over the newspapers and dismissed summarily, to boot. Secondly, if I give you a statement, no matter how closely I keep it to a professional evaluation of your work in this consulate, I'll seem to be encouraging you in your opposition and lining myself up on your side. Believe me, John," the consul said, and according to my husband, he sounded sincere, "if I thought it would help you, I'd do it. But knowing that it would *hurt* you, it's out of the question."

My husband nodded, collected his things, and walked out of his office for the last time. He came home and told me what had happened. We cancelled the bridge party I had intended to give and discussed the matter the better part of the night. A good deal of the time we spent speculating on the identity of the person at the embassy who had taken it on himself to track down John's story. We could fix on no one and to this day we have no hint as to who it might possibly have been.

In the morning John sent in his resignation and two weeks later we flew to America. We bought a car and set out West, looking for a small, quiet place, in which we could live cheaply and without neighbors. We had a lovely trip and we enjoyed the richness of the scenery and talking once more to Americans, after being so long abroad.

We found our little house, by luck. After five minutes of inspecting it and surveying the empty desert lying on all sides of it, we made our minds up and have not regretted the decision for a moment. I have rearranged the furniture to suit our tastes and had two large bookcases built for John's books. The hurricane lamps I bought the day John worked for the last time serve us wonderfully for our dinners in the patio under the starry desert sky.

There was only one incident in all the time that made me feel that perhaps our plan for ourselves was not going to work out, and it was entirely due to my thoughtlessness that it happened at all. Several months ago, on one of my trips to town, I bought a fashion magazine which had in it an article, illustrated by photographs, entitled, with typical vulgarity, "Fashionable Americans Abroad." There, pictured on a snowy terrace at St. Moritz, was the consul and his wife. They were both deeply tanned and smiling widely. They looked, I must confess, very handsome and young and lucky in their skiing clothes. Thinking, foolishly, that it would amuse my husband, I passed him the magazine, saying, "He still manages to get around, doesn't he?"

My husband looked for a long time at the photograph and gave it back to me, finally, without a word. That night, he went for a long walk across the desert and did not come back until just before dawn, and when I saw him the next morning, his face looked old and ravaged, as though he had spent the night in bitter struggle. The peace and forgetfulness that I had thought we were achieving were all vanished from his face and for once, in my presence, his defenses were gone and all the violence of his pride, his endless ambition, his baffled jealousy, were plainly evident, all focussed and brought to an unbearably painful point in the smiling image of the man he had once admired and served so faithfully.

"Never do anything like that to me again," he said, in the morning, and although we had not spoken a word to each other for nearly twelve hours, I knew what he meant.

But it is all over now, although it took the better part of three months, and during that time my husband said hardly a word to me, hardly even read—but spent the days staring across the desert and the nights staring into the fire, like a bankrupt going over his accounts again and again, running the losses through his head, in helpless, silent hysteria. But this morning I came in from town with a letter from Michael, who, alone among our old friends, continued to correspond with us. It was a short letter and my husband read it quickly, standing up, and without changing his expression. When he had finished he handed the letter to me.

"Read this," he said.

"Dear Children," the letter began, in Laborde's hasty scrawl. "Just a note to keep you *au courant*. The weather's beastly, the natives sullen, and the consulate is rocking. Goldilocks is out. Resigned suddenly, as of two days ago, with no explanation. Except that at every cocktail party and every bar where English is spoken, the guess is Kinsey. The first bit of poison leaked three days ago in a column in Washington. Goldilocks and bride, tear-stained, departed yesterday for an Alp, to ponder the irony of destiny. Burn this letter and keep a bed warm for me in the desert. Love . . ."

I folded the letter and gave it back to my husband. He put it thoughtfully into his pocket. "Now," he said, "what do you think of that?"

He did not expect an answer and I said nothing. He took a turn around the small patio, touching the sun-warmed adobe wall, and stopped in front of me once more. "Poor man," he said, and the pity was real and revivifying. "He was doing so well."

He took another turn around the patio and said, "What do you think happened?"

"I don't know," I said. "I suppose somebody sent a letter to somebody."

"Somebody sent a letter to somebody," he repeated, nodding gently. He looked at me for what seemed like a long time, searchingly. Then he touched my hand and smiled in a very strange manner.

"Do you know what I've been thinking?" he said. "I've been thinking it might be a nice idea if we both got into the car and drove into C—— and bought a good bottle of wine for dinner."

"Yes," I said, "that would be a very nice idea."

I went in and changed and then we drove down the long, straight fifty miles to C——. We bought a bottle of Bordeaux that my husband said was of a quality he hadn't expected to find so deep in the heart of America. He seemed delighted with the crowds on the streets and the things in the windows and insisted upon buying me a very pretty little cotton dress, in a green plaid design, that he saw in a shop.

We drove home and I prepared the dinner and we sat out under the stars and ate it slowly. The Bordeaux, my husband said, was exceptionally good, and we became quite tipsy over the unaccustomed wine, and we laughed unreasonably as we sat across from each other at the table and if there had been anybody there to see us, he would have thought that we were very happy indeed, that night.

* * *

Victoria put the folder down.

The story had never been printed. There had been three rejection slips and she had given up. The editors during that period were cowardly, she told herself. She had started four or five more stories and never finished them. Wishing does not make a writer, nor education, nor injustice, nor suffering. The house was sold, at a profit, and they moved to Los Angeles.

She looked at the photograph of her husband, grave, soberly lighted, falsely calm, falsely honorable. She was not sorry he was dead.

She looked out the window. It was still raining. The rain on the window drowned the drowning world outside. It had turned out to be a good day for funerals. A good day for questions, too. Victoria. Victory. Victory over what?

What sort of love could it have been that demanded that price for its survival? In a time of sharks, must all be sharks? Who was the monster who had sat, in the pretty new dress—proud, wily, subservient, dining under the desert stars, and had smiled in pleasure and complicity at the man across the table, enjoying the wine?

The blond hair had been wet that day, too, although Borden was young then and had not yet begun to use dye.